High Desert

With nearly a decade since Forrest's last foray into the seamy world of the LAPD, it may have seemed as if we wouldn't see Delafield again. But–she's back. Not with a bang, nor with a whimper, but with a full-throated cry of foul at the various hands she's been dealt since we saw her last... Delafield, who remains the complex and engaging character she always was.

-*Lambda Literary Review*

Hancock Park

A classic case of what a heck of a lot of crime fiction isn't— outstanding character-driven writing.

-*Reviewing the Evidence*

Sleeping Bones

An excellent novel by a two-time winner of the Lambda Literary Award for Best Mystery.

-*Library Journal*

Murder by Tradition

Lambda Literary Award winner Forrest (*The Beverly Malibu*) transcends the run-of-the-mill police procedural and courtroom drama with this thought-provoking fourth in a series featuring Los Angeles lesbian homicide cop Kate Delafield. Kate and her partner, Ed Taylor, are called to the scene of the stabbing death of gay restaurateur Teddie Crawford. Working with information from a blood-spatter specialist, the cops learn that the killer has been seriously wounded, and soon pick up Kyle Jensen at the hospital where he has gone for help. Although Jensen claims that he killed Teddie in self-defense after Teddie made a pass at him, Kate suspects that Jensen is a gay-basher and investigates on her own. Just as she is making headway, Kate learns that the only heterosexual male who knows of her sexual preferences will be representing Jensen. She fears that the defense will broadcast her lifestyle, thereby weakening her testimony about the scene of the crime and, worse, jeopardizing her job. Kate's effort to persuade the jury to accept her conclusion while keeping her integrity intact is the primary focus of this compelling story.

-Publishers Weekly

Lesbian LAPD detective Kate Delafield's fourth appearance should quash any doubts concerning Forrest's abilities as a mystery writer, mainstream or otherwise. Well-detailed police procedure, sizzling courtroom drama, and a firm belief in ethics characterize this story of the gory murder of a handsome, gregarious gay man by a muscle-bound "straight." In tandem with assistant district attorney Linda Foster, and supported by lover Aimee, Kate struggles against departmental homophobics to destroy the murderer's plea of self-defense. Quality writing; for most collections.

-Library Journal

Daughters of an Emerald Dusk

Pam Keesey: The third installment in the fascinating story of the women who colonized the planet Maternas, this is the follow-up to *Daughters of a Coral Dawn* (1984) and *Daughters of an Amber Noon* (2002). In the telling of this tale, set 50 years after *Amber Noon*, Forrest captures the ethereal, otherworldly, second generation offspring of the women of Maternas... Forrest has given us both an entertaining and thought-provoking account. Fans of *Coral Dawn* and *Amber Noon* will welcome this addition to the series and Forrest has still left us wondering what will happen to this colony of women next.

-Lambda Book Report

Daughters of an Amber Noon

April, 2006: Katherine V. Forrest's best-selling *Daughters of a Coral Dawn* was published in 1984 and became an instant classic. In *Daughters of a Coral Dawn*, 4,000 women, descendants of a single mother whose origins are the planet Verna, leave Earth to start their own civilization on a planet they call Maternas. But many of their sisters chose to remain on Earth. What happened to those women? Now, nearly two decades later, the saga continues. *Daughters of an Amber Noon* picks up where *Daughters of a Coral Dawn* left off...

-Just About Write

Curious Wine

...is a beautiful story about finding out who you are when you least expect it. Published in the early 1980s, it's a classic lesbian romance that's won the hearts of many a reader, and for good reason. *Curious Wine* is masterfully written. It's perfectly paced and surprisingly erotic, since it's very much a romance novel and not an erotic romance. What does that mean? To me, romance = relationship drives the story, and erotic romance = sex drives the relationship development. *Curious Wine* solidly falls in the "romance" category.

-The Lesbian Review

Delafield

A KATE DELAFIELD MYSTERY

Also by Katherine V. Forrest

From Bella Books
Curious Wine
An Emergence of Green
Daughters of an Amber Noon
Daughters of A Coral Dawn
Daughters of an Emerald Dusk

From Spinsters Ink
The Kate Delafield Series
Amateur City
Murder at the Nightwood Bar
The Beverly Malibu
Murder by Tradition
Liberty Square
Apparition Alley
Sleeping Bones
Hancock Park
High Desert

Delafield

A KATE DELAFIELD MYSTERY

Katherine V. Forrest

Spinsters Ink

2022

Spinsters Ink
P.O. Box 10543
Tallahassee, FL 32302

Printed in the United States of America on acid-free paper.

First Edition - 2022

Editor: Medora MacDougall
Cover Designer: Heather Honeywell

ISBN: 978-1-935226-89-5

PUBLISHER'S NOTE

Dedication

For Jo
For Everything

In the depth of winter, I finally learned that there was within me an invincible summer.

Albert Camus

1

May, 2012

"Joe, another one just arrived," Kate Delafield said, gripping her cell phone as she paced her living room.

"Did you send it on?" Detective Joe Cameron had picked up her call on his private line at Victorville PD as if he'd been waiting for it.

"Just now."

"Hold on a sec...Got it..." He muttered, "Looks like she's escalating."

Kate strode to the breakfast bar and looked down at the handwritten note she'd taken out of her mailbox, photographed and forwarded to Cameron. She read it aloud: "*'Any minute now will be your last.'* That's about as escalated as it gets. Before she kills me of course."

"Our offer stands." His voice was harsh with exasperation. "You have your whole police family behind you on this, Kate."

"I know, I'm grateful. But we both know assigning protection is a waste. She figures to just wait it out." Nevertheless, and certainly at his behest, patrol cars drifted past her house every few hours. In her view they served only to draw unwanted attention and she felt exposed enough out here in the high desert.

"Yeah, well," Cameron said, "she might get tired of waiting it out."

"Joe, I'm armed, alarmed, and on film. This way I won't endanger anyone else. This way I'm not doing anything different from how you holed up to wait for your brother." Blunt reminder of the choice he'd made a few years back when she'd helped him protect his family in a cabin not too far from here. "There's something new, is why I called. A Yucca Valley postmark."

"Jesus. Did you save the envelope?"

She shook her head at this rote question. "It hardly needs analysis or fingerprinting. We know it's Ellie Shuster."

She heard Cameron draw a breath. They'd worked together so many years she held a clear image of him at his desk in the Victorville Patrol Station, unchanged from their days together as homicide detectives at LAPD's Wilshire Division: his jacket off and hung on the back of his chair, tie loosened, sleeves of a crisp shirt rolled tidily up to the elbow, holding his cell phone to his ear with an index finger, head bent, making notes as he listened. "Kate," he said, "it's more than just the envelope and you know it. Coming from out of town, there was always the possibility—"

"—that like most threats they were just threats," Kate finished for him. She knew better. Had known from the start this was as real as death. "So now she's right here."

The missives, this one being number thirteen, had previously been sent from seven different California postmarks in roughly two-week intervals over the past five months, all handwritten in brief, stark variations of the same message: Eleanor Frances Shuster's only remaining purpose on this earth was to remove Kate Delafield from it.

"At least we can pinpoint some action. Put out another BOLO, check out all the local hotels and motels, distribute a circular with her photo—"

Kate felt a scintilla of hope about a wide area be on the lookout but it faded quickly. There had been no sighting of Ellie Shuster for five months. She had left no electronic footprints; she was now operating untraceably on a cash basis with money awarded to her by the state. She could be anywhere in the high desert, the entire Coachella Valley, even right there in Victorville with Cameron. She could be in disguise. Using her prison connections, she might have arranged for a hitman as proxy, and if so, anyone Kate met on the street could be her killer.

"What's it been?" he was saying. "Year and a half?"

"About that since her release. Five months and a week since the letters started."

"What took her so long? That's what I can't figure. Even factoring in her wait for the reparations payoff."

"The rage was building, is my guess."

"She had nineteen years for that," he argued. "Kate, you seem way too...I don't know, *unruffled* over a case that was a total Torrie Holden fuckup."

"Believe me, Joe, I'm ruffled. It doesn't matter about Torrie. I was the D-three, she was a D-one. The case was my responsibility. I suspected she was a fuckup before she proved it the hard way." Kate flexed the shoulder that reminded her daily of an arrest gone south in every dimension including the death of the seventeen-year-old suspect, and a crossfire bullet that had put her down and on leave for six weeks. A bullet that came from the weapon of then-partner, Torrie Holden. "Besides, Torrie's out of the frame." Long since dead of breast cancer.

"It was a strong case even without her mess-up," Cameron retorted. "Incriminating diary, motive, testimony..."

She gritted her teeth. He would not let go of his determination to persuade her into absolving herself of any blame. Like everyone else, he had no inkling of her actual culpability in Ellie Shuster's wrongful conviction. She tossed the note back onto the counter, wishing that instead of giving in to her electric fear when she saw the postmark, the need to immediately share with him this newest and most alarming communication, she'd ripped up the goddamn thing and thrown it to the desert winds. She said flatly, "We put the wrong person on death row. Destroyed her marriage. Took nineteen years from her life."

"The jury did. It took the Innocence Project—"

"Yes, yes, I know."

"—getting the case reviewed with new evidence and reneged testimony. Which you had no way of knowing back then."

How many times did he have to repeat all this? She'd read through the trial transcripts and appeals, examined her copy of the murder book innumerable times, run over it in her mind a thousand more times looking for anything that might have been missed. If Ellie Shuster hadn't done this crime, who did?

"Joe, I know all this and so does she. It makes no difference. She's out to have someone else know how it feels to have their life torn up the way we did hers. Feel what it's like to be on death row."

"Aimee would—"

"Leave Aimee the hell out of this."

A song from the radio next door suddenly impinged on her consciousness and she involuntarily laughed.

"*What* is so goddamn funny," Cameron snapped.

"Music from next door. The Police, 'Every breath you take, I'll be watching you.'"

"Yeah, that's really funny. How's your sobriety?"

"Holding," she said shortly, irked by the question, an unwelcome reminder of what had been out of her awareness however momentarily.

"How about I come over to see you tonight?"

"Be glad to see you anytime, Joe. You know that." She clicked off.

Mostly anytime. Mostly she could do without his useless, hovering anxiety.

She began to pace her house, her go-to routine in confronting the renewed ache and craving for the soul-deep soothe of alcohol. She gazed at the tile flooring, beige tinged with coral, that she'd installed throughout and splashed with woven Native American scatter rugs. At her armchairs-only living room, all four of them in pale pastel shades and with ottomans. The angular glass coffee table and end tables, the mounted TV on a wall she'd painted sunset citrus, the two other walls layered in rough-hewn shelves crowded with books. The kitchen alcove with its breakfast bar, ruthlessly utilitarian as were the two bedrooms, basic bed and dresser in each and with another complement of books. She liked looking at, savoring this house, the first place she'd created just for herself. Never mind the monetary cost, its much higher cost emotionally, everything in here was hers, her choice, no compromise. If her life was to be taken away, let it be here with Joshua trees and desert winds as her companions. And when it happened, just let it be quick.

Infinitesimally lightened by the survey of her house, she moved to the front window and went through her next checklist, the practical one, less comforting. Minimal danger from the left: a rock formation that could be navigated only with boulders noisily breaking loose underfoot. Neighbors to her right, all of them familiar if not personally known to her. Beyond the back deck, a few widely scattered dwellings, then open desert extending for miles to Joshua Tree National Park. Before her, rocky sand patchworked with cactus, cholla, ocotillo; across the road, a purely desert vista of Joshua trees, creosote, chaparral, and brittlebush overseen by the far distant San Bernardino Mountains.

Not in view but much in her awareness were the police-mounted rooftop cameras that rotated front and back of the house and one above the front door, the alarms active on windows and doors. Motion-activated lighting that at night would wash the house in illumination at the approach of an intruder. All of it solid protection unless she left the house. She could be shot on the way to her Jeep. But she was always armed, and the shooter would be starkly visible on this desert landscape. Not that it mattered. She guessed that Ellie Shuster, if she performed the act herself, would want to be clearly visible whenever she finally acted.

Kate was in the kitchen removing the cap on a bottle of Teavana iced tea when a vehicle drove up. No mistaking that it had stopped in her driveway; she heard every sound with distinct clarity here in a silence broken only by capricious wind, the drone of an occasional aircraft, the song track from next door. Moments later a knock at her door.

Ellie Shuster, finally coming to kill her?

2

Kate assessed the slender, deeply tanned woman standing on her doorstep. From the coif of blond hair that framed a hawkish, skillfully made-up face, the crimson sleeveless silk tunic over black tights and weighted down with gold chains, the waft of perfume, she guessed Palm Springs. Or Beverly Hills. Under the makeup and bleach, sun damage exposed a woman in her sixties and no killer or solicitor or Jehovah's Witness was she: a Mercedes convertible with dealer plates glowed candy apple-red behind her own Jeep on the crushed stone lane comprising her driveway.

Having completed her own inspection of Kate in one raking glance, the woman announced in a smoker's voice, "I'm Geneva Fallon. Could I have a few minutes of your time? Alice Bannon suggested you might be good for me to talk to."

"*Alice?*" This did not compute. "Of course. How is she?" She stepped back to allow Geneva Fallon into her living room, recalling that a Christmas card from her LAPD colleague from the early days had been their last contact. Five months ago.

"Fine, she's fine," the woman replied, stepping over the threshold. "Retired of course. But you would know that. Alice asked me to give you her regards."

A smile added considerable wattage to her face and persona, and Kate smiled back, not so much at her as at the surfacing memory from when she and the then recently appointed Sheriff Alice Bannon of the coastal town of Seacrest had together exposed a disappearance as a murder. Geneva Fallon's bona fides were solid.

"I apologize for dropping in on you like this," Fallon said, glancing around her, "but frankly, I thought if I phoned you'd just hang up thinking I was a robocall. Or a nutcase. I've come from Palm Springs," she concluded, as if the one-hour drive were a herculean trek.

The words *Alice Bannon* would have been just as effective on the phone and this clearly intelligent, expensively turned-out woman surely knew it. A display of wealth and self-assurance optimized an in-person approach for whatever this was about, and Kate was intrigued. It would be at least a distraction from constant disquiet over sobriety and mortality.

"Very nice," Fallon commented, gesturing to the wide picture window and the San Bernardino Mountains in purple-beige definition under whipped cream clouds. She slowly surveyed the two walls of books, nodding as if something had been confirmed for her.

There was no hum from the air-conditioning unit; the house was comfortable enough with morning air. From the radio next door came the raucous voice of Tina Turner demanding "What's Love Got To Do With It," less audible when Kate closed the door. She settled herself in her usual chair, surreptitiously pulling the .38 from the back of her khakis and tucking it behind her armchair pillow. Fallon lowered herself into the pale green armchair opposite her, sending another wave of perfume her way, and placed her Gucci handbag on the floor, the gold ornamentation around her neck and wrists so heavy the chains and bracelets shifted in delayed reaction. She slung her feet up onto the ottoman, multicolored rhinestone straps of her sandals glittering.

Raising her eyes from the costly footwear, Kate met a shrewd, dark brown gaze in open scrutiny of her. Fallon's hands were in her lap, the fingers of each hand flashing with diamond and ruby rings, fingernails manicured in shiny swirls of orange and red to match her toenails. *Fallon as in talon*, Kate thought as she focused on those fingers, certain she was far from the first person to come up with the rhyme. So far the woman fit every stereotype of Palm Springs wealth, privilege, and fierce determination to hold onto every remnant of youth. But this much effortful display on a Monday morning was impressive enough that Kate felt vaguely gratified by her own accidental choice of one of her newer polo shirts to go with freshly pressed khakis, choices she'd made for her appointment today in Los Angeles.

"You're from Seacrest, then?" Kate ventured although she could not imagine this obvious sun-worshipper ever living in a foggy oceanside town.

Fallon flicked that away with two flame-tipped fingers. "God no. Alice and I were at UCLA together. We've been friends ever since."

Why, Kate wondered. Why on earth would the Alice Bannon she knew, the bluff no-nonsense sheriff of a quiet little northern California town, a declared lesbian, maintain a decades' long friendship with this ostentatious woman?

Fallon addressed Kate in a quiet, husky tone: "I'm hoping you can give me some help. I'm recently widowed and my husband left a considerable estate, enough that I can make financial amends to…someone."

Kate asked, puzzled, "You need help with that?"

"I need a go-between. To get it done. To get it to her."

"I take it there's a reason you can't make the approach directly."

Fallon emitted a sarcastic snort. "You take it exactly right. I tried to. She…She was…Can you imagine anyone turning away no-strings cash?"

Kate shrugged. "Sure. Drug money. Stolen money." There was no such thing as no-strings money. It always changed hands for a reason. She felt a pulse of admiration for the woman who had rejected Geneva Fallon and however much of her no-strings cash. Affluent people tended to possess supreme confidence that money solved any problem, including the salving of conscience. Poor people were left to trust in God for salvation or punishment—or, in criminal cases, black-robed judges. For some crimes no reparation was ever possible, and even "God's will be done" became inexplicable as to what God's will could possibly have been.

Geneva Fallon had leaned over to retrieve something from her Gucci bag, and coldly, Kate contemplated her. What had this woman done? Why had Alice sent her? Under the poise conferred by wealth and grooming, she appeared to have been quite a looker in her day, the usual requisite for marrying into wealth. Had there been a lesbian connection between this woman and the party she was trying to pay off? That cliché of the lesbian world, a straight Geneva Fallon experimenting with a woman, with the foreordained, equally clichéd outcome? As if she were back in an LAPD interview room, Kate took the lead. "Let's begin with her name."

Fallon handed her a photograph she'd taken from her purse, and leaned back. "Natalie Rostow." She shifted in the chair and for the first time looked ill at ease.

Kate glanced at the image of a gray-haired, thin-faced, unremarkable woman perhaps a few years older than herself, placed the photo on the end table next to her, then asked, "And the reason for this animosity toward you?"

"Kate…may I call you Kate? Please call me Geneva."

Kate nodded, and Fallon lowered her sandals to the tiled floor and clasped her hands as she leaned forward and said earnestly, "No one else in my life knows about this except Alice." She gazed at Kate as if in supplication. "I assume you know the film *The Children's Hour*?"

Of course she knew it. "Lillian Hellman," she said, her nerves flaring alert, and gestured to her bookshelves. "The play's in there somewhere." Also *Scoundrel Time* by the same author, a memoir relevant to a long-ago homicide investigation with roots in the days of the Hollywood Blacklist. *The Children's Hour*, a notorious sensation in its day, had informed her adolescence, and then a twelve-year relationship—far too much of her life with its powerful message about the cost of lesbian exposure.

Fallon raised her eyebrows at this definitive knowledge. "I didn't see the movie till the eighties. Or I might have learned something. But it was too late."

"Too late," Kate repeated. She already knew where this was going.

The knuckles of Fallon's clasped hands whitened. "I like to think it would have made a difference. But I was such a nasty little bitch…" She took in and released a breath. "Since you know the story then you'll understand what I mean when I say I was Mary."

The two major characters, she remembered, were Martha and Karen. Which meant that Mary… Hackles rising, Kate asked carefully, "You spread lies about two teachers being lesbians?"

"Just one teacher. It was actually the truth." Her mouth tightened, her eyes dark pools of pained memory. "There were six of us. A high school wolf pack. We called ourselves the Six Shooters. Everyone was petrified of us, even the teachers. Susan Ricks was our ringleader. Died years ago." She grimaced. "Bowel cancer. Fitting."

Again she shifted in her chair and Kate offered, feeling obligated, "Can I get you anything? Iced tea? Water?"

Fallon waved that away, intent on getting her story out, continuing in a rush of words, "Natalie Rostow was our sophomore year English teacher. I could see her backyard from a corner of my upstairs bedroom window. I saw her kissing another woman in what she believed was complete privacy." Her raspy voice trembled. "I took Polaroids."

Kate stirred in her chair as inchoate memory surfaced from her time with Anne, her own tightly closeted years in the military and police worlds. "I take it she lost her job."

"Her job?" Fallon blinked several times. "I can only wish it were just that one job. This was before Anita Bryant and all the save the children business. Before firing gay teachers made the California ballot."

"You don't know what happened to her?"

Fallon's face was grim. "I do know. Nothing good. Today she's in Desert Hot Springs. Living in a trailer park."

She might be there because of any number of life choices, Kate thought, but did not offer this potential comfort.

Fallon's mouth formed into a moue. "Natalie Rostow would tear me limb from limb if she knew I have a private detective keeping tabs on her. But I'm just trying to fix this."

Fix this.

Gripping the arms of her chair, Kate had to look away. Anita Bryant happened in 1977 so this must have been in the early to mid-seventies. No one knew better than she did how life had been like back then. For her and Anne. This woman actually thought she could do something to fix—*fix*—the life she'd laid waste to.

Fallon saw or sensed something in Kate's body language because she spread her jeweled hands placatingly. "I know I've been on the wrong side of gay rights—"

Kate turned that away with an abrupt raising of both hands, uncaring about her graceless reaction. Yet another *mea culpa* about to spill from a heterosexual. She asked curtly, "What changed you?"

"Seeing that film. And Alice. Mostly Alice." She continued awkwardly, "It took me years to tell her about this. She's always been…so strong, such integrity, such a leader…In college I just threw myself at her. Trying to atone. I'm not sure she ever really understood or welcomed friendship from me…"

Undoubtedly not, Kate thought. Alice must have been at pains to endure a woman so antithetical to her values and unpretentious way of life.

"…But I respect her more than just about anybody I've ever known. Better late than never, I guess."

Kate did not reply to this homily. Before the sea change in the culture of the country with domestic partnerships and the 2008 California marriages, the Fallons of the world had never questioned the cultural consensus around them, the vicious contempt and homicidal attacks on sexual difference. Took no notice of the bodies that lay strewn in the wake of that hatred. Few today had any concept of the courage it had taken to confront such animosity, the cost in lost jobs, families, lives. God knew she'd never had such courage, and her cowardice adhered to her like a burial shroud. These days nothing enraged her more than straight people smiling their existential tolerance: *We didn't enslave you. Didn't herd you into concentration camps. We're even starting to accept you now, right? So you're winning!*

Get over yourself, Kate ordered, returning her attention to Geneva Fallon. At least this woman, for one, was attempting some sort of a make-good.

"Dust in the Wind" was mournfully emanating from next door, and Fallon was gazing in irritation out the front window as if in search of its origin. She said to Kate, "Does that music go on all the time? How can you stand it?"

It's the soundtrack of my life. She smiled. "You're right. I should go next door and tell the woman."

Fallon managed an awkward smile in return and again looked at the bookshelves. "Quite a collection."

"A friend bequeathed most of them to me," Kate said, flicking a glance at the shiny brass urn and ceramic coffee mug resting amid a select grouping of books, trying to imagine what Maggie would have made of this woman across from her. "What did you say to Natalie Rostow, what did she say to you? She recognized you after all this time?"

Fallon answered tonelessly. "Knew me in an instant. I got to say I was sorry and offered her money and all she did was scream at me to get out get out get out."

"She knew clearly what you were there for?" A rhetorical question. She would have reacted the same way to this monster out of her worst nightmares.

She nodded. "I tried to give her the cashier's check but this mannish old woman came limping out from somewhere and grabbed me and shoved me out the door. Slammed it so hard the trailer all but came down."

"You can't accept that? Let it go?"

"I accept that she won't have anything to do with me," Fallon said, lowering her gaze to the tile floor. "I don't accept that I still can't help her."

Kate looked at her with a glimmer of respect.

"Barbara Jameson—her partner—must have been very sick," Fallon was saying in another raspy rush of words. "She died a month ago and now Natalie Rostow's an old woman all alone in a decrepit trailer. We both know how it is to be old anywhere in this country, much less isolated and dirt poor. I could be living right next door to her if I hadn't married a man who'd just got himself into the oil business. We moved here from Bakersfield." She looked up at Kate. "I live in Old Las Palmas now."

Kate had been in Palm Springs often enough over the years to recognize the legendary area where fifties-era film stars had resided and a few of today's celebrities still did, the most exclusive neighborhood in Palm Springs.

Fallon continued, "My son and daughter run the company business in Bakersfield. Above all, I don't want them ever to know about this, find out their mother could ever do such a thing to another human being. I trust Alice and she told me I could trust you." Again she spread her hands, the bejeweled rings glistening. "I have more than enough for anything I could ever want. I don't care about Natalie Rostow knowing who's giving her this money, where it comes from. I just want her comfortable the rest of her days. It's something I should do, can do, I want to do it."

Kate asked, "How much are we talking about?"

"Two hundred and fifty thousand."

Fallon shrugged in response to Kate's stare. "If she lives another ten, fifteen years, a quarter of a million is not all that much."

Only in your world, Kate thought. "So how do I come into this?"

"Where you come in…" Again Fallon shifted uncomfortably. "To quote Alice, 'Kate Delafield is really, really good at figuring things out.' My detective agency told me Natalie Rostow regularly goes to a bereavement group at some gay center in Palm Springs. I was thinking…I was thinking a member of her community like you…"

"And after I've made contact, what then?"

Fallon sighed and rolled her eyes toward the ceiling as if tallying a multitude of frustrations. "That's where I most need your help. I can't figure out how in the world to get this money to her. Neither could Alice. I had no idea how hard it is to give someone a large amount of anonymous, untraceable cash these days. Alice promised you could come up with a way to get this done. There'll be a fee for you, of course."

"I don't need or want your money."

"That's what Alice said you'd say."

Geneva Fallon nodded as if in conclusion to her business, and rose to her feet, radiating another wave of perfume. Again she reached into the depths of her purse, extracted a card, and placed it on the coffee table. "Please think it over, Kate. If you're willing to help, if you come up with any ideas, give me a call."

She gave Kate her high-wattage smile. "Having met you, I see why I can absolutely trust what Alice Bannon told me about you."

3

A few minutes after the door closed behind Geneva Fallon and she drove away, "Nights in White Satin" stopped mid-song. Moments later Kate once more keyed off her house alarm system and answered the knock from her next-door neighbor.

"I all but mugged the woman for those sandals," Pilar Adams said, moving briskly past Kate in her flip-flops, her long-sleeved, oversize yellow shirt billowing over her white shorts.

"Not the brand-new convertible?" The vehicle under Pilar's rickety carport was an ancient Camry.

"What would I want with a convertible? She a friend of yours? Sure didn't look it."

Kate glanced sharply at her. "Meaning what?"

"You're real. She isn't."

Kate laughed. In her perilous circumstances, having a nosy, observant neighbor like Pilar Adams seemed an advantage. Newly here from Calgary—and this being May, therefore not one of the classic November to April Canadian snowbirds—she was in her late fifties, recently widowed, with a daughter off somewhere in Europe, and gay friendly—as were many visitors from a country where same-sex marriage had long been legal. Kate judged her a bit eccentric, but low on the crazy scale compared to other denizens of the high desert. She welcomed Pilar's occasional drop-in presence, did not mind the inquisitiveness, and the constant seventies' and eighties'-vintage music emanating from the neighboring house served to bring some of the world inside and reduce her isolation.

"Make yourself comfortable, Pilar." She went into the kitchen alcove. "I'll get us some iced tea and tell you about my visitor." She felt no compunction about revealing the conversation; she'd made no promise of anything, including confidentiality, to Geneva Fallon.

Seated across from Kate, Pilar sipped her tea, now and again rattling its ice cubes as she listened to the recounting of Geneva Fallon's visit, reacting only with an occasional headshake. When Kate concluded, she offered, "So, what does our LAPD detective make of all this?"

Kate stared at her. "How did you know I was LAPD?" She'd wondered why a question as to her former occupation had never come up in their previous conversations. Google, she answered herself. She'd been in enough newspaper stories to warrant any number of Google hits and flags.

"For God's sake everyone knows," Pilar said, looking disconcerted. "Besides, you *look* like a cop. I mean, you carry yourself like one. I'm just glad you're next door. I see those police cars come by, that alarm"—she pointed to the bank of lights by the door—"those cameras on your roof, I feel safer out here. You didn't know you're a celebrity hereabouts?"

Kate shook her head, aggrieved by the knowledge. She wasn't social, hadn't sought out anyone here. Being known as any kind of a cop past or present, she'd learned, was a pain in the ass. People either pestered you for advice or intervention or flung you into the same cesspool that held all the racist bigots in law enforcement. "I'm retired," she said. "Long out of commission."

"But not your experience or your brain. So what did you think?"

Kate made an effort to overcome her annoyance and be amiable toward her artless neighbor. "Well…for starters, that flashy new car, how she…well, she didn't strike me as a grieving widow."

"Me either," Pilar said grimly. "Just from the way she walked."

Picking up her iced tea, Kate gazed at the urn holding the ashes of her closest friend, then back at Pilar. In those observant blue eyes, framed by thick-framed glasses, an aching darkness put the lie to her breezy manner and casual attire. The widow Adams was anchored in the same morass of grief as she was, enduring an absence, an emptiness as unrelenting and pitiless as desert sun, pulled under by the raw reality of that word *gone*. Sudden sharp resentment of Geneva Fallon and her flashy wealth and the imposition of her visit descended, and Kate drank iced tea and told herself she was being irrational.

"Could this be a scam?" Pilar asked, pushing several strands of dyed auburn hair off her forehead. "Money laundering? Some kind of a joke?"

"Not if my friend Alice sent her. I'll drop her an email…" No, forget that. If she managed to somehow survive Ellie Shuster's vendetta, she would take a long-overdue drive up to see her. "Geneva Fallon doesn't seem the type who'd knock on a stranger's door with a story that makes her look like a McCarthy-era informer—"

"Or a bloody Nazi," Pilar muttered. "I don't know why you'd want to get involved when her victim literally threw her out of the house." Her voice rose. "Sometimes what people do is so despicable there's no reparation, it's unforgivable—or do you not believe that?"

"Of course I believe it. It's why most cops become cops." Taken aback by the hair-trigger vehemence, Kate suspected it was linked to the woman's own emotional history. She added, "I have all kinds of regrets about things I did—or didn't do," she added wryly.

"Really." Pilar had instantly switched back to avid, bright-eyed inquisitiveness.

Kate again considered informing her about Ellie Shuster for the sake of her neighbor's own safety. And again decided there was next to no jeopardy for Pilar and too many unknowns, both unintended consequences and negative ones. Including hounds from the press descending on them both.

She returned to the topic of Geneva Fallon. "I may be splitting ethical hairs, but the current offer of money is coming not from her but from"—she made air quotes—"anonymous. We're talking about an old woman living alone in bad circumstances with minimal resources. Whose instant reaction came out of trauma, out of rage."

"A good point," Pilar conceded. Her eyebrows had risen above her glasses but no frown lines appeared.

Botox, Kate decided, and not a very good job of it. "If I get involved," she said, "I need to figure out how."

Pilar again rattled her ice cubes and sipped her tea. "Getting a quarter of a million dollars to someone can't be that hard."

"Maybe she wins a contest. Like…Publishers Clearing House."

Pilar grinned widely as she set her tea down on her end table, teeth starkly white in her tanned face. "Publishers Clearing House," she repeated fondly. "My mother used to send entries in to them all the time. Back then they gave their winners a check the size of a billboard for at least a million dollars, there was a whole entourage of people, a banner, cameras…" She shrugged. "Nope. The company would probably sue you for fraud."

In head-shaking dismissal of her own idea, Kate added, "There'd also be this small problem of her not having entered the contest."

"So keep it simple. Put the money in a duffel bag, leave it on her doorstep. Watch from somewhere to make sure she collects it."

Kate smiled at her. "If you walked out your front door and found a quarter of a million in cash on your doorstep, what would you think? Seriously."

"Seriously…Drug money, is what I'd think. A drug lord had to drop it there for some reason and I'd never stop worrying he'd come back to collect it and horribly torture then murder me."

"Way too much Netflix," Kate teased.

"So okay, what would *you* do with money you found on your doorstep?"

"Call in a reporter as a witness, take it to law enforcement and wait till they clear it, if they ever do, assuming they don't make up some reason to appropriate it for themselves." Kate sighed.

"How about you have her dig it up in her rosebushes, if she has any."

"Right. Picture me sneaking into her front yard in the dead of night with a shovel and a bag of money and neighbors in their trailers only ten or so feet away, and some old codger catches sight of me and calls the cops and there I am spotlighted with my shovel and my bag of money and squad cars all around us and Geneva Fallon disavowing any—"

Pilar raised both hands. "Okay. I'm fresh out of garbage ideas. How about one of your own?"

"An inheritance," Kate offered.

Pilar shook her head, simultaneously pushing away strands of hair that had again fallen across her face. Not for the first time Kate wondered why women bothered with the constant nuisance of long hair. "No way," Pilar was saying. "She'll think it's some version of the Nigerian scam."

"So would I," Kate conceded. "It has to be from somebody she knows of or some entity she'd accept as credible. It's a real puzzle…"

Pilar said lightly, "So how about the former detective creates the Delafield Agency and takes her first job?"

"The Delafield Agency," Kate repeated, chuckling. "Now that's something to wrap my head around."

She got up from her chair. "Sorry. I have to cut this short, Pilar—I need to drive into LA."

Pilar drained her tea and got up. "So what's in LA that we don't have out here?"

"Friends." The woman was just *too* damn nosy. "Memories. Business."

"All that hideous traffic," Pilar said as she strode toward the door, "I wouldn't drive into that crap heap of a city if someone left a million dollars for me on Wilshire Boulevard."

Moments later her radio came on with the Eagles welcoming everyone to the Hotel California.

4

A few minutes early for her appointment, Kate switched off her windshield wipers and after the final mourning echoes of "Where the Streets Have No Name," her SiriusXM. She rolled down her window to savor the cool, moisture-perfumed air, fine mist that had greeted her a few miles east of the downtown interchange, thickening as she drove into the city, promising to be even denser toward the ocean had she not pulled off the Ten onto La Cienega Boulevard toward Olympic. The sky would be overcast till the midafternoon burn off, typical of this time of every year she had lived in Los Angeles.

Unlike Joe Cameron, she did miss aspects of the city and LA's moody, late spring mornings—"rainish," Aimee termed them—were high on the list. Cameron professed to regret nothing about his departure, regarding his years at LAPD as exile, needed recovery from a traumatizing torture-murder case in his hometown in the early days of his police career, a painful divorce, and escape from the family demons that had served to drive him from VPD to LAPD. With the healing passage of time, he'd found his initial elation over his promotion to

Homicide Special—the holy grail, the aspiration of virtually all detectives—shifting into cynicism and contempt for the politics, the game-playing, the frat-boy machismo of many of his colleagues and superiors. Who had been astounded by his request for transfer from their elite unit to a nothing town like Victorville, a stop-off on the way to Vegas. He'd sold his house in the Hollywood Hills and returned to what he termed "real police work without the TV crews."

Aside from her personal friendship with Cameron, Kate still retained a police relationship of sorts with him: her tiny Yucca Valley town of Ricochet lay within the jurisdiction of his San Bernardino County police facility. A tiny town where, she mused, desert byways indeed held streets with no name, and inhabitants had dodgy reasons for living out there. Reasons which, since she was no longer in the cop business, she did her best to ignore.

At the appointed time she got out of the Jeep and made her unhurried way along the wet flagstone path at the side of the modest stucco house, through the side gate and into the backyard. With a light knock on the partially open door she entered the cottage office and into immediate comfort, the unchanging familiarity of the two-seater leather sofa, two matching armchairs accompanied by small end tables, a functional desk, two overstuffed bookcases. Only one element had altered since she had been coming here: the occupant, who was placing yellow roses, a last cut from the depleted bushes in the front of the main house, in a vase atop one of the bookcases.

Calla Dearborn wore a white scoop-neck top and navy slacks on a tall, high-hipped frame that had thinned with a recent and dramatic loss of weight. No illness, she had assured Kate; only a change in diet recommended along with medication for elevated blood pressure common to older African-Americans. Her frizzy halo of hair glowed with far more white than gray these days, but her face with its dome forehead and pink-brown cheeks seemed unchanged with the years.

She gave Kate a warm, dimpled smile. "Have a seat, Kate. Good to see you again."

"You too, Calla." Kate placed a check beside the vase of roses, inhaling their fragrance, then sat in her usual chair.

Dearborn took the one opposite her, a lined pad and her malachite rollerball pen on the table beside her. She sat back, crossed her long legs, and inquired, "So, what's going on?"

Kate started to speak and instead laughed.

Dearborn's vestiges of eyebrows rose. "That bad?"

"I have to be topping the list of your most fucked-up therapy clients ever."

Dearborn lifted a hand to hold her jaw between thumb and index finger in a parody of deep thought. Then she dropped the hand to the arm of her chair and said with a smile, "I can't seem to find that list. I can only locate you on a quite different one."

"Which would be..."

"The one with integrity on it. Loyalty. Commitment. Courage. My most admirable list."

How on earth did Calla perceive any of these things in her? After all their sessions together? *Courage?* "Damned if I can see myself on any list like that," Kate muttered.

"Of course not. In contrast to the rest of us, you always see a very different person—"

Who the hell is that person?

"—because you're depressed."

Kate grimaced, didn't reply. *Who wouldn't be depressed?*

"I do understand some of your reasons for feeling the way you do. How about we go one step at a time? Where are you in your dreams?"

"Back with Anne," Kate said promptly, glad for the question.

Dearborn nodded. "Your first partner. Who died many years ago. The eighties, yes?"

"Right." Kate was no longer surprised by Dearborn's recall of the most minute details from far back in their sessions together. "I've gone all the way back to nineteen eighty-three..."

"Another door in your hallway of locked rooms. Before you tell me about the dream, is it recurring like your other ones?"

Kate nodded. Staring beyond Dearborn at the certificates of professional status on the wall behind the desk, she began slowly. "I'm at a burial service in a funeral home…" Then, in a flash flood of words, "There's just myself and Anne's coffin and there's a woman in Anne's coffin who's not Anne and the funeral home people tell me it's absolutely her but I don't know who this woman is and I keep insisting and insisting it's not her and I finally slam the lid down on the coffin…" She jerked her gaze to Dearborn. "That's really about it. Then I wake up."

Frowning, Dearborn asked, "How do you feel in this dream?"

"Agitated. Really agitated. But not horrified like I am in my nightmares."

"What do you make of it?"

"I know what it means. When Anne died, I was about two years a homicide detective—fast tracked after we won the discrimination lawsuits and women finally got promoted. The male cops acted like we were all pretend cops, treated us with absolute contempt. The homophobia—it was lethal. I was buried so deep in the closet you couldn't have found me with a floodlight. The afternoon my lieutenant called me into his office to tell me my"—she made finger quotes—"'roommate' had died in that freeway accident…September seventh…it was like I'd been slugged with a baseball bat. I just stood there telling myself over and over: don't react, don't cry, don't even speak…"

Dearborn said gently, "How awful for you, Kate. I see how this relates to the strange woman in Anne's coffin."

Kate placed both hands on the knees of her khaki pants as if to brace herself. "Anne's sister-in-law came down from Santa Barbara, and an aunt. Took her body…everything of hers I hadn't managed to grab and hide in the trunk of my car. The house was in my name, in those days it had to be. She was thirty-two years old, Calla. Never ever thought of a will. I didn't have any claim on anything of hers, I didn't know what they'd do if I told them we were…together. My police career—I felt like it was all I had left and maybe those people would turn on me and…and…I didn't, couldn't even take a day off work. After her family left, our house felt like it had been stripped, like she'd been razored out of my life. We had an old collie, Barney. He died about six months after she did and I got rid of the house, couldn't bear to be there any longer. All I have now of our twelve years is a box of stuff I managed to keep."

Dearborn's sable brown eyes were glistening with tears, her voice anguished: "Oh, Kate, you were so alone. So very alone."

"Yes." She'd never truly, fully realized it until this moment. She felt her own eyes welling and tried to pull herself back together in this aftermath of what she'd never revealed to anyone. "Yes, I guess I was."

"You're telling me your dream is about your denial of Anne."

At Kate's nod, Dearborn offered, "Those were hideous years, Kate. For so many of you."

"We all of us lived that way. We had to," Kate replied matter-of-factly. "All of us in the same closet."

Dearborn shook her head. "You've had Anne locked away all this time, all those good memories…"

"Yes, really good memories." Kate's reflexive smile dispelled some of the urge to weep. "I'm glad to have that room open. The crazy way we managed to find each other…all those years together in our little house in Glendale…"

Dearborn nodded. "How's Aimee with all that's going on with you?"

Kate instantly sobered. "Beside herself."

"And how are you with that?"

"Okay, actually. This way she'll stay away. I wasted so many years of her life—" *Like I did with Ellie Shuster's life.* "What's going on—more than anything I need to keep her safe."

"Just like before." Dearborn's expression had altered, her gaze narrowed.

Kate was expecting the reaction and challenged her. "All this time we've been working through my PTSD, all those nightmares linked to my homicide cases—if you'd been in my shoes, would you have taken those murder scenes home with you to share?"

"You know I can't bring anything that happens here home either—the ethics of my profession. Still, it's a very fair question, Kate. I get that my work hardly compares with the visceral impact of yours. But I like to think I'd have engaged any partner of mine in a discussion about my needing to not do it. Over our time together you've come to realize that you were the one who decided, you shut her off. Now, like before, you've taken it on yourself to protect Aimee without any consultation with her. Like before, it's at your very great expense."

More defensive with Dearborn's every word, Kate snapped, "This is *different* and you know it. This is a direct threat. It's *now* and it's *real*. And yeah, even though I agree with you about before, nothing I can do about what I did then, only about *now*."

"Of course this threat is real, I do know that. She knows that—"

Aimee didn't know anything about Ellie Shuster, but Dearborn didn't know it and didn't need to, Kate reminded herself.

"So how she feels about where you are now and what you've done with the condo—"

"Doesn't matter," Kate insisted.

"Doesn't matter," Dearborn repeated and shook her head. "How she feels doesn't matter. Her opinion doesn't matter." Her voice flattened. "You know it does. You've changed, grown, you've gained so much insight, you've—" She broke off and asked, "Kate, how are you feeling about the loss of her, about all this?"

Ambushed by the question, her heart lurching, Kate shifted in her chair. She and Aimee had been estranged before, three times in these last four years when periods of sobriety had been broken up by her renewed relationship with Cutty Sark. Aimee adamantly refused to be with her when she was drinking, Calla had also told her the last time that the refuge of this cottage office was closed to her till she was sober and solidly back in the disciplines of AA, offering referrals to other therapists. Each time she had fled to the harshness and peace of the desert, two hours away from the tormenting city where alcohol offered the one reliable refuge from the demons inhabiting her. But no separation had been like this one. Never with these stakes, never this long, and never with this vast distance, this arctic silence between them…

She said raggedly, "Calla, I was there for Anne and we made a good life together. With Aimee I can't change all those years with her, the best years of her life wasted on me." Her voice was a rasp. "I was in the closet and she wasn't. I locked her out of my job, that whole huge vital part of me. Even when I was with her, I wasn't. I was soaking my brain in Cutty Sark to drown what I saw every day. All those years with her I was nothing but a mess, I was a bloody drunk, I gave her *nothing*."

Dearborn's lips had thinned as Kate spoke, her forehead deeply scored with frown lines. She picked up her pen and tapped it on the arm of her chair as she spoke emphatically: "Aimee saw you, *she knew who she was with*. She made a *choice*, she stayed with you because of what she saw in you. You were no different from a boxer taking shots to the head and suffering the cumulative consequences. She *had* to see that happening to you and all along she stuck by you. Because you're *worth* it to her and she loves you for who you actually are."

"Calla, the job is no excuse for what I did to her. I was just a cop. No different from hundreds of thousands of other cops."

"That's utter rubbish and you know it." The tone was acid, the pen tapped more emphatically. "You were a *homicide detective*. With bodies and blood and smells from the most horrific crimes right up in your face every day, reaching right into your very soul. All the survivors, the mothers, fathers, husbands, wives, children—you were right there with them on the very worst day of their entire lives."

The words were like blows and it took Kate several breaths before she could say, "I should never have been with Aimee. Not ever."

"Oh, Kate." Dearborn shook her head. "That's your depression speaking. Let's get back on the topic of the condo. Can you at least see that what you did with it was a *fait accompli*? And your place in the desert—"

"I know." Raising both hands, Kate said, "I never even had a conversation with her. But I did what I had to do. Calla, I had to do *something*. Can't you see I had to do something *significant* to try and make it up to her…"

Like Geneva Fallon. How could I think I was in any way superior to her? How am I any goddamn different from her and what she did to that teacher?

Dearborn sharply tapped her pen. "Where are you, Kate? Where did you just go that you won't tell me about as usual?"

Kate ignored this constant challenge of Dearborn's and continued, "If we'd been legal, Aimee would have half the condo anyway and—well, she deserves a place of her own free and clear of me. You know the inheritance from my aunt bought that house in Yucca Valley. I don't need anything more. If I'm to stay sober I have to be the person I can live with, Calla. Given what's going on now."

Hands in her lap, Dearborn lifted and dropped the last three fingers of her left hand, an unconscious gesture Kate had come to recognize as a letting go, at least temporarily, of a particular topic.

"What about Dylan? How does he fit into all of this?"

She lightened at this mention of her nephew. "He's got his own life now, thank God. So immersed in transgender rights I don't see him or his partner or his mother all that much. Especially now that I'm living where I am."

"Do they—"

"They don't know, and I'm keeping it that way."

Again the three fingers rose and fell. "How is your sobriety, Kate?"

She gave the same response she'd given to Joe Cameron but in a less churlish tone: "Holding." She added, "Pure hell."

She had weathered another crisis two evenings ago. With her nerves incandescent filaments of need, she'd walked far into the moonlit, starry desert, gun tucked in her belt, asking herself why she should go back when the next five minutes could bring the end from the woman determined to kill her and what was the point of not drinking, what was the point of anything?

She told Dearborn, "Sometimes I want so desperately to just not feel again. For even a few minutes. To hold a drink in my hand and remember how it was to have that alcohol spreading through me and everything that hurt just fade away. But if I hold a drink, I'll drink that drink and I won't stop. Sometimes it's not one day at a time, it's five minutes at a time. I call my sponsor, he's always there for me." As he had been that night. One bar of cell phone signal might have preserved her life. For now.

Dearborn nodded. "I know I've helped you work through and lessen the nightmares, but he's more valuable to you than I could ever be."

"In that one way I suppose he is. Nothing like another recovering alcoholic cop who's ex-military like me. You know what Justin told me the other night? That I'd hit the trifecta. Born a lesbian and hated for it. Served in Vietnam and hated for it. Became a cop and hated for it. He's right there with me on everything."

Dearborn's eyes acquired an opaqueness while she considered this, and remained opaque while she asked, "How often are you going to meetings?"

"Several times a week. When it's bad and I need to get out of the house I go every day. I pretty much just listen when I'm there. Being there is what helps."

Dearborn's eyes sharpened on her but she offered mildly, "Perhaps you and Justin might concede that the world's a bit different now. Vietnam vets, today you're honored. You have a community of LGBT people, a transgender nephew who adores you. A police family who've made it clear they value all your years of service and want to protect you. We even have a Black president."

"Yes. All good stuff," Kate said. And shrugged.

Dearborn looked at her mournfully. "Are you sleeping?"

Again Kate shrugged. "I nap so I don't get too tired, so I can try and wake myself before I get too far into any dream. They're not as horrific now, thanks to you." She sat up in her chair. "I'll tell you exactly how I'm dealing with this, Calla. Every day, every minute, I'm *aware*. And that's different from not wanting to feel. I'm more *aware* than I've ever been. Every plant and bird and insect and living thing, with my every breath I'm *aware*. The one big reason I don't dull any of that with booze is Ellie Shuster and knowing I feel so aware because I could die any minute. Since Maggie passed, those people I visit in the hospice where she was, they're a gift. I'm so much right there with them I could even have a bed in the place. Just like them I've been given a terminal diagnosis."

Dearborn nodded. "I can see that. Except there's a possible cure for your particular terminal illness. There's hope Ellie Shuster may come to her senses and decide she really doesn't want to go back on death row for the premeditated murder of a police officer."

"She won't. Not with what was taken from her. She always said she was innocent—"

"Don't they all?"

"Yes, pretty much," Kate conceded. "I learned early on that 'I didn't do it' usually translates into 'I can't believe I did it, not me, I couldn't possibly have done it.' But something should have told me to hear her…"

"So you haven't come a single inch away from blaming yourself."

"Why would I? I was lead investigator."

Dearborn held up a hand. "I won't go there again, Kate, we've argued and argued about it. So let's take another perspective. She's what, mid to late fifties? She has a lot of life ahead of her."

"Right. But in her view, a half-life."

The fingers rose and fell. "Are you being physically active?"

"When I can," Kate deflected. Except for the sojourn into the desert, she'd not emerged for weeks from that chair next to Maggie's urn except for meetings, for hospice, for her appointments here.

"How's that anger you told me about last time?"

"Okay. Under control." But she involuntarily flexed her right hand. She'd almost broken it three days ago in a fury of counter pounding when she fumbled and dropped an iced tea. And she'd nearly kicked a cupboard door off its hinges when it didn't immediately open…

"From where I sit," Dearborn offered in her low, sonorous tones, "I see a woman who's estranged herself from the people who care about her. A woman in a vortex of negativity. I see a huge distortion of blame and shaming of self, self-destructive behavior—"

"*I'm* being self-destructive? Someone is out to *kill* me. All I'm trying to do is avoid collateral damage to the people I care about!"

Dearborn said calmly, "And how are you dealing with that, how are you proactively helping yourself cope with the anxiety, despair, the fear?"

"For one thing," Kate sniped, "I'm seeing you for my usual ice-cold shower of criticism."

Dearborn smiled. "If Maggie were still alive—"

"Right. I know." Kate grinned at an image of Maggie confronting her, hands braced on the waist of the cargo shorts she always wore. "She'd be ten times harder on me than you."

"Another one who tried to make you see the fine person the rest of us see."

Kate spread her hands. "Calla, I have to do what I have to do. I can't do anything more until Ellie Shuster acts. Realistically, there's no point in wasting police resources protecting me when she's had twenty years to figure out how she'll take me down. She could have shot me this morning on the freeway."

Dearborn sighed. "It's an awful, awful way to live, Kate. I am so sorry." She added, "But I have to tell you…I see your behavior as less pragmatism than fatalism."

You're right, Kate thought. But she said, "If I wanted to die, I could do it right here and now with the weapon I'm carrying. I'm doing the best I can."

"I know. I know you are, Kate. I hope it's at least helping you to talk to me about it. My door's open to you day or night. I want you to come in as often as you can."

"Thank you, Calla," Kate said. "This is the one place where I *can* talk about it. Where there's honesty I can trust. Where I feel seen. Understood. Right now you're more important to me than anyone else."

The two women looked at each other, and Kate saw and felt palpable warmth, a not uncritical but unconditional acceptance of her that she'd known only with Maggie.

Holding her gaze, Dearborn leaned forward as if to further the connection. "Then listen to me, Kate. Hear me. You tell me you're being realistic. The test is, if Ellie Shuster were hit by a bus today, where would you be? You face a terrible threat, I do see that, feel that. I fear for you like everyone else in your life fears for you. As you face this threat, the real question is: how much value are you truly, fully, actually placing on your one wild and precious life?"

Kate nodded. Got up, grabbed her shoulder bag, and left the cottage-office with Calla's words reverberating.

5

Turning off La Cienega onto Wilshire Boulevard, Kate ruefully reflected over Pilar Adams's remark about leaving a million dollars on this street if driving into LA were the requirement to collect it. The prestigious six-lane boulevard, for which her LAPD Wilshire Division was namesake, had always been the most elegant of the thoroughfares stretching from downtown to the ocean, but over the years she'd borne daily witness to its transmutation into an ever denser corridor of massive office buildings, impressive hotels and department stores, imposing religious edifices, expensive high-rise residences, and more and more vehicles crawling antlike between them, toward or away from downtown.

"Everything changes, nothing stays the same," Maggie chanted in Kate's head, her standard phrase whenever Kate had lamented changes to the city.

"If you were here you'd be bitching too," Kate retorted as a distant red light halted all progress. "Just try that drive in from your house in Encino these days..."

Finally she crossed Fairfax and turned onto South Curson Avenue. Glancing again at the street sign, she muttered, "Curse. On."

The block she sought soon appeared before her, a quiet, pleasant middle-class street just as it had been twenty years ago when a murder and suicide were so shocking in their ramifications that news vans were encamped for days. *Unbelievable* and *How could anyone do this* had been common refrains from residents to the TV and print reporters. She drifted the Jeep along the very same row of shaggy untrimmed palm trees in curb cutouts. The same concrete stairs that led up to the doorways of a mixture of older homes and small apartment buildings elevated from the street, their slanted front lawns shaded by a variety of small trees and bushes, bordered at street level by hedges or low walls of stucco and used brick. It was trash pickup day: black and bright blue bins for garbage and recycling sat curbside in the street, an occasional green bin for garden clippings in the mix. Despite the only sporadic presence of attached garages, open spaces were available as they had been back then, thanks to two-hour daytime parking signs. In a city of dramatic change, this block seemed unaltered over the years since she'd been supervising detective on the Shuster case. *Perfunctory* supervising detective, came the acid bath reminder.

Kate pulled into the curb across from where the Shusters had lived. She sat head down, unmoving, engine idling, gathering herself against the urge to simply drive on. Since the murder, not once had she driven down this street. Nor to certain other murder scenes that had eaten away parts of her over the years. A block on Grammercy Place; another on Wheeler with its infamous alley. A section of Hancock Park. Most of all, a particular stretch of La Brea, scene of a crossroads case early in her career, where the Nightwood Bar had lived and died. Where Dory Quillin had lived and died, bludgeoned with a baseball bat at age nineteen beside the VW van she had made her home, believing she would be safe behind a secluded lesbian bar. The women in the Nightwood Bar, especially Maggie, had come into Kate's life during that mid-eighties investigation, at first openly hostile—in those days all police were the enemy—only to have Maggie become her closest friend and the other women her enduring family over the decades.

Kate finally lifted her gaze to the green stucco duplex where fifteen-year-old April had suffered a fate similar to nineteen-year-old Dory—death by blunt force trauma—behind the Shuster house. The murder weapon for this homophobic murder had been far more symbolic than a bat: a heavy bronze crucifix. Kate gripped the steering wheel as stark memory broke through: the young body savagely ripped open by the sharp angles of the weapon, the grass around her submerged in crimson, T-shirt and cutoff jeans drenched, blond hair a reddish mass in her crushed skull, her eyes dull, dark, frozen. Far, far too similar to that other murder years earlier, that other crushed-in skull, those wide blue eyes of Dory Quillin fixed forever on her unimaginable killer.

That day twenty years ago she had taken one staggering step back from April Shuster's body, knowing in an instant that she couldn't do this. Couldn't possibly bear up under another case like the Dory Quillin murder. But caught herself before anyone saw her recoil, knowing also that recusal was impossible. Display or admission of what would surely be interpreted as weakness would finish her police career, transform her into just another female proven unfit for the job, tainted and diminished beyond recovery in the eyes of superior officers and colleagues.

In escalating distress as motive quickly emerged, also too similar to that earlier case, she'd improvised, directing partner Torrie Holden, around the murder scene, Torrie responding with alacrity at this wholly unexpected trust in her in a homicide that would have high visibility, that had already drawn a flock of news vans. Later in the day Kate had deferred to Torrie's detailed presentation of the case to Lieutenant Bodwin, expressing a confidence in Torrie more wishful thinking than reality, promising close supervision of a D-1 with two years' experience in homicide. With the approval of the divisional lieutenant and captain in place over what appeared to be a slam dunk case, Torrie had read it all as an initial test of her potential to take the lead on a future major investigation. As had everyone around her, admiring Kate for her generous mentoring of an up-and-coming female detective. No one had the remotest clue that for her the merest brush against the case was torture, her conscience-salving justification that, bottom line, it was indeed a slam dunk.

The arrest of the murdered girl's mother the same day had allowed her to further withdraw to the sidelines. She'd not interviewed the prime suspect, quickly drawn away from the one-way glass of the interview room, scarcely able to look at her, merely scanning reports and witness statements. On the basis of experience and on principle she had not questioned Torrie's contemptuous dismissal of Eleanor Shuster's furious denials. Erupting behavior that Torrie considered further evidence, behavior that had similarly manifested itself in the rageful, premeditated killing of daughter April. Since Kate had not personally collected or assessed all the available evidence, Torrie Holden had given courtroom testimony on what was observed at the crime scene and discovered subsequently as supporting evidence.

If the investigation of the murder of April Shuster had been flawed, it was because it had been compromised by the weakest of links—herself. She now knew that her abdication had led to assumptions, misjudgments, missed steps. Which, quite possibly, might have made no difference whatever—she would never know how the investigation might have gone down had she been supervising detective in more than name only. Only one person had known how eminently culpable she was: Maggie, who'd waved it off as justifiable self-preservation in the face of the rabid machismo of police culture and, after the arrest and conviction of Ellie Shuster, harmless. Aimee had had no clue. Nor, later, Joe Cameron. Not even Calla Dearborn, to whom she'd described the murder scene only as a component of her PTSD, uncertain about the reporting requirements of Calla's psychotherapy profession and any ramifications, given Calla's previous affiliation with LAPD's Behavioral Science Services unit.

Her worst misjudgment had been the naïve supposition that Torrie Holden being parent to a fourteen-year-old daughter would lead to maximum commitment and meticulousness. Not, as it turned out, to excessive emotional involvement, derailment of protocol, infuriated determination that maximum punishment be imposed for the unthinkable crime of filicide. Killing not just one teenager but two, in Torrie's mind, since the murder had led to the compounding heartbreak of the same-day suicide of sixteen-year-old Stella Hayden in the adjacent duplex.

Letting memory free-associate, Kate took her time looking over the sage green stucco duplex, a simple but handsome square, an anomaly amid its more graceful neighbors, many of them Spanish style with tile roofs and arched windows. The long vertical windows of the duplex were shaded by translucent cream-colored curtains, aesthetic improvement over the blinds that had been the window coverings when she was last here. The duplex's single front door led to a small foyer, she recalled, then adjacent doors to each identical two-story unit. Two bedrooms and bath upstairs; living room, dining area, kitchen and half-bath downstairs. Both units with back doors to a shared small lawn and hedged garden...

A shadow loomed over her window followed by a rap on the glass. Startled, Kate rolled down her window to a white-haired, hunched-over old woman leaning on a tall cane, peering in at her through oversize glasses fashionable in the seventies.

"I'm guessin' you know there was a murder in that place you're lookin' at?" she quavered.

"Yes, I know," said Kate.

"They let her go more'n a year ago, you know, the mother."

"Yes. Yes, I know."

The old woman's rheumy hazel eyes narrowed. "I wondered back then, you know, I wondered."

Kate's interest had sharpened with each exchange. She, better than anyone, had learned that progress in any sort of criminal investigation rested all but entirely on people's willingness to talk. And gossip. "You were a neighbor?"

A slight tilt of the woman's cane indicated a house behind her. "Right next door. Been there fifty-two years. New people in that duplex now, a'course. Right nice people. Better people."

She did not remember this neighbor, no surprise, but she would certainly have been interviewed, her statement amid the FIs in the murder book. Kate asked, "Did you know the Shusters and the Haydens well?"

"Hah. Not my kind of folk. Gospel music pumpin' outta there—"

"Both families?"

"More the Haydens. But they coulda had a cross tattooed on their foreheads, the lot of 'em. Sunday mornings them four and the two daughters'd all be marchin' off to their crazy church and I'd be out here doin' stuff for my place and them four parents'd look at me like I was a heathen sack of sin."

Kate nodded. Religious extremism was all over the reports, had been all over the news. The major motive at the trial.

The old woman was staring at her. "Who are you with all these questions, what're you doin' here? Another damn reporter? Rubberneckin'? Casin' the place?" She cackled at her last query.

"I was one of the detectives involved in the investigation back then."

The old woman backed away, immediately somber, shaking her head at Kate. "Don't remember you, you're not one that talked to me. The mother locked up all those years—you must feel like a pile of manure."

"I do," Kate said. The note this morning with its unnerving Yucca Valley postmark had been the impetus for this visit, but she was at a loss to actually explain her presence. Why *was* she here? What did she think she'd accomplish?

"So who did kill that poor girl?"

"It's under investigation."

The old woman heaved a sigh. "So nothin' new, you're tellin' me. Your people came 'round again when the mother got let go, but nobody since. Been months and months. I expect you're wantin' to take a look inside the place again."

"With new owners—"

"Away." She waved a shooing hand. "France or whatever they're tourin' this week. Been gone a month. I'm lookin' after their pitiful excuse for a dog."

She brightened at Kate's smile. "Well, you know, one of them bitty things that just bark. So, you wanna take a gander at the place again? Wait, I suppose I should look at some ID."

"I wish I could show you some," Kate said, opening her door. "I'm retired."

Looking Kate over as she stepped out of the Jeep, the old woman nodded. "Shoulda guessed. If you were still there I might be thinkin' about applyin' for a job myself."

"Thanks," Kate said with a grin. "My name's Kate."

"I'm Agatha. Lookin' your age ain't no sin," she said, shaking off Kate's assisting hand on her arm as they crossed the street. "I get myself around just fine with this cane. Up them steps too."

Inside the foyer, a sharp yapping began as Agatha inserted a key she pulled from the pocket of an ochre dress that looked like a monk's robe, heavy for a warm spring day. "Stand back so I can get Peaches before she runs out. Silly name for a silly dog."

The door opened to a frenzied miniature dachshund which Agatha scooped up and cradled as it excitedly jumped about in her arms and licked the grinning woman's neck and face. "She's a sweet little thing," she conceded sheepishly. "I'll give her some treats while you have your look."

Kate was already viewing with inordinate relief a living room transformed from her agonized memory of it. Gone were the religious posters crowding the walls, the furniture surfaces spilling over with stacks of doctrinal books, pamphlets, bulletins, symbols, and artifacts. Color-accented walls supplanted the previous universal beige paint; hardwood floors replaced carpet; a wood-burning fireplace, forbidden and useless long before these days of climate change, had vanished in favor of a solid wall. Rigorous simplicity was now the norm—leather furniture in pastel shades not unlike her own was a considerable visual improvement over the Shusters' fussy floral-patterned sofa and armchairs. And instead of the pervasive, sickening aroma of incense she remembered, the air now held the musty scent of absence.

"The Johnsons—them's the new owners—bought this whole place for a song," Agatha commented, watching Kate's scrutiny. "Two girls dead here, who'd want it? Stripped both units, redid 'em top to bottom. Only the backyard's pretty much the same."

Why wouldn't the first priority be altering the scene of a horrific murder, Kate wondered.

"Outta some sort of respect for the dead," Agatha offered as if reading her mind. "Can't get you in next door," she added. "I don't much see them people but they look okay, you might ask 'em. That's the place I can't see anybody buying. God almighty, sleepin' in that bedroom where Stella died?" Her gaze sharpened behind the oversize glasses. "What I heard, she found out about April and cut herself open like she was in a great big hurry to go with her."

Kate did not reply or react. The description was more accurate than Agatha could imagine. Inspection of that scene had been relatively brief, this time justifiably—the box cutter in Stella's limp, bloodied palm, no sign of a struggle, and a final entry in her diary couldn't have been more conclusive of suicide. But even the abbreviated view had permanently etched the image of staring blue eyes in a snow-white face, the throat, wrists, even the ankles slashed open, the bleached body outlined in a vast red pool on pale cream sheets. Every drop of blood in Stella's face and body appeared to have drained into her clothing and the bed.

"I'd like to go upstairs," Kate said. But an overall uneasiness about being in here escalated into uncomfortable awareness that this was an invasion of privacy. She was not a cop, she did not have an approved search warrant, she was in here illegally.

"Then go ahead." Occupied with the exuberant dog, Agatha lowered herself to the sofa and waved her on with a shooing motion.

Kate gingerly climbed a set of stairs, once carpeted but now gleaming hardwood, to what had been the parents' room, the area of most interest to her. It too had been transformed.

Teakwood dressers and a headboard, replacing heavy mahogany, enlivened a room further lightened by white carpet and white-curtained windows.

Kate focused on the far wall, site of her single contribution to the investigation, which now held a large feature clock with radiating rainbow spikes. Some hours after medical examiner Walt Everson had opined from April Shuster's torn flesh that the likely weapon would be a heavy, sharply angular bludgeon, she'd noticed the crucifix hanging slightly askew on this bedroom wall, a faint smear next to it. An on-scene swab test had revealed dried blood in the crevices, later determined to be from the murdered girl, the smear on the wall also hers. Clearly the initial act after the murder had been to hastily rinse and replace the weapon, accounting for the stain on the wall—transfer probably from blood-spattered clothing to the killer's fingers.

Even more damning had been the results of an additional thorough search and inventory of the house, its purpose to rule out the theory of an intruder. April's father, inspecting the contents of his arrested wife's jewelry box, had visibly recoiled from the sight of a tiny silver crucifix. The cross was suspended from a broken chain, and, he reluctantly admitted, the chain and its cross had hung around April's neck every day of her young life. Photographs of her confirmed this, but tests on the smaller cross had come up negative for the presence of blood. The prosecution presented a closing argument theory that the mother's initial act had been to symbolically rip the cross from her daughter's neck before bludgeoning her to death for her mortal sin against God. Afterward, unwilling to consign so revered a religious object to casual disposal, she had concealed it among her own pieces of jewelry.

Lost in thought, Kate examined the room. It fronted the street; April Shuster's bedroom was the one that overlooked the backyard murder scene, a key fact at the trial to explain why discovery of the body had not occurred for several hours. Time of death, reckoned by body temperature and lividity, had been estimated between eight and eleven that morning, confirmed by the pathologist. But Eleanor Shuster had not reported her daughter's death till early afternoon—a 1:11 p.m. timestamp for the 911 call—believing April was in Bible class and claiming that in the busyness of the morning she had not once glanced into the backyard from the expansive kitchen window. Eleanor Shuster's whereabouts included errands and a visit to an ATM, for which the defense had produced electronic receipts. But the prosecution effectively countered with their own timeline, asserting that she had performed those activities only after she had murdered her daughter, rinsed and replaced the bronze cross on the wall, and left the house to dispose of blood-soaked clothing that had never been located. No traces of blood had been found in the bathroom sink and drain by SID, but could well have been washed away by an open, gushing tap.

Overriding all the testimony pro and con was Ellie Shuster's motive, fury with her daughter. Vividly recounted in Stella Hayden's diary over an eighteen-month period, the growing rage over her discovery of their lesbian relationship was so damning, so undeniable—even though the defendant characterized it as farfetched exaggeration—and so convincing that an outraged jury had deliberated only an hour to pronounce a first ballot verdict of guilty of first-degree premeditated murder with the special circumstance of lying in wait. Subsequently, they required only one additional hour to condemn to death one of the few women ever consigned to the Central California Women's Facility in Chowchilla to await execution at San Quentin. Not that it would happen—for decades, death row had been in name only in California, the last woman executed in 1962. But the California Supreme Court, five years into the sentence, had reduced the death penalty to twenty-five years to life. Its reasoning: imposition of the death penalty was the result of an overzealous prosecution and an emotion-driven verdict based on the unsupported and insufficient evidence of a diary. And special circumstances did not apply to a crime-of-passion homicide. Parole was then made possible, but had been about as likely as it was for the Manson family. Until, fourteen years later, the Innocence Project intervened with its definitive DNA results.

Since the killer was not Ellie Shuster, Kate mused as she glanced into the retiled bathroom, maybe it was April's father. Perhaps the likeliest suspect now, his motivation would have been the same as his wife's. Back then he'd been alibied airtight by Mathew Hayden, Stella's father, and four followers who claimed they'd all been in an activities planning session in the church all morning. Also a clerk who received Shuster's cash payment for gas at a Chevron station on Olympic. But Shuster's alibi had now acquired quotation marks. Eleanor Shuster's defense had contended that Mathew Hayden and any of the worshipful flock would have supported a claim of innocence if Daniel Shuster or any of the churchgoers had mowed down children in a playground. The four followers had indeed finally reneged on their testimony to attorneys from the Innocence Project. Even though reneged testimony was insufficient in overturning a conviction, they'd offered this supporting evidence in sworn statements, declaring they'd taken Daniel Shuster's word for his innocence and had simply closed ranks to protect their members from any shadow of suspicion. The eyewitness cashier remained steadfast, but his testimony had been rendered worthless within the timeframe of the murder.

So the Haydens, Veronica and Mathew, as well Daniel Shuster, had now become viable suspects with the same homophobic motive. All had been members of the Church of the Eternal Word, headquartered in a small white frame structure on the modest western end of Pico Boulevard. Identified only by a simple cross, the church had boasted a congregation of a mere sixty, its single financier aged Brentwood millionaire Andrew Pulman. After the deaths of the two girls, amid blistering TV and newspaper investigative reports and editorials characterizing the church and its tenets as a clone of the Westboro Baptist Church, the building had been vandalized and then shuttered. Pulman had withdrawn his support and himself, remaining in seclusion in Northern California until his death eight years ago. According to Joe Cameron, who had queried the current case detectives, the Haydens and Daniel Shuster left the country immediately after the trial, reportedly to take up missionary work in homophobic Uganda—the perfect alternative location, Kate thought, for their medieval theology. To this day, to anyone's knowledge, they had never returned.

Coming back down the stairs, she asked Agatha, "Could we step outside?"

"Peaches would love it," the old woman replied, hoisting herself from the sofa with the help of her cane. Moments later she opened the kitchen door into the backyard and the harsh bray of a nearby leaf blower, Peaches straining before her on the end of an extendable leash.

Kate braced herself in the doorway, inhaling the scent of mown grass, and stepped outside onto lawn deeply shaded within a circumference of tall ficus trees. She noted the changes over the past two decades: a lavish scarlet bougainvillea now climbed up the far side of the duplex; a row of lantana, bird of paradise, and fan palms lined the foundation of the duplex. She walked across the strip of lawn to where the ficus trees formed a corner.

"This where the poor girl was killed?" asked Agatha from beside her, the dog straining at its leash as it scampered around the yard.

Kate nodded, standing on pristine grass exactly where once a gory corpse had sprawled. She looked carefully back at the duplex. With the body in place, none of the photographs and drawings made at the scene had been from this exact perspective. April was killed in full view of her own family's kitchen window and at clear viewing angles from bedroom and kitchen windows of both units.

If Daniel Shuster's alibi was now in question, she mused, where had he actually been? Where had the Haydens been?

"What I can't figure," Agatha said, "is with me livin' just there"—she pointed beyond the ficus trees with her cane— "why didn't I hear a thing? Nobody did. Wouldn't the youngster scream?"

"The theory is she was incapacitated by the first blow." She did not mention the other theory, that April had been rendered mute with horror at the source and ferocity of the attack.

"Thank you, Agatha," Kate said quietly, and gestured that she was ready to head back inside. "I think I've seen enough for now."

"Glad to do it. I'm thinkin' I'll stay awhile and let Peaches run off some a' that energy." She nodded at Kate. "You just let yourself out." Her face softened. "Comin' here again after all this time…You just do your best to find some peace with yourself."

6

Waiting to reenter the congestion on Wilshire Boulevard, Kate argued with her impulse to head into West Hollywood. *Aimee figures to be at work*, she told herself. *No harm done, I could just take a quick look… You're hoping she's home. To catch sight of her. But what if she's with someone…*

At a break in traffic, Kate turned the car away from West Hollywood and directed her thoughts resolutely toward her next destination. Calla Dearborn's voice intruded: *"You have a gift for compartmentalizing."* "A survival technique," she'd retorted at the time. To which Dearborn had countered, *"An avoidance technique."*

Survival or avoidance, these days the "gift" stood her in good stead. A prime benefit of her house in the desert was its complete absence of Aimee. And the feline companion they'd raised from a kitten. To the places she would not go near because of too much traumatized memory, she'd had to add the veterinarian's office on Highland where she'd taken the aged and suffering Miss Marple. Back in the condo, during the months of her most recent separation from her, she saw Aimee everywhere, heard her everywhere. Seated in her favorite armchair watching TV news and commentary in headshaking disdain. Out on the balcony tending to her garden of potted flowers and herbs. Drinking coffee at the breakfast bar as she read the *LA Times*. Dancing through the house to her music, moving about the kitchen. The smells of her shampoo and perfume seemed to permeate the bathroom no matter what sprays or oils Kate employed to banish them, and as for the bedroom…

After all their years together, Aimee adhered to every part of her. And was a component of the ever-present craving for the soothing balm of Cutty Sark. *So tell me again, Calla, if it's going to hurt like this forever, why* not *kill myself? Why* not *drink?* To these constant rhetorical questions she mouthed, "Later," her go-to word.

She turned off Wilshire toward Sunset, and soon afterward drove up the graceful curve of Hyperion Avenue to the wooded, secluded area that held Silverlake Haven. Pulling the Jeep under the oak tree where she usually parked, she said aloud, "Contrary to that 'everything changes' claim of yours, Maggie, your hospice is exactly the same. Same nice neat building, same plants and trees, same messy lawn. Same old dying."

She sat, chirping birds and the occasional tick of the cooling engine the only sounds in the peace of her surroundings, thinking that there was no compartmentalization here, no avoidance. This place, where the dearest friend of her lifetime had breathed her last, had never made the avoidance list. Ironically, returning here as a trained hospice volunteer had become a net positive amid all the negativity that infected her. Experiencing the place as the final repository of Maggie's living self seemed to provide a sort of necessary linkage between that last essence of Maggie and the bookshelf in the high desert where her ashes now rested along with the coffee mug she'd used most days of her life. Here was compartmentalization at its best.

Moments later, opening the tall oak door into the hospice, Kate entered the light-filled reception room. Marla, wearing her usual blue nursing scrubs, was at the reception desk working at her computer on the endless forms and reports required by medical and regulatory agencies.

She smiled at Kate. "Always good to see you."

"Good to see you too, Marla." She meant it in every sense. Along with being a very pretty Latina, to Kate her calm demeanor and qualities of character verged on the saintly.

"Loretta so looks forward to your visits, Kate."

"I'm glad she's still here. Anything I should know?"

"She's hardly eating…you know what that means. My guess is another week. All she talks about is Gloria. Any word on her?"

Kate shook her head. "Loretta insists she never left Minneapolis, never married or changed her name—she's right there. I can't understand why she'd not be easy to track down. But, still working on it. I'll find her."

Marla smiled and went back to her task, and Kate made her way quietly on through reception, past what appeared to be a Latino husband, wife, and teenage son gathered in earnest heads-together conversation around the fireplace area. Inhaling the astringent scents of medicine mixed with cleaning products, she waved to two white-clad attendants, Alicia and Marcus, who greeted her with wide smiles as she went into the rear corridor.

Loretta Giovanni's room was three doors down, one door closer than Maggie's room had been, and across the hall. Like Maggie's room it held two bedridden occupants. One lay asleep under a pale yellow blanket, mouth agape, an oxygen line attached to her nose, her breathing audible, her hair spread in white wisps on her pillow. Loretta sat propped against several pillows, gazing out the window into greenery where two hummingbirds whizzed around a bright red feeder.

Most residents, Kate had observed, spent these final few days and nights of their lives asleep or dozing under the influence of powerful painkillers and relaxants. They always reminded her of her mother's rose garden in Michigan in late fall, the perfect summer beauty of the roses in drooping collapse, the petals holding onto their color but transformed into delicate tissues hanging tenuously from green stems, soon to be pulled away by a stray breeze or simple gravity.

Kate knocked lightly and Loretta's head jerked around in several birdlike motions, her eyes a medicated haze, pupils dilated. Kate asked, smiling, "Remember me?"

"Of coursh," she slurred, and continued slowly, "Coursh I do. The retired poleesh detective."

"Is this a good time for a visit?"

"Alwaysh a good time. Thosh two little guysh"—she pointed a shaky finger at the zooming hummingbirds—"sho mush energy."

Smiling, Kate pulled a chair close to the bed. She had been visiting Loretta, who had kidney cancer, for the last three weeks. "How are you doing today?"

"Not sho bad. Jashon jush gave me morphine. How good of you to vishit twish in one week."

"I'm glad to, Loretta." She hadn't been here for five days but didn't bother correcting her; heavily medicated hospice patients often had a confused concept of time.

"Kate…my Gloria? Will I be sheeing her?"

Gazing at the fragile woman before her, the supplicating eyes, Kate made an instant calculation and concluded: *Why not?* She said with a smile, "I came here to tell you she's on her way."

Loretta smiled beatifically. "What wonderful newsh. Thank you sho much."

"Your son visiting you today?"

"Every day. Every day after hish work. You reading to me today?" The signal that her supply of energy for conversation had been exhausted.

Kate reached over and plucked an ancient paperback of *A Tale of Two Cities* from a drawer in the bedside table. She began, as she always did, at the famous opening lines about the best and worst of times; Loretta could no longer hold onto any details of the ongoing story. Kate was grateful it was an opening worth rereading for the third time.

Twenty minutes later, with Loretta lulled to sleep by her shot of morphine and the cadence of her voice, Kate quietly replaced the book in its drawer, drew the blanket up to Loretta's shoulders, and made her way from the room.

Marla beckoned to her, and she stopped at the desk. "Someone else wants to see you," Marla told her. "Monique came in just yesterday, heard you were here today and is asking if you could stop in."

Kate pointed to herself. "Me specifically."

"You specifically." Marla smiled. "You must know by now—everybody talks about you. The staff, the patients. A retired police detective is even better than a priest. You hear confessions but pronounce no judgments."

Kate grinned. "Yeah, but no absolution either." She glanced at her watch. Traffic was always the major issue, getting out of town before the rush-hour deluge.

Marla said, "She really pleaded. She's day-to-day with pancreatic cancer."

To hell with traffic. What did it matter? "Where is she?"

"Next to Loretta, room four."

"Okay, and just so you know," Kate said, "I told Loretta that Gloria's on her way. I'll try to make it happen."

Marla blinked, then said softly, "That's the best thing you could tell her." She leaned across her desk, gazing at Kate. "Over the years I've learned only two things ever really matter to the people here. One is love they found or lost. The second is regret over some act or decision or crossroads they didn't take."

"Love and regret," Kate said, mulling over this distillation of where she herself was these days.

"Working here makes me think the rest of us live our lives as if...I don't know, as if we're all like ants just crawling along," Marla said. "Oblivious. Clueless."

Kate nodded. "The people here teach me so much..."

"Me too, Kate. You bring a lot of comfort to them."

Kate smiled as she walked away. As she'd told Calla Dearborn, she was now out of the cop business but still in the confession business. Dying people protected family and friends by minimizing their pain and their fears of impending demise, but they told the truth to hospice volunteers. With these perfect strangers they could speak openly about death, dread, sorrow, pain, regret...anything.

The name in the placeholder on the doorway of room four read *Monique Lefleur*. The last name resonated with Kate, pinging a memory too nebulous for recall.

Monique lay alone in the room; the bed across from hers was made up and awaiting its next occupant who would surely arrive momentarily. This small hospice was always full.

Black hair lay in thin wisps on Monique's scalp, the hair color unusual in this place where gray or white heads were the norm. Abnormal to have hair at all with chemotherapy a standard treatment for pancreatic cancer. The woman was tiny, so thin that her skin, with its symptomatic jaundice, seemed draped over the bones visible above the blanket.

Walking over to Monique's bed, she said, "I'm Kate. You wanted me to visit?"

"Yes, yes, thank you," was the reply, the voice clear but faint. Kate very gently took the ice-cold scrawny hand the woman extended. "You perhaps knew my husband. Phil Lefleur."

Memory immediately broke through. Patrol Sergeant Phillip Lefleur, from the dawn of her police career. What would it be now, forty years ago? "For sure I knew him," she said. "He was in my division. He disappeared—"

"He didn't. I know exactly where he is."

Kate released the cold hand to contemplate her. What was she about to hear from this dying woman?

"Best you sit," Monique said, indicating the bedside chair. "I'm waiting on painkillers till I talk to you."

As Kate scraped the chair over close to the head of the bed to better hear the wispy voice, Monique pointed to her. "There was a woman officer. Maybe you. So very unusual to see women police back then."

Kate nodded. "Yes, it was unusual."

"Easier for me," Monique said, "if you tell me what you remember." She reached for the glass of water on the bedside table.

Kate summoned more memory of the sensational, notorious case, unsolved to this day as far as she knew. Despite the passage of so much time, police response to the disappearance had made an indelible impression on a newly minted police officer like herself.

She recalled, "The missing person report came during roll call and every single Wilshire officer was assigned—he was one of ours. I know we traced every minute of Sergeant Lefleur's last day on the job. Interviewed everyone he came into contact with, every friend and relative, people in every hangout he was known to frequent. I was assigned to field interviews near the house, so yes, it might have been me you saw…I remember it turned out he'd put in an ordinary shift and just went home…" Tactfully, she stopped, did not mention the neighbors' report of hearing what might have been a gunshot around the time Lefleur would have arrived at his home.

"Yes. Phil's car was in the garage, so it looked like he came home. It turned out no one saw him leave…You probably know they searched the house, even knocked out one wall. Tested everywhere for blood, especially in the car, even dug up part of the yard."

Kate nodded. "You say you know where he is…"

She raised a hand. "Before that, let me tell you why." She closed her eyes and grimaced in a spasm of pain that might be as much anguish from surfacing memory as it was physical.

"You probably won't remember we had a daughter. Eight years old. The night before, something woke me up. Around midnight. Phil was out of bed. Something told me to…I got up. He was in Isabel's room bent over her, the fly open on his pajamas, his…his…" She broke off, gripped her glass of water, sipped noisily through its bent straw.

Her hand groped toward Kate, and Kate again took hold of it, her own hand now as cold as Monique's.

"I was barefoot and my daughter's eyes were squeezed shut so neither of them heard or saw me. I don't know what possessed me not to scream…I just knew to back away. I ran into the living room, yanked a picture down off the wall so hard it crashed to the floor and smashed the glass. I flew into our bedroom. Of course Phil ran out to check on the noise and I came out of the bedroom like I'd just heard it too. He assumed it fell off the wall, so he tended to it while I went in to see about Isabel...She grabbed me, she was crying...I pulled her pajama bottoms down and...and looked at her, Kate. Nearly as I could tell, whatever he was doing to her, it wasn't..."

She closed her eyes. "I knew right away what I had to do, and I was awake all night lying next to that monster figuring how I could do it." She opened her eyes to stare unblinkingly at Kate. "You do understand why I didn't just call the police? Back then?"

Back then. Kate nodded and the two women contemplated each other in mute, total understanding. Back then a husband's ownership of a family was sacrosanct along with the belief that a bit of rough treatment was probably what the wife or kids had coming to them, and spousal abuse, even child endangerment, especially if it involved a police officer, was greeted with skepticism or tolerance, at worst by "Hey, brother, now don't you do that again." Monique Lefleur accusing a police officer with the rank of sergeant, in the absence of clear evidence? Her husband would simply brand her crazy, it would be an exercise in futility and self-destruction.

"The next morning I asked my mother to pick up Isabel after school saying Phil and I had to go out that night. I put on dark glasses and a hat and got a bus to the airport. Rented the most ordinary car, a Chevy, at the busiest counter. I had to use my license so all I could do was hope a busy clerk wouldn't remember me or my name. We had a two-car garage, I parked it in there. When Phil came home, I told him the car was Sally's, a friend who'd come in from Phoenix, and she'd gone out for a walk."

Monique grimaced again, took another sip of water. "He took off his police belt and bent down to open the gun safe like he always did. I pulled the gun out of the holster, pointed it at him and told him I was going to drive him to St. Basil's for us to talk with a priest about what he did with our daughter. He said I was crazy but I told him what I saw and I'd shoot him right there if he didn't do what I said, which I would have, and he could tell I meant it. He probably figured if I was driving he'd just humor me and get the gun away soon as we got in the car.

I told him he had to get in Sally's Chevy because our car had a police radio and he wasn't to call his cop friends. He didn't argue, he just shrugged and we went to the garage and he got in the passenger seat. I opened the driver door, braced the gun in both hands like I knew to do with the recoil, and shot him in the head. Shot him dead."

Kate let out the breath she didn't know she was holding.

Monique nodded at Kate's reaction and said dispassionately, "I was lucky. Some splatter. But the bullet stayed in him, didn't hit the car. I thought about that too, you see. If the bullet went through him and hit the car, I figured I'd just have to take it somewhere and wreck it."

There wouldn't have been all that much mess from the shot, Kate thought, if it wasn't a through and through. Back then cops did not have today's more powerful nine millimeters for service weapons. They wore .38s, a much lesser weapon, one she still had, now locked in the glove compartment of her car.

"We had rags and bottles of water in the garage, I grabbed some, took his gun belt from where he'd left it in the house, threw it in the car. I put a Dodgers cap on him. I figured people would hear the shot and think it was a backfire, engines backfired in those days. But even so I hurried. Opened the garage, drove away fast as I could in case somebody did call the police. I drove him up to a Mulholland lookout. Parked real close to the edge, opened his door—he was already leaning against it—and pushed him out over the side and down the hill. Then I cleaned up the car. He didn't fall all that far and I still can't believe somebody didn't find him over the years. But that's where he is, the gun and belt and the bloody rags there with him."

"Isabel…"

Monique's bony head rose off the pillow. She pointed. "You might give me what's in that cup now." Kate handed her the tiny paper cup with its pain pill. Monique downed it quickly with a single sip of water, lay back with a relieved sigh. "I reported Phil missing. Mother kept Isabel with her over the next week or so."

"How did you explain his car being there? And the rental?"

"I didn't. I'd parked the rental a few streets over near a Seven-Eleven, picked up a few things from the store and walked home making sure some neighbors saw me. I right away called the division, said Phil's car was there but he wasn't, and he should be because we were going to a restaurant that night."

The timeline wouldn't have made any sense, Kate thought. To get to Mulholland and back would have taken the better part of an hour after Lefleur got home.

"Everyone was right away suspicious I'd done something to him," Monique said as if aware of Kate's train of thought. "His family, the police. With Isabel gone from the house that whole day they didn't question her, thank God. But when it came right down to it they couldn't figure out why I'd do anything to him, how I'd do it without leaving some trace, how I'd go about disposing of someone twice my size. They did test me for gunshot residue but I knew from Phil that just washing my hands would get rid of it. They finally decided maybe somebody'd jumped him when he parked the car, somebody he'd arrested along the way. But all their questions…if it hadn't been for Isabel I'd have broken down. I didn't know to protect her before but now I vowed…" Her yellowish eyes looked distant, burdened. She looked exhausted.

"Monique, you had no inkling?"

"None. I was his second marriage—he had a wife and teenage daughter over in Phoenix before he transferred to LAPD."

A daughter who grew beyond his appetite for children, Kate speculated. She asked cautiously, "Isabel…how is she?"

The reply was a fading whisper: "I don't know what Phil did before I found him out, but her life's been a mess."

"You did your best," Kate offered.

"She still has no idea," Monique said, closing her eyes, then reopening them with obvious effort.

"What about the rental car? How did you get that back without—"

"Days later I drove it to Palm Springs Airport, flew back. Phil wasn't as much of a story in Palm Springs." Her voice was an exhausted whisper.

Kate nodded. Technology today versus back then…those early days seemed so primitive now. She remembered the cynical, world-weary remark her first partner, Ed Taylor, had made after she'd made detective: "We catch the dumb ones, Kate. The smart ones, they can get away with anything."

"Monique," she asked carefully, "what is it you want me to do with this information?"

The bony shoulders shrugged against the pillow. "I don't care. I wanted to finally tell somebody. Have someone know. Understand. You seem...just right. Thank you."

Her cold hand gave Kate's a final squeeze, released; she closed her eyes and her waxen face slackened peacefully into sleep.

7

Twilight was deepening as Kate pulled her Jeep off the dirt road leading to her house and onto her crushed stone driveway. Cameron's Rav4 was parked far to her left, two wheels in desert sand to leave ample room, and he'd used his key to let himself in; lights were on in the house. She opened her car door to muted voices from the stucco cottage next door. Not unusual—Pilar always turned off the music in favor of dusk-till-bedtime TV. The closing slam of her car door brought a sharp barking from inside her house, and she halted in astonishment. What on earth was Cameron doing here with a dog?

The front door opened to Cameron braced in the doorway, restraining a frenzied black and white border collie by its collar. "This is Dakota," he announced, grinning as she approached.

"Hello, Dakota," she said with a smile, holding out the back of her hand. "How nice of you to welcome me into my house." The dog ceased barking and became a quivering stillness to sniff her, then backed away.

Kate moved past Cameron and tossed her shoulder bag onto a chair, Dakota lurching after her, then punched in the code to reset the alarm system. "So, now you have a dog?"

"Just looking after her for a colleague." Releasing the dog's collar and giving her a pat, he added nonchalantly, "I was hoping you might keep her for a couple of weeks."

"*What?*" She whirled on him. "Is this another of your crazy notions about protecting me?"

Shaking his head, he raised a palm. "Cool it, will you? My crazy notion was Dakota would love being in the desert instead of cooped up in my place. And maybe you'd give her more physical activity than I can. I had this other crazy notion about you maybe liking some quiet easy company."

Mollified, somewhat abashed, she searched for a reason to refuse. She'd once had a dog, Barney, a painful memory. Thirty years ago. With Anne. "I'm a cat person," she offered lamely.

"Who doesn't know that. It's only a couple of weeks, Kate. She's a really nice dog. I even brought her food."

Kate glanced at the bags of Purina on the counter, at a bowl of water and one of kibble on her kitchen floor, then locked gazes with Dakota who sat on her haunches, head cocked. Disconcerted by the dog's unblinking, alert, preternaturally blue eyes flanking a streak of white running down her handsome dark head, she broke away and strode into the kitchen. "Coke?" she asked, already pulling one out of the fridge.

"Whatever."

She prepared herself an iced tea, taking her time, still groping for an excuse to reasonably decline Cameron's request. Finally she came back and handed him the can of Coke, took an armchair across from him. Dakota, still sitting in the middle of the living room, swiveled her head from one to the other of them several times, then trotted over to Kate and flung herself down at her feet.

Cameron burst out laughing. "I've heard border collies top the list for intelligence. Dakota's just figured out who owns the place."

Kate reached a tentative hand down to pat the dog's head; Dakota butted her hand in appreciation. "I've heard this breed needs a lot of exercise," she muttered.

"Yeah, well, be good for you," Cameron returned, pointedly surveying her.

He crossed an ankle over a knee and Kate, continuing to pat Dakota's head, wryly looked him over. He wore his usual garb, jeans and T-shirt, but on his trim, fit figure, the T-shirt was pristine white and neatly tucked into crisply pressed jeans. His navy blue Skechers looked fresh from the box, his graying hair fresh from a barber, his smooth cheeks fresh from a razor. Cameron had changed in some respects over the years but never his fastidious ways.

He picked up the latest note from Ellie Shuster from the end table beside him, waved it at her and inquired sardonically, "Anything else interesting about your day?"

"Aside from not being shot, stabbed, poisoned, or run over," she said, "a few things." She decided she didn't want to talk about Geneva Fallon, did not even want to think about the woman again today. "I saw my shrink, heard a murder confession—"

"From your shrink?" he asked incredulously.

She laughed. "From a hospice patient. About a Wilshire cop who disappeared four decades ago." She related in thorough detail her visit with Monique Lefleur, Cameron sipping from his can of Coke as he listened without expression or interruption. He'd learned to be a keen listener as well as a decent interviewer during their time together as partners.

"That's quite a story," was all he offered when she concluded. His unspoken question hung in the air.

"I did ask what she expected me to do. She said she just wanted somebody to know."

"Let me guess. You're going to do fuck all."

She looked down at the dog who'd just moved herself to cover one of Kate's feet with her warm black and white body. "The animal kingdom is survival of the fittest," she murmured, "but that never includes raping its young." She reached down, this time to stroke her soft fur approvingly. "I should dredge up an obscenity of a human being, a pedophile cop, inflict him on his survivors for the sake of closing a cold case? Let him rot where he is."

"Wouldn't be much to find anyway, between the coyotes and the elements," he said easily. "I'd say justice was done."

She was hardly surprised by his reaction. During their time together, Cameron had stepped outside the strictures of police conduct with a motivation borne out of bitter disillusion with the parameters of justice. Years ago he'd managed to rope her into a scheme to scare out of town a pathological stalker they both knew law enforcement could not stop until he escalated to the final step of murdering his victim. Deeply conflicted by Cameron's vigilantism during their time together, she now looked back at his actions, and him, with far more equanimity.

"Your hospice visits…" He shook his head as if unable to further voice his thoughts.

She'd told him many stories about the remarkable people she'd met at Silverlake Haven, the end-of-life confessions and memories they so openly entrusted to her. She said, "They talk, I ask a few questions, I mostly just listen. To listen—that's always what they want most from me. Few ever expect me to actually do something. I told you about Loretta…I can't understand why it's so goddamn hard to track down this sister of hers with just an Internet search. You'd think she was in witness protection."

Cameron pulled out his cell phone. "What's her name again?"

"You hardly have time for this, Joe."

"Right, Kate, my days are so much better spent with scumbags and assholes." He sat with thumbs poised over the tiny keyboard.

She smiled at him. "Gloria Elena Romano, Minneapolis. Anything you can find out…Loretta's got maybe a week."

She sipped her tea while Cameron typed onto his notes page, put the phone away. She said, "One other thing today. I visited the Shuster house."

His eyebrows elevated. "First time, right?" The question was rhetorical, and he continued in a quiet tone, "You had a bad murder at that house, Kate. A really bad one for us to get wrong." He indicated the Ellie Shuster note he'd replaced on his end table. "This the reason?"

She gave a slight nod. "I've never not taken her seriously, Joe. But that note puts her on my doorstep. You and I both know she can't be stopped unless I get really lucky. It's now or never to finally figure out what happened twenty years ago. Anyway, what else have I got to do with what's left of my time?"

He didn't speak for some moments, looking everywhere but at her while he sipped his Coke. She knew he was upset but there was nothing she could do or say.

He finally asked, "So, how did it go at the Shuster place?"

"The current owners are traveling." She gestured toward Dakota. "But it's my day for dogs. A neighbor looking after the owners' dachshund let me in."

"An omen." He grinned at Dakota, who looked quizzically back, her head cocked. "So, what did you find out?"

"We missed something somewhere," she said drily.

"So, it was well worth your visit," he said equally drily. "Kate, how about a fresh pair of eyes on the case? How about we look at the murder book together?"

"I'd be very glad for that, Joe," she said fervently, "if you have the time." She would never have asked. Opening a murder book with all its minutia and leads and alleyways was like being dropped into a thicket in the middle of a maze.

He glanced at his watch. "Anything decent to eat in that so-called kitchen of yours?"

"I've got a pepperoni pizza in the freezer. Would that offend your sensibilities?"

"Sounds good. How about I bunk with you and Dakota tonight, leave early?"

"Great," Kate said and sprang up lest he change his mind. This was the best news of the day, week, month.

Dakota also rose and trotted behind her into the bedroom, sniffing the bookcases and then avidly around the bed as if assessing it for future occupancy. Amused by the efficient, purposeful investigations, Kate watched her for some moments before unlocking the floor safe and lifting out her Shuster files.

"Dakota likes you," Cameron commented when she returned with her armload of documents, Dakota at her heels.

"Proof positive that dogs aren't as discriminating as cats," she retorted, dumping everything on the breakfast bar.

"Or police captains. Nice you still have friends in high places to give you murder books. All my years at Wilshire and I'll never be able to ask Walcott for a toothpick."

"I get why you left Homicide Special," Kate told him, pulling photographs from an envelope file. "But the way the captain vouched for you, covered for you during that vanishing act of yours so you wouldn't damage your chances for promotion—"

"Yeah. And I embarrass her by pissing all over the promotion. It's good she figures she still owes you for saving my ragtag ass."

It was arguable how much saving she'd actually done during that near-lethal encounter with his brother, but she'd long since given up debating the point. Cameron was correct that her possession of a complete copy of the April Shuster murder book was entirely due to Captain Carolina Walcott. It had been delivered to Kate the day after Cameron learned about the first threatening note and sent a report up the chain of command. Walcott knew she would want a copy of the book and had found a way to make good on the debt she felt she owed to Kate.

"Pull up a barstool," Kate said, spreading out three photos on the counter as an initial step for Cameron.

She looked quickly away from the grim face of thirty-seven-year-old Eleanor Frances Shuster, whose defiant glower from a frontal view booking photo belied her innocence. The other two photos, left and right profile, were only slightly less difficult to look at. Waiting to stuff them back in the file after Cameron finished his perusal, she reminded herself: *Avoidance was your downfall.* She forced her gaze back onto the woman who was deciding the duration of her life.

"That face of hers would have done her no favors at trial," Cameron remarked, still studying her.

Contemplating the cold blue eyes with twin frown lines incised between them, the drawn-back lips, the dark hair pulled severely into a twist, Kate silently agreed; the face mirrored rigidity, projected the fanaticism that had been the prime focus at trial. She searched in a separate file and pulled out a photo she'd discovered online in a newspaper archive, the Shusters' wedding announcement reproduced in the *Los Angeles Times*. She placed the printout before Cameron and did not have to look at it to remember the inconsistency between that buoyant smile at age twenty-one and the combative image in the booking photos taken sixteen years later. When Cameron reacted with only a grunt, she wondered if perhaps there was no inconsistency, only a purely personal reaction on her part. Everyone she had ever known with a similar gap between their two front teeth seemed to combine an engaging personality with an artless, endearing smile. Still, even allowing that the wedding announcement photo conveyed a much younger woman yet to be radicalized, the happily smiling Ellie Shuster disconcerted Kate, so at odds was she with the woman at her arrest and trial.

Kate went around the counter to preheat the oven for the frozen pizza. Cameron pushed the photos aside, opened the thick, indexed murder book and began to slowly leaf through segments arranged in a precise order honed over the years for maximum efficiency in trial preparation. Kate watched with covert interest as he spared only a glance at the sections he considered peripheral for now: the chronological record and crime scene log. He stopped at the many-paged crime report, followed in sequence by the equally substantive and detailed death report. He sprung open the rings of the binder and removed these two segments, closed the rings and pushed the open book back over in front of her barstool, saying, "This will do me awhile."

She sat beside him and leafed past property and evidence until, with a smothered sigh, she stopped at the crime lab reports.

Here was the source of Ellie Shuster's acquittal. Here lay the stark, fundamental difference between criminal investigation in the last decade of the twentieth century and today. That difference being DNA, the science. DNA, the laboratory test. No matter how rigorously police investigations had been conducted pre-DNA, today's lab tests continued to discredit, negate, put the lie to conclusions drawn from the most meticulous police work and all other evidence gathered for criminal convictions.

We should never have had the hubris to impose the death penalty, she reflected. All the innocent, terrified people who were marched to their death... There was no such thing as infallibility except when it came to Catholic popes. And look at the controversies around these so-called inerrant disciples of God.

If only...if only. Because we *did* have the means early on, she lamented for an uncountable time. We had those tests referred to by the initials of their lengthy scientific names, PCR and RFLP. We could swab for PCR, test blood samples for RFLP— they'd been available at the time of the Shuster case.

But, as always, the new had pushed against the institutional tide of the tried and true. Police procedure held the same reluctance to change as any other area of society. Indelible in her memory and the memory of every cop she knew was the landmark 1995 O.J. Simpson trial, with its exhaustive presentation over many days of conclusive blood evidence testimony. Groundbreaking, proven DNA science that should have convicted O.J. Simpson of first-degree murder. But all that laborious testimony, all the scientific evidence, scientific fact, had zoomed so far over the head of the jury that they had not once considered it. A case eight months in the presentation had taken four hours of deliberation for a not guilty verdict.

And the Shuster case had predated the O.J. Simpson trial by three years. In these lab reports before her there was not even a section for DNA. Only the form showing that blood samples taken at the scene had tested O positive in their entirety. Many blood samples had been collected from April Shuster as a matter of course because of the widespread cast of her blood during the assault, but HLA or RFLP testing had not been requested or done on any of them. Given all the other supporting evidence, and with no wounds on the mother, the report she now looked at had been deemed sufficient for trial.

She brought her gaze again to the angry face in the booking photo. Only Ellie Shuster's insistent, continual protestations of innocence, included in the automatic legal reviews that wound through the system in any death penalty case, along with her demand that samples be retested for the possibility of different

DNA on her daughter's body, had finally resulted in drawing the attention of the legal advocates at the Innocence Project. Their court filing for a laboratory retest, granted in the face of considerable skepticism, had led to the astonishing discovery that the O positive blood on April Shuster's body contained DNA from another individual who was not her mother. Clearly, April Shuster had either wounded her killer in an act of self-defense, or, more likely, the killer's hand had been laced open by the edges of the crucifix in the frenzy of the attack. Never a mother who had not had a single wound on her hands or her body.

Back when Kate heard this devastating news, no one had blamed the investigating officers or the prosecution. Given the circumstances of the day, the investigation and trial had been deemed proper and adequate. But she endlessly wracked both memory and conscience as to whether, had she retained her position as lead detective instead of abdicating to Torrie Holden, she would have ordered additional blood testing. Or would she too have been predisposed, like Torrie, by the preponderance of evidence pointing directly toward the mother? Out of her usual abundance of caution and her experience that defense attorneys leaped on the slightest excuse to tarnish an investigation with a "rush to judgment," her answer remained always the same: she would have requested the tests. If for no other reason than April Shuster's O positive blood was the most common type and therefore most likely to disguise a blend with an individual with the same blood type. It all led back to her emotional breakdown that day. Her panic, loss of focus, abdication, her unwillingness to take into proper consideration Torrie Holden's inexperience in exploring every avenue no matter where it led.

Staring at the lab report, Kate knew she should confess to Cameron her malfeasance on that crucial afternoon. And also knew she would say nothing. How could she reveal to this friend who trusted and admired her that she had betrayed her colleagues, superiors, the courts, the public? If she was to pay for her failure with her life, if her death was to happen in these coming days, then she would go to her grave leaving him with however much good opinion he had of her.

She got up, put the pizza in the oven.

"Hey," Cameron called from his immersion in the crime report, "how about some coffee? Your special blend?"

"Done," she said.

They ate as they read, washing the pizza down with extra strong black coffee. She had turned to the witness statements and notes she'd made over the past months, reviewing them quietly alongside Cameron, who was now focused on the follow-up reports. She worked with renewed hope that lay fully in Cameron; she had gone over the files too many times to have any expectations of herself and did not want to distract him. The only sounds in the house were the rustling of pages, the scratch of a rollerball pen on the pad Cameron had requested, and, occasionally, Dakota slurping from her water bowl or crunching mouthfuls of kibble.

Sometime late into the night, Cameron carefully replaced the pages he'd removed from the murder book, closed his notepad, got up and announced, "Done for now, Kate."

Knowing better than to ask if he'd found any flags yet, looking at the dog's imploring eyes, Kate said, "We need to take Dakota outside."

"Just about to suggest it." He clipped a lead onto her collar, handed the leash to Kate, and they left the house, Dakota in a bouncy trot beside Kate.

The night had turned markedly cool; as usual the desert temperatures had begun their multi-degree plummet with the setting of the sun. Cameron, having once taken up residence not far from here for several weeks while he contended with his lethal brother, knew the climate well and had welcomed one of Kate's jackets.

Under glittering configurations of stars, the trees and shrubs were ink stains on the contours of the land, the air holding the dusty scent of cooling sand. Cameron, moving in the faint silvery light with his head down to watch his step, hands in the back pockets of his jeans, murmured, "Nobody outside the family, nobody in the neighborhood got really looked at for this."

"I wouldn't go quite that far, Joe. But no motive, no evidence of sexual assault or ejaculation on the body."

"And no judgment here, Kate, just thinking out loud, looking at blanks that maybe didn't get filled in. We both know everything can't get into the murder book or we'd be writing *War and Peace*."

"I didn't take it as judgment. You make a very fair point. Penetration or seminal fluid don't have to be present for this to be a sex crime. With the mother and her religious frenzy out of the picture, the violence here…" She broke off; she was parroting what they both knew. "We did run a check on registered sex offenders in the area." But pretty much pro forma—they'd had their suspect. "The locale of the murder came into play. Getting into that backyard wouldn't be easy for some stranger."

"Unless the stranger was familiar. Anyway, it's still very likely religion for motive," he offered. "All four parents and dozens of other people being in that batshit crazy cult. Anything about the fingerprints you might remember?"

"Nothing," she stated. "You know we didn't have AFIS back then for tracking. Doors, windows, we did all the usual dusting downstairs, lots of unknowns—they had visitors from the church. We dusted both bedrooms and baths, the one with the cross on the wall top to bottom. The cross, nothing useful, a couple of two-point prints, mostly smears."

They halted as Dakota strained on her leash to investigate a creosote bush, deemed it suitable, and squatted next to it. "Too bad we can't let the girl run," Cameron said as he kicked copious amounts of sand over her proceeds, the sour smell rising in the thin desert air.

"In the morning, early," Kate promised. Nighttime brought out lethal predators, just as it did with humans. But snakes, coyotes, foxes—they all hunted for survival, Kate thought, not to savage each other out of pathology or on behalf of a belief system.

"I'm still working through all those FIs," Cameron said, shaking his head.

"We hardly had to knock on doors to get them," Kate told him. People had come out of the woodwork, resulting in dozens of field investigation cards. "The neighborhood went ballistic over those two families, how those two girls died. The fury—and the press and TV made it that much worse—we had to assign protection to Mathew Hayden for months, till the families sold the duplex and left."

Cameron nodded. "I do remember the outlines of the case. Jim Jones wasn't all that much earlier so everyone thought this was another fanatic with a cult, he'd brainwashed a follower into murder."

"I did too," Kate said. "People like Mathew Hayden, Jim Jones—according to them, burning people like me at the stake was acceptable because Lucifer would be doing the same thing to us when we arrived at the gates of hell. Preachers are still at it today."

"The absolute certainty of people with all the answers, Kate…like marching Terminators. Tell me about Mathew Hayden. All I remember is he had white hair."

"Snow white. First thing you'd notice. He didn't trick himself out like some of the other gurus or the prophets of old. No beard, just this very thick shock of hair that hung over his forehead."

"President Snow?"

Smiling at his reference to the villain in *The Hunger Games* film, she said, "More Elvis. Bony face, sky blue eyes. Always wore collarless white tunics to go with the hair."

"Sandals?" Cameron asked derisively.

"Loafers. Hand stitched."

"What did they believe in? Other than it being a fine thing to kill millions of gay people?"

"You could fit it into a nutshell. All the evil in this world can be overcome if we all just obey a few simple, fundamental tenets given to men—and I do mean men—chosen through the grace of God. And banding together will give true believers insurmountable strength."

There were also those less publicized aspects of a cult, she thought, no less powerful for how they met basic human hungers: fellowship, loyalty, safety, belonging to a family.

"Can life even for two minutes be that simple, Kate?"

"For her, maybe," she answered, gesturing to Dakota who strained at her leash to investigate a mesquite tree, the white streak down her head luminous in the starlight.

He asked abruptly, "Did Ellie Shuster testify?"

"No. No one ever thought she would. Her defense of 'I didn't do it' was up against a diary that implicated her and a belief system that thundered 'Death to homosexuals.'"

"So, no point in looking at the trial transcript."

"Ever order a trial transcript, Joe?" She had read the record at the courthouse.

"Never had a reason."

"They're a literal transcription of the trial and run about three bucks a page for duplication."

Cameron let out a soft whistle. "Legal defense, medical costs, it always helps to be rich."

"Always." They turned back toward her house. "The rich truly are different."

"From what I've seen so far, the key evidence really boils down to the Hayden girl's diary and a murder weapon that obviously goes to motive. Everything else seems like cross-stitching on those two components of the case. So, what about the diary writer? Stella Hayden, she a possible?"

"We did look pretty hard at her, at murder-suicide," Kate told him. "With teenagers, no such thing as too crazy. I discussed it with Torrie, kicked it around with Lieutenant Bodwin and the DA. But—there was just no motive, Joe. The girls were inseparable. To the exclusion of any other friends. No evidence of jealousy, not so much as a mention in that overwrought diary of Stella's. To the very last page she was all about the mother being constantly suspicious of them and trying to keep them apart, trying to poison April against her, wanting April to have other friends, all those Bible quotes about unnatural desires being an abomination in God's eyes and eternal hellfire, yada yada."

"Too bad the goddamn church couldn't have been put on trial," Cameron said, kicking a spray of sand. "Calling down death in a country where same-sex love is lawful, isn't that inciting murder, isn't that terrorism?"

"Everyone's afraid of calling out religion. Unless it's a country we don't like. If you're Taliban. Or Islam."

They had arrived back at the house. "I need to see about a bed for Dakota," Kate said, thinking about contriving something from extra blankets.

"I've got one in the car," Cameron said and strode off toward his Rav4.

Moments later she noticed a partially torn off sales tag on a new-looking blue plaid dog bed. The owner would surely have provided the dog's bed... Then she decided she wouldn't challenge whatever Cameron's motives were about bringing Dakota here. Cats, with their effortless, fluid grace, no matter their gender, were like being in the presence of constant feminine energy and beauty. Dogs had a different presence, even female dogs. Maybe having an animal companion more gender neutral for a while would be a less painful reminder of the women she'd loved and lost.

"Okay, I'll take Dakota for now," she told Cameron, and went off to her bedroom with the dog bed under her arm, Dakota following.

8

The next morning, Kate sat outside on a portion of the rock formation at the side of her house, a wide boulder with a flattened top. With "Who'll Stop the Rain" emanating from Pilar's house, she watched Dakota cavort in the morning sun in avid exploration of her new terrain. The border collie—three years old, she'd learned from Cameron—had been well trained from a pup; she answered to her name and returned, if impatiently, to Kate when called. A good thing, she thought, not to have to keep so lively an animal confined to a leash when they came out here during the day and evening.

Cameron had showered, used Kate's razor, and availed himself of the change of clothes he kept in his car as did many cops, an emergency stash for callouts in the event he was away from the job or his house. He was now on his way back to VPD and would return tonight for more immersion in the Shuster murder, he'd promised, and would bring dinner. Something healthy, he warned. She knew these back-to-back visits were not so much help with the Shuster case as escalated concern for her and payback for putting herself in jeopardy when he confronted his brother. No way in hell would she have allowed him to face Jack Cameron alone, but whatever his motive, she welcomed it. He was an armed and trained police officer, and however futile it all might turn out to be for her survival, his presence diminished some awareness and fear of that sword of Damocles poised above her head.

She picked up the folder she'd set beside her on the rock, a thick file painstakingly created some months ago, the result of a visit to the property room at Wilshire Division. She'd photographed Stella Hayden's diary, every single handwritten page of it, then constructed a computer file from the images on her phone. From there she'd printed out pages to highlight passages and make notes in the margins. At his request, she'd just emailed the file to Cameron.

All this time later the diary was no less hard to look at, so vividly did it conjure its young author. Teenage ecstasy all but lifted from the pages in the gushing references to April's eyes, her hair, her skin, her legs, her lips, emphasized by multiple exclamation marks and phrases, some visibly incised into the diary pages in tracings, the doodled embroidery around April's name. Stella Hayden had been body and soul ardently and forever in love, as only a sixteen-year-old can be, and an aching sympathy out of the secrecy in her own early life rose in Kate every time she looked at the all-too-revealing passages. As if being an emerging lesbian with rabidly fundamentalist parents had not made her sufficiently *other*, loops in the handwriting and a backhand slant identified her as the lefthander she was.

Looking up to watch Dakota, Kate once again plumbed the crosscurrents of theory that had preoccupied her these recent months. The killer of April Shuster had to be one of the other three parents or a member of the cult, and evidence had to exist somewhere to identify that individual. Certainly, there might be a wild card to prove her wrong, but real world homicides seldom provided fodder for mystery novels; they came out of primal motivation that pointed directly to a perpetrator. Mathew Hayden's cult, a fundamentalist bubble in one of the West

Coast's liberal bastions, was no different from any belief system anywhere that generated beheadings, honor killings, jihad, bombings of abortion clinics and gay bars; countless murders in the name of whatever god. If the killer of April Shuster could be identified, some justice would be done by issuing an arrest warrant. If it was for one of the parents and extradition from Uganda for a homophobic murder was impossible, he or she would at least then be an identified murderer, forever vilified like film director Roman Polanski, who had fled to France before he could be sentenced for his rape of a thirteen-year-old girl.

Peggy Lee began plaintively singing "Is That All There Is?" and Kate watched Dakota, grateful for the amusing distraction as she trotted over to investigate the foundation of Pilar's house and decided it was acceptable for urination.

Again looking down at the file, she reasoned that of the three parents, Stella Hayden's cult leader father seemed most obvious. His rage and mortification over an offspring guilty of the unnatural behavior condemned by the creed he preached could only be imagined. Like the other parents, he had gone into seclusion after her death, had not testified at the trial, and afterward promptly vanished to Uganda. The manner of April's death pointed to Old Testament righteous wrath, a pronouncement of death carried out with a symbolic murder weapon on a devil-possessed girl who had infected and corrupted his offspring.

If the choice of murder weapon fit the scenario, the source of it defied logic. The Shusters and Haydens did have access to each other's duplex, but why would Mathew Hayden, with a similar cross hanging in his own living room and a multiplicity of other religious statuary and symbols available to him, have gone into the Shusters' house to pull that particular cross off their bedroom wall? And why would he have spared his own daughter? Had he perhaps staged the suicide? Or known she would kill herself? Or ordered her to kill herself and orchestrated the act by having her write that final despairing page in her diary?

No, on all counts. The declaration would have been phrased as contrition for sin, not blame for April's mother. And not written in a diary he would consider an obscenity that would live on after his daughter. The diary had not been visible at the scene of her death; it had been extracted from under her pillow by the coroner's assistant, its plastic cover stained with blood soaking through the pillow.

A murder of Stella staged to look like a suicide was a possibility but seemed far too organized, too contradictory to the disorganized, unrestrained savagery of April's murder. Stella Hayden's death had every hallmark of a suicide and Kate was convinced that it was.

Whoever killed April had, without a qualm, let her mother take the blame. In a religious context, there was no mystery as to why. She would have been reviled for her failure to protect her daughter from the wiles of Satan, with any temporal punishment meted out to her a mere preliminary to the everlasting fires of hell.

Daniel Shuster? Same motivation as Mathew Hayden. That he would use the cross from his own bedroom as the implement of murder made more sense than it did for Hayden. Yet Kate found herself again quailing from the idea that a father would kill his own daughter and then allow his own wife to be sent to death row for an act he would consider justifiable filicide.

Veronica Hayden. Time of death for both girls was the same, a three-hour window, and she became most likely if the scenario were turned upside down, if Stella had died first. Stella kills herself, is found by her mother, who then seeks out April in a vengeful fury. Certainly the violence of April's murder fit the theory. But the last page in the diary did not.

Kate finally opened the file and turned to that last page and its huge, fervid, scrawling entries.

I TOLD April her mother would never understand!!! I TOLD AND TOLD April her mother would kill us both!!! And now she's gone and done it!!! How could she do this to us!!! It's all over and all her fault!!!

OMG!!! April…it's awful awful AWFUL. I CAN'T GO ON not even another day another hour I just can't. I won't. If we're both going to hell at least we'll be together. Your mother she did this to both of us. You just killed April and now you just killed me.

"Kate, you have a dog now?"

Kate all but fell off her rock, so lost had she been in reverie. She hadn't seen or heard Pilar leave her house, hadn't noticed the music stop. *Ellie Shuster could have killed me ten times over*, she snarled at herself as she hurriedly closed the file and slid it back down beside her.

"Just keeping her a couple of weeks for a friend," she said.

"The guy who spent the night?"

Kate laughed. "You don't miss much, do you. Meet Dakota," she said as the dog ran up to investigate this new presence.

Grinning, Pilar held out the back of her hand to her. "You're quite the lively one there, aren't you?" She pointed to the folder beside Kate. "This the first case for the Delafield Agency?"

First and last, Kate thought. "Just a file from an old case."

"How old?"

"Twenty years," Kate said, gathering up the folder and getting to her feet. "I have stuff to do," she said. She didn't want to say one more word about what was in the folder.

"Wait, wait," Pilar said, holding up a hand. "I've got an idea about the woman that came here yesterday."

Kate sat back down, welcoming the change of subject. She hadn't given Geneva Fallon a single thought today. "I'm all ears."

"It's actually your own idea. About an inheritance. So, all you need is a letter from a lawyer."

"Sure," Kate said and shook her head.

"Come on, you must know one. Everybody at least knows somebody who knows a lawyer. All you need is letterhead. Hell, you could design some yourself."

"I actually know someone who works in a law office," Kate said slowly. *Aimee.*

"There you go. The way I see it, you'll need two visits to convince her. One time to tell her now that you've located her, you need her to maybe fill out some paperwork and produce identification to be sure it is her, yada yada, before any funds can be released. Second time you give her the check."

"It's an idea," Kate agreed. And it was. With some modification…

Pilar pointed to Dakota, who had returned to her explorations. "You got a ball or a stick or something you can throw for this lively gal?"

Kate frowned. It had not occurred to her.

"I see you know squat about dogs."

Not true, but she simply shrugged; she was not about to reveal anything of her life history.

"Tell you what," Pilar said. "You go about your business and let me entertain her. I got nothing better to do."

"I'd be glad for that," Kate said. "Bring her back whenever you like."

She grinned as she got to her feet. So far, Cameron's notion of Dakota providing her with more exercise had got her all the way from her house to this rock and back again.

9

Kate refilled Dakota's dishes, washed several that Cameron had left in the sink from his breakfast of eggs and toast, performed a few other household chores. As she finished returning her house to what satisfied her as normal, as hers, Pilar tapped on the front window, gestured to Kate's doorstep and waved a farewell.

Kate opened her door and Dakota trotted in and over to her water bowl for a lengthy, eager slurping after her morning's exertions. After a survey of Kate as if to ask if any services were required, she settled onto her dog bed.

Feeling subtly warmed by Dakota's quiet presence, Kate also settled herself in an armchair with her feet up on the ottoman and picked up the file containing Stella Hayden's diary. Pilar's music station had apparently moved from music of the eighties to the seventies—"Good Vibrations" had ended and Olivia Newton John was beginning "You're the One That I Want." Not a good move, she sighed. Seventies' music had far more power to hurt because of what it evoked.

Suddenly feeling the impact of her late night with Cameron she leaned her head back against the chair. She would close her eyes for just a few minutes…

She awakened, startled to see on the wall clock that she'd slept, dreamlessly, for more than two hours. Becoming aware of what had penetrated her subconscious to awaken her, she froze, throat instantly tight with anguish. From Pilar's house, Roberta Flack: "The First Time Ever I Saw Your Face."

She gripped the arms of her chair knowing she could not hide anywhere from the soaring yet tender voice, the lyrics of longing and discovery and love and joy.

A drink. She desperately wanted a drink.

Coward. You coward. You've always been a coward. Always drowning what memory might do to you. Why do you still care about that or anything else when you could die today?

She sprang from her chair, tossed the file of Hayden diary pages onto the breakfast bar, and strode into her bedroom. From the top shelf of the closet she yanked down a gray metal box, carried it into the living room. Dakota raised her head as if to see if there was good reason to further bestir herself, lowered her head back down to her paws and watched Kate.

Returning to her chair, Kate placed the box in her lap and keyed in the combination to the lock. Anne's birthday. Resolutely, she pulled out all the contents and set them on the table beside her: bundles of photos and cards; *Surfacing* by Margaret Atwood; a motel room drink coaster; a miniature 1962 Mercury Comet; a framed certificate; a McGovern for President button; a napkin.

She picked up the napkin, gazing at its cartoon image of a woman seated in a martini glass, wearing only the high heels she kicked up in the air. It pre-dated Anne by four years; it was from her twenty-first birthday. With Julie. A carefree spirit a year ahead of her in college, a lesbian who had befriended her and taken her out for a coming-of-age birthday celebration. The night it all began, Kate thought bitterly. *When cowardice became my way of life.*

Memory flooded her of Julie driving them from the campus of University of Michigan in Ann Arbor that August evening, refusing to disclose anything about the birthday surprise she had planned for Kate. An hour or so later they were in downtown Detroit, then onto a side street of scruffy, graffitied buildings off Woodward Avenue where Julie parked her ancient VW Beetle. She led Kate to a shadowy nondescript door that drew no attention to its identity as any sort of a business, and Kate realized what the surprise was and stood frozen as the door opened and a wave of music and feminine voices and laughter swamped her senses, an intense wafting of cigarette smoke and perfume overlaying acetone fumes of alcohol.

She became aware that the place was small and dim from low light and smoke, had a well-stocked bar and a worn bar counter lined with backless stools; a scattering of Formica tables that surrounded a small dance floor. But her focus was riveted on the bartender who was leaning over the bar, laughing and flirting with a busty woman in a tight skirt and spandex top. By far the most blatantly butch woman Kate had ever seen, the bartender had black hair that gleamed with Vaseline, brush-cut, its inch-long sheaves standing straight up on the top of her head. She wore army fatigues, her shirtsleeves rolled up over muscular arms, a cigarette pack caught in one of the folds. So awestruck was Kate by the woman's flamboyant masculinity, a brazen courage beyond her imagining, she was caught momentarily breathless.

To Patsy Cline singing "Crazy," Julie took her by the hand and wove her through women swaying on the dance floor to a small table at the distant end of the bar. A waitress, in skirt and blouse and blue saddle oxfords, followed, placed napkins on the table, and asked for ID. Kate fumbled for her wallet, handed over her driver's license, feeling as if she had stepped under a floodlight of exposure. The waitress glanced at the license, smiled, wished her happy birthday, handed it back. Kate nodded numbly and when asked for her drink order, said the first thing that came to mind, scotch and soda. Julie ordered a daquiri and Kate remembered her saying of Kate's drink, "Good choice for your first legal drink," and "I thought you would really like it here."

All around her, women mostly her age wore jackets and ties and winged tip shoes, they wore pants with western shirts. They sat at tables or danced closely with women in miniskirts and low-cut blouses and dresses. Other tables held couples, male and female, clearly heterosexuals, avidly watching the scene on the dance floor, and Kate knew they were, in the parlance of the day, "slumming," here to gawk at "the queers."

Their drinks arrived, brought to the table on a large tray of assorted beverages by the masculine bartender. "On the house, compliments of Joanie over there at the bar," she said, adding when Kate began to demur, "Relax, just take it, okay? She's a hooker. They come in here, like to toss their money around on women."

Kate nodded as a siren went by somewhere close. Julie said, "Let's dance."

"No," Kate said.

"No?"

"No."

Julie's dark eyes widened in her gamin face and her lips twisted downward. "Oh God. Don't tell me. You don't want to be here."

"Julie, these places get raided all the time. You *know* I'm going into the military. I *can't* get arrested. I *can't* take a chance—"

"The military," Julie said contemptuously. "You know that won't happen. You can't even give me a reason for doing something so stupid."

Kate did not answer. Julie had never taken this ambition of hers seriously because Kate had never given her the reason she was so determined to enlist. That she'd always been a disappointment and a despairing suspicion to her parents with her unfeminine behavior, her otherness. This one thing, she could do this one thing to atone to her mother, deceased now four years, and to finally win her war veteran father's approval: she could wear the uniform of her country.

"I'm not leaving, Kate," Julie said. "If the cops come," she sneered, "you'll just have to run your chickenshit ass out the back door."

She picked up her drink just as a woman in khaki pants and boots and a western shirt strode up to their table, politely asked Kate if she and Julie could dance. Julie leaped to her feet before Kate could nod assent and took her hand and followed her onto the dance floor.

For the next hours Kate sat in the shadows of the bar, further concealed by her navy pantsuit, nursing drinks and chain-smoking Pall Malls and watching as if to memorize the women on the dance floor and at other tables, at the jukebox dropping in quarters. Songs repeated, clearly dance favorites from the romantic fifties that would forever evoke that bar, that night: Patti Page singing "Allegheny Moon," Jo Stafford crooning "You Belong to Me," Connie Francis wailing "Who's Sorry Now," the Everly Brothers harmonizing "Cathy's Clown." No one approached Kate; the tension in her face and body must have given off clear negatives. Julie, laughing and drinking, completely ignored her, dancing with any number of partners, including some of the very femme women. As the evening wore on, she sat huddled at a table with a fresh-faced young woman in pants and a plaid shirt, with slicked back red hair and a face full of freckles.

Kate also watched the woman at the bar who had paid for her first drink, dark-haired, boyish, leather miniskirt, fringed buckskin vest, a small feathery bag dangling from her shoulder, the sex trade written all over her.

What's she doing here, Kate wondered, and answered her own question: she was here for a quiet drink in a place where she would not be accosted by men. The woman at the bar now sat facing the room, her back resting against the bar. Her eyes passed over Kate without stopping, settling on someone on the dance floor. A short, slender butch woman, wearing black trousers and a black-checkered jacket over a white shirt, broke away from her dance partner and strutted toward her. She conferred with the woman, pointed to the collection of bottles lining the back of the bar. The bartender lifted down a bottle from the top shelf, carefully poured a drink into a shot glass. The very expensive stuff, Kate guessed. The butch sat down and as the two bent their heads together in conversation, Kate returned her attention to the activity in the bar. But a few minutes later the pair at the bar caught her again: they were leaving together.

A patron nearby was also observing them; she said to her companion, "A hooker who's lesbian. I hear lots of them are actually lesbians."

"So how can she *stand* being with men?"

"Maybe it means nothing. Sex with a guy, just exercise compared to making love with a woman."

Her companion snorted, "I'd rather lie down in a pit of snakes."

"One thing I guarantee you, that little butch she picked up won't be paying for it."

Kate shook her head. The hooker led the kind of subversive, daring, unapologetic life she found unimaginable.

She looked around the room again, this time taking it in with fresh pangs of awareness and grief. She was in a world of the exiled. Where she could not be. Where she dared not be.

Julie returned to the table. "Ready to go," she announced. "Sorry I ruined your birthday."

Kate slid the napkin from under her drink as she got up, tucked it in her jacket pocket. "You didn't. It's a birthday I'll never forget."

The next weekend, Julie said she was returning to the bar. Kate had simply nodded. She never saw Julie again.

And did not step into the lesbian world for another seventeen years. Until she was a homicide detective and Dory Quillin was murdered behind the Nightwood Bar.

Kate carefully placed the forty-five-year-old napkin back in the gray box, a box she had not opened for decades. But she knew exactly where a certain photo would be in the collection she had piled on the table. Pulling it out, braced, taking a breath, she looked at the favorite of all her images of Anne and found the sight of the beloved face smiling at her so excruciating that she squeezed her eyes shut. Then forced them open and gazed, anguish slowly dissipating, the tension in her face softening as memory overcame her.

Like other bereft people, Kate had been ambushed by glimpsing an agonizing similarity to a loved one in someone on a street, in a restaurant. But this had happened to her only with her parents, never with Anne. To this day she seemed singular with her cap of caramel hair laced with gold, coffee-with-cream brown eyes, a front tooth that crossed slightly, endearingly, over its neighbor, features that all tilted upward in a face that reflected innate buoyancy. "Somewhere I had to have an Asian ancestor," Anne had once joked as Kate lay with her in bed their first days together, her fingertips tracing the slanted shape of her eyes. And Kate had responded, "No, you must be a relative of Doris Day." Walking into a room with Anne in it was like walking into sunlight—how Kate imagined it would be in the presence of that luminous movie star.

She placed the photo gently in her lap and picked up the tiny 1962 baby blue Mercury Comet, a replica of Anne's car, ten years old when they met. Touching its intricate taillights, she reflected that in her sessions with Calla Dearborn she had come to recognize the path she'd been placed onto by birth circumstance, the color of her skin, her sexual orientation, other forces that had subverted and molded her life. But her relationships with women seemed comprised of the uniquely accidental. Ellen O'Neill, accidental witness to murder—on her very first day on the job in a Wilshire Boulevard high-rise office building, in a case her partner, Ed Taylor, had deemed "amateur city." Andrea Ross, accidental presence at the Nightwood Bar on the day Dory Quillin died. Aimee Grant, accidental presence at the Beverly Malibu apartment building on the day film director Owen Sinclair had met his grisly fate.

But her meeting with Anne had been the most miraculous of the accidental. In a sense, she realized, she had been on the job that day too, the last day she would ever be in uniform. At a bar whose name and location she could not now remember, with six other ex-marines, a mustering-out party in San Diego after her official discharge that afternoon from the Marine Corps at Camp Pendleton. She and her fellow ex-marines had been among those with no family to meet them as they became civilians once again in an ungrateful nation torn apart by political and generational conflict. They had all served in Vietnam and none of the group was more bitter about their service than she. The year she'd endured in Da Nang would scar her forever. And four entire years of her life were gone, squandered to win approval from a father who only five years later would take whatever pride she'd earned from him to the grave. Every single day of those years she'd served her country she'd spent perfecting the art of subterfuge, hiding her true self away from the relentless witch hunts for homosexuals which would have destroyed her future had they ensnared her. The one benefit to her time in the service: she'd applied to and been accepted by LAPD, one organization in her hostile country that placed value on her military discipline and training.

Several drinks into her time in the bar, her life transformed. Lance Corporal Lionel Gardner took her by the arm, she turned around on her barstool, and he said: "Captain Delafield, I'd like you to meet Anne Gardner, my sister. She just got here from LA."

The first time ever I saw your face. Her very first stunned thought had been that the last name Gardner was perfect: she was like a bloom in a garden. Her smiling, radiant face and her long-sleeved dress, gold with bands of taupe around its hem and cuffs, ignited a joy that had been lost somewhere inside her for years. A moth to flame, she was drawn to her instantly.

Sitting with Anne at a small table in a heightening glow of attraction and desire, Kate had been so enclosed in a two-person bubble, so impervious to the noise of the bar, that afterward she had no memory of a single other person or conversation or even what she ate or drank during the time with Anne. Anne, she remembered, had ordered a Coke; she would not be twenty-one for three more months. Nor was she a smoker; from the instant she saw Anne wave away tendrils of smoke that reached her, she had not reached for the Pall Malls in her pocket.

Like herself, Anne was from Michigan. Two years ago she'd "thrown caution to the winds and horrified my parents" by taking her savings and hitching a ride with friends heading west on a month's vacation along Route 66. She'd found a boarding house in LA, landed a part-time job, attended community college. Now she was evening cashier at a Glendale restaurant and had switched to Occidental College in Eagle Rock to earn a teaching credential. She was impressed by Kate's collegiate and military career, impressed that Kate would be attending the Police Academy, not all that far from her boarding house in Elysian Park. Kate warmed under her approval; she could not remember the last time someone had looked up to her in admiration instead of down at her for actually having volunteered, enlisted to serve in so despised a war.

Then Anne had glanced at her watch, exclaimed, "I have to go. Where's Lionel? We've got a two-hour drive."

"Maybe," Kate had ventured, all but quivering with hope, "you could find some time to show me around when I get there?"

Anne had extracted pen and paper from her purse to write down her number. "Call me when you're settled. When are you getting to LA?"

"Motel tonight, bus tomorrow."

"Would you be able to drive back with Lionel and me today?"

She merely nodded. She would have given everything she owned to be with her for a few hours more.

On the trip to Los Angeles, her duffel bag in the trunk, she had deferred to brother and sister, sitting quietly in the backseat of the rickety 1962 Comet, avidly listening to them talk family news and laugh over reminiscences of childhood. They dropped her off at a Travelodge on Sunset Boulevard in Echo Park...

Kate put the Comet replica back into the box and picked up the Travelodge drink coaster.

Three days. She'd forced herself to wait that long before calling Anne, too anxious that she would appear overeager or show interest that could be construed as "unnatural." She would settle for Anne being a friend, anything to remain close to her.

It was a Saturday when she called; Anne did not have classes. They met for coffee before Anne had to go to her evening job at the restaurant not far from the motel where Kate would stay until she got through the maelstrom of her first days at LAPD and found a furnished single.

"Let me help you look for a place," Anne offered at the end of their hour together. An hour when, with every minute that passed, Kate knew her destiny was heartbreak because she loved everything about this woman who gave off signals of wanting friendship but no hint of mutual attraction. Yet faint hope mixed in with her fear: the sharing of life history and values did not include mention of male relationships for either of them.

Was it the next night? No, the night after that, a Monday. Anne's restaurant was closed, and she had driven Kate back to the Travelodge from their dinner together, had come into the motel room for coffee Kate had offered to make in the room's miniature coffee maker.

She had closed the door and turned. To find Anne halted in front of her, head down, and then her hands blindly reached for and gripped Kate's arms. She raised her face, and those remarkable soft brown eyes met hers, wide, vulnerable, asking. Kate grasped her shoulders and drew Anne to her and they held each other, and then their lips touched so very lightly, long moments of tentativeness before they fully kissed, as if neither could trust what was happening. In similar slow progression clothes had come off, as if each required wordless permission.

Then they were naked together in the bed and for Kate the night became a blur of unutterable softness and silk and scents and her body enveloped in an acceptance she had never known. The leap of ecstasy the first time Anne's legs rose and wrapped in embrace of her, in urgent want of her. Bliss and endless desire. Her senses swathed in Anne's floral perfume, then more earthy scents. Her escalating passion met by unguarded desire, and as the night deepened, the heady gratification of Anne's trembling, her sounds of climax so orgasmic that she had needed nothing more for herself. Not until Anne's hands, her fingers, her mouth, had come to her, proving that need was not want. Again and again...

Kate placed the coaster back in the box. Before Anne there had been infatuations, crushes. But for me, she thought, looking again at the photograph of Anne in her lap, it was the first time ever I saw your face.

She picked up a stack of cards, birthdays, Christmas…

Dakota emitted a sharp bark and leaped instantly toward the door. Kate, startled from her reveries, alarmed, glanced out the window to see the mail truck pull away. She rose from her chair, came to Dakota and patted her on the head. "Good girl," she said. "You'll earn your keep yet."

She went out to retrieve the mail, the dog at her heels. There were the usual circulars during this presidential year, a gas bill. And an envelope addressed to her in Ellie Shuster's handwriting. This time with no postmark.

She stood staring at it, her heart thudding, then involuntarily whirled to look all around her. Her tension eased. Logically it had to have been placed in her mailbox yesterday when she was in LA. Cameron, she'd ask Cameron if the rooftop camera's range could be extended to take in her mailbox.

She slit the envelope open with a fingernail.

Soon. Very soon.

She crumpled the note. Forget the camera. Forget Cameron—she would damn well not tell him. Nothing, there was absolutely nothing he could do and this unpostmarked note might even freak him into demanding that he move in with her. No way was that going to happen. This was her mess, he had no idea how much this was her mess. She'd do what she should have done yesterday, rip this note to shreds and scatter it to the desert winds. Except no, she would not litter the sere, pristine, peaceful landscape laid out before her. She roughly shoved the note and its envelope into a pocket and stalked back to her house, Dakota hanging back, reluctant, disappointed by their destination.

She flung the note into the trash, returned to her chair, thinking that she could actually thank Ellie Shuster for one thing: her life seemed to be flashing in front of her eyes, and some of it was well worth revisiting.

A framed certificate on her end table caught her eye and she picked it up, seizing on anything as a distraction. She stared at it, then ran her fingers gently over Anne's teaching degree from Occidental College, remembering how she had snatched it off the living room wall just as Anne's relatives arrived to claim her possessions. The day Anne became a teacher was the day their lives had become so very much more complicated...

Ellie Shuster receded as she settled herself in her armchair and let memory flood her, those first days of soaring joy over Anne in her life and the blissful nights at the motel before they'd found a furnished single for Kate in a nondescript apartment building near the Police Academy. She could not come to Anne's boarding house of course, and they both deemed it too risky to move in together while Kate was on probation. Between their jobs and school they spent as much time in Kate's apartment as they dared.

Probation ended, she had been assigned to Juvenile as were most women police. Months later, savings from her military service, her status as a veteran, and now a uniformed police officer at LAPD had combined to barely qualify her for a loan on the modest two-bedroom and one-bath house in Glendale. They'd had to have the second bedroom. Anne kept her clothes in its closet, arranged a collection of perfumes and hairbrushes on its dresser, lingerie in the drawers. This protected them from Anne's relatives and in the event of unexpected visitors to the house. And of course there were the separations at Christmas and occasionally on Anne's birthday. All unavoidably necessary, and painful.

Anne was teaching in elementary school; Kate had a promising future in law enforcement, planned to go to law school. Growing ever more paranoid about their visibility and protecting each other as years passed, Anne had paid by far the greater price. Kate was reassigned occasionally and able to keep her personal interactions with police colleagues to a minimum but Anne could not; her contacts with other teachers and parents were numerous and required. Anne left teaching jobs after three or four years, sometimes sooner, offering varied reasons for her departure, before parents and especially colleagues could connect too many dots to her personal life. Some were schools and children and colleagues she especially loved, and she was tearful for days afterward. But she knew that as a teacher of children six to ten years of age, any hint of the private life she shared with Kate would bring them disgrace, lay waste to their careers and their lives.

As Kate looked through their cards to each other, sentimental cards, humorous cards, the *Love Forever* signatures, she thought: Natalie Rostow was a teacher and Geneva Fallon destroyed her. The same thing could have happened to us at exactly the same time. Just as easily, just as *accidentally*.

She didn't give a fig about Geneva Fallon, but didn't she have a duty of care to Natalie Rostow? For the sake of Anne, in memory of Anne...

She found the card Fallon had left, picked up the phone. Remembering Pilar's remark about this being the Delafield Agency's first job, she smiled as she punched in the numbers. She would take the job.

10

As Kate pulled the Jeep onto Old Woman Springs Road for the drive into Palm Springs, she shook her head over how much had landed on her plate so quickly. She was on her way to pick up a cashier's check from Geneva Fallon; attend an AA meeting that would be available while she was in town; check out the bereavement meeting at the LGBT Center in Palm Springs. And oh yes, maybe get killed by Ellie Shuster. She glanced in the rearview mirror. Nope, she was not being followed. So put that one down for possibly later on the agenda.

No bravado here, she thought sourly. Bruce Willis she was not. All that bullshit fearless swagger, the choreographed slugfests to the death in all those macho films—all predicated on the prime directive: survival. How about a film where the hero doesn't care one way or the other? Where the *act* of death is the only fear and not the *fact* of death?

Months, she had been months in a hopeless, scalding hot spotlight of fear with nowhere to hide from the constant awareness of impending death burning along her nerves. No way to make peace with it as she might with tracking a terminal illness that debilitated her body. She was a mouse trapped by a toying cat. Or in a car tracked by a relentless helicopter. Even her house was no refuge. Like Cameron's monstrous brother, Ellie Shuster could arrive in the nighttime and firebomb her house.

She turned on her Sirius XM, then turned it off; she did not want to hear more news of atrocities in Syria or Romney advancing toward the nomination to run against Obama. And she'd had enough for now of music sliding under her guard. Dakota would have been good company for the drive, she lamented. The dog had leaped up at the first jangle of her car keys, trotted with her to the door. "Sorry, girl," she'd murmured, patting her on the head. "I can't bring you in anywhere and no way can I leave you in a hot car."

She focused on her sun-infused surroundings and the vibration of the road through the car seat into her hips and thighs. Aimee loved the desert too, she thought with a pang. But neither she nor anyone she'd ever known, not even Maggie, would fathom the soul-deep connection she felt with it now, this affinity for the harsh, forbidding, stark land all around her. Direct overhead sun baked the spiky, leathery green plant forms studding the sand, a few remaining red and yellow spring blooms braving it out in the channel along the road until their inevitable scorching into strands of blond stubble.

She turned onto Highway 62 and soon the road became a swath curving through rolling foothills of the San Bernardino Mountains, jagged with granite outcroppings, its studs of brush and scrub like bits of nougat. Here and there the terrain was overlaid by a stubborn coating of green that pitiless sun would soon bleach into a meld with rock and sand. Maybe, she thought, I love this place because it matches my soul.

Emerging into view a few minutes later were windmills, tall, stark white apparitions alongside the road, topped by two intersecting curved arms. They would soon multiply, these power generators, row upon row of them spread over the rolling landscape against the blended beige folds of the San Jacinto Mountains, signature symbols of Palm Springs, loved or despised by the residents. Count her among the former. Some of the windmills sat motionless on their broad bases, seeming cemented in the earth; others spun their arms at varying speeds in the fluctuating winds of the San Gorgonio Pass as if in some arrhythmic alien dance. They were anomalous, otherworldly, and she loved their hallucinatory presence on the desert landscape.

She ventured into Palm Springs so rarely that she gazed around her with renewed interest as she sped toward the city center. She was now on Indian Canyon Road, soon to become Palm Canyon Drive as it traversed the heart of the city, then trekked east through four more Coachella Valley towns. The turnoff to the Tramway was off somewhere to her right; it would be crawling with cars headed toward a scenic ride on the rotating car that rose 8500 feet up a San Jacinto mountainside with views of the Coachella Valley to the Salton Sea. She'd been on it with Aimee...she pushed the memory away. A sea of vehicles was now accompanying her, many with out-of-state license plates, one last influx of tourists before summer heat pulled them back to their cooler climes.

Her phone rang through her Bluetooth connection as she came alongside the Old Las Palmas area where Geneva Fallon lived. Cameron, she saw from the ID. She punched the accept button.

"Kate, so what's going on?" A casual question, requiring reassurance.

"Quiet here," she said easily, braking for a red light. "I'm on my way to an AA meeting." He did not have to know where she was or anything about Geneva Fallon and Natalie Rostow.

"Sounds good. I've got info for you on Gloria Elena Romano. Kind of surprising info. Not much wonder you couldn't find her."

"Don't tell me—she's been locked up for however many years?"

"Nope. She's been dead for however many years."

"*Dead*? How...how could her sister not know? You're sure it's the same—"

"The very same, Kate. The sister who asked you to find Gloria is the surprise. She *has* to know. Minneapolis PD ran Gloria's name, and Loretta Giovanni's name came up as driver of the car in the accident that killed her sister."

Stunned, staring at the Bluetooth connection on her dashboard, she was reminded where she was by a horn blast. "So when was this?" she asked, accelerating with an apologetic wave to the driver behind her.

"Twelve years ago. The millennium. New Year's Eve. DWI. Pled out to vehicular manslaughter, six months' jail time, community service."

As Kate silently absorbed this, Cameron suggested, "Medication maybe? The drugs they're giving her at that hospice must be…"

"Possibly," Kate said, but she was shaking her head, remembering Marla's remark yesterday at Silverlake Haven that the preoccupations of the dying were ever only two: love and regret. Monique Lefleur had killed a husband without a millisecond of regret, out of protective love for her daughter. Loretta Giovanni had so loved the sister she lost that she had altered guilt-ridden reality into the outcome she craved.

Cameron said, "When you go to that hospice of yours you should take along a screenwriter."

Still nonplussed by Cameron's news, Kate could only manage a lame, "Everyone's life is a novel."

"From where I sit, more Stephen King than happily ever after," Cameron observed. "Kate, what do you know about your neighbors?"

"They're neighbors."

"Okay," he said with exaggerated patience. "How about the woman next door—"

"Pilar," she supplied.

When he did not reply, she understood that he was waiting for the last name and rolled her eyes. "Adams. Pilar Adams."

"What do you know about her?"

"From Calgary. Widowed, quite recently I think. A daughter in Europe."

"What else?"

"What else should I want to know?"

"For chrissakes, everything. For starters, is she renting? Did she buy the place?"

"Joe, the woman's nosy as hell." Her tone matched his in exasperation. "I ask any kind of personal question, she'll kick the door open right into my personal business. Why would I care? Why do *you* care?"

"It's called covering the bases," he said caustically. "Call me suspicious and paranoid, but anything around you, you need to check it out. Sometimes I can't believe you were ever a detective. This woman just happens to turn up just as Ellie Shuster tells you she's right here—"

"So Pilar's a hired assassin?" She was trying not to laugh at the image of the woman in one of her oversize tunics aiming an automatic weapon at her.

"Or an informer paid to keep an eye on you. Which would explain her wanting to be in your business all the time."

"I'll keep it in mind," she told him, again rolling her eyes.

"I just want you to be careful, Kate. Damn careful. I'll see you tonight." He clicked off.

She was irritated by his irritation. But she was now on Palm Canyon, her attention diverted to the Sun Center on her immediate right, an L-shaped mini mall, location of the LGBT Community Center. It was on the upper floor, she saw, noting the pride flag colors superimposed over a grouping of palm trees, clearly the organization's logo. She turned off, into a spacious lot. She still had half an hour before the AA meeting she had found online, and her meeting with Geneva Fallon was later still. She sat, fingering her car keys, still absorbing the news from Cameron, realizing that the falsehood she had given to Loretta about her sister being on the way had been more of a kindness than she could have imagined. Loretta could now peacefully pass away, wishful thinking intact.

She got out of the car smiling, wondering how the Center viewed its first-floor entrance right next to a medical marijuana dispensary. Her own Yucca Valley location hardly needed any dispensaries; its isolated hamlets and widely spaced domiciles were a refuge for potheads, and the sweetish aroma of marijuana occasionally reached her on a desert breeze. Pulling open the door leading up to the Center, she entered a lobby with an elevator and wide staircase, and chose the stairs.

Glass doors led to a reception area pleasantly cluttered with chairs, tables of brochures, a reception desk; a hallway led to a series of offices, some with glass partitions. "Can I help you?" inquired a rotund, bearded man in a plaid shirt and cargo pants seated at a desk that overlooked the parking area. He looked to be in his seventies, a volunteer, she surmised.

"I understand you have a bereavement group meeting here today?"

"Yup. From three to four. They sign you up when you come in."

"I'd just like some information about it for now."

"Sure." He pointed to a table crowded with flyers and racks of brochures. "Stuff about our programs is right over there and you might take a look at the bulletin boards down the hall. First time here?" he inquired as she continued to look around. She nodded and his face broke into a broad smile. "Welcome. My name's Dave," he said. "Any questions, anywhere I can direct you, I'm your man. You live here?"

She was smiling back; his warm welcome was infectious. "Yucca Valley."

"We have a lot going on now, worth your drive in. Our women's programs, it's not the boys' club it used to be. I know you're interested in the bereavement meeting, but there's a free counseling program too that's really good."

Meeting his gaze she said, "Don't you wish we'd had even a fraction of this when we were growing up."

He said fervently, "You got that right, sister."

She collected a few brochures from the table and made her way down the hallway to the bulletin boards where a tacked-up pastiche of additional brochures greeted her along with more flyers, announcements and business cards. People bustled past her, coming and going down the hallway. She was well aware that

Palm Springs' LGBTQ population had reached a national high in percentage, the city a cultural center, party scene, and national destination for such events as Dinah Shore weekend, the gay and lesbian film festival, many other community activities. This demonstration of LGBTQ presence was fulsome testimony to changing times and she felt her spirits rise for the first time in… longer than she could remember. If she did indeed die today, she had lived long enough to experience a world that was in a different place, a far better place for her and her LGBTQ family than the closet where she'd been trapped—and had trapped herself, she admitted—for most of her life.

She returned to her car to find the sun-exposed driver's seat and steering wheel searing to the touch. Without getting in, she managed to start the engine and turn the air conditioner to full blast. Then she pulled the aluminum windshield screen from the trunk for when she parked at her next destination, only a few blocks down Palm Canyon.

AA meetings could be anywhere, she reflected a few minutes later as she turned the Jeep in to the parking lot of a mall dominated by a huge Steinmart. She'd found them in the backrooms of stores, in church basements, union halls, clubhouses, anywhere. She often marveled that an organization comprised of addicts from every sector of society, with wide open membership and no dues, had managed to form a cohesive, reliable network that stretched from coast to coast with widely available meetings easily found via a pervasive Internet presence.

This would be a substantial gathering of about fifty, she judged as she entered the noisy room, a storefront, crowded with an animated older group, predominately men, wearing the Palm Springs uniform of shorts and shirts, and a few women in capris and colorful tops. The room was set up with a long table and chairs, additional chairs along the room's perimeter. Every meeting she'd ever been to was similar to this, sometimes rows of chairs with a makeshift stage for a larger group or chairs arranged in a circle if the group was small. A table near the door was laden with the usual large coffee machine, stacks of Styrofoam cups, platters of cookies.

"Welcome," said an elf of a man who looked to be his sixties, his spindly legs sticking out of many-zippered cargo shorts, his T-shirt emblazoned with the gay pride flag. "Your first meeting here?"

"First one here," Kate replied, smiling, "but hardly my first rodeo."

"Glad to have you. Grab a coffee, grab a seat before the Mission Hills van gets in."

She nodded thanks and carried a brimming paper cup of black coffee to a seat close to the door as the room quickly filled to capacity. The meeting opened with the usual ceremony and reading of the twelve steps, and she eased back into her chair in a room filled primarily with gay, lesbian and trans people. She could see herself in everyone here, parts of herself in all these addicts sitting in various attitudes of attentiveness. Could see the same alleviation of loneliness, a major component in the compulsion to drink, that she had always felt even during her days of coupledom with Aimee. There was openness here, an almost tangible comradeship; there was hope in this room. And a belonging she had never felt as much as she did when she was with those like herself, whose bodies and souls, like hers, had been seduced, gripped, and then absorbed into addiction.

A tiny man in a plaid cotton shirt and white shorts was now speaking, Canadian, she could hear from his oots and aboots. Like Pilar, he was here outside the usual season of November to April. He was sharing his personal epiphany, the moment he understood that alcohol not only solved nothing, it had served to damage people beyond himself. Part of his amends was the vow to stay sober so he could help the next guy stay sober.

She had never spoken in any meeting, shrinking back in debilitating shame and regret and awkwardness. But she attended faithfully because she knew she had family here, unconditionally supportive family. Family that was literally keeping her alive.

An hour later she retraced her route on Palm Canyon, following her GPS map into Old Las Palmas. A vague memory gleaned from who knew where told her the area dated from the thirties, and the small but exclusive neighborhood looked every year of its vintage. She gazed at sprawling homes with their fully mature foliage and an architecturally designed variation and opulence that had once brought fame to this playground for movie moguls and luminaries, some celebrated to this day on city streets such as Dinah Shore Drive, Gene Autry Trail, Kirk Douglas Way. The individuality of the homes, the ostentation of Spanish style mansions with their multitude of peaked tile roofs, the angular mid-century modern boxes with their distinctive flat roofs—it was a bygone world now mostly preserved by moneyed vestiges of a bygone generation, aging denizens like Geneva Fallon.

She parked in front of a huge white stucco hacienda with cathedral windows and multiple peaked tile roofs, the place set off from the street by a low wall overhung with scarlet bougainvillea and lined with ficus and palm trees, their fronds glittering silver in the haphazard breeze. She texted Geneva Fallon as previously instructed, then got out and made her way through an entryway topped by carriage lamps. A brick walkway bisected a vast expanse of grass—such an absurdity, ludicrous in the desert, she snorted. Why did people feel compelled to replicate what they knew regardless of where they were, to force their square pegs into nature's round holes? At least the people where she resided lived like the interlopers they were, on a prickly landscape that scarcely tolerated human occupancy.

Geneva Fallon, wearing a metallic gold top over capris that looked to be brocade, appeared at her front door as Kate approached and stepped aside for her to enter. Kate took in the affluence she'd expected: a vast living room with white walls and a ceiling of dark oak beams, a fireplace sculpted into much of one wall, arched windows that overlooked a huge blue-tiled pool. Ornate white and gold cabinets lined the room; there was a white granite wet bar with red barstools. Cream-colored sofas and armchairs, reposing on bright red and blue carpets, surrounded a series of glass tables.

"My children are here. They're out by the pool," Fallon said.

Alerted by the tone of voice, Kate halted in mid-step and turned to her. Fallon was rotating from one gold-sandaled foot to another in palpable anxiety as she reached into the drawer of an antique table beside the door. She withdrew an unmarked white envelope. "Here you go," she said.

"I thought we were going to discuss my idea to—"

"I trust you. Just take it," she said, pushing the envelope at Kate.

Kate finally understood what was happening here. Fallon had come to the door before the doorbell could ring and alert anyone else in the house. She did not want her children to know, to have to explain Kate's presence.

Kate pulled the check from Fallon's hand and said brusquely, "I'll let you know." She pushed heedlessly past Fallon to the door. She wanted out, out, out of here.

"I would appreciate that," Fallon said as Kate strode down the walk, calling after her, "I know this will get done, I trust you completely."

Her back to Geneva Fallon, Kate raised a hand in a contemptuous acknowledgment.

She started the engine to engage the air-conditioning and then sat in her car fuming, snapping the envelope with an index finger. It was unsealed. She opened it.

There were two cashier's checks, one with a Post-it attached. One for two hundred and fifty thousand dollars. The other, with the Post-it, for ten thousand. *For you with many thanks*, the Post-it read.

Kate crumpled the Post-it and thrust it in her litter bag. She looked at the larger check, shaking her head over this equivalent of a suitcase full of money, cashier's checks as good as cash. She could keep it all for herself and no one would ever know the difference. She could donate it, she could do anything she wanted with it. Geneva Fallon had found someone to complete her errand; she was now happily all done with Natalie Rostow, obligation fulfilled, guilt assuaged, conscience cleared. Whether or not Kate called her with any sort of report was immaterial. The ball had landed in Kate's court and Geneva Fallon had walked away. Kate returned the checks to their envelope and locked it in the glove compartment.

A security vehicle drifted alongside as she straightened up, the uniformed driver's assessing eyes on her as he drove by. She knew she easily passed his checklist: right skin color, right gender, okay late model car, okay for her to be here.

She threw the gearshift into drive and burned rubber away from Geneva Fallon and out of Old Las Palmas.

11

Kate drove back to the LGBT Center. According to the clock in her car, fourteen minutes remained in the meeting of the bereavement group, a few more if, like AA meetings, there was minor social interaction afterward. She located a parking space close to the entry to the Center, backed into it to face the door, and waited with the engine idling to feed the air conditioner.

She had brought with her the photo of Natalie Rostow that Geneva Fallon had given her, and she picked it up from the passenger seat. She wanted an in-person look at Rostow, her need to physically assess the woman undoubtedly the lingering effects of cop mentality, she conceded. She also had the address of the mobile home in Desert Hot Springs, taken down during the brief conversation yesterday that set up the drive into Palm Springs today.

Still smarting over her meeting with Geneva Fallon—if she could even call the thirty seconds of take-this-envelope-and-get-lost a meeting—she admitted that she was being irrational.

Nevertheless she indulged her resentment that a member of the superior rich had finessed her into a commitment, then treated her like a minion carrying out the get-it-done orders of a mafia don. For two cents she'd march into the Center and hand the checks over to the bearded guy at the front desk and consider it mission accomplished, the money well spent to support community programs. But she knew, and grew even more irritated with the certainty, that on principle and for the sake of Natalie Rostow and her own conscience she would do no such thing. She would carry out her commitment.

The door of the Center finally opened to seven people emerging in a flock, five women, two men, all of them advanced in years, three of them on canes, Natalie Rostow easily recognizable among them. A small woman with a neat cap of gray-white hair, she wore well-fitted white capris on trim hips and legs and a lavender T-shirt with print Kate could not discern. Her arm was wrapped around a stooped woman on a cane, in sisterly comfort more than affection; the other woman's face was blotched with red, her eyes wet, presumably from the discussion in the bereavement group. Rostow assisted her along the curb to where a driver waited by the door of a van whose sign announced one of the assisted living facilities in town. After a farewell pat on the woman's shoulder, Rostow turned and made her way to a dark blue Datsun Pulsar that dated from somewhere in the nineties, Kate guessed.

She followed her out of the lot, over to Indian Canyon, remaining at a distance. Reviewing her thought process about a possible approach to Natalie Rostow, the alternative she'd come up with as she'd sat fuming in the parking lot at the LGBT Center, she knew she had to make a decision before she approached the turnoff. She remembered the *Soon, very soon* note from Ellie Shuster in her mailbox and with a loud, fierce growl of "Stop being an idiot, you could die today," she turned away from the road to her house and sped up until she was behind the Datsun.

Natalie Rostow's mobile home was on the far end of Dillon Road, part of a community off Smoke Tree Road. When the

Datsun pulled into the carport alongside the trailer, Kate drifted her Jeep past to take a longer look at the place.

Four hundred square feet at most, she judged, and a standout amid its neighbors, sandy beige with a slightly peaked roof and two vertical front windows framed in dark brown below a small, graceful clerestory window. A stairway led up to the doorway and a tiny covered patio with two white chairs and a small table, bookend to the covered parking spot on the other side of the trailer.

She turned the Jeep around and parked in front of Rostow's home. Then made her way through a small yard landscaped with fine crushed rock and sand and cactus, and up the stairs.

Natalie Rostow immediately answered her knock as if she'd been standing just inside the door.

"My name is Kate Delafield." To the stony expression in the blue eyes magnified by thick glasses, she added, "I'm not a preacher and I'm not selling anything."

"You followed me here." The tone was flat, accusatory.

"For a good reason I'd like to explain. May I come in? I'm a retired LAPD police officer, if it helps."

"That may impress some people," Rostow conceded, leaving *but not me* implied. She stepped aside.

The living room, a fan turning under its peaked ceiling, was immaculately tidy. A decorative gray stripe around the top of snow-white walls matched a gray sofa enhanced by fluffy white pillows. There was a cream-colored loveseat, a coffee table with a marble top, two stylish ceramic lamps adorning miniscule end tables, a geometric black and gray carpet covering much of what appeared to be hardwood or laminate floor. A small TV sat on a bookcase filled with paperbacks. In an alcove, a gold mirror reflected a dining table with a white top and two gold chairs with bright red seats. The tiny kitchen held handsome dark gray cabinets and appliances and a counter with a gray-white Formica top on which were a coffee maker, a container of cooking implements, a knife set. Only Geneva Fallon, Kate thought acidly, would ever consider this very pleasing home "a decrepit trailer."

"I need coffee," Rostow said, stepping lithely toward the kitchen. "You too?"

"Me too, and black is fine," Kate said gratefully. "May I sit down?"

"Of course. Anywhere."

The coffee maker was preloaded, apparently set up before Rostow made her trip in to the bereavement group, and a few minutes later its rich aroma permeated the air and she came into the living room carrying two mugs.

Kate, seated on the loveseat, sipped excellent coffee, nodded appreciation, set the mug down on the marble table. Without preamble, she extracted the envelope from her shoulder bag as Rostow seated herself on the opposite sofa.

"Geneva Fallon asked me to bring this to you. I understand how very upset you were at the sight of her—"

"Do you really." Rostow set her coffee mug down on the coffee table with a whack and crossed her arms.

"—and that your partner, Barbara, threw her out."

"It's blood money," Rostow uttered, not looking at the envelope, her tone granite.

"Most definitely. And I'm here to offer it one more time. Or to have it distributed to your choice of our gay and lesbian organizations throughout the valley." She slightly emphasized the "our" to further identify herself. She extended the envelope to Rostow. "Your decision."

"Well, that's a new variation on an ultimatum," Rostow said coolly, but with the barest hint of amusement. She uncrossed her arms, took the envelope and in the same motion flicked it onto the marble table between them. Picked up her coffee and sat back in the sofa. She gazed at Kate. "You seem an odd sort of emissary."

Tell me. She thought about explaining, then said merely, "It's complicated."

"Are you a friend?"

"Not on this earth," Kate said, "or any other planet."

The lines in Rostow's face deepened in the barest hint of a smile. "Tell me more about what you think of her."

Kate did not reply.

Rostow said impatiently, "For God's sake, why are you doing this?"

Kate said with equal impatience, "Look, just give me a decision and I'll be out the door."

"Tell me this: what does she expect in return? Forgiveness?"

"Absolutely nothing. Nothing," she repeated. "What she did to you bothered her enough to make a gesture. Millions haven't, don't even acknowledge what they did to us, much less consider restitution. My problem with her is the one I have with most rich people. They actually think they deserve what they have and can buy what they want because they're superior. It never occurs to them that they're just goddamn lucky. Geneva Fallon already has what she wants. The instant I took this envelope from her you got crossed off her list."

Rostow's laugh was involuntary, contemptuous. "People don't change, do they. What she did to me is the person she actually is. But I give her half an ounce of credit for having half an ounce of conscience."

"As do I," Kate said, and drank much of her coffee; it appeared she would not be here long enough to savor it.

"Barbara guaranteed me it was worth it to throw her out on her ear. Since your alternative is donations to LGBT organizations, I take it she's offered more than the paltry sum Barbara guessed it was."

"What did she guess?"

"Five hundred, maybe five thousand at most. So, I'm curious—what's on the check? What was the damage she did to my lesbian life worth to her?"

Kate held Rostow's gaze and remained mute.

Rostow shrugged, picked up the unsealed envelope, opened it, looked at the top cashier's check.

"Jesus God!"

"Believe me, she can afford it." Kate was trying not to smile at the gasping whisper, the wide-eyed, slack-jawed amazement on Rostow's face. "Maybe you'll increase that half ounce of credit to an ounce."

"Maybe two ounces." Rostow, quickly recovering, pushed the check back into the envelope, dropped it on the table. "I like you," she pronounced, getting up. "Let me refresh that coffee. Unless you're in a hurry?"

"I'm not," Kate said. "And I like you too." This spirited, self-possessed woman was good for her morale, good to be around.

"Call me Natalie. I never let anyone call me Nat. Short person that I am, it makes me feel even more like gnat the insect."

Kate smiled. "Except for people I arrested in my police career, no one's ever called me anything but Kate."

When Rostow returned with mugs of coffee refilled to the brim and resumed her seat on the sofa, Kate said quietly, "You asked why I took this on. My partner back then could have been you, Natalie. Anne was a teacher too, primary school. We were very careful. And always afraid."

"I thought I was really careful too. How lucky that nothing happened to Anne."

"Something did." She felt as if she could tell this woman anything and continued heedlessly, "She died in an accident on the Hollywood Freeway. She was thirty-two."

"Oh, Kate, I am so sorry." She looked genuinely distraught. "How terrible that must have been for you back then."

"We did have twelve good years. I'm very sorry about Barbara. How long—"

"Twenty-seven for us. They were good years, too."

Kate asked, choosing her words, "After Fallon did that to you, what…how did you manage?"

"I didn't. My teaching career—gone. The woman I loved—she told me I had to leave. My parents were horrified. Friends and colleagues were no longer friends and colleagues. Geneva Fallon dropped an atomic bomb on my life."

Geneva Fallon, Kate thought, was lucky that Natalie Rostow had only screamed at her. I probably would have killed her.

"Two women, two wonderful women came to the house while I was packing up and told me they were there to help…" Tears welled and she picked up her coffee.

In the pause, Kate offered, "I had help from women at key times too. I can't imagine where I would be without them."

"In my case, I'd be dead. I had reservations at a motel, I already had the bottle of vodka and three bottles of aspirin I was going to take when I got there."

"Who were they? How did they know about you?"

"They never did tell me who it was that sent them, to this day I don't know. I suspect it was someone in administration in the school system. That's the only way they would have known my address. They were Betty Berzon and Terry DeCrescenzo."

She looked at Kate as if expecting recognition of the names. "They were co-founders that year of the Southern California Women for Understanding." When Kate still showed no sign of knowing the reference, she said impatiently, "A lesbian organization that brought mostly professional women together for networking and to do community work. Betty Berzon was a psychotherapist instrumental in getting homosexuality declassified as a mental disorder. Both women have written books..." She scowled at Kate. "You don't know this? Where have you been all your life?"

Kate answered shortly, "Being a closeted police officer."

Rostow's face softened slightly, and she nodded. "In the eighties, Terry DeCrescenzo founded GLASS—Gay and Lesbian Adolescent Social Services—the first refuge anywhere for our throwaway youngsters."

Mute with admiration at all this achievement and its impact, Kate just nodded. "I don't know my history as well as I should," she muttered, chastened.

"For sure," Rostow said in a tone that did not disguise disapproval. "They took me in. To their home. Betty treated me for suicidality. They got me a job as a researcher for a historian they knew, and I went on from there into technical writing. Then I met Barbara and the sun came back into my life."

"I'm very glad to hear it," Kate said. "What did Barbara do?"

"She was co-owner of a bakery. Till a drunk came through a red light and crippled her. Between insurance money and workman's comp and my income, we got this place and managed.

It's a little harder now she's gone, but I have a good home here, not much expense." She glanced at the envelope, back at Kate. "I do manage, I have enough. A whole coterie of women live here, we all look in on each other. We're all colors, all creeds, a lot of us lesbian." She smiled. "Though I've always suspected that most women are lesbians. Some of us just don't realize it yet."

Kate smiled back at her. "It's a good thought. Tell you what, Natalie..." She pointed to the envelope. "Why not use this money to make life a little easier for all these women around you?"

Natalie Rostow contemplated her. "That's actually not a bad idea. In fact it's a good one. Melanie needs a caregiver and can't afford one. Our clubhouse needs a little work. Actually, a lot of work. That car of mine—it's on its last legs, I could use an upgrade..."

"So put the blood money to good use and tell everybody it's life insurance." One of the approaches she'd been thinking of using. That, or a phony inheritance.

"Kate, I saw two checks in there."

"The other's a cashier's check for me, ten thousand. I wouldn't touch it with a flagpole. I'd like you to give it to the LGBT Center."

"Why don't you—"

"I'd rather it came from you. Maybe to fund that bereavement group you go to?"

Rostow nodded. "A good idea."

Kate finished her coffee and rose to her feet. "I have to go. I just remembered I have a dog to walk and feed."

"Whereabouts are you?"

Kate gestured. "Over in Yucca."

"It was rude of me not to ask more about you. Will you come back and visit?" Rostow rose and went to the kitchen counter, wrote on a pad, and gave the page to Kate. "I think you'd like the women here and I'm sure they'd like you."

Kate looked down at the page; it had Natalie Rostow's phone number. She took the pad and wrote her own phone number on it. And finally read the message on Natalie's lavender T-shirt that she had noticed in the parking lot of the LGBT center: *When I am an old woman, I shall wear purple.*

She grinned. "Thank you, Natalie. I definitely will."

If I live long enough, she thought, looking wistfully around her. It was a lovely place to be. A peaceful place to visit with this cultivated, interesting woman and her circle of friends.

12

As Kate drove along the road toward her house, an image emerged through the dusk: Pilar Adams peering into the front window, waving and gesticulating. When Kate pulled into her driveway and opened her door, she heard the reason for the behavior.

Pilar, an oversize maroon sweatshirt hanging over her capris in the evening chill, greeted her with a raised hand and a grin. "Figured you'd be along so I thought I'd just keep her company awhile."

"Thank you," Kate said earnestly, unlocking her front door to escalating barks. "I didn't expect to be away nearly so long. She's got the loudest bark—I hope she didn't drive you crazy."

"She's a good girl, she only started up about an hour ago. I got her nice and quiet till she heard your car drive up. It's no trouble. What else have I got to do?"

A thought rose and Kate turned to Pilar and blurted in a sudden surge of hope, "Did you happen to see anyone drive up— maybe walk up—and put something in my mailbox yesterday or today?"

Two frown lines deepened between Pilar's eyes. "Well, no, but…Any idea when this was? I can't imagine I wouldn't have noticed."

Neither could Kate, and she was deflated by the response. The possibility of a description of Ellie Shuster's car, however vague, or even of the woman herself, hair color and clothes if she was on foot or in disguise, had vanished.

"Maybe it was middle of the night," Pilar offered.

Kate nodded. That made more sense. Unless Shuster had been cunning enough to approach at least partway on foot on this all but deserted road, Dakota would have barked just as she had at the mail truck.

"Is this a problem to you, Kate? Why you've got all those cameras on your place?"

She answered truthfully, "It was an envelope with no signature or return address." As she reached to turn off her alarm system, she regretted that she'd ever asked the question.

"Something nasty?" Pilar asked avidly.

"I need to tend to Dakota. Thanks for looking in on her." She closed the door firmly behind her, the dog cavorting around her. She expected Cameron momentarily, was in fact a little surprised he wasn't there already. He'd texted an earlier ETA as she left Desert Hot Springs. But a few minutes to feed the dog and settle herself were welcome. This had been a full day. Overall a good day, she thought wryly, petting Dakota who was still spinning in glad greeting, for someone whose days were numbered by more than the calendar.

Cameron turned up shortly after eight o'clock, takeout and soft drinks in his arms, elbowing his way through the door Kate had left ajar when she heard him drive up. His thin face tense with irritation, he grumbled, "They got on my ass about goddamn fucking paperwork."

Dakota, having barked at his arrival, abandoned her enthusiastic welcome in favor of another go at her food bowl. Amused by the dog's sensing of Cameron's mood, Kate watched with approval and sharpening appetite as Cameron unpacked and opened cartons of shrimp with brown rice, sesame chicken, green beans with mushrooms and a pint of keto salted caramel ice cream which he stashed in the freezer. She said, "Whatever happened to that theory about computers ushering in a future of no more paper?"

Cameron snorted, "People really believed that? I'll take back the world of paper. It's endless email, bureaucratic crap, more and more goddamn reports, more fucking demands, more more more." Tossing his Padres baseball cap onto a barstool, pushing up the sleeves of the white loose-weave cotton sweater that hung over his jeans, he turned to her and suddenly grinned. "So how about some plates for this stuff? And how was your day, Kate, beyond you still being in one piece?"

Kate grinned back. As a confidante, Cameron was no Maggie but she was grateful for him. "Every day's a good day, Joe. The food looks great," she added, tantalized by the tangy aroma of soy sauce. Pulling plates and bowls out of the cupboard, she elected to try to deflect his mood by filling him in on her two meetings with Geneva Fallon.

They sat at the counter and ate their dinner and then bowls of the ice cream Cameron retrieved from the freezer, all the while Kate relating every detail she could remember from Fallon's arrival in her candy apple-red Mercedes convertible to the outcome today with Natalie Rostow at the trailer park in Desert Hot Springs.

Cameron grunted a few times in reaction but did not once interrupt her. Clanking his spoon into his ice cream bowl when she finished, he took a long swig of his Diet Coke, then gazed up toward the ceiling as if trying to decipher a message written on the plaster. "Let me summarize," he said. "In the last two days you've had someone confess to murder, someone else ask you to find a woman she killed twelve years ago, and today you handed over two hundred and sixty grand cash money to a stranger living in a trailer." He lowered his gaze from the ceiling to focus on Kate. "Are you making this stuff up? Maybe writing a book and trying subplots out on me?"

She laughed. "Fate's just making use of me, Joe. Maybe this is some sort of karma. Between Vietnam and all my years on the job, any idea there might be a god with a hand in anything got knocked right out of me. So it's nice to think I can set anything right. I'm just an agent."

He grinned. "The Delafield Agency."

Startled, she said, "That's what Pilar next door called me yesterday."

He leaned back on his barstool, crossing his arms. "You've always been the Delafield Agency. On the job people saw you were a straight shooter, they trusted you. You just never saw yourself that way. Still don't."

Of course she didn't. No way could he see that her whole life was a series of wrong way driving. She didn't argue, offering facetiously, "You and my shrink are sitting in the same chair."

"What a surprise," he mocked. "Then there's Aimee. You never mention Aimee. I happen to know she hasn't gone anywhere."

Fighting off the powerful impulse to ask how and what he knew, she said warily, "No point. She needs to stay far away till this gets resolved one way or another. No one should come near me who isn't one of us."

"You know what I think?"

She didn't want to know and didn't reply.

"After all these years I believe I understand a few things about you, Kate," Cameron said, stacking their dinner plates and bowls. "Well, maybe it's more like, I kind of know how you are. So this is what I'm guessing: Aimee doesn't have a clue about Ellie Shuster."

It was a statement, not a question, and she looked at him sharply, scowling. She couldn't tell him it was none of his business. She'd made Cameron's personal life her own business and he'd done the same for her in every way that mattered. She said, "All our time together, especially after I took that bullet in the shoulder, she stressed over me on the job. I don't want this in her face. I don't want her knowing about something as bullet-to-the-heart real as Ellie Shuster. I don't want her calling me every two seconds to see if I'm still alive."

"So you leaving her to come here, dumping her over a cliff—that's better, Kate? Your logic is total crap. How can a threat on your life be any different than if you had a terminal cancer diagnosis?"

I don't need this, she thought, her anger rising in a scorching burn. "It *is* different, Joe," she snapped. "You damn well know it's different."

"Maybe it is. But the one thing that's never changed is you thinking you always know what's best for people who care about you. Our opinions never seem to matter."

"In that case I don't know why you even bother with me," she muttered, struggling to conceal the magnitude of her wrath. He'd now formally joined the ranks of Calla Dearborn and Maggie Schaeffer. Neither of them could ever seem to understand that the foremost and best gift she could give to the people she loved was to protect them. She was sick to death of arguing about something so simple and clear. *To Protect and to Serve*—the motto of the LAPD, the entire purpose of her time in the military, the enduring dictum of her entire life. Why did he not damn well understand after she'd for chrissake lived that motto to the hilt helping him when that homicidal ex-con brother of his had been fixed like a laser on murdering him?

He reached out to her, put a hand on her arm. "Kate, one of these days this will end." He squeezed her arm. "I just wish…"

We knew how and when, she wordlessly finished for him and covered his warm hand with her own, her anger dissipating.

He again squeezed her arm then released it, picked up and flicked on his phone, began scrolling. "I did more stuff today on the Shuster case, read through Stella Hayden's diary—"

"Without a translator?" she joked, immeasurably eased by his brief physical contact. She picked up their dishes and carried them and the empty cartons into the kitchen.

"Yeah, tough going, like hieroglyphics, that handwriting of hers and all the symbols…"

So this was why he was late getting here, she realized, staring across the counter at him in consternation. Just as she'd suspected, the murder book had hooked him and he'd spent his day on the Ellie Shuster case. Not much wonder they were on him about late reports on his own open cases.

"Joe, it won't make me feel better if you lose your job trying to help me," she told him.

"Never happen," he said flatly, not looking up from flicking pages on his phone. "Don't worry about it."

"You're the fair-haired boy like always?" she probed lightly.

"They're okay with how I spend my time," he countered, his tone brusque. Looking up, his lips thinning with annoyance at the mere suggestion of job negligence, he said, "What matters is the important stuff getting done. It gets done."

Of course it did. In her experience he was goal oriented and strategic in his priorities. With that extra bonus present in good police detectives: relentlessness about the who and why of every homicide case assigned to them. Searching for conclusive answers to cases that remained indelible even when the active investigation was suspended and assigned to the cold case files.

"You say I never mention Aimee," she said. "You never mention anyone."

"Yeah, well, aside from jacking off to computer porn, you're it these days."

She laughed. "Thanks."

Staring at the page on his screen, he said distractedly, "Two dates and they want commitment. I just ain't there."

The truth, she knew, was that so far no one measured up to his adored ex-wife who radiated enough pheromones and animal magnetism that she'd impacted even Kate. Plus, he still could not bring himself to be serious about any woman after never suspecting—highly rated detective that he was—the rampant cheating that had gone on under his nose for seven—"*SEVEN!*" he had once roared drunkenly at Kate—of the fifteen years he and Janine had been married.

Cameron said, "I know you've been through Stella's diary—"

"A dozen times," Kate said.

"This bit here…" Cameron held his phone sideways, magnified text with two fingers, handed it to Kate. "She wrote this nine days before her suicide. What did you make of it?"

Kate read aloud, "'*Miss Hall, I hate hate hate you. You're every bit as bad, no, the garbage you put in her head is the worst, just as awful as all the preachy stuff from her bitch mother.*'" She frowned. "It's of a piece with everything else that's in here."

"Yeah, but…" He began more scrolling on his phone.

"Here. Here," she said, pulling over the stapled pages of the copy she'd made of the diary.

"Yeah, good, much easier," he said, seizing it and leafing rapidly through to the page shown on his phone. He extracted a notebook from his back pocket. "So we don't have to go through it again, I made a list…" He flipped to a back page. "Stella's mother and father, they're always Mother and Father, never Mom and Dad, and from what I see in here—" He tapped the diary, "—she saw them only as authority figures, dictators making her do only what they wanted, never what she wanted. Same deal with April's father, he's the Beast, her mother is the Bitch, sometimes the Queen Bitch. There's a preacher from the church she calls Thundermouth, his wife's Mrs. Mealymouth…" As he continued reading from his list, Kate was nodding familiarity and he told her, "I know you know all this, just bear with me here. There's Donkeyface, Pruneface, Toadface, Broomstick, Pinhead, Darth Vader…"

Kate began to laugh at this distillation out of the diary pages, and he joined her. "Yeah, she's pretty colorful. So, okay, we know all these people had to be members of the church because the church was the entirety of her parents' lives. According to the interviews I read last night, any relatives of theirs refused to have anything to do with this band of fanatics. So all these people were at her house all the time bowing and scraping to her father and in lockstep with spewing all their homophobic hatred."

He turned the page in his notebook. "Then we have her teachers, Peabody's one of the few she likes, her history teacher. Miss Lincoln for English, fun and nice, but silly. Miss Fujikawa who made Stella angry over her math grades. Mr. Francis, Mr. Turnbull, Miss Guerrero, all mentioned in passing, they taught classes she shared with April."

"Okay, so where are going with this?"

"Right back to Miss Hall. She doesn't figure to be a member of the church, Kate—Stella gave every single one of those people nicknames."

"Then she was one of the teachers."

"No, that's the thing. It just doesn't figure. Remember the changes in the LA school system by the late nineties? Programs for gay kids taking hold…"

She nodded, a memory surfacing of the women at the Nightwood Bar marveling over the astounding courage of a woman who was enduring a national firestorm of condemnation over her creation of the first school support group in the nation for gay kids. The mideighties, Project 10, she finally remembered. Virginia Uribe.

He repeated the passage from the page of the open diary, "'…the stuff you put in her head is just as awful as all the preachy stuff from her bitch mother.' No way a teacher would have done this. But April talked to somebody in authority and this Miss Hall told her something Stella didn't like, and maybe, just maybe it had nothing to do with being lesbian."

"The school psychologist," Kate said, marveling at the acuteness of his observations.

"Bingo, and here's the day's big news," he said, his face, his voice triumphant. "I called the high school. The murder-suicide was twenty years ago, but believe me, it's legend at that place. The woman I spoke to in administration—" He consulted his notebook. "Mrs. Fernandez, she knew all the teachers in this diary, exactly who I was asking about. Miss Hall was a consulting psychologist who retired a decade ago. No current contact information. That's as far as I got in tracking her before I got slammed with the goddamn paperwork."

"This is great stuff and I can take it from here, Joe. What's her full name?"

"Marietta Hall. She—" He broke off, staring at Kate. "What, what?"

Gaping at him, she was groping for her power of speech, certain her face had gone white. "Dory Quillin," she finally managed to say.

"Who? Who's she?"

"A murder victim. Marietta Hall was the psychologist who treated her. Dory Quillin, the Nightwood Bar."

Cameron now was nodding; she'd often spoken about this case during their time together at Wilshire Division. She sighed inwardly. Would that decades-ago murder at the Nightwood Bar ever stop encroaching on and haunting her life?

"I didn't see it," she lamented. "Miss Hall…I never connected those dots like you did."

"Easy to understand why. Go through a case this many times, you get too deep in the weeds. It took a fresh pair of eyes to see something out of pattern."

She nodded, accepting this. It happened. Most often to cold case detectives ferreting out new information from old evidence.

She said slowly, "It figures April Shuster either went to or was sent to that psychologist, and she was given advice that Stella took great exception to. It may not be in the least relevant to the who of April's murder—"

"But it's a trail."

"Which I'll follow. I'll find her, Joe."

Tomorrow. Which could not come soon enough. LA was again drawing her in, a magnet.

13

Pacific Gardens was an easy find in West LA, off the Ten, on well-traveled Bundy Drive between Pico and Venice boulevards. The handsome two-story building, partially concealed by a boxwood hedge and crowned with graceful clusters of queen palms, was dark red brick, a classy contrast to the surrounding mixed-use buildings with the stucco cladding pervasive throughout the city. Google Earth had shown a facility that took up an impressive amount of real estate with its shaded paths and gardens, and Kate now saw that it boasted a driveway leading down to free underground parking. An aged, white-haired attendant seated in a camp chair, a newspaper spread in his lap, waved her into one of many open slots.

She rode a tiny wood-paneled elevator to the main floor, its doors opening to a stylish bronze table bearing a lavish arrangement of leafy succulents overflowing a bright blue ceramic bowl. A polished blond wood bench lined the wall adjacent to the elevator; a reception area with a boomerang-shaped granite counter, crowded with brochures and flyers, occupied the opposite side of the room. At the counter a tiny middle-aged Asian woman looked up at her from behind a bulky desk computer.

"I'd like to see Marietta Hall," Kate said, searching the cluttered counter for a visitors' sign-in book.

"How nice. Such a treasure to the people here, a real favorite," the woman gushed. "Go into the main room," she said, gesturing, "take the hallway to your right and her unit's straight down, one-twenty-four. You'll need to knock," she added, and Kate deduced that unlocked rooms were the norm.

The place wasn't a prison, she reminded herself after thanking the woman, nor did it need the safeguards of a hospice. It was a well-located, upscale assisted-living facility without a memory ward, so no lockdown. Aside from screening for intruders, why would they care who visited?

The lobby opened into a carpeted central area dominated by a railed-off section holding several dozen tables of varying sizes, padded chairs around them, bright red menus propped up by an assortment of condiments. Kate paused, gazing around with interest. A dozen elderly men and women were talking and laughing as they played cards at an oblong table in an alcove partitioned off by vertical shafts of pale wood. A similar alcove, furnished with armchairs, was lined with bookcases, its two white-haired occupants bent over their books. There were no food aromas nor was there any hint of the medicinal and disinfectant odors pervasive at Silverlake Haven.

Along the carpeted hallway toward Marietta Hall's unit, Kate slowed to inspect a bulletin board comprised of a large monthly calendar listing times for excursions to museums, films and theater productions; get-togethers on the premises, social functions and lifestyle lectures. Lining the corridor were paintings and photographs of redwood forests, pine trees, fields of sunflowers, bowls of daisies. All the units Kate passed bore nameplates identifying the occupants, and one-twenty-four's read *Dr. Marietta Hall*.

Kate's brief light knock was answered by a husky call of "I'm coming…" But it was some moments before the door swung open.

Eager for information yet all too aware of the memories that would be dredged up by this visit, Kate had been dreading it. But the sight of Marietta Hall, her imposing height scarcely compromised by the walker on which she leaned with both hands, drew an involuntary grin. The wild frizzy dark hair of yesteryear was now wild frizzy white hair. The lines in her round face had considerably deepened, her lips reduced to a thin line framed by wrinkles. But the lake-blue eyes, bright, lively with awareness, were unchanged. As Kate took in the floor-length housecoat decorated with tiny silhouettes of Mickey and Minnie Mouse against an iridescent yellow background, her grin widened. The attire evoked the radically unconventional therapy office on San Vicente that she had visited more than two decades ago, its walls as dazzlingly yellow as Marietta Hall's housecoat.

"Well, as I live and breathe," came the same low, Garboesque tones Kate remembered. "Of all people I never imagined I'd ever see again…Detective Kate Delafield. Come in, come in."

"Detective no more, I'm retired," she informed her, entering a room that resembled a hothouse. Potted plants, some flowering, many of them ferns, a half dozen tree-like and ceiling-high, all but overwhelmed the warm room and produced a rich, humid, fecund smell. Adding to the jungle-like atmosphere were wall hangings of birds of spectacular plumage. She stood relishing this re-creation of the psychotherapy office she well remembered and how discomfited partner Ed Taylor had been when they had come there to interview this woman. "It's good to see some things haven't changed," she said, shaking her head in wonder.

"Well, it appears that a lot of life has happened to you," Marietta Hall remarked, having finished her own inspection of Kate.

"I feel a mere hundred years older," Kate joked, taking in the large window, shaded by a metallic awning, that looked out onto a path winding its way through an expanse of grass. Beside the window an electronic chair stood starkly vertical, its seat slanted to the floor, having delivered Marietta Hall to her feet to answer the door. A wheelchair was within reach of the electronic chair, an armchair at conversational distance. The single side table held an assortment of prescription bottles, a glass of water, a disorderly stack of paperbacks, a pair of glasses, a few tissues, a cupholder of pens sitting on a pad of paper. On the coffee table were miniature glass and ceramic sculptures of birds and animals lined up in neat rows according to species. There was a wall unit with a TV, its other shelves stacked with books and magazines. An archway led, presumably, to a bedroom and bath. In an enclave beside the door a miniscule kitchenette contained two cupboards over a sink, a small refrigerator, hot plate and tiny microwave. All she would need, Kate thought, with meals being served to the residents.

"Dr. Hall, it's a very nice place," Kate said. "You look to be really comfortable here."

"Marietta, call me Marietta and I'll call you Kate. It's good here. I did one truly sensible thing in my life—took out a top-notch long-term care policy. I'll never be a burden to anyone but the people here, and they're well compensated for looking after me. Have a seat, Kate. Coffee's freshly made. Take anything besides black?"

"Black's fine." Seeing that Marietta could not manage two coffees plus her walker, Kate followed her to the kitchenette.

Finally seated in the armchair, she watched Marietta's electronic chair slowly lower her into a comfortable sitting position, her legs elevated on its footrest. "Rheumatoid arthritis," she told Kate, gnarled fingers clutching her mug. "I get around this little place of mine and watering these plants gets me on my feet, a good thing. But any distance, it's the walker. The wheelchair—well, I need some assistance with…this and that."

Kate nodded, assuming "this and that" to be going to meals, showering, and dressing. Sipping good strong coffee out of a mug adorned with penguins, she guessed that Marietta was well into her seventies if not beyond; she had looked to be in her fifties when they first met. "I'm getting a bit creaky myself," she offered in commiseration.

Actually, aside from her hovering hooded figure of death and considering her years of smoking, eating crap food on the job, drinking whatever and whenever, and with no physical activity outside her daily routine, she was in better physical shape than she deserved. Reading glasses were now a necessity, her knees sometimes hinted at lesser days to come, and her left shoulder was a constant nuisance, stiffening overnight and aching well beyond the reach of Advil on rainy days. There was also that view in the bathroom mirror each morning, tired blue eyes looking back at her in a face baked by the years like clay in the sun, framed by ever unruly hair that was now a pale gray. Her body thinner because of not much of an appetite, a good result for a bad reason. But, more than anything else these days, the vista she now looked out on was the metaphoric landscape in her rearview mirror. Generating nostalgia, wistfulness, occasional joy; more often regret, sorrow, grief. No way could the woman seated across from her, who was contemplating her with a shrewd, inquisitive gaze, know that the case they'd shared all those years ago had been a watershed in her emotional life. The murder of Dory Quillin had drawn her out of her closeted isolation after Anne's death and into a lesbian community of chosen family.

"So how have you been, Kate?"

"I've had my ups and downs," Kate replied with a wry smile. "And you?"

Marietta chuckled, a rich, deep, chocolatey sound. "Ups and downs are known in my trade as living a human life. Granted, more intense for you than most of us, given your line of work."

Kate nodded, noting that Marietta had not answered her question. Revealing anything personal during the therapeutic process was proscribed by her former profession and the directive had evidently followed her into retirement. Continuing to sip her coffee, procrastinating over her reason for being here, an inexplicable reluctance, she confessed in deflection, "Retirement was hard at the time. But a good thing...I came to see how the job was hacking more and more out of me. From what the woman at the front desk said about you, I take it you're still in the therapy business."

Marietta raised a hand. "I seem to have turned into a combination of Dr. Phil and Ann Landers. If I didn't lock my door, they'd be flocking in here at all hours."

Kate was chuckling and nodding. In view of where she was, she elected not to bring up any of her own experiences with the dying at Silverlake Haven and instead offered, "I've had people ask if I can help get their driver's licenses restored. To do something about barking dogs, rude teenagers. A woman in my own condo asked me to talk her kid into going into rehab."

"I hope you did that last one."

"Yes, actually. Easy enough to come up with a version of scared straight after all the drunks and druggies I've seen being zipped into body bags."

"I can only imagine. Out of curiosity, Kate…how did you find me? I've been here several years now; I seldom have visitors."

Kate heard this sadly, thinking of the people she had visited at Silverlake Haven, abandoned by family and friends wearied by the constant reality of death and dying. She answered, "Through a colleague of yours, Calla Dearborn. I've been seeing her for years."

"Ah, yes, Calla, one of our best," she said with a vigorous nod and added meaningfully, "One friend who never let me down when times got tough. You couldn't do better, she's splendid." Wincing, stirring uncomfortably, she adjusted the chair's footrest to a lower position. "I'm assuming the case we have in common is what brings you here, something about the murder at the Nightwood Bar." She added so softly, as if to herself: "I think of Dory to this very day."

Kate suddenly found herself more than willing to meet Marietta Hall on this common ground. "She haunts me," she uttered, the three words tumbling out of her.

"I deeply understand that, Kate. You viewed her in death. Worse for us who knew her in life. I'll never forget her. She was a special spirit on this earth. Mercurial, pugnacious, charming, smart, a rebel to her very core…"

"I did know that. It came across from everyone who knew her," Kate said. "I interviewed a woman Dory was with for about a year, Neely Malone. She was trying to tell me what Dory meant to her and she quoted a phrase from Shakespeare, that Dory was life's bright fire."

"How perfect," Marietta said mournfully. "I just wish I could have done something, anything…"

"I know. But that interview I did with you all those years ago, your sessions with her, how you pursued her all over the place trying to get her to tell you the truth of what happened to her. How elusive she was—"

"Quicksilver."

"You knew, you absolutely knew what happened with her father when no one else did, even though you couldn't get her to tell you."

"The signs were classic. But, Kate, I'm sure all she could see was that revealing it would destroy her family."

"In this case, if only it had. You did all you could. You have nothing to regret."

Marietta grimaced. "Wishful thinking is not the same as regret."

And guilt is quite different from regret, Kate reflected, thinking of Ellie and April Shuster and her dereliction of duty.

The forking lines around Marietta's lips smoothed with her faint smile. "I remember the partner you had at our interview."

"Ed Taylor."

"Yes. A misogynist and homophobe, as I recall—"

"Add racist to the list."

"Even though I'm heterosexual, he's the kind of male that makes me wish for a world of only women."

"I've often wished for that too, and for the same reason. Marietta, it's not Dory that brings me here," Kate finally began, and took a deep breath. "I need to know about a high school student who was sent to you about twenty years ago. April Shuster."

Marietta flung her head back against the headrest and closed her eyes. "Oh Goddess," she uttered, "that one." Then she jerked forward to stare at Kate. "But she wasn't your case. I followed all the newspaper reports, I'd hoped she was yours when I first heard about the murder."

"Actually, she was my case. And wasn't." She took a breath and expelled the truth: "I deferred to my inexperienced partner to be lead detective. To this day no one knows the real reason I did that. It was because of Dory. I couldn't..." she fumbled, "I... so close after Dory...I couldn't...just couldn't...deal with it."

"Oh, Kate, I understand. No one could understand that better than I do," Marietta pronounced in her husky tones, her eyes moist, and she picked up her coffee mug, cradling it in both hands as if seeking the comfort of its warmth.

Kate sat silently, tearful, unmoving for an expanse of time, aware only of her intakes and exhalations of breath, the smell of the greenery in the room, the lightness spreading through her shoulders as a twenty-year weight lessened with this sharing.

Marietta put down her mug. "I read about the acquittal. That must have been a horror."

"Ever had a client of yours commit suicide?"

Marietta winced. "Two, actually."

"Then you maybe understand how I feel about the years taken out of this woman's life."

"I won't bother arguing that it wasn't your fault; I'm sure Calla's done her futile best with you. Since it wasn't her mother, who did kill April?"

Kate smiled thinly. "Given the nature of the Church of the Eternal Word, the possibilities are numerous."

Marietta said mockingly, "Challenge the god I believe in? In his name I kill you, blasphemer."

Kate shrugged her agreement with this cynical truth.

"It's been...how long since the acquittal?"

"A year and a half."

"I've been right here. You're here only *now*?"

"I didn't know about you till now. Long story, I'll get to it. Marietta, I need to ask some questions about April."

"Yes." She spread her hands. "Of course. But you know the rules of my profession."

"I do. All I can offer are extenuating circumstances." She enumerated on her fingers: "April's been dead twenty years. The church has long since disbanded. Her father and Stella Hayden's parents are somewhere in Africa. The lead detective in the case has died. Ellie Shuster has chosen me to blame for her conviction and a letter hand-delivered right to my mailbox promises she's about to kill me."

"Oh Goddess." Marietta blinked at her. Then heaved a sigh. "Oh, Kate, Kate, you so don't deserve this." She shook her head. "Not that *deserve* means anything with someone entrenched in their own reality. Well, in an ideal world common sense would always prevail over any rule book. Besides, who cares if my governing agency pulls my license? What do you want to know about April?"

"Every single thing you can remember."

Marietta lowered her frizzy head, massaged her face with her fingertips, blew out a breath, leaned her head back. "Kate, with all this going on I'm doubly glad you're seeing Calla. About April, I remember quite a lot. First off, I can tell you she was no Dory Quillin. With April, self-assertion was a foreign country. She was a walking bundle of anxiety, fear. You at least got a look at her—"

"Covered in blood," Kate interrupted bluntly. "Her face and skull crushed."

"Oh Goddess. But you've seen photos—"

"I haven't. I practiced all the avoidance I could on this one." Photos of the living April Shuster, as well as Stella Hayden, remained in a sealed envelope locked in her safe.

"Well then, the basics. Dory's eyes were blue—"

"Yes I know." She wanted no further description of Dory, of the lifeless body that had pierced her to her soul, the eyes she had seen forever frozen in horror over her killer.

But Marietta was oblivious, inexorable. "Such a…a *lacerating* blue they were. They pinned you till she looked away. Now April, her eyes were light brown, and when she looked at you they went skittering away as if she was afraid she might reveal something, you might actually see something hidden in her. She was a very pretty girl, Kate, heart-shaped face, turned-up nose, but pretty like a porcelain doll. Rigid, she was so very rigid. Now Dory…Dory was like…" She flapped her hands as if they were an aid in her groping for words. "She was like a lighted candle was inside her. Like a stained glass window with sunlight coming through. But April, her whole body was jittery, as if her feet were always on ice. She was so afraid…"

"Of what?"

"Everything. Imagine being that girl. Imagine your whole existence dictated by that…that…*cult*. Living in a closet inside a jail." Her eyes were sparking in anger, her tone scathing. "A Tibetan monastery wouldn't be as regimented as the home life of that poor youngster. In my book she was an abused, emotionally battered child. But…" She raised a hand, dropped it. "You know how it is, Kate. Parental rights, freedom to call any nutty belief a religion…"

Kate nodded; no need to say more when they both had been daily witness to the destruction caused by these "rights" being taken to extremes.

"April had a girlfriend…" Marietta rubbed fingers together in a gesture that she was searching for a name.

"Stella. Stella Hayden."

"Yes. I remember that Stella was April's one and only friend. Her family lived right under the thumb of that cult leader next door in their duplex." Marietta's voice rose. "From the moment she woke up in the morning she was battered by people who used the Bible like a weapon. Have you ever read the Bible, Kate?"

"I can quote Leviticus," she said drily.

Marietta snorted. "That's enough to know how people use it to justify anything. I've always wished someone would come along and proclaim Shakespeare the reincarnation of Christ, and his plays the new gospel. I mean, why not? It's the greatest and wisest literature the world has ever known. It holds every guidepost to human behavior and morality."

"I wish," Kate said, struck by the concept. But then, she thought, people would still find ways to interpret and distort the plays to suit their purposes. She asked, "Given April's home life, how did she ever come to identify as lesbian?" Then, realizing that she had only Stella Hayden's diary for this assumption, she quickly asked, "Or did she?"

"She did. She found a book—"

Kate's sharp laugh was involuntary. "A book," she repeated. "The true weapon of mass destruction. No wonder they burned them throughout history. Do you happen to remember which one?"

"Sure. *Annie on My Mind*, Nancy Garden. My recollection is she found it—someone left it on a desk in one of her classrooms. Probably a kid I was treating. Back then, the novel was number one on my recommend list for teens struggling with their lesbian identity."

Kate shifted in her chair. What a different turn her own life might have taken had she found a book like that in high school. Or a Marietta Hall. "Her sexual orientation...had she acted on it?"

"How I wish she had," Marietta said wistfully. "But what she took from the book wasn't affirmation. Only confirmation of her worst fears about evil desires inside her and committing a sin that would consign her to the fires of hell." She sighed. "I wish I could have done something, anything...But, she was so thoroughly indoctrinated...The fact that she was willing to listen to me at all—well, even that much was amazing."

"Why was she sent to you? I assume it wasn't voluntary."

"It was, actually. In those days I was at the school two afternoons a week. A teacher came to me out of concern for how isolated and troubled April seemed. So I approached her on my own, very casually, told her I was talking to a number of the girls at the school and asked if she'd like to come in and talk to me, tell me about herself. And she did."

"How many sessions did she have with you?"

"Only three. And let me tell you, they were more distressing than you can imagine. The whole time she would sit perched on the edge of her chair like she was about to bolt. I did challenge her—very, very delicately—about her view of herself, and every time she answered with a Bible quote. But the way she was always early for our meetings, Kate, I got the feeling there was something inside her trying to get out, that God wasn't nearly enough company for her. I was kind as I could be. I think she was glad for any sort of approval of her, caring about her." She was looking dolefully past Kate into the distance of her memories. "A tragedy, she was a tragedy in so many ways, and the worst one is, I got trapped by my goddamn rule book. I had to tell her that by school policy—by goddamn *policy*—I could only see her the three times before I had to notify her parents. And that was it, I never saw her again." She raised both hands. "Dory haunts you, April haunts me. How many times since have I regretted that I didn't throw the goddamn rule book out the window even if it did cost me my career."

Kate asked softly, "When was the last time?"

"A week before she died."

Marietta picked up her mug, drank coffee, and Kate picked up hers as well. She finally broke the silence to ask, "Did she talk about her parents?"

Marietta's round face seemed to darken with her scowl. "Her father was the disciplinarian. They never laid a finger on her, mind you—I asked, almost hoping they did so I could make a report to CPS and spring her out of that environment even briefly, show her something else was possible. Punishment consisted of sensory deprivation, locking her in her room which her father described as isolation to expiate her sins and pray for forgiveness."

"Jesus," Kate muttered.

A flicker of amusement crossed Marietta's face. "If he ever turns up, I'll be the first to tell him he has a lot to answer for."

"What about the mother?"

"The mother." Marietta frowned. "She's why I never questioned her conviction for the murder. What came out at trial. According to April, she was always trying to break up her relationship with Stella Hayden. I knew that was true."

"What did she tell you about that?" Kate asked eagerly. "What do you remember?"

Marietta said regretfully, "April didn't go into much detail. Only that her mother was always telling her that Stella monopolizing her was not a good thing and she should make other friends."

Eloquently confirmed in Stella's rage at Ellie Shuster. "Do you think April's mother was suspicious of the nature of the relationship?"

"She may have been, but I can't confirm that for you."

"Did you ever have any contact with Stella?"

"Only indirectly. I remember seeing her in the cafeteria with April and one other time. What a study in contrasts. April so feminine, Stella so much more on the androgynous side. Dark hair, dark eyes, angular face. She was taller, huskier. April was so passive, but Stella, she kind of, I don't know, *bristled* with a kind of belligerent energy."

"I got vibrations of that from her diary," Kate said with a faint smile. "She used as many exclamation marks as she did words."

"Sounds very teenage. The other time I saw her I happened to be in the gym. She was playing basketball and she hip-slammed some poor girl so hard she went flying into someone else and a whole bunch of them all went down in a howling heap. It was actually pretty funny, but the coach benched Stella and she was furious, looked at that coach like she was shooting lightning bolts."

She was smiling now, and Kate too smiled at the image. She reached into the shoulder bag she'd placed on the floor beside her, extracted the sheet of paper tucked into a side pocket. "Marietta," she said, "what led me to you is something Stella Hayden wrote about you in her diary."

"Me? I'm in *Stella's* diary?" She stared at Kate. "That diary was all over the news. Wasn't it key evidence at the trial?"

"It was. If you're wondering why you weren't contacted, the mention of you is so obscure in its context that I missed it and I've been through that diary at least a dozen times—"

She broke off with the thought: *But if I'd seen it at the time, so close to Dory's murder...* "Miss Hall" might well have caught her eye. Something else to add to her lengthy regret list.

She explained, "Your name looked to be included with her ridicule and hatred of a number of members of her church and a few teachers. The last police partner I had at Wilshire Division, he's a very good detective and a fresh pair of eyes. He saw the slight difference in context just yesterday, questioned who this 'Miss Hall' might actually be. Even went the extra step to check with the school." She added bitterly, "He saw it, I didn't. Add stupidity to my list of transgressions."

Eyes widened in consternation, Marietta placed her coffee mug carefully on the table beside her. Then fastened her gaze on the page in Kate's hand. "What on earth would Stella Hayden have to say about me in her diary?"

"Something that makes no sense to me."

Kate handed her the page. Marietta seized it, grabbed the spectacles from the side table and set them on her nose, read aloud the passage Kate had outlined: "*'Miss Hall, I hate hate hate you. You're every bit as bad, no, the garbage you put in her head is the worst, just as awful as all the preachy stuff from her bitch mother.'*"

Kate said, "Knowing you'd have been completely supportive of April's lesbian identity, this mystifies me."

"You're right—of course it's not about her lesbian identity. All I did was support her, defend whole aspects of herself she was trying to smother under church doctrine."

Kate said baldly, "Stella was in love with her. The diary was very much confessional, very passionate." She added as a surprising thought struck her: "Did April even know it?"

Marietta shook her head. "If she did, she didn't tell me. I remember Stella coming up in conversation only once, when I asked April about the friends she'd had in her life. That's when she told me that Stella was it, they'd been inseparable for as long as she could remember. That's when she mentioned her mother's disapproval."

"Any idea what would bring this outburst from Stella?"

"Sure. Possessiveness. Because I agreed with April's mother and told her so. I floated the idea that April should open herself to both girls and boys her own age in the church." She waved the diary page at Kate. "Stella knew I was threatening her exclusiveness with April. I figured if I couldn't get April to reassess her view of the world as a sinful place, other friendships could be nourishing even in the claustrophobic world she lived in. It was even possible," Marietta said with a melancholy smile, "that getting out from under the thumb of one single-sex friendship with a girl who was so aggressive, so overpowering, so overwhelming, might bring other options. It's possible April might even have been bisexual."

Kate gave an emphatic nod. "I'm with you on that. I have a trans nephew. Dylan's given me quite an education."

"I'm afraid that's about all I can remember." Marietta thrust the copy of the page from the diary back at Kate as if it were burning her. She looked at the wall clock. "Sorry to say they'll soon be coming to get me for the book club."

Kate tucked the page back into her shoulder bag. "One more thing," she said. "Since I'm now a retired detective, and I never was anywhere near being a good one where this case is concerned, from where you sit, might you have any theories as who might have killed April?"

"What an interesting question." She sat back in her chair. "Take our coffee mugs out to the kitchen for me, will you, and let me think a moment."

When Kate returned after rinsing the mugs in the tiny kitchen sink, Marietta said, "I'll tell you who I don't think it was: her father. Unless they had some sort of hideous relationship that never came out at the trial or my conversations with April, I don't believe Daniel Shuster would have killed his daughter and then sat back to let his wife take the blame."

"I don't think so either," Kate said.

"But it could have been either one of the Hayden parents. Especially if they got wind of their daughter's feelings about April. The father could have held April to blame and killed her, never dreaming his daughter would commit suicide over it. Then justified himself by blaming April's mother for raising her daughter in sin. It would be a good reason why he fled to Africa."

"Yes, I've thought of that scenario too."

Marietta shook her head. "Kate, honestly, it could have been any member of that nutbag church. April told me lots of them were in and out of the duplex all the time. What if one of them caught the girls fondling each other in the backyard or something like that, wanted to spare the church leader and the parents the embarrassment of such a thing, and killed April in the name of God?"

"Also possible. What about Stella killing April and taking her own life?"

"Possible too. There's no exaggerating the power of teenage passions and drama and how they can teeter on the edge of insanity. All I have to do is think about my own adolescence. Remember those poltergeist tales that were so popular when we were younger, Kate? They were actually parables about teenage hormones making youngsters capable of conjuring up supernatural creatures."

Smiling ruefully, Kate just shook her head and picked up her shoulder bag.

"Even if you found out who did it, Kate, how would you ever prove it after all this time?"

"At this point, I'd just like to know who it was."

"Will you let me know? Will you keep in touch?" She added hopefully, "Maybe come back for a visit?"

"Marietta, I would love to," Kate said with sincerity.

"And will you take very best care of yourself? If your former partner is involved in the case, I assume you're under police protection."

"I am. I'm doing my best."

"I'll hold you to that. Give my best to Calla, and how about you come visit me maybe next week?"

"It's a date," Kate said. "I'll call you."

A few minutes later, keys in hand, riding the elevator down to her car, Kate thought about the two women who had suddenly converged in her life. First Natalie Rostow and now Marietta Hall. And how much she was looking forward to seeing both of them again.

If I live.

For the first time in many months, maybe years, she thought that maybe she might actually want to.

14

Several hours later, having fed and taken Dakota out for a brief walk, Kate sat down at the breakfast bar with a mug of freshly made coffee and opened her computer. To the creamy voice of Rita Coolidge singing "Higher and Higher" emanating from the radio next door, she surveyed the day's usual dozen or so emails. Most if not all would be spam and she skimmed them, index finger rhythmic on the delete key. But the finger froze as one leaped out at her from a familiar address: *Grant@ PeeryandHromadko.com*. Aimee, using her work computer at the law firm where she had worked for years as a paralegal. Messages seldom came from either her work or private email, and those that did usually pertained to some query about the condo recently transferred to her ownership. The subject line read *Maggie*.

Kate, I got a call last night from Patton. She doesn't have your new cell number or email address. I didn't give them to her, just told her you'd changed them and would be contacting her. I don't like being in this position, so please do so with her and your other friends, Kate.

She called to ask if you and I and Rainey, Ash and Tora could all get together for a remembrance of Maggie and the Nightwood Bar next week on the anniversary of her death.

I'm happy to host it here at the condo of course. Or we could meet there if it's better for you. Since you're the one with her ashes, your choice whether you bring Maggie here or we come there or somewhere else if you prefer. I hope you're looking after yourself.

Aimee

"Goddammit." Sitting back on the barstool she glared at the bookcase and the shelf containing the urn. "Did you have an ashy hand in this, Maggie?" she snarled.

She could not bear to go to the condo. Nor did she want anyone close to her coming anywhere near this place. But she could not imagine taking Maggie anywhere else. *Hey*, she reminded herself, *next week you might be dead.*

Dead would certainly solve the problem. A lot of problems. For starters, Aimee, permanently lodged in her heart and her bloodstream. Alcohol. The always clawing want of alcohol. Her nightly dreams. This place and Maggie's ashes would then go to Aimee with the stipulation that her ashes and Maggie's be scattered together wherever, the four winds, for all she cared. So what was actually keeping her here? Why was she even waiting for Ellie Shuster?

In one word: Aimee. She'd done enough damage to Aimee without adding suicide to the list. She knew, far better than most, that suicides often left nuclear devastation in their wake. A problem solver for the deceased bequeathed haunting guilt and endless agonizing to shocked partners and family and friends over what action they might have taken to intervene, to prevent this most irrevocable, most final of acts.

She looked back at the message, the other names it contained: Patton, Ash, Tora, Rainey. Rainey's partner, Audie, a case in point, dead by overdose a decade ago; mourned yet unforgiven to this day by Rainey for truncating their lives together by first deciding that she would forego radiation and chemotherapy, then believing she would spare them both her protracted dying from late-stage breast cancer.

Again she looked at the message. *Your* friends, Aimee had written, not *our* friends. *The* condo. Not *my* condo or *our* condo. Just...*the* condo. Calla Dearborn might call this a sign of transition. A good thing, a good sign, she supposed. Then why did she feel such unease about this particular transition? Wasn't it exactly what she wanted?

Ash, Tora, Patton, Rainey. Still here, still in her life. All of them from the Nightwood Bar, that multicultural lesbian haven tucked away on a hillside behind a motel on La Brea but long since gone, its denizens having drifted away like feathers pulled away into the wind. Away from the dim, smoky, convivial twilight realm they had once shared, to live their lives more freely, openly, within redrawn lines of a more accepting world. Including, of course, Andrea.

Her mood turned melancholy as memory surfaced of the woman who, unlike Audie, had survived breast cancer. Andrea Ross, recovering from a double mastectomy when Kate met her at the Nightwood Bar. In retrospect, their briefest of brief but piercingly beautiful affair had been healing for them both. So much better that Andrea too had vanished into the winds of change before Kate had fallen down a bottomless well of love for her.

Dakota rose from her dog bed, shook herself, settled down again, and Kate smiled at her, glad again for her easy companionship. She surveyed the bookshelves where Maggie's ashes resided, bookshelves filled with volumes of a different kind of companionship: Maggie's lesbian novels and many she herself had chosen, her virtual community. Patton, Rainey, Ash, Tora—these four loyal friends were her very necessary tangible community. She focused again on Maggie's urn, wistful, reflecting that friendships seemed more essential now than ever. Unlike the unconditional love from a parent or the entirely conditional partnership of a lover, friends like Maggie were safety nets to catch and hold easy the foibles and mistakes of a lifetime, the sorrows. To regret that a mere four friends remained from the glory days of the Nightwood Bar was to say that only gold nuggets remained from a mining claim.

Only yesterday she had discovered that a community of women her own age had formed in companionship and mutual support in a patch of Desert Hot Springs. If she formed a friendship with Natalie Rostow—and she sensed that a friendship could be a reality if she pursued it—she would be on the periphery of another promising mining claim.

She sipped her coffee, wondering about this sliver of possibility amid all the jeopardy she faced, then put down the mug with a grimace. Caffeine—such a weak-kneed substitute for the sharp, rich bite and spreading comfort of Cutty Sark. She needed help again, support. Time to get another bracing appointment with Calla Dearborn. Get herself to another meeting. Call her sponsor.

Even if she were to succumb to her urges to put a bullet in her brain, she had a loose end, a very loose end, to tie up beforehand. Now that she had an angle, however oblique, toward resolving the April Shuster homicide and moving it out of the cold case files to a closed case. A final gift to her three-decade home at LAPD.

She picked up her cell phone, smiling as Olivia Newton John ooh-ooh-oohed into "You're the One That I Want."

"Captain Carolina Walcott...is not available," singsonged the mechanical voice. Nor had Kate expected her to be. She left a message identifying herself and the case her call pertained to. Not five minutes later Walcott returned her call.

"Always good to hear from you, Kate," she said hurriedly, and Kate heard the echoing sound of voices as if she were striding along a crowded hallway. "I'm on my way back from a press briefing at the PAB, then I've got a conference call. There'll be time to talk once I'm back in my office."

"Of course, Captain. At your convenience. Thank you."

Walcott's agenda, her mandated presence at the Police Administration Building, reminded Kate of why she had never wanted to advance beyond a D-3. Politics, crisis management, bureaucratic bullshit, she'd never had any ambition or stomach for any of it. The higher you climbed the more exposed you became, and she'd spent much of her public life wanting less visibility than she inevitably suffered when cases of hers attracted the media. Maggie had called her on it as she called her on everything, saying that her craving for privacy was nothing less than a rationalization of the closet. If so, then so be it. Past history.

Walcott, she thought, shaking her head in wonderment. No one navigated the rancid politics and internecine warfare of LAPD's hierarchy with more savvy and skill than Captain Carolina Walcott, or wore the LAPD uniform with more authority. Assertive posture that rose from muscular hips and thighs into ramrod shoulders, a jutting jaw and tight lips and an aquiline nose that suggested descendancy from the mating of an owl with a hawk. Dark, penetrating eyes in a coffee brown face that warned you to be plain and straight with her because she would see clear through your bullshit. For the final captain in her police career, she could not have had a more admirable commanding officer than Carolina Walcott.

Kate got up from the breakfast bar, tucked her gun into the belt of her jeans and pocketed her cell phone and notepad, grabbed her coffee. Alerted, Dakota rose and trotted over to her. Kate guided her onto the back deck, holding her collar as she made herself comfortable in an Adirondack chair. Surveying the vista of desert scrub and Joshua trees out of habitual caution, she let herself simply absorb the ambiance of another pleasantly warm breezy day in the desert, inhaling the chalky smell of sand and the aromas of plant life rising in the heat of the sun, savoring the solitude and tranquility where she had sight lines only to far distant neighbors. Pilar's radio reached her just faintly; it projected out the front of her house. Back here the quiet was mostly broken by the crackling of brittle stems of desert brush in washes of wind.

She released Dakota's collar, patted her head. "Can I trust you not to run off?"

The dog gazed at Kate with her assessing, spectral blue eyes, shook herself, trotted from the deck down into the sand, chose a patch to squat and relieve herself, returned to lie down at Kate's feet.

Her phone vibrated in her pocket. Too early for Walcott. Maybe Cameron?

The caller ID read Silverlake Haven. She braced herself as she answered.

"It's Marla, Kate. Loretta passed about an hour ago. Very peacefully."

She felt only relief. But she asked intently, "Was her son—"

"Larry got here. We called him when her vitals declined. She was gone not fifteen minutes later."

Neither of them commented further. It was all too common at Silverlake Haven, death occurring immediately after a loved one's arrival as if the dying person were willing the presence of love to be in the room as the final impetus toward release from life.

"Thank you for telling me, Marla."

"Another reason I called—Monique. She's in a coma, I don't believe she'll last the night. She asked us to give you a message. Just two words: thank you. Said more fervently than you can imagine. What did you do for her?"

Kate could hear the approval in her voice. "Just the usual, Marla," she said easily. "Heard her confession."

"Well, it helped. She seemed much at peace with herself when you left. Will you be in again soon? We have someone else asking for you. A guy, a vet from the Vietnam era."

"A vet? Why isn't he at the VA?"

"I wondered too. But his family want him here and are paying out of pocket for it."

Kate shook her head. Silverlake Haven was a good facility, but they would be paying out of pocket through the nose. Without insurance or Medicare coverage, the Ritz Carlton would hardly be more expensive. This dying vet, though...she could be of value to him, offer something of herself, having shared one of the most transformative times in either of their lives. "Tell him I'll be there in the next day or so," she said. She hoped. "Thanks for the call, Marla."

Placing the phone on the table beside her, having decided to jot the major points of her agenda with Captain Walcott, she picked up her notebook. APRIL, she wrote in caps as a heading. APRIL. She looked at the word. *APRIL.* Stared. New pieces began falling into place. With Dakota snuffling in sleep beside her, she sat back and thought. Made more notes in point format alongside her agenda with Walcott.

Two hours later, with the music from next door silenced, Pilar having made a noisy departure in her ancient Camry, Kate moved back into the house with Dakota.

She was sitting in the living room armchair with a fresh mug of coffee, deep in thought, gazing sightlessly toward the distant San Bernardino Mountains, when Walcott finally called.

Kate's mood turned mellow, reminiscent as she picked up the phone. She could so easily picture the captain in her office, seated behind a desk smothered in files and reports, heavy glass cat paperweights compressing and identifying each stack, each of the cats a different color and in a different pose. Her personal favorite had been the snarling black marble feline that sat atop the largest pile, the one Walcott termed garbage-in. Behind the captain on a credenza would be a half dozen gold-framed photos of her husband and two sons, these flanked on either side by handsome teak woodcuts of Toni Morrison and Martin Luther King.

"Sorry, Kate," she said. "You know how it is."

"I do, Captain. I appreciate you finding the time to call me back."

"I just wish it were about anything but the April Shuster case," she said crisply. "I've got twenty minutes or so before the next storm blows in. First off, how are you doing? Keeping safe?"

"I'm okay. About Shuster, if you're wondering why I've gone so far up the chain of command about a reopened case with detectives assigned, it's the circumstances. Ellie Shuster is literally on my doorstep, she put her last note directly in my mailbox. I have to figure it's her final one."

"Dear God. Look, Kate. We can put you in protective—"

"Thanks, and I'll think about it," she interrupted, to circumvent wasting time on a discussion she did not want. "I do have new information and what I think is a solid theory. I need your help to check it out, see how solid it really is."

"I'm listening."

"I fully understand why Joe Cameron is in your bad books, but he's just taken a look at the murder book—"

"He's not been on my shit list for some time, Kate. I'm more and more thinking Joe's the most sensible guy I know for taking himself out of this cesspool. You were here for the best of it."

"Right," she said, smothering a laugh. "It was a picnic."

"Riiiight," Walcott repeated, and Kate could hear the smile come into her voice in the drawn-out syllable. "Talk about words bypassing my brain—all you had were the Watts riots, Rodney King, O.J. Simpson, the Ramparts mess—just one clusterfuck after another."

Walcott had not mentioned—nor did she need to or perhaps want to—the comet that had struck Wilshire Division, the drive by shooting of the Notorious B.I.G. and the associated murder of Tupac Shakur, a disaster that had miraculously missed the two of them while smashing other careers and reputations, and that would forever swirl amid the infamous legends of LAPD. But all the breakdowns Kate had witnessed were, by her lights, inevitable. Any objective observer could simply compare the nation's two largest cities and draw the logical conclusion from NYPD's seventy-seven precincts to LAPD's twenty-one divisions; NYPD's thirty-five thousand sworn officers to LAPD's nine thousand. LAPD had never been anything but the thinnest of thin blue lines, creating never-ending crisis management for a beleaguered chain of command responsible for the policing of a city sprawled over one of the world's largest metropolitan areas.

"Just so you know," Walcott continued, "my last briefing with the case detectives on Shuster was a couple of months ago. Let me tell you what I know first, Kate. Carlson and Wiggins have their spotlight on Stella Hayden's father, what's his name—"

"Mathew."

"Right. Their theory is Mathew found Stella's diary. Went

ballistic over how a lesbian daughter would go down with his followers and April *has* to be to blame for corrupting any daughter of his. So in a frenzy he grabs the cross from her parents' bedroom and smashes the devil out of her. Maybe he shows his daughter what he's done, maybe she finds April herself. Either way, with or without his knowledge, she kills herself."

"All very plausible, yes," Kate said and chose not to say that it did not explain the missing bloody clothing.

"A few more items to finish the current theory. Stella's diary incriminates April's mother, she's arrested. April's father believes she did it, the cross he found in her jewelry box is even more evidence, and Mathew Hayden is just fine with all of it because if the mother been a better disciple of God then April wouldn't have been possessed by the devil and corrupted his daughter. After the trial, with all the bad press over the girls' deaths his church is kaput in this country, so off they go to Uganda to get a fresh start for the cult. Just so you know, we've tried tracking the three of them since the acquittal, but it's been twenty years and they may have changed their names, and besides that, no one in Africa gives a damn about our little murder. If Mathew ever brought himself back here, we could test for a match to the other DNA we found on April's body. Without that, all we have is a maybe plausible theory."

Kate took her cue about the case detectives' due diligence. "After thirty years on the job," she told Walcott, "I know a dead end when I see one."

"So what have you got? This case is such a bastard, I'd be glad to entertain anything."

"What I have is all due to Joe. He looked at the murder book with those fresh eyes of his, saw a crucial detail everybody missed." Carefully, consulting her notes, she described the anomalous nature of the "Miss Hall" he had picked out in Stella Hayden's diary and the revelation of her as the school therapist.

"Bloody hell!" Walcott exploded. "She's a *therapist*? Fucking *hell!*"

Kate held the phone away from her ear as more expletives

ensued. Walcott, a former homicide detective, knew as well as she did what a key source of information had been missed.

"Kate, is this a tip you're offering or have you had contact?"

"Contact. I know Marietta Hall from a case previous to Shuster. She was a key interview then too."

"She gave you information? Without a subpoena?"

"I was persuasive," Kate said lightly, hoping Walcott would let her move on from the topic.

"You must have been. Any therapist I ever interviewed, it was like trying to extract the secrets of the confessional out of a priest. So what are you telling me?" Walcott's voice had lowered with intensity.

"Some framework first." Again she consulted her notes. "A teacher, I'll get her name if we need it—" She had all but kicked herself when she realized she hadn't followed up with Marietta for this detail. "—this teacher reported to Marietta about April appearing isolated and visibly troubled. So Marietta approached her with a story about various students talking to her about their lives and would April like to have a conversation. The fact that she came to Marietta speaks for itself, how desperate she must have felt. They had three separate sessions and then she fled when Marietta told her she was mandated by school policy to advise the parents if they continued. A week later she was dead."

Kate picked up her fresh mug of coffee and in the pause Walcott asked, "Did she say who she was afraid of?"

"She was afraid of everybody, Captain. She was in a vise, caught between two forces, a homophobic religion she fervently believed in and a female best friend—her only friend—in love with her."

"Was she…Had she acted on…"

"Was she lesbian? It's not clear in the diary what April might have felt or did—Stella was way too hung up on just her own teenage emotions. From what April told Marietta, I'm guessing she had to be on that pathway or she wouldn't have been so conflicted. So we have a fifteen-year-old girl convinced she's already condemned herself to hell for a physical relationship with Stella Hayden—or that she will be if she acts on what she really wants."

"Well, Stella didn't help matters any," Walcott muttered. "That diary…God, talk about obsession…Did your therapist suggest anything about this Stella maybe being bipolar?"

Kate was shaking her head as she said, "No way would she know. With only three sessions with April, she didn't see any of the evidence we saw. And Stella had her own demons, Captain, given the father she had. She—"

Walcott interrupted impatiently, "I assume the therapist told her there was nothing wrong or unnatural about a lesbian orientation?"

"Of course. Emphatically. Even back in those days. But she couldn't make a dent in fifteen years of daily immersion in homophobic rants." Kate consulted her notes for the phrases she'd written down. "Why I'm calling is the other advice Marietta gave April. I believe it's absolutely key to all this. She agreed with April's mother, who strongly advised April to bring other friends into her life, male friends as well as female."

Walcott asked cautiously, "What exactly are you telling me here, Kate?"

"April was killed only a week later. The most likely scenario is she took that week to think about this advice and maybe her mother even reinforced it. Then she told Stella she wanted to step away from their relationship in favor of other friends, possibly including a closer walk with God. I would imagine them having a violent argument. That Stella didn't, couldn't win. You've seen the crime scene photos—"

"Yes. As savage a killing as I've ever seen," Walcott said, and Kate could imagine the grimace on her face from the tone of voice.

"Rage, from losing her grip on what made her life worth living. It explains why she went into the Shusters' bedroom for that crucifix—she wanted *their* crucifix—and she confronted April. Ripped off the crucifix she had around her neck, then smashed April to death with the bronze cross. Rinsed it and slapped it back on the wall, and more in stone-cold vengeance than in any attempt to frame her, put April's necklace in her mother's jewelry box. Went back to her side of the duplex and into her own bedroom, didn't bother to change clothes, maybe she even wanted April's blood on her. Which would explain why we never could find any bloody clothes. She slashed herself in so many places that any wounds in her hands from hitting April with the crucifix looked like part of the suicide." Kate concluded, "That's what I have, Captain."

Walcott was silent for some moments. Then said slowly, "It fits, Kate. It does. Assuming all this is true, we have a new primary suspect who's dead and now we have an even worse problem of proof. Stella was so obvious a suicide the ME had no reason to retain anything for testing. We have no way of matching Stella's DNA to the foreign DNA we found on April."

"But we do." Kate realized her voice had risen, told herself to cool her excitement. "That's the main reason I'm calling you, Captain, for your direct intervention in this. Stella's DNA is right there with the April Shuster case evidence. From the day of the murder everyone working on the case had only photocopies of Stella's diary because it was key evidence—it's been preserved in its paper packaging except for when it was produced as an exhibit in court to prove its existence. It was too much to include in the murder book, so I used my phone to make copies from it when I was in the evidence room. Only April's bloody clothing and test samples from the crime scene were ever tested. Same thing for the Innocence Project, that's what they tested too— and we only verified their tests. But Stella's diary was under her pillow where she died and has a cover soaked in Stella's blood."

Walcott hissed a breath. "Kate, I'll move heaven and earth to get that test done. If you're right about this, you'll be the first to know and the news networks and Corey Lanier will be next."

Corey Lanier. Kate rolled her eyes. How fitting. The persistent-as-a-mosquito veteran *LA Times* police beat reporter, her *bête noir* in cases past. She'd never broken Kate down for comment on any of her cases, but never for lack of trying. She would probably relish tracking her down for one last bite.

"God I hope you're right. It all fits, and I'm betting you are." Walcott continued, "There'll be immediate news bulletins on a case this notorious. April's mother will know who killed her daughter as soon as we can get the news out there."

"Thank you, Captain." While it would answer the question of who had murdered April Shuster, she doubted it would make much difference to Ellie Shuster about culpability for her incarceration.

"Please thank Joe for me, tell him he's welcome if he would ever want to visit. Never mind, I'll call him myself when I get some time. One more thing, Kate. Don't blame yourself for anything. In this murder, that therapist is a needle—not in a haystack but in a goddamn wheatfield. This is no one's fault. It took the case cooling off for years for someone to see something so miniscule."

Walcott clicked off.

Kate dropped her phone on the counter and her head into her hands. *I would have seen it.*

She raised her head to look at her Marietta Hall notes. She would be visiting the woman again soon, and if she was right about the DNA on April's body belonging to Stella Hayden, then at all costs she needed to figure out a way to prevent Marietta from climbing into the same pit she occupied. Forever racked by the image of two simple dots that if joined together would have led to the proper blood tests and saved Ellie Shuster nineteen years of anguish, imprisoned with her seething rage.

She picked up her phone, texted Cameron: *Call when you can for news.*

God, she wanted a drink. "Dakota," she called, "let's go for a walk."

But Cameron called back instantly. "I'm in transit—"

"Where to?"

"The station. So I've got maybe ten minutes. What news? Are you okay?"

"I'm okay." She brought him up-to-date with a condensed version of her two conversations, Marietta Hall and Captain Walcott, concluding with, "You'll be glad to know you're back in Walcott's good books. You'll be hearing from her."

"Let's see…" he muttered vaguely, distractedly, as if he hadn't heard this last statement of hers. "She'll for sure get that diary hand-delivered to serology. They'll need what, at least an hour for extraction…The test for quantity, the same…PCR, that's the one that takes the time…electrophoresis…analysis, the final report. What the hell time is it now, Kate?"

"Just after four." She could only surmise that he did not want even a glance at the clock in his car to interrupt his thought process.

"With Walcott throwing all her weight behind this—and you just know she'll be claiming the life of one of our own is hanging on it—it'll go straight to the head of the line. I figure tomorrow afternoon, Kate."

"Good to know, Joe." She'd already factored all this in and come to a similar estimate. She might be four years gone from LAPD, he might be far more up to date on the current science, but the major variable when it came to lab tests had never changed in every major city: backlog.

"Smartest thing you ever did was call her. But wow, Kate. If there's a DNA match, the case detectives will want your head on a post when they hear."

"After they've boiled me in oil," she agreed. But saving them embarrassment over a break in the case that did not circle them in was not worth the stakes. They would have done their own due diligence, reviewed the diary, reinterviewed Marietta Hall, followed procedure. In their place she would do the same. Afterward, they might not have taken their confirmation any higher than lieutenant, which meant the comparison test sitting in line at the serology unit for days, weeks—even months, for all she knew. She'd had no real choice; she'd absolutely had to involve Walcott.

"How's Dakota doing?" he asked in a jarring change of subject.

"She's good," she said warmly, welcoming the topic. "Can't ask for a better friend. She looks out for me, asks for what she needs but doesn't try to tell me what to do."

He chuckled. "I won't take that personally." He asked, casually, as if it were the idlest of queries, "Would you be keeping her if you could, if, say, her owner was okay with it?"

"I would, actually." She didn't have to think about it. "I already consider her a friend."

"She's yours."

Having suspected this from the moment Dakota had greeted her at the door of her house, she still felt a leap of joy. She asked, perfunctorily, "What about the owner?"

"He can be persuaded."

She held no doubt that he had chosen the dog especially for her from a rescue organization and had rolled the dice from there, trusting that his fabrication about her caring for Dakota for a few weeks would be enough to develop a strong bond. It had taken only a day. "Thank you, Joe. I can't tell you how much I appreciate this. All of it."

"Everything you've done for me, we're nowhere close to even, Kate. How about I come over tonight?"

"Dakota's still not enough protection?" she joked.

"I figure there's one more day till Ellie Shuster finds out who really did this. I'm thinking maybe it'll shift things, change the equation."

It wouldn't. She'd had months and months to think through the probabilities. Why would it? Even so it would be good to have him here while she strategized her next moves, given this development and what she'd further deduced. "I'd be glad to have you, Joe. We'll give Dakota a good long walk."

"Great. I'll bring some Pollo Loco." He clicked off.

15

It was bound to happen. Of course she would be asked to visit someone in the same room and occupying the same bed in which Maggie had died. It was to be expected in a place as small as Silverlake Haven, and in fact it had already happened to her several times before. But Walt Masterson in that bed—someone, like Maggie, entwined with the significant history of her life—it was upsetting, disorienting.

Acute leukemia, Marla had told her. Agent Orange, she'd immediately surmised: the stealth assassin implanted in the bodies of many who had served in Vietnam, the defoliant war crime inflicted on the country's citizens. Standing quietly in the doorway, a hand on the doorframe as if for support, she took her time inspecting him.

His head, devoid of hair undoubtedly from chemotherapy, was turned away. Either he was asleep or his gaze was fixed on the trees and bougainvillea blossoms beyond his window. The shoulders were bony in his blue short-sleeved pajama top; the arms resting on the blanket were wiry and prominently veined.

From what she could see of his face, it appeared compressed to the fundamentals of bleached skin over bone. But, even with his life now reduced to a matter of days in this place for the dying, he still gave off an aura of toughness. To her he looked the very essence of a Vietnam vet.

"Walt, company!"

His attention summoned by a woman in the bed nearest the door calling to him, he jerked his head toward her and she was staring into pale blue eyes that pierced her.

"Staff Sergeant Walter F. Masterson," he said and raised a hand stiffly to his forehead in formal salute. "Second battalion, fourth marines, Chu Lai, nineteen sixty-five." The voice was reedy, with a slight Southern twang.

She returned the salute. "Captain Kate Delafield, second battalion, first marines, Da Nang supply corps, sixty-eight and sixty-nine."

With a nod to the emaciated woman in the adjacent bed who was peering at her with watery, puzzled eyes, she strode into the room and pulled up a chair to Walter Masterson's bed. He had continued to hold his salute and she told him with a grin, "At ease, Sergeant." Seated, she extended a hand. "How did you know who I was?"

He took her hand, trying and failing to firm up his grip. "Marla described you. Anyway, no offense, you look like you could be a vet."

"No offense taken. I think," she added, continuing to grin, liking him on sight.

"You're here sooner than Marla said."

Holding onto his hand, she replied lightly, "I was that eager to meet you."

Which was somewhere in the vicinity of the truth. As soon as Cameron's Rav4 had disappeared down the road this morning she'd made haste to leave. Had topped up Dakota's food and water, the dog gazing at her with eyes so mournfully aware of what this portended that Kate had knelt down to her and stroked her ears and head in consolation. "I'll be back just as soon as I can," she promised. "Soon as I get the DNA results."

At this moment LA was the easiest and safest place she knew to be. She'd located an AA meeting in Hollywood and had already attended the hour-long gathering. This visit to Silverlake Haven, combined with the trip in and back, would take her well into the afternoon and give her a productive passing of time when she would not have to be on guard this day when Ellie Shuster might finally learn the truth of her daughter's death.

"How come you're here and not at the VA?" she asked him, releasing his hand but resting hers close to his.

He tried to lift his head from the pillow only to have it fall back, and she saw how weak he was. He began to speak, shook his head as if dismissing those words, began again. "It's complicated. I'll be interred with my comrades in arms but... let's just say that I've spent considerable time in VA hospitals these recent years and I felt...well, conflicted about where I wanted my final surroundings to be."

From his diction, the acute perceptiveness in his eyes, she gathered that this very ill man was deeply intelligent. "I think I might have some understanding about that," she told him. It had never occurred to her to care about exactly *where* she might want to be when she died. But forty-three years after the war in which she had served, what kind of allegiance did she now feel to anything associated with it? For whatever reason, he had asked to see her, and she said, casually, searching for ground on which to meet him, "So what's your best memory of being in country?"

"Best memory...Well, let me see," he said, gazing off somewhere beyond her, stroking his chin with two skeletal fingers as if a goatee had once been there. "The heat. No, maybe that teeming thundering rain. Nope, the bugs biting me right where I couldn't get at them under all my gear. No...maybe it's everybody in my company strung out on any junk we could find to get through our days in country." He shook his head and looked directly at her. "No, it has to be the sounds. Of destruction. Artillery. Bombs. Helicopters. Villagers screaming and running for their lives from us. Captain Delafield, *you* tell *me* why the hell we were ever there."

Hammered by his words and all they evoked, she groped for a response while she caught her breath. She temporized with, "First of all, my name is Kate."

He nodded. "And I'm Walt. So, what's your own best memory?"

No way could she match his irony, so she offered, "Mine's afterward, a reunion of us twenty years ago, in DC. Seeing where we were in our lives, what our time there did to us all…" She stopped, caught in melancholy over the images.

"I'm betting it was nothing good," he suggested, eyes narrowed in contemplation of her.

"Nothing good," she confirmed, trying to retrieve herself from a plummet into the past. But she was back there at the Inn on Liberty Square, wrenched with grief over the death of the gay marine who had come to be like a brother to her, bearing witness to the lasting trauma to Rachel and Bernie, the two nurses who remained in the heart of her memory every day since that adrenaline-fueled year in Da Nang. "Then going to the Wall," she breathed. "We gave everything we had, Walt, and when I saw all those names…" Her voice caught. "All those young boys, those *kids*, dead for absolutely *nothing*."

"Not quite nothing, Kate." He covered the hand that lay next to his. "We were called by our country and we served. What we did, bottom line, was give the world some truth. You know we were the first TV war. And the political narrative we were all told to swallow—that we were heroes and saviors— every night on TV it was exposed as bullshit. It tore the country apart, Kate. People saw with their own eyes how our leaders were lying sacks of shit."

Nodding, Kate quoted, "'Better to die for something than live for nothing'—remember that catch phrase from the sixties? So what's changed? It never ends. Never will as long as you guys run things. It's you men who make war."

"Can't argue with that. Well…at least our war ended the draft," he contended, and the liveliness in his eyes told her he was reveling in the exchange. "Today it's rockets, surgical strikes, terrorism. Dozens, maybe hundreds die. Isn't that better than the thousands and millions dying from bombs and combat?"

"Yes, but those weapons—" Kate's phone dinged in her pocket. "Sorry," she muttered. "I have to see what this is."

A text from Walcott.

Your thesis proves correct. Diary's DNA a match with Stella Hayden's blood on April Shuster. Press conference to announce at 5:00pm. Do you want to be there?

She quickly typed *Hell no.*

The answering ding was immediate. *Pro forma question.*

Again she typed. *Thanks for everything you've done for me, Captain.*

Kate, you are the very best. Wish you were still here. Will be in touch.

"Something's come up," she told Walt Masterson, pocketing her phone.

He was watching her. "I can see that. You have to go."

"I'm so sorry, Walt, but I do. I can't guarantee it, but I'll try to be here tomorrow to continue." Rising from her chair, she added with a smile, "Promise me you'll live that long."

He nodded, grinning. "I will if you will."

It wasn't a promise she could give, and she said, smiling wryly: "I'll do my best. Do you know I'm a retired cop?"

"Yeah, and I don't hold it against you," he joked.

She pointed to the TV mounted on the wall equidistant between the two bedsides. "Turn that on at five o'clock and you'll understand why I have to leave now."

Sitting in her Jeep under the trees outside Silverlake Haven, engine running, Kate texted Cameron: *News. Call when you can.*

Her phone rang in her hand. Glancing at the ID, she clicked on the call. "Natalie, I'm glad to hear from you," Kate said, and she was. Her trip home could wait.

"I didn't want you to think I'm one of those people—that I was blowing smoke when I asked if you'd come back and visit."

"You hardly seemed the type," Kate said honestly.

"Good to know," she said, and Kate could hear the smile in her voice. "I'd love you to join our group in the clubhouse here next Sunday, all of us lesbians who've retired here. Take a look at the new furniture that's being delivered tomorrow."

"Sure. I imagine you're quite the hero around there these days."

Natalie's laughter warmed her. "I am, Kate. And I'm loving it. Question is, how am I going to explain you to these pals of mine?"

"A lonely soul you met at the grocery store?" Kate suggested. The image of Maggie in her hospice bed at Silverlake Haven floated into her head. "Or maybe at your bereavement group. I'm thinking maybe that might be a good idea for me too."

"I recommend it. We could go together. See you here next Sunday then, Kate, around two o'clock." She clicked off.

Kate was wending her way through the downtown interchange, still smiling at the exchange with Natalie Rostow, when Cameron called back. From the scene of a vehicular fatality, he told her, awaiting arrival of the medical examiner.

"Teenage male is all we can tell from what's left of him in the rollover. Talk about gunning it, you should see the rubber where he lost control. Solo driver, at least he didn't take anyone with him. Kate, will I ever get used to people who just piss their lives away?"

"Probably not," she assured him dourly.

"So what's your news? Test results?"

"Yep." Making her way through traffic, she filled him in on the report she'd received from Walcott, the test results that matched Stella Hayden's DNA to the blood samples from April Shuster's body.

He heaved an audible sigh, and she visualized him slumped in his police vehicle, gathering his emotions as well as his thoughts as he gazed at the wreckage of human and machine awaiting various investigative and cleanup crews.

"So twenty years later," he finally said, "the answer to April Shuster turns out to be raging teenage hormones."

Not remotely that simple, she thought, but chose not to pursue further discussion for now. "At least we know. And everyone has you to thank, Joe. If it weren't for your—"

"We did it together," he interrupted, clearly irritated. "Like always. You did the spade work. You're the one who took the two and two and put it together."

This she decided to argue. "*You're* the one who made all the difference, those fresh eyes of yours on the case. I looked at that diary of Stella Hayden's I don't know how many times and never saw what you saw, never would have." The fact that she surely would have twenty years ago would not have escaped Cameron, but he'd either dismissed bringing it up it as counterproductive or had tactfully elected to avoid mentioning it. She reiterated, "This day could never have happened without you."

"Okay, whatever. Just call me Joe Poirot," he joked. "Now the key question is how much difference it makes to April's mother."

She clutched the steering wheel, knuckles white, staring out into the sea of traffic, shaking her head in dismay, exasperation. *April's mother.* The two words had been an electrical jolt of realization. Why had she not placed Ellie Shuster in this exact context before? With all its weight and fraught emotion? Easy answer: she'd been too focused on only the facts of the murder, only the avenues toward hard evidence. Too focused on the scenario to factor in the endless agonies a mother would suffer over a savagely butchered child.

"It figures to be hours here," Cameron said into her self-flagellating silence, "but soon as the body's gone I can come over."

She loosened her grip on the wheel, gathered herself, and said with genuine regret, "I'll be in town." Regret that she couldn't be with him when he was so deserving of her praiseful presence. Regret that she'd had to lie about her plans for tonight. It was imperative she be home and that she be alone. Before he could ask, she added another untruth: "Pilar's looking after Dakota."

"I'm guessing you'll be at the press conference?" His tone conveyed skepticism over the very idea.

"You know me better than that. Walcott and the case detectives can do the victory dance. Regardless of anything we contributed, for them it's a win. It's closure of a really bad, really ugly black eye of a case. Right now I want to be safely out of sight till all this goes down. I figure staying here in town a day or two, maybe seeing some old friends from the Nightwood Bar—"

"Maybe Aimee?"

A wave of fury inundating her, she snapped, "Why do you always go there?"

It was his turn for silence until she finally offered, "You and me, we'll get together soon and…" She could not bring herself to utter the word *celebrate*.

"We'll put a cork in it," Cameron finished for her. "Ellie Shuster might give it up, go away now. Let you be."

"Maybe she will." Another untruth. She could not fathom the reasoning behind his suggestion of this outcome. What difference would identifying April's killer possibly make to Ellie Shuster beyond inflicting more agony, more rage? The bottom line remained the same: they'd got it wrong. Disastrously wrong. Bottom line, they'd not only taken away nearly two decades of Ellie Shuster's life, they'd made those decades a living hell of being branded a child killer.

"Call me when you can," Cameron said. "And, Kate, at least now we know. Case closed. So it's a good day." He rang off.

16

Staring at Kate through the screen door of her house, Pilar Adams repeated Kate's request: "You're asking me to come over...to watch a news conference with you. What's it about?"

Kate, standing on Pilar's front stoop, her loose shirt flapping in a warm, vagrant breeze, nodded confirmation. "A case of mine when I was a police detective." She gestured to her own house. "The why of all that surveillance gear. It's on in about five minutes."

Peering at her in wonderment through her thick-framed glasses, Pilar shrugged, opened her screen door and followed Kate across the gravel driveway between their two houses.

Pilar glanced around Kate's living room, hands on the waistband of her cargo shorts, looking uncharacteristically awkward, uncertain. "Where's Dakota?"

"I left her snoozing on the back porch." She added, "She's safe—I've never seen any coyotes around here." Not wanting Dakota indoors as a distraction, she'd moved the dog's bed outside and attached the lead to her collar to one of the porch posts. She'd also turned off her cell phone.

Kate had already placed a bowl of chips on the coffee table. She gestured to one of the two armchairs she'd positioned before the wall-mounted TV which was already tuned to channel five, the sound muted. She headed toward the kitchen. "I've got iced tea in the fridge."

Continuing to glance narrow-eyed around the living room, Pilar yanked up the sleeves of her blue pullover as if preparing herself for whatever strangeness might occur and dropped herself into the chair where Kate had directed, simultaneously picking up a potato chip. "You're being very mysterious," she said with as much petulance as curiosity.

Kate waved a hand at the TV screen. "Well, like they say, a picture is worth a thousand words."

"Especially coming from a woman of very few words."

Kate ignored the jibe, employing the rattle of ice from the icemaker tumbling into two glasses to fill the silence. She'd judged from the news broadcasts during her drive back from LA that the press conference would be given prominence on local newscasts. The day had not been especially newsworthy beyond the usual city politics and squabbles, the continuing national events and international controversy over Russian involvement in Ukraine and Crimea.

She returned to the living room, halting to look around acutely as if seeing it for the first time. Or the last time. *Mine*, she thought in a sudden surge of affection for her home, the living room bathed in citrus tones in late afternoon desert sunlight. *All me, all mine.* She placed the iced teas on the coffee table. Sat down adjacent to Pilar just as the clock ticked over to five o'clock.

KTLA CHANNEL 5 BREAKING NEWS flashed onto the TV screen. Adrenaline surging, she unmuted the sound to a disembodied voice:

"Coming to you live from the Police Administration Building in downtown Los Angeles, we have reporters on the scene for breaking news. We bring you the latest developments in a sensational two decades-old murder case that continues to shock this city...Here is Wilshire Division police Captain Carolina Walcott right now, she is just about to join Chief Beck..."

Kate watched Carolina Walcott, in her dark blue captain's uniform and hat with the gold braiding, notes in hand, march purposefully to a podium emblazoned with the seal of the LAPD: three symbolic figures standing between the scales of justice positioned in front of an American flag. Kate sat as quietly as she could, hands braced on the arms of her chair, her gaze shifting between the television screen across from her and sidelong at the woman seated next to her. Who sat frozen with her potato chip halfway to her mouth as Walcott placed her notes on the podium and her sonorous tones filled the room.

"Thanks to the hard work and diligence of current case Detectives Daniela Carlson and Cleveland Wiggins, in collaboration with retired Detective Kate Delafield, one of the original case detectives, as well as her partner of more recent years, Detective Joe Cameron, we have resolved our reopened investigation into the 1994 homicide of fifteen-year-old April Shuster. We are now able to announce that we have established a match to key DNA related to the case. Blood samples found on murder victim April Shuster, unrelated to her, have now conclusively identified her killer. That killer, we can now state with certainty, is next-door neighbor and best friend to the victim, sixteen-year-old Stella Hayden, who committed suicide within minutes of the homicide..."

Pilar had lowered the potato chip but continued to sit frozen as Walcott concluded her statement. Kate, every sense alert, only vaguely heard Chief Beck, who had taken the podium. "Our system of justice did its best with what we knew in 1994. But we got it wrong. Only now, thanks to advances in technology along with the determination on the part of dedicated Wilshire Division detectives to seek the truth, have we—"

"*Ellie Shuster!*" The name was flung in a shout from the cluster of TV and print reporters. "*What about April's mother?*"

Chief Beck raised a hand, broke off his statement to nod at Walcott, who was already stepping up toward the podium, dark eyes flashing. Her hands seizing the edges of the podium, sternness accenting her hawk-like features, she leaned close to the cluster of microphones. "From the time of her acquittal,

Eleanor Shuster has chosen to live in privacy and seclusion. As is her absolute right. We fully respect that right, we ask that others do so as well. She deserves to live out her life as she deems best under these tragic circumstances. Our hope is that she will see or hear about this news conference and finally know the truth about the murder of her daughter. Of course, should she ever wish to come forward we would welcome her into a full discussion of this development."

To the din of *"Why did it take so long?" "How come you couldn't figure this out twenty years ago?"* and more shouted questions, Kate picked up the remote control and clicked off the TV.

Pilar Adams had not moved. Kate also sat quietly, for several long minutes, during which she was aware of little more than the heightened beat of her pulse and the slow passage of time. When Pilar finally did move, to place her potato chip back in the bowl, Kate rose from her armchair, turned it so that it faced Pilar, then reached carefully behind her and removed from the small of her back her .38 Smith & Wesson service revolver. Placed the gun on the table beside Pilar.

Pilar had watched her during this entire process, and now stared at the gun as if the weapon, lying on the table with its handle angled toward her, were a cobra.

Kate resumed her seat, feeling every hair on her body standing on end. She said quietly to the staring woman: "I know."

Color had drained from Pilar's face from the start of the press conference. Still focused on the gun, she did not look up. She uttered softly, tonelessly, "Tell me what you think you know."

"I think it's too easy these days for police or anyone in this country to run a background check, so that's why you claim Canada as your place of origin. But I heard a Canadian speak in one of my AA meetings—and realized you have no trace of anything Canadian in how you speak, not even so much as an inflection. You sound more like American Midwest. We were talking a few days ago about how to give away Geneva Fallon's money and you told me your mother used to send entries into Publishers Clearing House. But that company doesn't do business in Canada. It never existed there. Your name, you claim to be from Calgary, but how likely are parents from a western Canada city to give a baby a name like Pilar? I wrote out some notes for when I spoke to the captain you just saw on TV. Printed your daughter's name in caps. That's when I saw it. Pilar is an anagram for April."

She still had not looked up. "What else," she said, almost inaudibly. She picked up the gun, fitted it into her small hand as she said, "I need to know how someone can recognize me when I can't even recognize myself."

Kate watched her, feeling as if her bones were shrinking with the increasing tension in her body. "First I need to tell you that not many people would figure this out. I doubt I would have thought twice about you if my previous police partner hadn't asked, insisted I think about your presence here. Even so, maybe it took a detective like me with decades of experience in putting very small pieces together in building a case for court. So, I added your falsifying your origins to other clues. The short length of time you've lived next to me. Your face, the grief I see in your eyes all the time. The music coming from your house—seventies and eighties, nothing from the last twenty years when you were incarcerated. Your glasses are their own kind of disguise. Your hair never grows or changes, it's a wig. Whatever you've done to your face…" Kate shook her head. "You look nothing like any of your photos."

"Teeth," she said, and she finally looked up, baring them at Kate, white and perfectly even. Her blue eyes were arctic cold. "Amazing how teeth can change a face. That separation between my front teeth had to go. A dentist up in Red Bluff didn't give a shit why I wanted all those perfectly good teeth pulled, he was glad to get the money for implants. They changed the shape of my mouth, my jaw. A cosmetologist in San Francisco did electrolysis on my eyebrows, a little Botox. I actually do need to wear glasses now. But as for this—" She reached up with the hand not holding the gun, pulled off the wig that concealed short dark hair lightly threaded with gray. Tossed the wig into a messy tangle on the floor.

Her gaze on Kate, she raised the gun until it was horizontal to her vision, turned the barrel with a series of clicks, inspecting it. "It's loaded," she marveled. "So, no trick. Or is the safety on—"

"There's no safety," Kate uttered, grimly aware of the incongruity in her response. "Not on a revolver."

Index finger lightly touching the trigger of the .38, she asked in sardonic wonderment, "What's the deal? Can't bring yourself to do your own suicide?" She ran a hand roughly through her newly freed hair, then pointed the gun at Kate. "What gives? If you knew who I am—why the hell didn't you have me arrested?"

Kate managed not to recoil as the barrel of the gun leveled on her head. "Because there's no way I can do that. No way in hell can I have you spend one more minute in handcuffs or a jail cell and continue living with myself."

Pilar shook her head. "Why not? I don't get it. Why all the camera and alarm stuff to protect yourself? You aren't even the right cop, the one who did this to me. You're not the one who testified—"

"No, but—"

"That *bitch*," she spat, leaning toward Kate, the gun wavering with the vehemence in her voice. "Didn't matter what I said, what anybody said. I was guilty from minute one. Every time she looked at me it was like she wanted to grab my face and shit down my throat."

"She was a mother, like you. And couldn't get past it. But it wasn't just Detective Holden." Kate gestured toward the blank TV as if the press conference were still in progress. "You're more right about coming after me than you could ever know. Detective Holden should never have been lead investigator on your case. I was supervising detective, your case was my responsibility. I put her in that position. You didn't get the investigation you deserved."

Kate pointed to the gun. "Whatever you do or don't do, it stops now. It's eighteen months since your acquittal. Eighteen months of living with knowing my part in what happened to you. Five months and two weeks of waiting for you to carry out your threat. My days have been nothing but misery. Even so, it's taken all these months to get to this point where I now realize I can't do what I would need to do to stop you—and live with myself. So why continue with the protection? Do I want to live? I suppose I must, or I'd have taken care of that already. So, what's the difference? Whatever happens to me happens right here and right now."

The woman looked at her, eyes still blinking from taking in what she had heard. Then she pointed the gun at Kate again and a grimace of a smile sketched itself across her face. "Thank you for giving me a better rationale for killing you. Back then I did see you with that detective, but I've had some qualms about taking out someone who never even spoke to me. Still, you were part of the case. So, how simple is this? You've made it way too easy."

Eyes on the gun, bracing herself, the thudding of her heart echoing in her ears, Kate gripped the arms of her chair to stop herself from raising her hands in instinctive, futile self-protection.

"But there's a flaw in your generosity," Pilar said. "Your cameras will show me coming in here—"

"They won't. They're switched off."

"Doesn't matter. I shoot a cop, I no longer have the courtesies of the LAPD. They'll know it's me, I'll go right to the top of their most wanted list."

"I did think of that. I fired a shot into the sand this morning—"

"That was you? I figured it was one of the wingnuts around here."

"So I've got gunshot residue on my right hand. All you have to do is put my gun in it."

"This is unbelievable." Shaking her head, Pilar lowered the gun into her lap, retaining a loose grip on the handle. "Damn thing is heavy," she muttered.

Kate expelled a breath. "Guns mostly are," she said in a voice that surprised her with its steadiness. "And most people never expect the recoil."

"Good to know," Pilar said with irony.

"If I could ask a question…" Kate said.

"Better late than never," Pilar mocked. "Ask away."

Again Kate gestured to the TV. "Did the proof—what you saw today, did it surprise you?"

Seemingly struck by the question, Pilar looked away for some moments, frown lines between her eyebrows. "No and yes." She shook her head. "All those years, of course I wondered…But it had to be Stella or Pastor Mathew. I put absolutely nothing past Pastor Mathew—no limits on what he'd do in the name of his God. He actually believed the drivel he spewed. I sort of hoped it was him."

"Why?" Kate couldn't help but ask.

"Why, you ask." Her gaze lost its focus. "Well, it comes down to which murderer you wish your daughter were last looking at, doesn't it. The minister sending you to hell where he thinks you belong? Or your best friend, the person you love? She was afraid of Stella, but she did love her."

"You knew she was afraid of Stella?"

Pilar contemplated Kate. "Okay. Knowing I have your kind permission to kill you today, let's talk. First of all, my name is now actually Pilar," she said in a firm but softer tone, "like it says on all my phony documents. I prefer having a version of the name I gave my daughter, and I gave it to her right away. One look at my brand-new baby girl, I could see she was fresh and sweet and beautiful as April. Her father insisted on something biblical, so she's got a middle name. But I never ever spoke it, not once."

She placed the gun back on the side table, looked levelly at Kate. "Who else am I ever going to talk to about any of this?" She reached for her iced tea, sat back and crossed her legs, a battered flip-flop dangling from the upper foot. "It's as much up to you as it is me how long you live. What else would you like to know, Scheherazade?" She smiled at her own witticism.

Kate eased back in her chair. About to ask her to begin with a revisit to the chronology of that haunting day in 1994, she decided against it. This was not an interview room and she would not inflict the pain of those hideous memories on Pilar. If

Pilar went there, fine. "I want to know about April, but first tell me about Stella."

"Stella." She looked up to the ceiling and sighed as if seeking a clue for where to begin. "You know those heavy-breathing romance novels where the lovers are always"—she made air quotes—"besotted? That was Stella. I think she got it from her father. Her father was besotted too, but not with God. With himself. Stella needed to be with April every minute. Every second. She was over to our place all the time, they did everything together, she had to go everywhere with her…"

"A real problem for you," Kate said carefully. Needing liquid for her dry throat, she picked up her iced tea with a fairly steady hand and sipped, her body releasing more of its tension.

"Nicely understated," Pilar said wryly, placing her own glass back on the coffee table. "Of course I knew they were spending way too much time together. April and Stella had a lot in common, but it didn't take a genius to know both girls needed other friends, other interests. But if April even talked to another girl, Stella would all but flap around in her misery and she'd make April even more miserable. My daughter was always too easily cowed, too soft-hearted. She couldn't bear hurting anyone. And when it came to boys, her father and Pastor Mathew made things worse, they were Stella's unintentional allies. If I ever so gently tried to push April toward some perfectly nice kid in the Bible study group, Daniel would push her right back the other way as if every teenage male were a potential rapist. As for Pastor Mathew, he was delighted that his own daughter showed no interest in—" Again the air quotes, "—fornication."

"Your husband didn't see what you saw in the girls' relationship?"

"I prayed to God he didn't. With him I acted as if everything was normal. If I breathed a word about their friendship being out of the ordinary, I didn't know what might happen to the two girls. What kind of exorcism Pastor Mathew might take it into his head to—"

"I understand," said Kate. "You were in an impossible spot."

"You have no idea. Worse still, I had no idea how well-off I was in my impossible spot. There was this therapist at April's school. Somehow she saw that April seemed to be…troubled, I guess. I thought she was a godsend when she reinforced my advice to April about having other friends, other interests. What she told April seemed to toughen her up more toward Stella than I ever could." She shook her head, closed her eyes briefly. "How many times have I wished the woman had never…" She sighed. "April finally pushing her away, it's what sent Stella right over the edge."

She looked at Kate. "That therapist should have testified at the trial."

"I know," Kate said. "Why didn't she? Why didn't your lawyer call on her?"

"He advised against it. Was adamant she'd strengthen the prosecution's case. According to him, the therapist all but said my daughter was in an unnatural relationship, so it gave me even more motive to kill her." Her smile was bitter, her shrug eloquent.

She contemplated Kate. "About the trial, answer me this. I found out how good a detective you were in your day, there's stuff on the Internet about some of your cases. That cop friend who visits you all the time, anybody can see how much he respects you. So how come I got second best? How come I got Detective Holden instead of Detective Delafield? Why did you hand off April's murder?"

Kate answered quietly, "Because I was too close to the time of a murder that gutted me. A murder like hers. The teenager's name was Dory Quillin—"

"One of your cases I read about," Pilar interjected.

"She got to me. To this very day she still gets to me. I could have formally withdrawn from your case. I should have. Not just handed it off."

"Well, either way I'd get a different detective, wouldn't I."

Kate managed a faint smile. "Maybe one that wouldn't have hated you quite so much as Torrie did."

Pilar shrugged. "Everybody hates a child killer. Everybody."

"Your husband, did he never…" Kate groped for tactful words.

"Stand by me? Come to my defense?" To Kate's confirming nod she uttered, "Daniel," her tone acid. "After everything we'd been through together, all those years, that fucking little wimp turned his back on me. He adored April as much as I did, he knew damn well I could never do anything to hurt her and never ever that kind of butchery. But he only ever listened to Pastor Mathew. Just the fact that she died meant I was a bad mother and no matter who killed her or how, it came down to being my fault."

Grief, Kate thought. Daniel Shuster was in grief, and no one knew better than she how irrational grief could be. "Pilar," she said, "about April, did you yourself ever think the two girls—that she was in your view unnatural?"

She nodded without hesitation. "Today I'd say so. My daughter never looked at boys the way I did when I was her age, never showed any interest. Not the way she did with Stella. Back then, if I'd seen them in bed together, even kissing, I'd have probably gone out of my mind. But no matter what I wouldn't have killed her. I mean, they were *teenagers*. They were *kids*. You know how crazy teenagers can be, I was a mess at her age too. The household April grew up in, we four God-obsessed parents, *that's* what's unnatural. Who knows, if she ever got away from all the Bible and God business, got away from Daniel and me to think a little bit for herself, maybe she'd have been heterosexual. Or bisexual. Or whatever. It's possible, isn't it?"

"Of course it is." For herself, being anything other than lesbian had never been possible, not from the earliest age she could remember. But she had grown into the realization that for many people, especially those able to resist religious and societal pressures, sexuality was on a sliding scale.

"How did you ever get drawn into—" She groped for a phrase.

"All the crap from the Church of the Eternal Word?" To Kate's nod she shrugged. "Long story. But then, you have all the time you want."

"I'm in no hurry," Kate confirmed drily. "Newspapers back then—I never looked at anything beyond headlines, so I don't know much about your church. Just some of its…ah, beliefs."

Pilar smiled. "Nice of you not to say *crackpot* beliefs. Especially when my church believed people like you should be put to death." She picked up and munched a few potato chips as if gathering thought. "Pastor Mathew *was* the church. Grew up Mormon but went off on his own as soon as he knew he could run his own circus his own way. Only a follower can really understand why we just lined up behind him…" She picked up several more chips.

Seeing that Pilar was reflecting over what she would reveal, Kate remained silent in what felt like a less charged atmosphere. She could indeed understand what Pilar had just said—like the rest of the country she'd been sickened witness to the nine hundred suicide/murders, a third of them children, perpetrated by cult leader Jim Jones in his Peoples Temple in Guyana.

Dakota stirred on the back deck. Hearing the rattle of her collar, paws on the wood flooring, Kate could picture her getting up from her bed, shaking herself, settling back in. Pilar grabbed the bowl of chips, extended it to Kate.

"Unless you don't want these to be your last meal?"

Kate reached to the bowl and scooped up several. "They happen to be a staple of mine."

An expression between a smirk and a smile on her face, Pilar set the bowl down and sat back. "Hardly a surprise. You're not exactly a conventional woman. You walk your own walk. About the church, you may not believe this, but Pastor Mathew was not a con man."

"But a narcissist," Kate suggested.

"Well, sure, that's obvious. It still doesn't explain him to anyone who wasn't there, who didn't…" She flapped a hand in a frustration of seeking words. "He had, like, this glow around him. A radiance. You wanted to be around it all the time. For sure he was like any other preacher—righteous, pious, all those things. He walked and talked and lived with such total conviction…"

She ran both hands through her spiky hair and gripped her head as if to physically corral her thoughts. "People don't understand how reasonably intelligent people could ever be taken in by someone like him, all the shit he preached. But I've had years and years to think about all this and his genius…I tell you it *was* genius…" She looked defiantly at Kate as if Kate were about to argue her choice of word. "The way he drew in people from all backgrounds—okay, lots of us wouldn't rank very high on the IQ charts, but we had teachers too, programmers, lawyers…you'd be shocked by the caliber of people who followed him. All these years thinking about the people I got to know in our church back then, I finally, *finally* figured out what we had in common: none of us had a clue about how hollow our lives were till we saw him, heard him."

The thick lenses of her glasses heightening the intensity in her eyes, her voice rose as if volume were an assist in her need for explication. "He *fed* us what we didn't even know we needed, hungered for, understand? Call it whatever you want, but we had to have it. He was an *equalizer* for us, you get what I mean? People who came to the church, we'd all felt, I don't know, *diminished* in some way all our lives, we were out there just blowing around in the wind—"

Leaning toward Kate in her animation, she pointed to herself. "People like me, people like Daniel, with zero expectations about anything to do with us, Pastor Mathew tucked people like us under his wing and spread gold dust all over us, made us feel all righteous and superior because we were with *him*. He gave us an enemy to fight, do you see? Evil people like you who were out to destroy everything God-given and holy about the world. All the unbelievers out there who didn't know any better. We were an army of righteous rebels on a path that was straight and true and right. And filled with light from *him*. I tell you, it was potent, heady stuff."

"I can see that," Kate said quietly. And she could. "His wife, Stella's mother—"

"*Veronica,*" Pilar spat. She grabbed her iced tea, took a drink, thumped the glass back on the table. "Little wifey—just *perfect* for him. What a dishrag," she mocked, rocking back in her armchair. "Scuttled around after him…How a kid like Stella could ever come out of a woman like her…" She waved a hand as if to wipe away Veronica Hayden's very existence. "So, you'd think Stella would be like Pastor Mathew, right? And in some ways she was. But, basically, she wasn't. Assertive like him, sure, but his preaching never applied to her. Stella did whatever she damn well wanted to do." She shook her head. "Tell her she was a sinner bound for hell, she'd act like, okay, that will be happening to me tomorrow, not today. Somehow, some way, Stella saw that she had *choices*. Most people do what they're told, don't ever think beyond the small box they're in—I for sure never did. I'll tell you something, Kate: I met hundreds of women over all those years in prison and I learned how easy it is for people to be led down bad roads, be taken in by con men, preachers, politicians. We're most of us susceptible. But not Stella." She shook her head in wonderment. "Not ever. You can see how it would be logical for me to think Preacher Mathew killed my daughter. I hated him for that, but I hated him more for not going after his own daughter instead of mine."

Stella Hayden was like many lesbians throughout history, Kate thought, assertive women who flouted cultural norms and beliefs and broke ground for the rest of us. In growing curiosity about this well-spoken, obviously intelligent woman across from her, she asked, "How did you meet, you and Daniel? Were you Mormons too?"

"Methodists. From Idaho. A farm near Pocatello for me, Daniel came from Boise. We met at a state fair. Life was farm chores for both of us, schoolwork, church work, it's how we grew up. All we knew, all we expected. Marriage for me only meant a different farm, different church—this time Baptist. Until we found Pastor Mathew at a revival meeting."

Kate gazed at her in wonder. "But you sound…" Again she searched for tactful words.

"Not stupid?" Pilar suggested caustically. "Yeah, well, I hold all sorts of degrees—from the school of life. Everything I know, it's from three years of high school and my grandfather." She shrugged. "And okay, a lot of it from my time up north."

Meaning prison. What all had happened to this woman during her nineteen years of incarceration?

Before she could ask another question, Pilar said, "My grandfather…" and her face softened in reminiscence as she continued, "Grandad grew up on the farm where I was born.

Five brothers and sisters, he was oldest. Sold his acres to his two brothers and went off to law school in Boise, his dream. Two years go by, a combine falls on both my great uncles at harvest time, his dream's over. Came back to take over the farm. Had to, we were all dependent on him, including my father. I only got to know him when he was an old man." Her voice was filled with regret. "Living in a little cabin on the property so he wouldn't be a bother. Law books all around him, other books of all kinds he'd collected over his lifetime. It's because of him I found out about Willa Cather, Mark Twain, Walt Whitman..." Her eyes had moistened with memory. "He went nearly blind those last few years. I'd go over to his place and read to him from whatever he wanted, and he'd talk to me about the law, he so loved the law. He'd recite poetry he'd committed to memory, especially a Scottish poet, Robert Burns..." Her voice choked.

"Your grandfather sounds like a great person," Kate offered, realizing that she'd had no figure in her life like him, not even the father she'd adored.

"The best person ever. I was just sick about deserting him when I got married. I know it hurt him too, but he told me he was glad for me. Looking back, it left a big hole in both our lives. He was such a lonely man...died not six months later. What a great lawyer he'd have been if only..." She paused. "...if only he hadn't got trapped in his life." She added bitterly, "Didn't we all." Her gaze drifted away to Kate's front window and the openness of desert.

Kate followed her gaze to a landscape turned orange in late afternoon sun, and her somber nod conveyed that she too was a card-carrying marcher in that particular band. "How did you end up in LA?"

"Andrew Pulman."

Again Kate nodded. "I do know who he is." The tech millionaire funding angel for the church.

Pilar sighed. "The way things happen, sometimes I think we're all just a bunch of billiard balls banging around some cosmic pool table. Pulman visited a daughter in American Falls, she insisted he had to hear Pastor Mathew. He was an instant believer—goes to show you how even millionaires can get taken in. He guaranteed Pastor Mathew financial support if he'd bring his church to California. We sold our farm, followed him, we didn't even have to discuss doing it. I became church accountant—" She waved a hand in deprecation of the title. "It hardly took skill to do the church's books, believe me. Daniel was his assistant, confidant, errand boy, all around factotum. Andrew Pulman paid for it all, the church building, our salaries, found the duplex for us. The parishioners funded whatever else was needed."

"From what you say, it sounds to me…" Kate began, broke off, offered lamely, "Prison really changed you from those days."

Pilar laughed. "You have a real gift for understatement. Yeah, you can definitely say that. Nothing like getting away from the master hypnotist. Having the curtain pulled back on the great and powerful Oz. Anyway, who needs God when you have prison guards ordering you around twenty-four hours a day? *Faith*," she uttered, as the word were an obscenity. "The big shiny bubble that explains everything. Isn't life simple when scripture dictates what you do and everything that happens good or bad becomes God's will. Or what someone claims is God's will. But all it takes is one tiny pinprick and the bubble pops—" She slapped her hands together so sharply that Kate startled in her chair. "Poof! Gone! You see some little guy scuttling around, he's creating all the lightning and thunder around the great and powerful Oz."

Kate was silent for so long that Pilar finally said, derisively, "What, don't tell me I took away all your faith just as you're about to meet your creator?"

Deeply immersed in thought, Kate answered soberly, slowly, "I think…what faith I have…I've always pretty much placed in other people…in institutions." Whatever tenuous religious belief she might ever have had, it had dissolved in the jungles of Vietnam along with a great many other illusions. "It's faith that's sometimes been misplaced…betrayed. Maybe more often than not. Even so…"

Digesting these words, Pilar was nodding. "Even so you wouldn't have it any other way."

"I guess not. No."

"And I'd guess thirty years a cop proves it." Pilar was gazing at her in either wonderment or incredulity, Kate couldn't tell. "You never lost faith in trying to make right from wrong."

Kate met her gaze. "And sometimes making things worse, getting it even more terribly wrong." She took a breath, broached the topic she dreaded. "Pilar…your time in prison…"

"Worse than you imagine, Kate. But…sometimes…better than you'd imagine."

Pilar shoved the coffee table aside, pulled an ottoman over to her armchair, kicked off her flip-flops and raised her feet onto its leather surface. And Kate, seeing she was settled in, leaned back to just listen.

"Death row, where I was for a while…you probably know it's nothing like the rest of the prisons at Chowchilla, out there in farm country. A separate unit for us worst of the worst, or we'd have all been attacked, probably shanked our first day in the main facility. Especially child murderers. Hell, it was all I could do not to take on some of those monsters myself. One of them shot all four of her boys. Jessica, she smothered both her little daughters…"

She shook her head vigorously, as if pushing away memory that had become all too tangible. "I'm sure you've heard all about this stuff, how damaged and pathetic most of those women are. Talk about pathetic—I saw the Manson women. Susan Atkins, Leslie Van Houten, Patricia Krenwinkel," she said, pronouncing each name with a moue of distaste. "They weren't on death row, but they were in isolation like me, dead women walking, they knew damn well they'd never get out if they had a million parole hearings. When I saw them I counted myself lucky Pastor Mathew wasn't into drugs with his followers like the Manson creeps. Who knows what kind of deranged stuff he might have cooked up…"

She shrugged. "A lot of women I got to know were all drugged up when they did what they did. Some were dumb as, well—so dumb they didn't even know what they did was wrong. Some had been raped and beaten up from as early as they could remember, finally turned on and murdered their psycho husbands or boyfriends. And lots of them were just like me, pretty much pulled into the lives they led. Like me, they found out they were different people away from all the shit they'd been shovel-fed. All those women I met showed me so many paths we can be led down."

She looked at Kate with a half-smile. "Some of us, you know, found other women to love. And were damn happy to give the finger forever to men. Some of us were like me, lived for the prison library. Read all the time, worked every hour we could on our appeals."

Her smile widened. "Any other questions?"

"Yes," Kate answered grimly. "You asked why I didn't have you arrested once I knew who you were. But I only put everything together and figured it out in the last day or so. You've lived next door to me for the last two months or so. Why..." She looked at Pilar, irritation rising as she remembered the endless days of trepidation, fear.

"Why haven't I killed you already?"

Kate didn't bother to respond.

Pilar said, "And here I thought you were such a smart detective..."

She reached beside her, picked up the gun, rose from her armchair, carried it to the end table next to Kate, set it down. Returned to her armchair.

"If I could have done it," she said vehemently, "I goddamn well would have, Detective Delafield. Did it never occur to you that even though I didn't murder my daughter, I blame myself for the part I played in the life she led? It never occurred to you that making threats was the only thing left for me to do? I didn't kill you for the same goddamn reason you gave me for not having me arrested."

In an adrenaline flood of relief that made her bones feel like water, Kate tore her stare away from the gun and uttered, "After everything you went through, everything that should never have happened to you—"

"Okay, shut up about that, will you? Okay, you're sorry. I get that, for fuck's sake. But only on TV is it easy to kill someone—you know that. Only if you're a psycho is it easy to kill someone. You couldn't live with yourself if you had me arrested. I couldn't live with myself if I murdered you."

"So you contented yourself with tormenting me," Kate said, still trying to settle a roiling of emotion.

"Well, yeah, to some extent that was satisfying. Watching all that stuff being installed on your house, those cop cars driving past, that cop friend of yours here all the time and giving you Dakota, I knew I was at least making you squirm. I'd pretty much got it out of my system after that last note and was going to see how long before…"

"I stopped squirming?"

Pilar looked at Kate with something like hostility. "I hope you're not expecting an apology," she said.

"I absolutely don't. I won't." She now realized, with the vaporizing of that ever-present sword looming over her life, that some form of penance had been necessary for her part in the incarceration of this woman.

"Pilar, after this, after today," Kate said. "We've both arrived at a different place for us both…What's next for you? Where from here?"

"Well, I've actually thought about that. I know I have to stay invisible. The early days out of prison—you'd think they'd be great, right? I was finally free. I'd been totally exonerated. But they were a nightmare. I had no home, nowhere to go. I was nearly forty years away from Idaho, parents gone, nobody there I cared about or who cared about me. Daniel was gone, not that I ever wanted to see him again, everybody I knew from the church I wanted nothing to do with. So, family gone, friends gone. And I had a pack of hounds after me. News reporters, people who wanted me to write a book with them, make a movie, a TV series. They couldn't imagine I just wanted to get away from it all, and not, for chrissakes, relive everything all over again. They were like leeches. I finally hit the road just to get away from them. The happiest day in my life out of prison was when the reparations money came through. Took long enough, almost a year, but then I could do whatever I wanted. Change myself. Hire somebody to go back into my case and find whoever he could who'd been part of doing this to me, taking away all those years. That's when I found you. Where you were living. I drove down here, could hardly believe my luck to find the house next to you empty. I bought it for cash, cheap, figuring I could walk away when the time came, easy."

She shifted in her chair, gestured with outstretched arms to the desert beyond the windows. "But guess what? I really like it here. I really like the desert. I'm an oddball and a misfit just like the oddballs and misfits who live out here. Including you. Would it bug you if I stayed living next door?"

Kate looked at Pilar Adams, a woman as alone and bereft as herself. A woman coming to terms with what was left of her life, like she was. The two of them were an odd couple, but a matched couple if there ever was one. Kate said, "I'd be glad to have you as my neighbor. But only if you don't change your mind about killing me."

Pilar's lips quirked up at the corners. "I guess I *could* always change my mind—that's true. So here's a really good idea, Kate: instead of making you any promises, how about you live your life from now on like every day's your last day."

"Then I won't have to change a thing. I've been doing that the last five months, thanks to you. I do have one request." She smiled. "I like your music, but you might turn the volume down a tad."

"Done. I have one request too. You breathe not a word, not one word, to anyone about who I used to be. Not to that cop friend of yours, not to *anybody*."

"Done. About that, I have another issue. I've got that cop friend all but living with me because of you, I have Dakota here because of you. Cops in this whole county are on alert because of you."

"Yeah…" Pilar shook her head, pursed her lips. "From now on I'd so like the idea of them not looking for me. I don't want anybody looking for me ever again. How about I put one last note in your mailbox that I'm done with this, I'm leaving you alone? We can collaborate on it. Or you can just dictate what it should say."

"That would work."

"You're keeping Dakota though, right?"

Kate nodded. "From now on she can look out for both of us."

Pilar said musingly, "I've been thinking about getting a cat…"

"I'd love that. I had one for years, Miss Marple. I miss her."

Pilar chuckled. "Okay, with that name in mind, maybe I'll name mine Sherlock."

"Sherlock. I like it."

Both women rose, and Kate had to catch herself on the arm of the chair, almost collapsing with her body's release of tension, fear, adrenaline.

Pilar walked over to Kate, extended a hand. "So, Kate, we have a deal."

"Pilar, we have a deal."

Kate grasped her hand.

17

Arms crossed, waiting, Kate stood at her living room window gazing out at the desert landscape and the distant San Bernardino Mountains, sharp-edged, gray-purple clarity on this hot, dry, cloudless May afternoon, the fourth anniversary of Maggie's death. Behind her, the house was in full readiness for its very first influx of visitors, as expectant as she was. Thanks in no small part to Pilar, whose involvement Kate had not had to enlist—she'd as usual poked her nose into the atypical activity around Kate's property. But so energetically and creatively had she suggested furniture rearrangement, artful displays of Nightwood Bar memorabilia, even menu items, that Kate had quickly appreciated her collaboration. And invited her to meet the group. But Pilar had declined: "A day like this is way too private, way too special to all of you." She was right, of course, and Kate suspected that she also wanted distance between herself and anything that reminded her of her daughter, even a memorial for a stranger.

Pilar. In the aftermath of their confrontation after the press conference Kate felt as if a fifty-pound weight had been amputated from her back. She no longer had to endure the literal weight and meaning of the gun she'd carried on her body every day for all those months. The cameras and alarms on her house were gone, every spotlight on her was now extinguished. She had always felt scalded under the searchlight of public attention, shunning opportunities to attain higher rank during her three decades at LAPD for this reason if no other. These recent months of enduring the focus of Cameron and her police colleagues had been a daily torment of wearing a bright target on her back. Now it was over, all over. Now she was truly free from her police career, she was truly gone from LAPD.

For her and Pilar, they had found mutual resolution and absolution. What remained was the reality of the two of them isolated in their circumstances and facing the plain truths of aging. With words unspoken, they were now looking out for each other. Her nosy, inquisitive neighbor had been exposed as an admirable, self-actualizing individual; reemerged, after nearly two decades of imprisonment, into life on her own terms. Pilar returned Kate's admiration; she never ceased telling her how safe and protected she felt with Kate next door. And after years of incarceration in the company of women, she had learned, she said, to prefer their company. As her latest favor to Kate, only a few minutes ago she'd clipped the lead onto Dakota's collar, taken her out for a long walk. Afterward, she promised, she would entertain Dakota at her own place until all the visitors had departed.

One of those visitors would be Aimee, and Kate once more glanced down at her attire for the day, belted gray pants and a pale blue shirt. For all her indecision over their selection, they were merely a dressier variation on the pants and shirts she usually wore. But it had been a chasm of seven months since she'd seen Aimee, and she felt unmoored about her, disassembled by the unexpected dissolution of the threat from Ellie Shuster. Never had she factored in any possibility of redemption—and why would she? No way could she have expected any outcome other than the end of everything. For months she had braced herself, quashing any hope, too guilt-ridden over her part in a tragic miscarriage of justice. But now…now, with her rationale for avoidance of Aimee all these months suddenly evaporated, she felt an awkward uncertainty she could not shake off. So reminiscent of those early days when she returned from Vietnam and the high adrenaline front lines of a war, disoriented in the absence of unceasing action, tragedy, jeopardy. For months she'd been off-balance, dislocated.

After the press conference there had been emails, one from Aimee, a message cool in its tone: *Just saw the Walcott press conference. Guess you were more involved in that case than I knew. Nothing new under the sun with you. But glad it's resolved. It had to be a hard one for everybody. See you next week.*

Cameron's congratulatory text had been first to pop up. Others came in over the next days from acquaintances and colleagues she had not heard from in years, most of them forwarded to her by the case detectives at Wilshire who had graciously offered their gratitude for closing a case that had tarnished everyone associated with it. Also in her mailbox were requests for press and TV interviews, the media's ability to track her email address, no matter how often she changed it, a continuing aggravation even this far into retirement.

The whirlwind of events since the press conference had only magnified her sense of dislocation. Predictably, the media had seized on the announcement of the DNA results to resurrect Mathew Hayden and his Church the Eternal Word for renewed excoriation, again comparing him to the notorious Fred Phelps, pastor of the Westboro Baptist Church, opining that his homophobic ravings had been responsible for turning his own daughter into a murderer. A thesis Kate knew to be intrinsically true if simplistic; the secrecy and isolation of the girls' lives had served to intensify Stella's obsessiveness over April.

For front page headline news, the story had quickly run out of oxygen, the media spinning frustrated circles around itself trying to verify, if not amplify its speculations. Despite the powerful outreach of the networks and its investigative reporters, Eleanor Shuster could not be located. The lead actors in the glory days of the church, if they actually had been tracked down wherever they were in Africa, apparently offered no comment. Former parishioners who did speak on the record delivered variations on "Evil happens to those who try to subvert God's law."

All that was forthcoming from the current case detectives was "No comment." Nor could anything be elicited from Captain Carolina Walcott beyond her refrain, "The press conference speaks for itself." Nor could another key player originally involved in the case, a certain retired Detective Kate Delafield, be contacted for interview. Knowing that the media would be quick to trace her to her location, Cameron had invited her and Dakota to stay a few days with him in Victorville to escape the media onslaught, and she'd been quick to accept.

Kate's main pursuer and nemesis, police reporter Corey Lanier at the *Los Angeles Times*, stated in her weekly wrap-up column that in the aftermath of the press conference she had tracked down and managed to speak in person with a next-door neighbor. Who had advised that Kate Delafield, so far as she knew, was away and would be traveling in Canada for the next several months. When Pilar had called her cell phone to jauntily pass on word of this subterfuge, they'd both laughed uproariously, Kate imagining how Lanier would choke on her press credentials if she ever realized she'd actually been talking to Eleanor Shuster.

Kate could not imagine Cameron's reaction should he ever guess Pilar's true identity. Odds were that this would never happen—he'd seen only a few old photos in the case file and, like Corey Lanier, now had no reason to ever look beyond Pilar's cosmetic alterations. He'd relaxed his vigilance, persuaded that Kate was safe by the wording in the handwritten letter she and Pilar had composed to confirm his belief that the truth about the murder of April had recentered the blame and mitigated Ellie Shuster's rage over the events that cost her so dearly.

Kate had photographed and transmitted the letter to Walcott and Cameron the day after the press conference, claiming she'd found it in her mailbox after returning earlier than she'd planned from LA. She too was convinced, she'd told Cameron, that she was no longer under threat, and therefore would not be endangering anyone else.

In the note Kate had attached to the photo of the letter sent to Walcott, she requested an end to police surveillance and withdrawal of all BOLOs for Ellie Shuster. Further, now that the case was closed, she had no interest in pressing any charges related to the previous threats made to her life. Walcott responded with one of her typically terse emails: *Your choice. No argument here.* And added, *Do look after yourself, Kate.*

But Cameron's vigilance over her had not totally disappeared, evidenced by his first question when he called her after receiving the email with the letter. "After all this blows over, maybe you'll get back with Aimee?"

His stepping yet again on this exposed nerve so infuriated her that she barely managed to keep savagery from her tone when she replied, "I don't see you in a hurry to get hooked up with anyone."

"Yeah, well, now things may get different for me too."

Well aware of what a caring and true friend he had been to her over the past nightmarish months, she fully realized it now. He had put his life on hold for her. Her anger melted into more gratitude.

Three days after the press conference, the media heat having tapered to the vanishing point, she'd moved herself and Dakota out of Cameron's spare room and back home. Then drove into LA with an agenda. To begin with, a leisurely visit to Walt Masterson at Silverlake Haven, the hour with him filled with more comradeship and reminiscence. Followed by a high-spirited, laughter-filled appointment with Calla Dearborn, so giddy were they both over the sudden release of the pressurized tension between them over the past five months. It was the first such day Kate could ever remember with her therapist of many years, and afterward Dearborn had cheerfully promised a return to the usual skewering at their next appointment.

From there to West LA to perform a more subdued postmortem with Marietta Hall in the aftermath of the April

Shuster case. But then they'd had lunch in the dining area at a communal table with other female residents, and other topics of conversation came to the forefront, life in Los Angeles, their shared history and memories. Introduced to other residents in the community, she'd joined in their laughter over their stories about Marietta, and Kate had left the place, and the city, lighter in spirit and with a newborn sense of anticipation in knowing she would return soon to this city that carried so much history of her life.

Her visit to Natalie Rostow the following day had resulted in another easy, convivial afternoon in a clubhouse with women in her own age group, all of them lesbian, and she'd been warmly welcomed as Natalie's friend to participate in their games of cards and in their comradeship. And invited back.

Seeing a car in the distance coming toward the house, Kate turned away from her window to her CD player. The crashing guitar chords that opened the Eagles' "Take It Easy" filling the house, she straightened and, hands on her hips, once more she surveyed her living room, its carefully arranged memorabilia. The Nightwood Bar sign, rescued from the bar's front window, in glowing lavender neon high on a bookshelf. Directly under the sign an end table was draped with a sequined lavender cloth, on it Maggie's urn, surrounded by flickering votive candles, each glass container in a color of the rainbow flag.

The sign was symbolically located; there had been bookshelves in the bar, beside the pool table. In the years following the Dory Quillin murder she had both borrowed from and supplied lesbian books to those shelves. There had been game tables too, with Scrabble and chess boards, cards and trivia, and one of those was duplicated on a table beside an armchair.

The breakfast bar and coffee table were laden with platters of shrimp, chicken wings, coleslaw, potato salad, a cheese assortment and crackers, olives, tortilla chips and salsa. Glasses were grouped beside a pitcher of water and a tub filled with ice and soft drinks. In this re-creation of the Nightwood Bar only the aroma of coffee permeated the room. There was no alcohol on offer, and she directed a self-satisfied grin at Maggie's urn. Something else was different since the press conference: these past several days there actually had been patches of time where she hadn't ached for alcohol, hadn't even thought about it. It wasn't all that significant, it wasn't even a milestone, she knew that—she'd been here before. But still it was something. Something good.

At the sound of a car door slamming she moved toward the door, voicing aloud: "Maggie my friend, you'd be hooting with glee about all this."

First to arrive were Ash and Tora, both women in flashy purple tights and bright pink thigh-length T-shirts emblazoned with LATINA PRIDE in rainbow colors. Not only did the pair seem ageless, they were the only lesbian couple she knew of who had remained together through all the years since the demise of the Nightwood Bar and the passing of the owner-bartender being celebrated today. They greeted Kate with warm whirling hugs and, in Tora's case, cries of "Chica!" and affectionate if painful slams of her fists on Kate's forearms.

"Wow, look at this place! Maggie, you'd be proud!" she shrieked, breaking away from Kate and dancing over to the urn to the lilting rhythms from the CD player, Ash gazing at her with tolerant affection.

Next came Patton and Kendall, arriving in Patton's battered F-150. Patton leaped out of the truck looking thinner than when Kate last saw her; the denim shirt hanging off her bony shoulders was tucked into baggy jeans all but falling from her narrow waist. She wore a green plaid tam over her short, springy gray curls; she had never replaced the yachting cap she'd worn for years. Its ashes reposed in the urn, mixed in with the other symbols of love that had decorated Maggie's body that day of her passing at Silverlake Haven, including a replica of Kate's police badge.

Maggie's passing. Such a euphemism for what had actually happened that day. It occurred to Kate that she had become a prime repository of deep secrets. Secrets of her own and secrets of such unusual weight that she had entrusted not one of them to Aimee or Calla Dearborn or any other sort of confessor. The true cause of Maggie's death. The promise she'd sworn to a CIA officer, long since dead, to hold secret the true origin of a prehistoric bone found at a murder scene in LA's legendary La Brea Tar Pits. And now she was guardian of the true identity of Pilar Adams.

These sober thoughts fled as Patton's butch buddy Kendall was next to emerge from the truck, in all black except for white loafers and a loose-fitting snow-white tie dangling from the open collar of her black shirt. Patton ran to Kate and hugged her; Kendall gave her a mock salute and knocked knuckles, then slapped palms. Patton greeted Ash and Tora, who were already piling their plates at the food bar, then gazed at the living room in evident delight. "What a neat place you got here, Kate," she exclaimed, and strode to the table with Maggie's urn. She doffed her green plaid tam in a deep bow, hung her cap over the urn. "Hey, Maggie, I'm here," she said softly, tears glistening, then removed the cap and replaced it on her head.

"Hey, look who's arrived," Kendall called from the window. "It's Rainey." She added in a shocked voice, "What the fuck? Somebody's with her."

It had to be a new partner. She would not have brought a friend, none of them would have. But no one, including Kate, could imagine her partnered with someone other than Audie even though she had been dead for years. If there was ever a one-woman woman, it had to be Rainey.

Two women did indeed climb out of a Subaru Forester, both in flowing beige tunics over earth-toned pants. Rainey had changed her hairstyle; beaded dreads were gathered in a thick ponytail flowing in black rivulets between her shoulder blades. The other woman wore a turban that glowed gold in the sunlight, as did her large hoop earrings. Kate stared fixedly at her as the two made their way to the house, her strikingly beautiful dusky face tugging insistently at memory.

Not taking her eyes off this exotic visitor, she was greeted by a quick hug from Rainey. The other woman, staring back at her, said, "I'd tell you that you haven't changed a bit, Kate, but it would be a bare-faced lie."

The voice, low, musical, jolted Kate's memory into recognition before her mind registered and finally identified the image of the face. "Andrea Ross," she breathed.

"The very one," the woman answered, raising her eyebrows as if in surprise at the immediate recognition. "I wondered if you'd even remember."

How could I ever, ever forget? "You haven't changed, and that's the truth," Kate uttered, and involuntarily spoke her next thought: "You're just more beautiful than I remember."

Andrea smiled. "And you still do have a way about you, Detective Delafield."

"I've retired, but my memory hasn't. I remember interviewing you at the Nightwood Bar, rudely asking about your racial heritage. You telling me it's…Jamaican…Japanese…"

Andrea was nodding. "Mixed with Spanish and a bit of English," she said with a laugh.

"I remember you had all those leafy plants in your house—"

"Good God," interrupted Rainey, shaking her head and elbowing Kate. "You two have history on top of history. Aren't you going to ask how I found her, Kate?"

"How did you find her?" Kate asked dutifully, dully, still staring confoundedly at Andrea Ross. Back then, she'd thought Andrea's face in profile belonged on a coin. If anything she had become more regal with age.

"At the hospital."

Rainey was an oncology nurse at Cedars Sinai. Shocked, dismayed, Kate managed to restrain herself from glancing down at Andrea's chest. They had met only weeks after her double mastectomy. Andrea chuckled at the expression on Kate's face. "Yes, my old bugaboo. Got it beat again though, Kate. Stage one uterine, they caught it. Rainey's been helping me with post-operative treatment the last two months. We got to talking—"

"Yeah," Rainey cut in. "About the old days and can you believe it, she mentioned Maggie and her bar and it came out she went there for only a couple of weeks, but it was when Dory…Anyway, she knew you and Maggie…So, well, of course I asked her to come along today—she belongs with us."

"Of course she does," Ash said from behind them where she had been listening, and reached around Kate to grab Andrea's hand. "I remember you. Sitting in the bar off by yourself all the time. We could tell you were working through something, we knew to leave you alone."

"It's why I kept coming back, how all of you were. It was a tough time for me," Andrea told her softly. "I was post-operative, had partner troubles. It felt so good and safe just to be in the bar. With all of you."

"Yeah, till somebody got murdered," Patton said.

"Well, there was that. But we all got to know the very good detective who was on the case," she said with a faint smile at Kate.

To a further chorus of welcomes and exclamations of "Sure I remember you" and "You've hardly changed at all" from Ash and Tora, Rainey took Kate's arm and drew her aside.

"Aimee?" she asked quietly.

"On her way," Kate assured her, unsurprised that Aimee would delay her arrival to not be a distraction for these special friends who preceded her presence in Kate's life. To give Kate the spotlight to greet precious friends of many decades who had first opened the lesbian world to her.

Nodding toward Andrea who was being crowded by an admiring Patton and Kendall, Rainey said, a smile spread across her ebony face, "Let me guess. There's some really major history between you two."

"Some," Kate conceded. *Only one incomparable night. Much too little.*

"A real looker," Rainey went on. "Way out of my league. But you, you had a lot going for you back then."

"I must have," Kate said with a grin. "Where did it all go?"

"Where did any of it go?" Rainey replied with a wistful smile. "And so goddamn fast?"

"Go get yourself some food," Kate told her, pushing her by the shoulder, "before it's all gone. Tora's about to finish off the chicken wings all by herself." She again glanced out the window.

"Here she is. I see Aimee's car down the road." It was the same three-year-old Prius, deep blue, on the same color spectrum as Aimee's blue-violet eyes. Kate moved toward the door to greet her away from the group.

Vehicles having already taken over the driveway, Aimee pulled off the road in front of the house. Kate walked toward her, then stopped as Aimee emerged from the car and stood motionless, a hand poised on her open door, studying Kate. Then she smiled, as did Kate, both of them realizing they'd been taking the same inventory of each other. Awkward about protocol as she again approached Aimee—should she hug her?—the situation was resolved by Aimee's usual grace; she reached for Kate's hand.

When they first met more than two decades ago during a murder investigation at the Beverly Malibu apartment building, she'd thought Aimee bore resemblance to Candice Bergen. Since then, Aimee's dark hair had leavened with silver-gray and served to highlight the fine features of her face. Kate gazed at her. *Something has to be very wrong with me that I managed to so totally fuck it all up with this woman. I must have a death wish.* Beginning in Vietnam, then thirty years a cop. She'd ask Calla Dearborn next meeting.

"You look..." Aimee began. "You're thinner."

"You look the same," Kate offered neutrally, "only better. Thank you for your tact. I know I look like an old boot."

Aimee shrugged, squeezed her hand. "Nothing wrong with old boots. Kate's still in there somewhere. You've lost a lot of weight, though."

Five months of stress and no appetite was the best diet on earth. She said, "Maybe the booze. Lack of it."

"I'm glad to hear about your sobriety."

The remark held the overtones of rote. But how many times had she proclaimed progress with alcohol, Kate thought as they walked toward the house, Aimee's warm soft hand in hers.

At the door, Aimee said quietly. "Okay if I stay and we have a talk after everyone's gone?"

"I'd be glad for that," Kate said.

But a sudden alertness rose in her, lurching into agitation. Aimee had not waited for an invitation to stay and talk; clearly, she had an agenda. Was there now, finally, someone else in her life?

18

The afternoon had been raucous, the group seated in a semicircle around the urn, reminiscences of Maggie and the romantic entanglements—hers and theirs—in days of yore at the Nightwood Bar bringing shouts of laughter and ribald teasing interspersed with singalongs to the tracks Kate had selected, a shuffled mixture including the Eagles, Carole King, Diana Ross, Fleetwood Mac, the Beatles. Ash and Tora rose and danced to some of the songs, others got up only to refill their plates and glasses from the breakfast bar or to dash to the bathroom.

Out of hospitality Kate sat next to Andrea Ross, since she had the least continuity with the group, and Aimee had chosen a chair next to Rainey. As the afternoon wore on and the decibel level reached ever higher crescendos, Kate wondered what more alcohol could have added to the high spirits, the joyful sisterhood. Amid the din, when Andrea leaned over to say close to her ear, "Good thing we're not in the city, somebody would be calling the cops," Kate laughed in delight.

Carole King finished "You've Got a Friend," and then Cher's low, chesty voice began "If I Could Turn Back Time."

From its first notes the song seized Kate by the throat. Every other sound in the room vanished as if the mournful lyrics had pulled all of them into the essential gravity of the day, the irrevocable passage of the years, the grievous loss of the extraordinary woman they were commemorating. The woman who in some ways had been den mother to them all. Kate gazed at Maggie's urn, eyes stinging, aware that everyone here was reliving the true meaning of the Nightwood Bar, the life-saving, life-giving harbor Maggie had given them in an utterly inimical world. As Cher sang, tears glittered in the eyes of all the quiet women around her, including Andrea, including Aimee.

Kate's gaze settled on Aimee. More than a decade younger than anyone in the room, she had fewer reasons to turn back time; she had emerged into a society of loosened condemnation of the women surrounding her now. Her tears were more for Maggie, whom she had come to love, than the meaningfulness of the bar. Perhaps those tears also emerged, Kate reflected, from a fervent wish that she'd been somewhere else, anywhere else except visiting her aunt at the Beverly Malibu apartment complex on the day Homicide Detective Kate Delafield arrived to investigate the murder of film director Owen Sinclair.

All the what-ifs. All the roads not taken that might have kept us together…if I could only turn back time.

Andrea reached over and covered Kate's hand, squeezing it. She had already learned from the general conversation of Kate's closeness to Maggie; and if she also knew Kate's history with Aimee, and Kate had to assume that Rainey had at least sketched an outline, she did not care in the least who saw this gesture of familiarity, affection, consolation. Aimee darted a glance at Andrea's sudden movement in the frozen room, turned back to her contemplation of the urn.

Patton was first to sing the recurring title of Cher's song, blindly reaching for Ash's hand, and others of the group joined her. Soon they all linked hands, everyone singing the final chorus.

A few minutes later, as if this had been the signal that all the business of the day had been concluded, Rainey announced she was due back in the city. The gathering broke up in a bustle of activity, enthusiastic hugs, and promises to see each other again soon. Then they were all gone in a caravan of cars. Except for Aimee, who was now at the breakfast bar extracting a Diet Coke from the tub of soft drinks, the few remaining cans floating in a pebbly sea of all-but-melted ice cubes.

"I know you want to clean up," she said with a gesture at the detritus of plates and glasses and napkins and silverware, the askew furniture that needed restoration to its usual place in the room.

"You know me so well," Kate said with a calmness she did not feel. The time had come. "It can wait."

Aimee gave her a knowing half-smile. "Why don't I just give you a hand—"

"It can wait," Kate repeated, and dropped herself into her usual armchair to emphasize that their conversation took precedence. And to confine her body, quash the compulsion to attack the disorder in her house, her skin all but crawling in abhorrence of the chaos around her.

Over the past hours she had observed Aimee taking in details of the house with surreptitious but keen interest in what Kate's individual taste had led her to choose for herself, as if these might hold clues to new or unknown facets of her. The survey had been thorough, extending well beyond furnishings to a contemplation of carpets, objects on the walls, photographs on shelves and tables—her parents and Maggie—even her kitchen counter appliances. Kate supposed she had ventured into the bedroom at least one of the times she'd gone to the bathroom because that's what she herself would have done had the group gathered in what was now Aimee's condo. Seeking any hint, any sign of the presence of another woman. Or some token of herself, a photo, a piece of jewelry, for reassurance, continuity. Something that showed she still meant something. There were, as of this morning, two photos of herself with Aimee that Kate had retrieved and placed in the bedroom for the first time since she'd been in this house. Before today, any image of Aimee would have been a scalpel to her heart.

It seemed rude to leap in and say what's on your mind, what is it you want to say to me, so Kate asked perfunctorily, "How's work?"

"A changing landscape," Aimee answered, and a rigidity in her seemed to ease with her welcoming of the question. Pulling a chair closer and across from Kate, she placed her drink on the nearest table and seated herself, crossing her legs with an easy, sensual grace so customary that Kate had to suppress what would have been a visible wince of pain. Aimee had always been a fascinating blend of assertiveness and sentience, with an innate femininity that was not femme, a touch of androgyny in the sculpted planes of her face. Those long, graceful legs draped in the fabric of her camel-colored pants, those hands clasped in her lap, those long, slender fingers… That graceful neck within the cream-colored silk shirt, the open collar revealing flashes of a thin gold chain, its opal pendant between delicate collarbones…

Finally settled in the chair, Aimee continued, "Right now we have two big cases with the Court of Appeal in Sacramento, both of them civil rights. Nothing but infuriating, frustrating, depressing." She shook her head, currents of silvery hair parting with the movement. "It's not just people with no scruples— they're always a given. It's people entrenched in certainty. We present evidence up to the ceiling about what they're doing to harm other people, they dig up some expert-for-hire to contend the opposite. Even when some of these people agree that maybe changes are needed for how we live with each other, they say okay, but just not today. Or, not on my turf. Or, okay, let's change things, but only this teeny tiny little bit. It's not just corporations fighting regulations, Kate. It's people who'll stop at nothing to hang onto the world they know even when they know goddamn well they're setting it on fire. I swear, if we were given proof a comet would hit LA in a month, there'd be people claiming it's just a conspiracy to drive us all out and have people of color come in and take our city. Remember when I thought I might like to be a lawyer?" She erased that with an abrupt swipe of her hand. "Thank God I'm still a paralegal. What I'd tell some of these defendants, some of these boneheads on the bench, I'd be in jail all the time for contempt. Or disbarred."

Kate had been nodding agreement throughout this diatribe. "Remember what Maggie used to say—"

"*'Everything changes, nothing stays the same,'*" Aimee chorused along with her. "Kate, you must be happier than ever to be retired." Then she looked at Kate and winced, sympathy softening her face. "I mean, especially with what's come out about that old case."

Kate had been asked about April Shuster, as she expected, almost as soon as everyone assembled. "It's been twenty years," she'd told the group. "Homicide cases that have direct proof almost never get to court, they're pled out. So it's circumstantial evidence that goes to trial. All the good science that's come in since then, at least we can use science to revisit some of our worst mistakes."

Patton, bless her, had further deflected the topic with her usual bombast: "If the murder of that girl happened today, somebody would have it on film. All the surveillance everywhere, pretty soon they'll be filming every breath we take. One of these days, Kate, nobody will get away with anything and all you cops will be out of a job." And with the group's laughter, some teasing about Kate retiring just in time for Big Brother, that had been the end of the topic.

She told Aimee now, "People hunger for certainty. What I've learned from my life is there's not much certainty anywhere. At least we can go back to the so-called good old days and make what reparations we can."

Picking up her glass of tea, long since warm with the melting of the ice cubes, she looked at the rich brown color and could not prevent the sparking along her nerve endings in an all too familiar craving, wishing to hell it were Cutty Sark, especially right now.

All but slamming down the drink, suddenly losing all patience, she snapped, "So, are you seeing someone?"

Whether Aimee's answering snort of amusement was over the brusqueness of her tone, which Kate instantly regretted, or at the question, she couldn't tell.

"Well, in a way, yes I am," she answered. "A therapist." She picked up her Coke and drank from it.

"Oh." In a confusion of emotion, Kate grabbed her own drink again, just for something to do.

"Oh," Aimee repeated sarcastically. "Just oh? That's all you have to say?"

"You caught me by surprise. I'm glad for you," Kate said hastily. "Hopefully it's helping you as much as Calla's helping me."

Aimee had never been to individual therapy. Couples therapy yes, twice with Kate. Each time to a different therapist of Aimee's choosing, through recommendation by colleagues in the legal field. Each time the series of appointments concluded with Kate's vow to take ownership of her excessive drinking and to be more forthcoming and present in their relationship. Which she had tried and ended up failing to do; she could not sustain abstinence from drinking after some of her worst days on the job, and could not bear to relive or bring herself to inflict the realities of it on this woman she loved. Aimee's commitment had been to develop additional friendships and activities to be less focused on Kate, to be less judgmental. Which she had successfully done.

Aimee said, directly meeting Kate's gaze, "I realized I needed to…to explore a few things. See someone new that neither of us had been to, someone independent of you, just for myself. Frannie at work recommended Susan. I've been seeing her these last seven months."

Kate nodded. That much continuity was indicative, positive. "So she's helped."

"She really has. Helped me look at myself, gain some perspective on where I am in my life. Given how long you and I were together, you can guess our relationship was a main topic."

Kate took a breath. Then a sip of lukewarm tea. "So, what have you…come away with?" She could not look at Aimee.

"That I should think seriously about her advice." Her voice was calm, even. "That at this point we both should get on with what's left of our lives."

After a time, into a vast, echoing silence, Kate met Aimee's gaze but treaded carefully: "This is what you wanted to tell me today? That you're thinking about it?"

"No. She gave me this recommendation a month ago and we've spent the time since then working through it. I need to tell you I've given it a lot of thought, Kate. I know you're not drinking. And no, there isn't anyone else for me but that doesn't matter." She took a visible, audible breath. "I don't want us to try again. I want…I *need* to get on with my own life."

"I'm in a much better place than I was," Kate managed to protest. Then, seeing Aimee's stiffening face, she added flatly, "But it's your choice."

"Yes. It is. One of the things I've come to know is, this time it has to be my choice whether we try again. Not yours again. One of the insights Susan finally had me see is that in all our time together I abdicated a role I should have kept. Some of it was because I'm so much younger than you, I felt in some ways inferior and thought maybe you knew better. But even so I conceded too much of myself for what I thought you needed. Our life together was on your terms. I didn't ask for what I needed."

"You did ask," Kate pointed out, shaking her head. "So many times, you asked."

"Asking wasn't enough. Insisting is what I needed to do."

Kate said softly, "In those days I don't know that I would have been able to give it to you. Had you…insisted."

Aimee nodded. "I get that. But I should have given you…not exactly an ultimatum but more like a line in the sand about how invested we were in each other. Something more like a visible crossroads. Where we both would have had a clear path to stay or leave, you see, to really question where we were. Instead of things deteriorating like they did. At least I could have held onto more of myself."

"Aimee, it was all my fault—"

"Don't go there," she interrupted, a sharp command. "Don't. Your days as a cop—they were the worst. I knew it. Damn it, Kate, I knew it and I should have helped you. I should never have stepped aside, let you carry it all by yourself. I should have insisted, demanded you let me help you any way I could."

If only I could have let you in…Was it even ever possible…

As she was still in this thought, Aimee said, "Kate…I've always wondered…about Anne."

"Anne?" she queried in astonishment.

"Yes. Anne. Along with everything else, Susan helped me understand the grief you carried alone—all your years together, and back then you couldn't share that loss with anyone. *Anyone.* You did talk about her over the years, this and that, but never what you went through all by yourself when she died."

"I couldn't," Kate said in a thick voice. "I couldn't bear to think about it, much less…"

"I really get that now," Aimee said softly. "Here's a question I came here today to ask: would Anne have let you go down that solitary road you've been on the whole time we were together?"

No. She's the love of my life. I'd have done anything she asked. I would sell my soul for one more day with her.

She looked away from Aimee. "I…don't know," she said. "I have to think about it."

Aimee, who had been watching her, smiled and waved a hand. "That's good enough. It's a good enough answer."

Numbly, Kate understood that it was. Her non-answer had been an answer.

"Are you okay here?" Aimee asked, sitting back and glancing around the room. "Any notion about coming back to the city?"

Kate shook her head. "I like it out here. I've got a dog, a border collie, her name is Dakota—"

"A dog? Not a cat? You have a *dog?*" Aimee added with a laugh, "Now I know you've really changed! So where is she?"

"With a neighbor for the day." Smiling, she gestured toward Pilar's house. "Things are okay for me here. I have an AA sponsor in Joshua Tree. Meetings I go to. Some new friendships."

Aimee smiled back at her. "You do seem to fit in, you seem comfortable, easier in your skin here. This solid no-frills house, it suits you, Kate."

"And I'm really glad you've got the condo."

Aimee simply nodded, and Kate took note that she had finally abandoned her previous and constant protestations that deeding a rapidly appreciating West Hollywood condo to her was far too generous a division of their possessions. To Kate, all that mattered was that she herself believed it to be eminently fair, and obviously therapist Susan had helped Aimee to see that perspective as well.

In the quiet between them, Kate surveyed herself as if from a cloud. Her shoulders had eased back, her spine relaxing, and with an almost buttery sensation pervading more and more of her body, she realized how much tension had gathered within her. Not just in these last few minutes. For months. And years.

She felt released. She felt sad.

She felt free.

"I'm so very grateful for you," Kate said. "For all our time together. You're a gift I never deserved."

Aimee shook her head as if recognizing the futility of arguing with this. She said, her voice tearful, "I think you know I'll always love you."

Tears moistening her eyes, Kate could only nod. There had been years and years of being happy together. Aimee too was a love of her life. They were the major presences in each other's lives, and even though too much that was irretrievable had now passed during their time together, these were facts she needed to keep uppermost whenever she went to that place of accusing herself of wasting Aimee's life.

Aimee leaned forward and, spotting where she had stashed her purse when she arrived, rose from her chair. "I know that whole cliché about people in our situation saying we should remain friends and they really don't mean it. I really, truly mean it. I'd like to see you as often as we can, maybe when you come in to see Calla, we can have dinner or something. Once we both get on with our lives. We've had so much good together..."

"We have. I'd like that, and I mean it too."

At the door, Aimee turned to her to ask with a smile, "So who was the Egyptian queen Rainey brought with her? I saw the way she kept looking at you."

Kate smiled back. "Somebody from the dark distant past. Before you."

"So, yet another secret. I have a feeling you haven't seen the last of her." Aimee's smile widened. "How do I know this? Because you collect women whose first name starts with A. Anne, Aimee, Andrea."

Kate laughed, and it felt good. "I'll tell you all about her next time I see you. Lots of other stuff too."

Aimee reached for her. "Promise?"

"Promise."

Kate took her into her arms for a farewell hug.

19

"Well, I have to say your little shindig was pretty raucous," Pilar said to Kate. "But good fun hearing that old-time music, how happy you all sounded together."

They were outdoors and wore hooded sweatshirts against the evening chill, watching Dakota roam between their two houses in search of a suitable spot for her offerings. When Kate didn't, couldn't answer because her throat had closed up in her distress, Pilar turned to her, frowning at what she saw in Kate's face. She put a hand on her arm. "You look like the world's come to an end."

It has, Kate thought dully. Her loving final moments with Aimee had dissipated with the departure of Aimee's car, had boomeranged into anguished depression. She managed to utter, "These visits down memory lane…"

Pilar snorted, squeezed her arm, released it. "Tell me about it. Memory lane's the shortcut to hell."

Yes it is, and so what the hell, Kate thought. Why not tell her. Why not.

But her tremulous voice betrayed the defiance of her thoughts as she confessed: "The woman I've been with and loved for twenty-three years—we just broke up for good."

Pilar, shocked, disconcerted, stared at her with comically widened eyes, then gestured toward the road. "The one who just left? You did? But you're *here*, you've been by yourself..." She sputtered, out of words, shaking her head.

"We were separated. It's been months. We've been off and on, on and off for quite a while."

"Sounds to me, Kate," Pilar offered slowly, "like the two of you have been in a dress rehearsal and finally opened on Broadway."

For one performance only. "Yeah, I guess you could put it that way."

Pilar took Kate's arm again, this time steering her into the space between their houses. "Let's go sit on that back porch of yours awhile. Let Dakota run a bit more. Besides, I've given you so much of my history, you owe me at least some of yours."

Kate allowed herself to be led; she welcomed, was grateful for the company.

For the next hour or so, gazing out at a starlit sky in majestic splendor over an ink black world, backlit by the light from her house, with Dakota lying at her feet, she talked and talked and freely answered questions about her years with Aimee, her parents and Michigan origins, her military life, her police life.

"It's so true what they say," Pilar reflected. "Every life is a novel. Yours is quite a tale."

"And yours is amazing," Kate returned with a smile. Her revelations, she realized, had been more soul-easing for her than a bottle of Cutty Sark.

Calla will give me a gold star for this, she thought. *For finally trusting someone enough to let go of...of what? Of myself.*

Her eyes filled with tears of gratitude for Calla, for the years of leading her so patiently—and sometimes so impatiently, she amended with affection—to this insight.

Then she gazed at the woman sitting quietly beside her in the darkness. Maybe she could learn to trust her with even more of her secrets. With more of herself.

"You know how nosy I am—" Pilar began.

"You? Nosy?" Kate teased.

"Hey, woman, this time your back door was wide open and I couldn't help but hear when I was out with Dakota. So I know you're a hospice volunteer and you have a transgender nephew."

Kate nodded. "I'll ask Dylan and his girlfriend to come out for a visit and you'll meet him. He's a great kid, you'll love him. As for my hospice work—it's maybe the best thing I've ever done."

"I was thinking maybe…" Pilar continued with an impish grin, "Well, I have lots of experience being on death row, so I was thinking…" Amid Kate's laughter she asked, "What's it take? What would I have to do?"

"You listen," Kate answered. "You just listen, bear witness. You'll get some good training but honestly, you mostly listen."

Pilar nodded dubiously, and Kate said, "I think you'd be wonderful. I'd be glad to introduce you to the program."

"I'll give it more thought. But right now I think I just might like to do it." Pilar got up from her Adirondack chair, stretched her hands high above her head, bent backward. "I'm beat. How about we three go into Joshua Tree for lunch tomorrow at a dog-friendly place?"

"Can't do lunch. How about dinner? With all that's been going on, I didn't tell you more about my visitor in that candy apple-red Mercedes. I tracked down Natalie Rostow and gave her the quarter million bucks."

"You *what*? You did *what*?"

"Yeah, I'll tell you more over dinner tomorrow," Kate said, grinning at Pilar's reaction. "I'm going to Desert Hot Springs tomorrow to visit her again, have lunch."

Pilar whistled. "Jesus, you really are a living, walking novel. And this Natalie, there's a woman whose life is for sure a wham bang story."

You have no idea, Kate thought. "She's promised to fill me in on lots of lesbian history she believes I should be embarrassed not knowing. I'll ask her here. Maybe you'd like to meet her."

"Who I'd like to meet is the Black woman in the caftan that came to your party. Talk about killer gorgeous!"

"Pilar," Kate teased, "are you trying to tell me something?"

"Maybe," Pilar said, with a Cheshire cat grin that faded in the darkness as she strode off the porch. "Tomorrow's a new day—and anything's possible."

"Yes," Kate said, taking Dakota's collar and leading her toward the warmth of their home. "Anything is possible."

Acknowledgments

Over the ten Kate Delafield mysteries, I've expressed appreciation in each of them to those whose input and advice made the books truer, richer, better. Topping that list for much of the way has been my loving companion of the last three decades, Jo Hercus. Her years as a hospice volunteer brought authenticity to key scenes in this book and the previous one, *High Desert*. Her wisdom and experience as a psychotherapist have infused vital aspects of my stories, especially the concept and development of Calla Dearborn. Any novelist should be lucky enough to have a resident Google search engine like Jo, along with all those other attributes so necessary in a spouse of a strange creature like a writer. Foremost would be her patience, her forbearance each time I departed the planet, absorbed into the lives and worlds of my fictional characters. Jo, my love to you, and my gratitude.

Kate began life amid the Third Street Writers Group in Los Angeles, with midwives Montserrat Fontes, Janet Gregory, Gerald Citrin, Jeff McMahon, Karen Sandler, Naomi Sloan, all of them acknowledged in those early books. Gerry, Naomi and Jeff—gone now, but never forgotten. Monsy, spiritual leader of our gang, has continued as an advisor all these years on all my books, and many thanks go to her and to her Gillis, another saintly partner to a writer. What grand memories we three share from those exhilarating good old days.

My love and my gratitude, beyond calculation, beyond adequate words, to Sheila. For the unwavering belief in me from the very earliest days that I could succeed as a writer. For everything I have ever achieved with my books since then, she made it all possible.

My very special appreciation goes to these advisors for their constancy over the years:

My brilliant writer-brother and dearest friend, Michael Nava.

Cath Walker, for an eagle editor's eye and sharp mind that prevented many a transgression from wending its way into print. In plain English, I owe thanks for saving my ass. So many times.

Elaine Wolter. Not only for what she contributed to my portrait of transgender Dylan Harrison, but also for the person she is, the mother of every LGBT child's dreams. My wish for our next generations of gay, lesbian, bisexual and transgender children is that they be fortunate enough to have so nurturing, loving, and accepting a parent as Elaine.

Retired Sergeant Mitchell Grobeson, for all he did to transform LAPD with the pioneering lawsuit that advanced our civil rights, for all he added to my understanding of this complex paramilitary organization.

Jason, for the police professionalism and integrity she added to those early books.

Retired Detective Supervisor Mary F. Otterson for her essential input and validation, for her personal example during the most formative stages of Kate Delafield.

These many years later I remain grateful to Louise of the United States Marine Corps, for everything she contributed to my understanding of Kate's closeted tenure in the Corps and her year in Vietnam.

Natalee Rosenstein, editor in chief at Berkley Books, for her shepherding of four of the books, for always sterling editorial advice.

Agent extraordinaire Charlotte Sheedy, with admiration and gratitude for her pioneering presence beginning with her agenting of legendary Isabel Miller's *Patience and Sarah*, and for the years I was fortunate to spend under her wing.

On this present book, I'm especially thankful for the advice and essential contributions from Claire McNab and Sheila Jefferson, for those Sunday afternoons in their living room amid my own little writers' group as Jo read aloud from the earliest of drafts.

Thank you again for the valuable input from Michael Nava, Cath Walker. Thank you to Lin Phillippi and Kerrie Terry, KG MacGregor, Barbara Wilson.

My many thanks go to Medora MacDougall for the valuable, top-notch editing on this novel and *High Desert*.

Introduction to Sally

Elizabeth von Arnim

First published in 1926

This edition published in 2023 by
The British Library
96 Euston Road
London NW1 2DB

Preface copyright © 2023 Alison Bailey
Afterword copyright © 2023 Simon Thomas

Cataloguing in Publication Data
A catalogue record for this publication is available from the British Library

ISBN 978 0 7123 5474 5
e-ISBN 978 0 7123 6886 5

Text design and typesetting by JCS Publishing Services Ltd
Printed and bound by CPI Group (UK), Croydon, CR0 4YY

Contents

❁

The 1920s

✦

- **1921:** According to the 1921 census, there are approximately 1.7 million more women than men in the UK.

- Unemployment rates in the UK remain above 10 per cent throughout the 1920s, with a peak of 23.4 per cent in May 1921.

- **1923:** The Matrimonial Causes Act makes adultery by either husband or wife acceptable as the sole ground for divorce.

- **1926:** *Introduction to Sally* is published.

- **1927:** *The Jazz Singer*, the first feature-length 'talkie', is released, effectively marking the end of the silent film era.

- **1928 (July):** The Representation of the People (Equal Franchise) Act 1928 extends eligibility to vote so that women over 21 can participate, achieving electoral equality with men.

- About 30 per cent of the population regularly goes to church throughout the 1920s, rising through the period, though declining in the 1930s.

- **1929:** When famous actress Mary Pickford cuts her long curls into a bob, it makes the front page of the *New York Times*.

❀ ❀ ❀

Elizabeth von Arnim
(1866–1941)

❀

The author now known as Elizabeth von Arnim was born Mary
Annette Beauchamp in Australia in 1866, and moved with her family
to England when she was three years old. Her cousin, born more than
twenty years later, was the renowned New Zealand short-story writer
Katherine Mansfield, whose real name was Kathleen Beauchamp.

The name 'Elizabeth von Arnim' was never used during the author's
lifetime. Her works appeared as being 'By the author of Elizabeth
and Her German Garden', which was her first, very successful novel
in 1898. Later her books appeared as being by 'Elizabeth' (inverted
commas included) and only when she was republished in the 1980s was
she given the name by which she is best known now, Elizabeth von
Arnim.

The surname came from her first husband, Count Henning August
von Arnim-Schlagenthin, making her a countess. They lived in Berlin,
and it was here that she wrote her heavily autobiographical first novel,
which led many of her readers to believe she was German. The couple
had five children, but in 1908 Arnim left her husband, whom she
referred to as the 'Man of Wrath'. He died a couple of years later, and in
1916 she married Frank Russell, the brother of the philosopher Bertrand
Russell. As he was Earl Russell, her second marriage also entitled her
to use the title Countess. This marriage was equally unhappy, and the

couple separated in 1919. She would use the marriage as the basis for her 1921 novel *Vera*.

For more than four decades, Arnim wrote comedies, tragedies and tragicomedies with equal skill. She died of influenza on 9 February 1941, aged 74, and is buried in Maryland having moved to the US at the outbreak of the Second World War.

She is now perhaps best remembered for the poignant and touching novel *The Enchanted April*. The Women Writers series has previously reissued *Father* (1931), and readers will find a similar combination of comedy and more serious considerations in *Introduction to Sally*.

Preface

Sally, or rather Salvatia, the long-awaited and much-wanted daughter of Mr and Mrs Pinner, is the flame-haired and seemingly golden-hearted centre of our story – yet she remains a somewhat enigmatic figure. Rarely allowed to express her own views, she is the beautiful canvas onto which everyone she meets (especially if they are male) projects their desires and expectations. In the manner of a fairy-tale character she is hidden away because of her entrancing beauty which creates mayhem and for which she feels she must apologise. Portrayed as an innocent – sweetly and politely acquiescent to the bidding of all – she is nevertheless the unwitting and bewildered cause of possessive (even obsessive) behaviour and distress. In her encounters with others she is objectivised, used and treated almost as a plaything. Love is anything but selfless here.

Throughout the book von Arnim explores the nature of social class and the pervasive assumptions based on verbal and societal indicators including the role of formal education and learning. It is the exploration of these small gradations of class and the specific reference to the servant problem that are perhaps the most obvious indicators of the 1920s setting. The reader is asked to consider both what we value about ourselves and how we measure the value of others. Like Sally's husband we might wish to reject the charge of snobbery – despite behaviour to the contrary.

In the telling von Arnim also reflects upon the institution of

❀ ❀ ❀

marriage and considers the significance and power of feelings and emotional responses. Yet all is delivered with a rather mordant wit and a satirical eye for the absurd. Moreover, the author makes it clear that this is merely an introduction to Sally and that her life holds much more. For the reader, who might feel complicit in the focus on Sally's physical beauty, this is a note of optimism for the future, as Sally gradually takes action and asserts her will.

Alison Bailey
Lead Curator Printed Heritage Collection 1901–2000
British Library

❀ ❀ ❀

Publisher's Note

❀

The original novels reprinted in the British Library Women Writers series were written and published in a period ranging, for the most part, from the 1910s to the 1950s. There are many elements of these stories which continue to entertain modern readers, however in some cases there are also uses of language, instances of stereotyping and some attitudes expressed by narrators or characters which may not be endorsed by the publishing standards of today. We acknowledge therefore that some elements in the stories selected for reprinting may continue to make uncomfortable reading for some of our audience. With this series, British Library Publishing aims to offer a new readership a chance to read some of the rare books of the British Library's collections in an affordable paperback format, to enjoy their merits and to look back into the world of the twentieth century as portrayed by their writers. It is not possible to separate these stories from the history of their writing and the following novel is presented as it was originally published. We welcome feedback from our readers, which can be sent to the following address:

British Library Publishing
The British Library
96 Euston Road
London, NW1 2DB
United Kingdom

Introduction
to Sally

❀

I

❁

Mr. Pinner was a God-fearing man, who was afraid of everything except respectability. He married Mrs. Pinner when they were both twenty, and by the time they were both thirty if he had had to do it again he wouldn't have. For Mrs. Pinner had several drawbacks. One was, she quarrelled; and Mr. Pinner, who prized peace, was obliged to quarrel too. Another was, she appeared to be unable to have children; and Mr. Pinner, who was fond of children, accordingly couldn't have them either. And another, which while it lasted was in some ways the worst, was that she was excessively pretty.

This was most awkward in a shop. It continually put Mr. Pinner in false positions. And it seemed to go on so long. There seemed to be no end to the years of Mrs. Pinner's prettiness. They did end, however; and when she was about thirty-five, worn out by her own unquiet spirit and the work of helping Mr. Pinner in the shop, as well as keeping house for him, which included doing everything single-handed, by God's mercy she at last began to fade.

Mr. Pinner was pleased. For though her behaviour had been beyond criticism, and she had invariably, by a system of bridling and head-tossing, kept off familiarity on the part of male customers, still those customers had undoubtedly been more numerous than the others, and Mr. Pinner hadn't liked it. It was highly unnatural, he knew, for gentlemen on their way home from their offices to wish to buy rice, for instance, when it had been bought earlier in the day by their wives or mothers. There was something underhand about it; and he, who being timid was also honest, found himself not able to be happy if there were a shadow of doubt in his mind as to the honourableness of any of his transactions. He never got used to these purchases, and was glad when the gradual disappearance of

his wife's beauty caused the gradual disappearance of the customers who made them. Money, it was true, was lost, but he preferred to lose it than to make it by means that verged in his opinion on shady.

As Mrs. Pinner faded and custom dropped off, he and she had more time on their hands, and went to bed earlier; for Mrs. Pinner, who had an untiring tongue when she was awake, and inveigled her husband into many quarrels, was obliged to leave off talking when she was asleep, and he, pretending it was because of the gas bills, got her to go to bed earlier and earlier. Besides, he wished more heartily than ever that she might have a child, if only to take her attention off him. But he longed for a child himself as well, for he was affectionate without passion, and it was his secret opinion—all his opinions were secret, because if he let them out Mrs. Pinner quarrelled—that such men are born good fathers. Something, however, had to be born besides themselves before they could show their capabilities, and Mrs. Pinner, who was passionate without affection, which in Mr. Pinner's opinion was rather shocking, for she sometimes quite frightened him in bed, and he was sure it wasn't at all respectable for a wife to do that, especially as next day she didn't seem to like him any better than before, hadn't been able to produce what was needed.

Certain it was that he couldn't become a father without her. In this one thing he depended utterly on her; for though she believed she ruled him through and through, in every other matter at the back of his soul Mr. Pinner always secretly managed very well for himself. But here he was helpless. If she didn't, he couldn't. Nothing doing at all without Mrs. Pinner.

Therefore, as a first step, every evening at nine o'clock, instead of at eleven or twelve as had been their habit in the busy, tiring years, after a day of only too much leisure they went to bed. There they tossed, because of its being so early; or, rather, Mrs. Pinner tossed, while he lay quiet, such being his nature. And whether it was these regular hours, or whether it was God, who favours families, at last taking pity on the Pinners, just as Mr. Pinner was coming to the conclusion that he had best perhaps now let well alone, for he and his wife were drawing near forty, Mrs. Pinner inexplicably began to do that which she ought to have done twenty years

earlier, and proceeded to go through those bodily changes, one after the other and all strictly according to precedent, which were bound to end, though for many months Mr. Pinner didn't believe it, in either a boy or a girl; or perhaps—this was his secret longing—in both.

They ended in one girl.

'I'm blest,' said Mr. Pinner to himself, seeing his wife's complete, impassioned absorption, 'if that kid ain't goin' to be my salvation.'

And he wanted to have it christened Salvation, but Mrs. Pinner objected, because it wasn't a girl's name at all, she said; and, as she had no heart just then for quarrelling, they compromised on Salvatia.

❁

Thus was Salvatia projected into the world, who afterwards became Sally. Her parents struggled against her being called Sally, because they thought it common. Their struggles, however, were vain. People were unteachable. And the child herself, from the moment she could talk, persisted in saying she was Sally.

She grew up so amazingly pretty that it soon became the Pinners' chief concern how best to hide her. Such beauty, which began by being their pride, quickly became their anxiety. By the time Sally was twelve they were always hiding her. She was quite easy to hide, for she went meekly where she was told and stayed there, having not only inherited her father's mild goodness, but also, partly from him and more from some unknown forbear, for she had much more of it than Mr. Pinner at his most obliging, a great desire to give satisfaction and do what was asked of her. She had none of that artfulness of the weak that was so marked a feature of Mr. Pinner. She never was different at the back of her mind from what she was on the surface of her behaviour. Life hadn't yet forced her, as it had forced Mr. Pinner, to be secretive; it hadn't had time. Besides, said Mr. Pinner to himself, she wasn't married.

From her mother she had inherited nothing but her looks; translating, however, the darkness into fairness, and the prettiness into beauty,— beauty authentic, indisputable, apparent to the most unobservant. Mr.

Pinner was divided between pride and fear. Mrs. Pinner concentrated entirely on her child, and was the best of prudent mothers. There, in their back parlour, they kept this secret treasure, and, like other treasures, its possession produced anxiety as well as joy. Till she was about twelve she did as other children, and went off to school by herself every day, illuminating Islington, as she passed along its streets, like a flame. Then the Pinners got a fright: she was followed. Not once or twice, but several times; and came home one day happy, her hands full of chocolates she said a gentleman had given her.

The Pinners began to hide her. Mrs. Pinner took her to school and fetched her away again every day, and in between hid her in the back parlour. Mr. Pinner did Mrs. Pinner's work as well as his own while she was gone, and just managed to because his wife was fleet of foot and ran most of the way; otherwise it would have broken his back, for he wasn't able to afford to keep an assistant, and had little staying power. At night, when the dear object of their love and fear was asleep, they earnestly in bed discussed what was best to be done so as to secure to her the greatest happiness together with the greatest safety. Their common care and love had harmonised them. In the child they were completely at one. No longer did Mrs. Pinner rail, and Mr. Pinner, after a time, be obliged to answer back; no longer was he forced, contrary to his nature, into quarrels. Peace prevailed, and the affection that comes from a common absorbing interest.

'It's all that there Sally,' said Mr. Pinner, content at last in his married life, and unable—for he had few words—to put what he felt more glowingly.

❁

But when Sally was sixteen Mrs. Pinner died; died in a few days, of a cold no worse than dozens of colds she had caught in her life and hadn't died of.

Mr. Pinner was left with no one to help him, either in his shop or with Sally. It was an immense misfortune. He didn't know which way to turn.

He lived within the narrowest margin of safety, for in Islington there were many grocers, and he was one of the very smallest, never having had any ambition beyond the ambition for peace and enough to eat.

It was impossible for him to run the shop without help, and without the shop he and Sally would starve, so there was nothing for it but to let her take her mother's place; and within a week his custom was doubled, and went on doubling and doubling till the local supply of males was exhausted.

It was a repetition of twenty years earlier, only much worse. Mr. Pinner was most unhappy. Sally couldn't help smiling back when anybody smiled at her,—it was her nature; and as everybody, the minute they saw her, did smile, she was in a continual condition of radiance, and the shop seemed full of light. Mr. Pinner was distracted. He hired an assistant, having made money, announced that his daughter had gone away to boarding-school, and hid her in the back parlour. The custom dropped off, and the assistant had to go. Out came Sally again, and back came the custom. What a situation, thought Mr. Pinner, irritable and perspiring. He was worn out keeping his eye on Sally, and weighing out coffee and bacon at the same time. His responsibilities crushed him. The only solution of his difficulties would be to get the girl married to some steady fellow able to take care of her. There seemed to him to be no steady fellows in the crowd in his shop, except the ones who were already married, and they couldn't really be steady or they wouldn't be there. How could a married man be called steady who eagerly waited for Sally to sell him groceries he would only afterwards have to conceal from his wife? While as for the rest, they were a weedy lot of overworked and underpaid young clerks who couldn't possibly afford to marry. Sally smiled at them all. She had none of the bridling, of the keep-off-the-grass-*if*-you-please, of her mother.

'For mercy's sake,' Mr. Pinner would hiss in her ear, tugging her elbow as he hurried past, 'don't go keepin' on makin' pleasant faces at 'em like that.'

But what faces was she to make, then? All Sally's faces were pleasant from the point of view of the beholder, whatever sort she made; and if she, by a great effort, and contrary to her nature, frowned at anybody, as likely

as not she would be gaped at harder than ever, and asked if she wouldn't mind doing that again.

Mr. Pinner was distracted. Even the clergy came to his shop,—came with breezy tales of being henpecked, and driven out by tyrant wives to purchase currants; and even the doctor came,—old enough surely, Mr. Pinner thought, to be ashamed of himself, running after a girl he had himself brought into the world, and pretending that what he was after was biscuits.

What he was after was, very plainly, not biscuits, nor were the clergy after currants. One and all were after Sally. And it horrified Mr. Pinner, who took round the plate on Sundays, that a child of his, so good and modest, should be the innocent cause of producing in the hearts of her fellow-creatures a desire to sin. That they desired to sin was only too evident to Mr. Pinner, driven by fear to the basest suspicions. These married gentlemen—what could it be but sin they had in their minds? They wished to sin with Sally, to sin the sin of sins; with his Sally, his spotless lamb, a child of God, an inheritor of the kingdom of heaven.

For a year Mr. Pinner endured it, struggling with his responsibilities and his black suspicions. The milk of his natural kindliness and respect for his betters went sour. He grew to hate the gentry. His face took on a twist of fear that became permanent. The other grocers were furious with him, accusing him among themselves of using his daughter as a decoy; and unable to bear this, for it of course got round to him, and worn out by the constant dread lest worse were yet to come, and some fine day a young whipper-snapper of a lord should be going for a walk in Islington and chance to stroll into his shop and see Sally, and then good-bye to virtue—for was any girl good enough and modest enough to stand out against the onslaughts of a lord? Mr. Pinner asked himself, who had never consciously come across any lords, and therefore was apt to think of them highly—Mr. Pinner determined to move.

He moved. After several Sundays given up to fruitless and ill-organised excursions into other suburbs, he heard by chance of a village buried far away in what seemed to him, whose England consisted of Hampstead Heath, Hampton Court, and, once, Southend, a savage and uninhabited

district in Cambridgeshire, where the man who kept its one shop was weary of solitude, and wanted to come nearer London. What could be nearer London than London itself? Mr. Pinner hurried to Woodles, leaving Sally under the strictest vows not to put her terribly complicating nose out of doors.

He thought he had never seen such a place. Used to streets and crowds, he couldn't have believed there were spots in the world so empty. It was raining, and there wasn't a soul about. A few cottages, the shop, a church and vicarage, and a sad wet pig grunting along a ditch,—that was all. Three miles from a branch-line station, embedded in a network of muddy lanes, and the Vicar—Mr. Pinner inquired—seventy-eight with no sons, Woodles was surely the ideal place for him and Sally. Over a bottle of ginger beer he made friends with the shopkeeper, and arranged that he should come up to Islington with a view to exchanging. He came; and the exchange, after some regrettable incidents in connection with Sally which very nearly upset the whole thing, was made, and by Christmas Islington knew the Pinners no more.

❁

All went well at Woodles for the first few weeks. It was a hamlet, Mr. Pinner rejoiced to discover, lived in practically exclusively by ladies. These ladies, attracted to it by the tumbledownness of its cottages, which made it both picturesque and cheap, had either never had husbands or had lost them, and accordingly, as so often happens in such circumstances, were poor. Well, Mr. Pinner didn't mind that. He only wanted to live. He had no desire to make more than was just necessary to feed Sally. More merely meant responsibility and bother, and of those he had as much as he could do with because of Sally. He settled down, very content and safe among his widow and virgin customers, and spent a thankful Christmas, entering with hope into the New Year.

Then, one day towards the end of January, two young men rent the peace of the sunny afternoon with the unpleasant noise motor-bicycles, rushing at high speed, appear, Mr. Pinner thought, kindly even towards

these, not to be able to help making, and a lady customer who chanced to be in the shop remarked, 'It has begun.'

Mr. Pinner inquired politely what had begun, and the lady said term had, and Mr. Pinner, who didn't know what she meant but was unwilling to show his ignorance, said, 'And high time too.'

After that, hardly an afternoon went by without young men hurrying through Woodles. Sometimes they were on motor-bicycles, sometimes they were on horses, sometimes they were in cars, but always they hurried. Where did they all come from? Mr. Pinner was astonished, and wondered uneasily whether Sally were not somehow at the bottom of it. But she couldn't have been, for they never so much as glanced at the shop window, from behind whose jars of bulls'-eyes and mounds of toffee he and Sally secretly observed them.

Then, gradually, he became aware of Cambridge. He hadn't given it a thought when he came to Woodles. It was ten miles away—a place, he knew, where toffs were taught, but a place ten miles away hadn't worried him. There he had changed, on that first visit, for the branch-line that took him within three miles of Woodles, and the village, asleep beneath its blanket of rain, had been entirely deserted, the last word in dank and misty isolation. And when he moved in, it was still asleep—asleep, this time, in the silence of the Christmas vacation, and only faintly stirred every now and again by the feeble movements of unmated ladies. It was so much out of the way that if it hadn't been for Cambridge it would have slept for ever. But young men are restless and get everywhere. Bursting with energy, they rushed through Woodles as they rushed through all places within rushable distance. But they rushed, they didn't stop; and Mr. Pinner consoled himself with that, and also with the knowledge he presently acquired that it was only for a few months—weeks, one might almost say, in the year, that this happened.

He bade Sally keep indoors during the afternoon hours, and hoped for the best.

❀

– 10 –

Then, on a gusty afternoon in early March, when the mud in the lanes had turned to dust and was tearing in clouds down the street, the door opened violently, because of the wind, and a young man was blown in, and had to use all his strength to get the door shut again.

No sound of a motor had preceded him; he appeared just as one of the ladies might have appeared; and Sally was in the shop.

She was on some steps, rummaging aloft among the tins of Huntley and Palmer, and he didn't immediately see her, and addressed himself to Mr. Pinner.

'Have you any petrol?' he asked.

'No, sir,' said Mr. Pinner quickly, hoping he would go away at once without noticing Sally. 'We don't keep it.'

'Do you know where I can—'

The young man broke off, and stood staring upwards. 'Christ'—he whispered under his breath, 'Christ—'

'Now, now,' said Mr. Pinner with extreme irritability, only too well aware of what had happened, and in his fear slapping his knuckly little hand on the counter, 'no blasphemy 'ere, sir, if *you* please—'

But he needn't have been so angry and frightened, for this, if he had only known it, was his future son-in-law; the person who was to solve all his problems by taking over the responsibility of Sally. In a word it was, as Mr. Pinner ever afterwards described him, Mr. Luke.

II

At the date when he went into the shop at Woodles in search of petrol, young Luke, whose Christian name was Jocelyn, was a youth of parts, with an inventive and inquiring brain, and a thirst some of his friends at Ananias were unable to account for after knowledge. His bent was scientific; his tastes were chemical. He wished to weigh and compare, to experiment and prove. For this a quiet, undisturbed life was necessary, in which day after day he could work steadily and without interruption. What he had hoped for was to get a fellowship at Ananias. Instead, he got Sally.

It was clear to Jocelyn, considering his case later, that the matter with him at this time was youth. Nature had her eye on him. However much he wished to use his brains, and devote himself to the pursuit of scientific truth, she wished to use the rest of him, and she did. He had been proof against every other temptation she had plied him with, but he wasn't proof against Sally; and all the things he had thought, and hoped, and been interested in up to then, seemed, directly he saw Sally, dross. A fever of desire to secure this marvel before any one else discovered her sent him almost out of his mind. He was scorched by passion, racked by fear. He knew he was no good at all from the marriage point of view, for he had no money hardly, and was certain he would be refused, and then—what then?

He need not have been afraid. At the word marriage Mr. Pinner, who had been snarling at him on his visits like an old dog who has been hurt and suspects everybody, nearly fell on his neck. Sally was in the back parlour. He had sent her there at once every time young Luke appeared in the shop, and then faced the young man defiantly, leaning with both hands on the counter, looking up at him with all his weak little bristles on end, and inquiring of him angrily, 'Now what can I do for you to-*day*, sir?'

At the end of a week of this, Jocelyn, wild with fear lest the other inhabitants of the colleges of Cambridge, so perilously close for cars and bicycles, should discover and carry the girl off before he did, proposed through Mr. Pinner.

'I want to marry your daughter,' he stammered, his tongue dry, his eyes burning. 'I must see her. I must talk—just to find out if she thinks she wouldn't mind. It's absurd, simply absurd, never to let me say a word to her—'

And Mr. Pinner, instead of pushing him out of the shop as Jocelyn, knowing his own poverty, expected, nearly fell on his neck.

'Marry her? You did say marry, didn't you, sir?' he said in a trembling voice, flushing right up to his worried, kind blue eyes.

He could scarcely believe that he heard right. This young gentleman—a car, and all—nothing against him as far as he could see, and he hoped he could see as far as most people, except his youth. ... But if he hadn't been so young he mightn't so badly have wanted to marry Sally, Mr. Pinner told himself, his eyes, now full of respect and awe, on the eager face of the suitor, for from experience he knew that everybody had wanted to do something badly with Sally, but it had hardly ever been marriage.

'If your intentions is honourable—' began Mr. Pinner.

'Honourable! Good God. As though—'

'Now, now, sir,' interrupted Mr. Pinner gently, holding up a deprecating hand, 'no need to get swearing. No need at *all*.'

'No, no—of course not. I beg your pardon. But I must see her—I must be able to talk to her—'

'Exactly, sir. Step inside,' said Mr. Pinner, opening the door to the back room.

❁

There sat Sally, mending in the lamplight.

'We got a visitor,' said Mr. Pinner, excited and proud. 'But I'm blest, sir,' he added, turning to Jocelyn, 'if I knows what to call you.'

'Luke—Jocelyn Luke,' murmured the young man as one in a dream, his eyes on Sally.

'Mr. Luke,' introduced Mr. Pinner, pleased, for the name smacked agreeably of evangelists. 'And Salvatia is 'er name, ain't it, Salvatia? 'Er baptismal name, any'ow,' he added, because of the way Sally was looking at him. 'Sometimes people calls 'er Sally, but there ain't no *need* to, Mr. Luke—there ain't no *need* to at all, sir. Get another cup, will you, Salvatia?—and let's 'ave our tea.'

And while she was getting the cup out of some back scullery place, wondering at suddenly becoming Salvatia, her father whispered to the suitor, 'You go a'ead, sir, when she come back, and don't mind me.'

Jocelyn didn't mind him, for he forgot him the instant Sally reappeared, but he couldn't go ahead. He sat dumb, gaping. The girl was too exquisite. She was beauty itself. From the top of her little head, with its flame-coloured hair and broad low brow and misty eyes like brown amber, down along the slender lines of her delicate body to where her small feet were thrust into shabby shoes, she was, surely, perfect. He could see no flaw. She seemed to light up the room. It was like, thought young Luke, for the first time in the presence of real beauty, suddenly being shown God. He wanted to cry. His mouth, usually so firmly shut, quivered. He sat dumb. So that it was Mr. Pinner who did what talking there was, for Sally, of the class whose womenfolk do not talk when the father brings in a friend to tea, said nothing.

Her part was to pour out the tea; and this she did gravely, her eyelashes, which just to see was to long to kiss, lying duskily on her serious face. She was serious because the visitor hadn't yet smiled at her, so she hadn't been able to smile back, and Jocelyn accordingly didn't yet know about her smile; and Mr. Pinner, flushed with excitement, afraid it couldn't be really true, sure at the same time that it was, entertained the suitor as best he could, making little jokes intended to put him at his ease and encourage him to go ahead, while at the same time trying to convey to Sally, by frowns and nods, that if she chose to make pleasant faces at this particular young gentleman she had his permission to do so.

The suitor, however, remained silent, and Sally obtuse. Her father had

– 14 –

never behaved like this before, and she had no idea what it was all about. It was hard work for one, like Mr. Pinner, unaccustomed to social situations requiring tact and experience, and he perspired. He was relieved when his daughter cleared away the tea and went off with it into the scullery to wash up, leaving him alone with his young guest, who sat, his head sunk on his breast, following the girl with his eyes till the door was shut on her. Then, turning to her father, his thin face working with agitation, he began to pour out the whole tale of his terrible unworthiness and undesirability.

"'Ere,' said Mr. Pinner, pushing a tin of the best tobacco he stocked towards his upset visitor, 'light up, won't you, sir?'

The young man took no notice of the tobacco, and Mr. Pinner, listening attentively to all he was pouring out, couldn't for the life of him see where the undesirability and unworthiness came in.

'She's a good girl,' said Mr. Pinner, not filling his pipe either, from politeness, 'as good a girl as ever trod this earth. And what I always say is that no good man is unworthy of the goodest girl. That's right, ain't it? Got to be good, of course. Beg pardon, sir, but might I ask—' he sank his voice to a whisper, glancing at the scullery door—'if you're a *good* man, sir? I should say, gentleman. It's a ticklish question to 'ave to ask, I know, sir, but 'er mother would 'ave wished—'

'I don't drink, I don't bet, and I'm not tangled up with any woman,' said Jocelyn. 'I suppose that's what you mean?'

'Then where's all this 'ere undesirable come in?' inquired Mr. Pinner, puzzled.

'I'm poor,' said the suitor briefly.

'Poor. That's bad,' agreed Mr. Pinner, shaking his head and screwing up his mouth. He knew all about being poor. He had had, first and last, his bellyful of that.

And yet on being questioned, as Mr. Pinner felt bound in duty to question, it turned out that the young gentleman was very well off indeed. He had £500 a year certain, whatever he did or didn't do, and to Mr. Pinner, used to counting in pennies, this not only seemed enough to keep a wife and family in comfort, but also in style.

Sally came back, and Mr. Pinner, inspired, lifted a finger, said "Ark,' gave them to understand he heard a customer, without actually saying he did, which would have been a lie, and went away into the shop.

Sally stood there, feeling awkward. Jocelyn had got up directly she came in, and she supposed he was going to wish her a good evening and go; but he didn't. She therefore stood first on one foot and then on the other, and felt awkward.

'Won't you,' Jocelyn breathed, stretching out a hand of trembling entreaty, for he was afraid she might disappear again, 'won't you sit down?'

'Well,' said Sally shyly, 'I don't mind if I do—' And for the first time Jocelyn heard the phrase he was later on to hear so often, uttered in the accent he was to try so hard to purify.

She sat down on the edge of the chair at the other side of the table. She wasn't accustomed to sitting idle and didn't know what to do with her hands, but she was sure it wouldn't be manners to go on mending socks while a gentleman was in the room.

Jocelyn sat down too, the table between them, the light from the oil lamp hanging from the ceiling beating down on Sally's head.

'And Beauty was made flesh, and dwelt among us,' he murmured, his eyes burning.

'Pardon?' said Sally, polite, but wishing her father would come back.

'You lovely thing—you lovely, lovely thing,' whispered Jocelyn hoarsely, his eyes like coals of fire.

At this Sally became thoroughly uneasy, and looked at him in real alarm.

'Don't be frightened. Your father knows. He says I may—'

'Father?' she repeated, much surprised.

'Yes, yes—I asked him. He says I may. He says I may—may talk to you, make friends with you. That is,' stammered Jocelyn, overcome by her loveliness, 'if you'll let me—oh, if you'll let me. ….'

Sally was astonished at her father. 'Well I never did,' she murmured courteously. 'Fancy father.'

'Why? Why? Don't you want to? Won't you—don't you want to?'

'Wouldn't say *that*,' said Sally, shifting in her chair, and struggling to find the polite words. 'Wouldn't exactly say as 'ow I don't *want* to.'

'Then you—you'll let me take you out? You'll let me take you somewhere to tea? You'll let me fetch you in the car—you'll let me, won't you? To-morrow?' asked Jocelyn, leaning further across the table, his arms stretched along it towards her, reaching out to her in entreaty.

'Father—'

'But he says I may. It's with his permission—'

'Tea too?' asked Sally, more and more astonished. 'It ain't much *like* 'im,' she said, full of doubts.

Whereupon Jocelyn got up impetuously, and came round to her with the intention of flinging himself at her feet, and on his knees beseeching her to come out with him—he who in his life had never been on his knees to anybody.

'Oh, Salvatia!' he cried, coming round to her, holding out both his hands

She hastily pushed back her chair and slipped out of it beyond his reach, sure this wasn't proper. No gentleman had a right to call a girl by her Christian name without permission asked and granted; on that point she was quite clear. Salvatia, indeed. The gentle creature couldn't but be affronted and hurt by this.

''Oo you gettin' at, sir?' she inquired, as in duty bound when faced by familiarity.

'You—you!' gasped Jocelyn, following her into the corner she had withdrawn into, and falling at her feet.

❁

Mr. Pinner was of opinion that the sooner they were married the better. There was that in Mr. Luke's eye, he told himself, which could only be got rid of by marriage; nothing but the Church could make the sentiments the young gentleman appeared to entertain for Sally right ones.

Whipt by fear, he hurried things on as eagerly as Jocelyn himself.

Suppose something happened before there was time to get them married, and Mr. Luke, as he understood easily occurred with gentlemen in such circumstances, cooled off? He didn't leave them a moment alone together after that first outing in the car when Jocelyn asked Sally to marry him, and she, obedient and wishful of pleasing everybody, besides having been talked to by her father the night before and told she had his full consent and blessing, and that it was her duty anyhow, heaven having sent Mr. Luke on purpose, had remarked amiably that she didn't mind if she did.

After this, Mr. Pinner's one aim was to keep them from being by themselves till they were safely man and wife. He lived in a fever of watchfulness. He was obsessed by terror on behalf of Sally's virginity. His days were infinitely more wearing than in the worst period of Islington. Mrs. Pinner was missed and mourned quite desperately. It almost broke his back, the hurry, the anxiety, the constant gnawing fear, and the secrecy his future son-in-law insisted on.

'What you want to be so secret for, Mr. Luke?' he asked, black suspicion, always on the alert where Sally was concerned, clouding his naturally mild and trustful eyes.

'You don't want a howling mob of undergraduates round, do you?' retorted Jocelyn.

'Goodness gracious, I should think I didn't, Mr. Luke,' said Mr. Pinner, holding up both his little hands in horror. 'She's got a reg'lar gift, that Sally 'as, for collecting crowds.'

'Well, then,' said Jocelyn irritably, whose nerves were in shreds. And added, 'Isn't it our job to keep them off her?'

'Your job now, sir—or will be soon,' said Mr. Pinner, unable to refrain from rubbing his hands at the thought of his near release from responsibility.

'I wish you wouldn't keep on calling me sir,' snapped Jocelyn. 'I've *asked* you not to. I keep *on* asking you not to.'

He was nearly in tears with strain and fatigue. Incredibly, he hadn't once been able to kiss Sally,—not properly, not as a lover should. Always in the presence of that damned Pinner—such was the way he thought of his future father-in-law—what could he do? He couldn't even talk to her;

not really talk, not pour out the molten streams of adoration that were scalding him to death while that image of alertness sat unblinking by. What was the fellow afraid of? He had asked him at first straight out, on finding how he stuck, to leave them alone, and the answer he got was that courting should be fair and above board, and that he was obliged to be both father and mother to the poor girl.

'Fair and above board! Good God,' thought Jocelyn, driving himself back at a furious pace to Cambridge and throwing back his head in a fit of wild, nervous laughter. His father-in-law—that little man with trousers so much too long for him that they corkscrewed round his legs. His father-in-law. ...

But what was that in the way of grotesqueness compared to his being her father? There, indeed, was mystery: that loveliness beyond dreams should have sprung from Mr. Pinner's little loins.

❀

The widows of Woodles, and also the virgins, were extremely curious about Jocelyn's daily visits, and tried to find out his name, and which college he belonged to. They were in no doubt as to the object of his visits, having by that time all seen Sally, and wished to warn Mr. Pinner to be careful.

They went to his shop and warned him.

Mr. Pinner, looking smaller and more sunk into his trousers than ever, thanked them profusely, and said he was being it.

'One has to be on one's guard with a motherless daughter,' they said.

Mr. Pinner said he was on it.

'And as your daughter promises to grow up some day into rather a good-looking girl—'

'There ain't much promise about Sally, mum—it's been performance, performance, *and* nothing but performance since she was so 'igh.'

'Oh, well—perhaps it's not quite as bad as that,' said the lady addressed, smiling indulgently. 'Still, I do think she may grow into a good-looking girl, and so near Cambridge you will have to be careful. Your visitor is an undergraduate, of course?'

And Mr. Pinner, afraid of Jocelyn, afraid of his threats of hordes of young men descending on the shop if the engagement were known, said, slipping on the edge of an untruth, but just managing to clear it, 'Couldn't say, mum.'

She forced him, however—the woman forced him. 'What?' she exclaimed. 'You can't say? You don't know?'

So then he told it without blinking. 'No, mum,' he said, his harassed blue eyes on her face. 'I don't think the young gentleman *did* 'appen to mention 'is name.'

And in his heart he cried out to his conscience, 'If they forces me to, 'ow, 'ow can I 'elp it?'

❀

Between these two men, both in a state of extreme nervous tension, Sally passed her last days under her father's roof, amiably quiescent, completely good. She did as she was told; always she had done as she was told, and it was now a habit. She liked the look of the young man who so unexpectedly was to become her husband, and was pleased that he should be a gentleman. She knew nothing about gentlemen, but she liked the sort of sound their voices made when they talked. At Islington she had preferred the visits to the shop of the clergy for just that reason—the sound their voices made when they talked. She would have been perfectly happy during the fortnight between her first setting eyes on Jocelyn and her marriage to him, if there had been a few more smiles about.

There were none. Her father was tying her up with trembling haste, as if she were a parcel to be got rid of in a hurry. Her lover's face was haggard, and drawn in the opposite directions to those that lead to smiles. Dumbly he would gaze at her from under his overhanging brows, and every now and then burst into a brief explosion of talk she didn't understand and hadn't an idea how to deal with; or he would steal a shaking hand along the edge of the tablecloth, where her father couldn't see it, and touch her dress. He looked just like somebody in a picture, thought Sally, with

his thin dark face, and eyes right far back in his head,—quite blue eyes, in spite of his dark skin and hair. She liked him very much. She liked everybody very much. If only somebody had sometimes smiled, how nice it all would have been; for then she would have known for certain they were happy, and were getting what they wanted. Sally liked to be certain people were happy, and getting what they wanted. As it was, nobody could tell from their faces that these two were pleased. Sometimes in the evening, after her lover had gone and the door was locked and bolted and barred behind him, and all the windows had been examined and fastened securely, her father would calm down and cheer up; but her lover never calmed down or cheered up.

Sally, who hardly had what could be called thoughts but only feelings, was conscious of this without putting it into words. Perhaps when he had got what he wanted, which was, she was thoroughly aware, herself, he would be different. There were no doubts whatever in her mind as to what he wanted. She was too much used to the sort of thing. Not, it is true, in quite such a violent form, but then none of the others who had admired her—that is, every single male she had ever come across—had been allowed to be what her father called her fiancy, which was, Sally understood, the name of the person one was going to marry, and who might say things and behave in a way no one else might, as distinguished from the name of the person one went to the pictures with and didn't marry, and who was a fancy. She knew that, because, though she herself had only gone to the pictures wedged between her father and mother, she had heard the girls at school talk of going with their fancies,—those girls who had all been her friends till they began to grow up, and then all, after saying horrid things to her and crying violently, had got out of her way.

As though she could help it; as though she could help having the sort of face that made them angry.

'I ain't made my silly face,' she said tearfully—her delicious mouth pronounced it fice—to the last of her girl friends, to the one she was fondest of, who had hung on longest, but who couldn't, after all, stand the look that came into the eyes of him she spoke of as her boy one day that he chanced to come across Sally.

'No. No more you didn't, Sally Pinner,' furiously retorted the friend. 'But you would 'ave if you could 'ave, so you're nothin' but a nypocrite—see?'

And the friend forgot herself still further, and added that Sally was a blinkin' nypocrite; which was, as Mr. Pinner would have said had he heard it, language.

❁

So that Sally in her short life had already caused trouble and uneasiness, in spite of having been so carefully kept out of the way.

Wherever there were human beings, those human beings stared at Sally and began to follow her; or, if they couldn't follow her with their feet, did so with astonished, eager eyes as long as she was in sight. Holy Communion was the only one of the Sunday services Mr. Pinner let her go to in Woodles, because it was sparsely attended, and the few worshippers were women. But even at that solemn service the Vicar, who was seventy-eight, found it difficult altogether to shut out from his consciousness the lovely figure of grace shining like morning light in the shadows of his dark little church. He was as instantly aware of Sally the first Sunday she came to the service as every one else always was the moment she appeared anywhere, and she had the same effect on the old man as she had had on the young Jocelyn when first he saw her—he caught his breath, and for a moment was near tears. Because here, the old man perceived, at the end of his life he was at last beholding beauty,—fresh from God, still dewy from its heavenly birth; and the Vicar, who had long been a recluse, and lived entirely among his memories, which all were sentimental and poetic, bowed down in spirit before the young radiance come into his church, as before the Real Presence.

❁

Such was Sally when young Jocelyn married her—mild inside, and only desiring to give satisfaction, and outside a thing that seemed made up of light. As Mr. Pinner had wished to hide her, so did Jocelyn wish to

hide her, and wanted to be married in London, the least conspicuous of spots; but technical difficulties prevented this, seeing that he wanted to be married quickly, so he took the Vicar into his confidence, and got a special licence, and thus avoiding banns and publicity was married early one bright March morning, while Woodles, unaware of what was happening, was still washing up its breakfast things.

By this time Jocelyn was acquainted with Sally's inability to give a plain answer to a question, and half expected her to reply 'I don't mind if I do' to the Vicar when he asked if she would take him, Jocelyn, to be her wedded husband. She didn't; but if she had he wouldn't have cared, nor would the Vicar have cared. Whatever she did, whatever she said, was to these two dazzled men the one perfect gesture, the one perfect word.

But Sally, young and shy, said very little. Hardly had she spoken during the brief courtship. To the Vicar, full of awe of his office and his age, she scarcely dared raise her eyes, much less lift up her voice. It was enough, however; the old man was enthralled. Far from being surprised at Jocelyn's determination to take his name off the books of his college and chuck his promising career and marry Sally and go up to London to pick up his living as a journalist, a profession for which he hadn't the slightest aptitude, the Vicar understood perfectly. The college authorities, on the other hand, unaware of his reason for ruining himself, were amazed at such deliberate suicide. They had not seen Sally. The Vicar, who had, was convinced the young man was doing the one thing worth doing,—giving up everything to follow after Truth.

'For is not Truth Beauty, and Beauty Truth?' asked the Vicar, too old to bother any longer with material considerations.

Jocelyn and he were unanimous that it was.

❁

The Vicar, indeed, was an immense comfort to Jocelyn the second and last week of his engagement, for Mr. Pinner was no comfort at all. Not that Jocelyn needed comfort at this marvellous moment; but he needed understanding, some one to talk to, some one who could and would listen

intelligently. Mr. Pinner didn't listen intelligently; he didn't listen at all. All he did was to say heartily, 'That's right,' to everything Jocelyn said, and such indiscrimination was annoying. It was a deep refreshment to get away from him and go up to the Vicarage, and there, slowly pacing up and down with the old man on the sunny path where the first daffodils were, talk with some one who so completely understood.

The Vicar concluded, from the frequency with which his young friend came to take counsel of him, that he was an orphan, but he asked no questions because he was long past the age of questions. The age of silence was his, of quiet resting on his oars, of a last warming of himself in the light of the sun, before departing hence and being no more seen. By this time, his mind being faintly bleared, he connected Sally with the *Nunc Dimittis,* and thanked God aloud, greatly to her confusion, for she couldn't make out what the old gentleman was talking about, for being allowed to see, before departing in peace, the perfect loveliness of her whom he called the Lord's Salvatia. Fitting and right was the young man's attitude in the Vicar's eyes; fitting and right to leave all things, and follow after this child of grace.

His unpractical attitude was immensely grateful to Jocelyn, who knew, though during this strange fortnight of thwarted love-making and arm's-length worship he managed to forget, that one of the things he was leaving was his mother.

He hadn't mentioned it, but he had got one.

III

Not a father, for he had long been dead, but a mother, whose single joy and pride he was. There she sat at home by the fire on his wedding night, thinking of him. No complete half-hour of the day could pass without the thought of Jocelyn getting into it. Her only child; so brilliant, so serious, so hard-working, so good. She loved brains. She loved diligence. She loved the man of the house to be absorbed in his work. What a halo he was about her head! Everybody round where she lived knew about him. Everybody had heard of his successes,—'My son, who is a scholar of Ananias. ... My son, who is a Prizeman of his University. ... My son, who won this year's Rutherford Prize. ...' Great was her reward for having devoted her life to him and his education, and for having turned a deaf ear to those suitors who had tried to marry her when she was a young widow. She wasn't even now, twenty years later, an old widow, but she was a widow who was less young.

She lived in one of those suburbs where much is done for the mind. She was popular in it, and looked up to. She was, in fact, one of its leading lights,—cultivated, lady-like, well-read, artistic, interested in each new movement that came along. And of a most pleasing appearance, too, being slender at an age when the mothers of the grown-up are sometimes so no longer, dark haired among the grey, smooth among the puckered, and her eyes had no crow's feet, and were calm and beautifully clear.

She was serenely happy. The *milieu* suited her exactly. She had come to South Winch twenty years before from Kensington—real Kensington, not West or North, but the part that clusters round the Albert Hall—on her husband's death, because of having to be frugal, but soon discovered it was the very place for her. Far better, she intelligently recognised, to be a leading light in a suburb, and know and be known by everybody,

than extinguished and invisible in London. Besides, spring came to the suburbs in a way it never did to London, and it was the custom in South Winch, where people were determined to think highly, to think particularly highly of spring. At the bottom of her half acre there was only an iron railing separating her from a real meadow belonging to the big villa of a prosperous City man, and spring, she told the Rector, who was also a Canon, did things in that meadow it would never dream of doing near the Albert Hall.

'Look at those dandelions,' said Mrs. Luke. 'I do think the meanest flower that blows in its natural setting is more beautiful than the whole of those thought-out effects in Kensington Gardens.'

And the Rector—the Canon—said, 'How true that is,' and remarked that she was a Wordsworthian; and Mrs. Luke smiled, and said, 'Am I?' and wasn't altogether pleased, for Wordsworth, she somehow felt, was no longer, in the newest opinion, what he was.

While Jocelyn, then, was worshipping Sally across the supper-table of the private sitting-room he had engaged in the hotel at Exeter, where they were breaking their journey to Cornwall, which was the place he was going to hide his honeymoon in, and Sally, unable to make head or tail of his speech and behaviour, was becoming every minute more uneasy, his mother sat, placid in the security of unconsciousness, by the fire in Almond Tree Cottage, a house which used, before the era of her careful simplicity, so foolishly to be called Beulah.

'A cottage,' she observed to her sympathetic friends, 'is the proper place for me. I'm a poor woman. Five hundred a year'—why hide anything?— 'doesn't go far these days after Income Tax has been deducted. Jocelyn has his own five hundred, or we would really have been in a quite bad way. As it is, I can just manage.'

And she did; and in her clever hands frugality merely seemed comfort gone a little thin, and nobody liked to ask her for subscriptions.

The house was small and very white, and had a small and very green garden, with a cedar on the back lawn and an almond tree on the front one. Two front gates that swang back on their hinges, and a half-moon carriage-sweep. Railings. Shrubs. The yellow sanded road. Houses

opposite, with almond trees too, or, less prettily, in the front gardens of the insensitive, monkey puzzles. The hall door was blue. Such curtains as could be seen at the same time as the door were blue too. At no season of the year was there not at least one vivid flower stuck in a slender vessel in the sitting-room window. And in the sitting-room itself, on the otherwise bare walls, was one picture only,—a copy, really very well done, of a gay and charming Tiepolo ceiling—Mrs. Luke was the first in South Winch to take up Tiepolo—in which everybody was delicately happy, in spite of a crucifixion going on in one corner, and high-spirited, fat little angels tossed roses across the silvery brightness of what was evidently a perfect summer afternoon. Books, too, were present; not many, but the right ones. Blake was there; also Donne; and Sir Thomas Browne; and Proust, in French. A novel, generally Galsworthy, lay on the little table near the fire, and, by an arrangement with a circle of friends, most of the better class weeklies passed through the house in a punctual stream.

Sitting in the deep chair by the fireside table on Jocelyn's wedding night, her dark head against the bright cushion that gave the necessary splash of colour to the restful bareness of the room, her lap full of reviews she was going to read of the best new books and plays, so as to be able to discuss them intelligently with him when he came home at Easter— only a few more days to wait,—his mother couldn't keep her eyes from wandering off these studies to the glowing little fire of ships' logs and neat blocks of peat, for her thoughts persisted in flying, like homing birds, to the nest they always went back to and so warmly rested in: Jocelyn, and what he was, and what he was going to be.

Other mothers had anxieties; she had never had one. Others had disappointments; she had had nothing but happy triumphs. He was retiring, it was true, and stayed up in his little attic-study when he was at home, and wouldn't go anywhere except to a Beethoven concert— together they had studied all that has been said about Beethoven, and she had plans for proceeding to the study of all that has been said about Bach—or for long tramps with her, when they would eat bread and cheese at some wayside inn, and read aloud to each other between the mouthfuls; but how much richer was she herself for that. And the

comfort of having a *good* son, a son who cared nothing for even so-called harmless dissipations! When she looked round at other people's sons, and saw the furrows on their fathers' foreheads—she smiled at her own alliterations—and heard a whisper of the dread word Debts, and knew where debts came from—betting, gambling, drinking, women, in a ghastly crescendo, how could she ever, ever be thankful enough that Jocelyn was so good? Never once had he betted, gambled, drunk, or—she smiled again at her own word—womaned; she was ready to take her oath he hadn't. Didn't she know him inside out? He kept nothing from her; he couldn't have if he had wanted to, bless him, for she, who had watched him from long before he became conscious, knew him far, far better than he could possibly know himself.

Many, indeed, were her blessings. Great and conscious her content. Her dark head on the vivid cushion was full of bright—why not say it?—self-congratulation, which is the other word for thankfulness. And how not congratulate herself on the possession of that beloved, brilliant boy? While, to add to everything else, the neighbour, whose meadow of buttercups she so freely and inexpensively enjoyed from over the railing on dappled May mornings, was showing unmistakable signs of wishing to marry her. His year of widowerhood had recently come to an end, and the very next week he had begun the kind of activity that could only be described as courting; so that she had this feather, too, to add to a cap already, she gratefully acknowledged, so full of feathers. Poor? Yes, she was poor. But what was being poor? Nothing at all, if one refused to mind it.

A third time she smiled, shaking her head at the neat peat blocks as if they had been the neighbour. 'Come, come, my friend—at our ages,' she could hear herself saying to him with gentle and flattering raillery—he must be at least twenty years older than herself—when the moment should arrive. But it was pleasant, this, to sit in her charmingly lit room—she was clever at making lampshades—and to know that next door was a man, well set up in spite of his sixty odd years, who thought her desirable, pleasant to be certain she had only to put out her hand, and take wealth.

And who could say, she mused, but that it mightn't be the best thing for Jocelyn too, to have a solid stepfather like that at his back, able to help him financially? She had spent happy years in the little white house, and it had rarely worried her that she should be obliged to take such ceaseless pains to hide the bones of her economies gracefully, but later on she would be older, and might be tired, and later on Jocelyn might perhaps want to marry and set up house for himself—after all, it would only be natural—and then she would be lonely, besides being ten years—she thought in ten years would be about the time he might wish to marry—less attractive than she was now, and getting not only lonelier with every year but also, she supposed, less attractive; though surely one oughtn't to do that, if one's mind and spirit—?

Whereas, if she married the neighbour …

❈

He came in at that moment, on the pretext of bringing her back a book she had lent him, though he hadn't read it and didn't mean to, for it was what he, being a plain man, called high-falutin. He didn't tell her this, because when a man is courting he cannot be candid, and he well knew that he was courting. What he wasn't sure of was whether she knew. You never could tell with women; the best of them were artful.

He came in that evening, then, to make it finally clear to her. She was a charming woman, and much younger, he imagined, than her age, which couldn't, he calculated, with a son of twenty-two be far short of forty-two, and he had always greatly admired the pluck with which she faced what seemed to him sheer destitution. She was the very woman, too, to have at the head of one's table when one had friends to dinner,—good-looking, knowing how to dress, able to talk about any mortal thing, and a perfect lady. And after the friends had gone, and it was time to go to bye-bye—such were the words his thoughts clothed themselves in,—she would still be a desirable companion, even if—again his words—a bit on the thin side. That, however, would soon be set right when he had fed her up on all the good food she hadn't ever been able to afford, and anyhow she was

– 29 –

years and years younger than poor Annie, who had been the same age as himself, which was all right to begin with, but no sort of a show in the long run. Also, Annie had stayed common.

So the neighbour, whose name was Mr. Thorpe, arrived on Jocelyn's wedding night about nine o'clock in the restrained sitting-room of Almond Tree Cottage, determined to make his purpose clear. That he should be refused didn't enter his head, for he had much to offer. He was far the richest man in the parish, his two daughters were married and out of the way, his house and cars were bigger than anybody's, and he grew pineapples. He couldn't help thinking, he couldn't help knowing, that for a woman of over forty he was a catch, and he went into the room, past the reverent-eyed small maid who held the door open, expanding his chest. A poverty-stricken little room, he always considered, with nothing in it of the least account, except the lady.

Yes; except the lady. But what a lady. Not a grey hair in her head, which he had carefully examined when she wasn't looking, nor, he would wager, any tooth that wasn't exclusively her own. And a trim ankle; and a pretty wrist. Ruffles, too. He liked ruffles at a woman's wrist. And able to talk about any mortal thing. Annie, poor creature, had made him look like a fool when he had his friends to dinner. This one would be the finest of the feathers in a cap which, he too gratefully acknowledged, was stuck full of them.

'All alone, eh?' he said cheerily. 'That's bad.'

'I'm used to it,' said Mrs. Luke, smilingly holding out her slender hand, on which a single ruby—or was it a garnet? probably a garnet—caught the light. She had on a wine-coloured, soft woollen dress that Jocelyn liked, and the ring and the dress went very well together.

A pretty picture; a perfect lady. Mr. Thorpe, determined to waste no time in making his purpose clear, bent his head and kissed the hand.

'Being used to a bad thing doesn't make it better, but worse,' he said, drawing up the only other really comfortable chair—Jocelyn's—and sitting down close to her.

And he was about to embark then and there on his proposal, for he hated waste of anything, including time, and Mrs. Luke was already

drawing up her shoulders to her ears in an instinctive movement of defence, for she would have liked to have had longer to turn the thing over in her mind, and discover really whether his splendid illiteracy—it was so immense as to appear magnificent—would be a source of pleasure to her or suffering, whether the pleasure of filling up his mind's emptiness would be greater than the pains of such an exertion, whether, in short, she hadn't better refuse him, when the little maid came in with the silver salver she had been trained to present letters on, and held it out before her mistress.

'Letters, eh?' said Mr. Thorpe, nettled by this interruption. 'I should give orders they're to be left in the—well, you can't call it a hall, can you, so let's say passage.'

The little maid, alarmed, sidled out of the room.

'I would indeed, if it weren't that I can't bear to wait a minute when it's a letter from Jocelyn,' said Mrs. Luke, holding the letter tight, for she saw it was from him. 'You wouldn't be able to wait either, would you,' she went on, smiling more brightly even than usual, for the mere touch of the letter made her more bright, 'for anything you loved.'

'No,' said Mr. Thorpe sturdily, seizing this opening. 'No. I wouldn't. And that's why I've come round—'

But she didn't hear. 'You'll forgive me, won't you my dear friend,' she murmured, slitting the envelope with an enamelled paper-knife lest she should harm the dear contents, 'but I haven't heard from that boy for over a fortnight, and I've been beginning to wonder—'

'Oh, certainly, certainly. Don't mind me,' said Mr. Thorpe, aggrieved. 'Mark my words, though,' he added, sitting up very square and broad in his chair, and giving the knees of his trousers a twitch each, 'one shouldn't overdo the son business.'

She didn't hear. Her eyes were running down the lines of the letter, while she muttered something about just wanting to see if he were well.

'Damned stuck up young prig,' Mr. Thorpe was in the act of saying to himself, resentfully watching this absorption, when he was interrupted by a complete and alarming change in the lady.

She gave a violent shudder; she dropped the letter on the floor, as

though her shaking hands couldn't hold it; and then, fixing her large grey eyes on his, opened her mouth and moaned.

He stared at her. He couldn't think what was the matter.

'Sick, eh?' he asked, staring.

'Oh, *oh*—' was all she said, turning her face from him, and burying it in the cushion.

❁

Well, what does one do with a woman who buries her face in a cushion? Comforts her, of course, thought Mr. Thorpe, again seizing his opportunity. The young ass couldn't be dead, or he wouldn't have written. But he might—

Mr. Thorpe paused at the thought, and withdrew the hand already put out to pat. Yes; that was it. Better not comfort just yet. For the young fool had no doubt run into debt, and was being threatened with proceedings, and was trying to persuade his mother to pay, and Mr. Thorpe didn't want to begin his betrothal with having to shell out for somebody else's scapegrace son.

His hand, accordingly, slowly redescended on to his knee, where it rested motionless while he stared at the figure in the chair. Pretty figure. Nice lines. Graceful, even in her upset. She only needed very little, just the weeniest bit, fattening up. But she shouldn't have spoiled that son. Women were fools about their sons.

Then, noticing that the letter was lying at his feet, and the lady, her face in the cushion, was incapable of observing what he did, he put on his eyeglasses, picked it up carefully so that it shouldn't rustle, and, remarking to himself that all was fair in love and war, read it.

Having read it, he as carefully replaced it on the carpet, took off his eyeglasses, and began to comfort.

For it wasn't debts, it was marriage; the best thing possible from Mr. Thorpe's point of view—clearing the field, leaving the mother free to turn her thoughts to other ties. And a good job too, for the young ass had gone clean off his head. What a letter. He ought to be ashamed

of himself, writing sick stuff like that to his mother. Married this very day. Given up Cambridge. Chucked his career. Finished with ambitions. Going to earn his own living in London. Mother bound to love—no, it was put hotter than that—worship the girl, who was more beautiful than any angel—

Tut, tut. Silly young ass, caught by the first handsome slut.

'Better tell me about it,' said Mr. Thorpe, leaning forward and laying his hand with unhesitating kindness on Mrs. Luke's shoulder. 'Nothing like getting things off one's chest. Count on me. Whatever your son's done I'll help. I'll do anything—anything at all, mind you, to help.'

And Jocelyn's mother, completely overwhelmed by the incredible sudden smash up of everything she had lived for, did, on hearing this kind, steady male voice through her misery, turn to Mr. Thorpe as the drowning turn to any spar, and, making odd little noises, stooped down and tried to pick up the letter.

But her hands shook too much. He had to pick it up for her.

'Read it—,' she said in a sobbing whisper.

So he took out his eyeglasses, and read it again.

❁

'Now what you've got to do,' said Mr. Thorpe, folding it up neatly when he had finished, and laying it down on the little table, 'is to make up your mind that what's done can't be undone.'

Mrs. Luke, her head buried in the cushions, moaned.

'That's it,' said Mr. Thorpe, a hand on each knee and an eye on her. 'That's the ticket.'

'I know—I know,' moaned Mrs. Luke. 'But just at first—the shock—'

'Shock, eh? I don't know that there's much shock about marriage,' said Mr. Thorpe. 'Shouldn't be, anyhow.'

'But so sudden—so unexpected—'

'People will marry, you know,' said Mr. Thorpe. 'Especially men. Once they get set on it, nothing stops 'em.'

'I know—I know—but Jocelyn—such a boy—'

'Boy, eh? Age has precious little to do with it,' said Mr. Thorpe firmly. 'In fact, nothing.'

'But his prospects—his career—all thrown away—ruined—'

'Marriage never harmed a man yet,' said Mr. Thorpe still more firmly, aware that he was being inaccurate, but also aware that no one can afford to be accurate and court simultaneously. Accuracy, Mr. Thorpe knew, comes after marriage, not before.

'Mark my words,' he went on, 'that clever son of yours won't stop being clever because he's married. Who's going to take his brains from him? Not a loving wife, you bet. Why, a good wife, a loving wife, doubles and trebles a man's output.'

'How kind you are,' murmured Mrs. Luke, who did find this comforting. 'But Jocelyn—my boy—to keep it from me—'

'Bound to keep something from his mother,' said Mr. Thorpe. 'Mothers are all right, and a man has to have them to start with, but the day comes when a back seat is what they've got to climb into. Only as regards their children, mind you,' he added. 'A woman has many other strings to her bow, and is by no means nothing but a mother.'

'Oh, but we were everything, everything to each other,' moaned Mrs. Luke, stabbed afresh by the mention of a back seat. 'Always, always. He never *looked* at another woman—'

'Damned prig,' thought Mr. Thorpe. And said out aloud, 'Time he began, then. Though having a woman like you about,' he added, placing his hand with determination on hers, which hung limply down holding a handkerchief while her face was still turned away, 'ought to keep him from seeing the others all right. You're a wonderful woman, you know—a remarkable woman.'

His voice changed. It took on the unmistakable note that is immediately followed by love-making.

'I—think I'll go and lie down,' said Mrs. Luke faintly, recognising the note, and feeling she could bear no more of anything that night. 'I—I really think I must. My head—'

She struggled to get up.

He helped her. He helped her by laying hold of both her wrists, and drawing her upwards and towards him.

'Head, eh?' he said, a gleam in his eyes.

'How kind, how kind—' she murmured distractedly, finding herself on her feet and very close to Mr. Thorpe, who still held her wrists.

She wanted her letter. She looked about helplessly for her letter, keeping her head as far away from him as she could. There was her letter—on the table—she wanted to snatch it up—to get away as quickly as possible—to hide in her bedroom—and her wrists were being held, and she couldn't move.

'Kind, eh? Kind, you call it?' said Mr. Thorpe through his teeth. 'I can be kinder than that.' And he put his arms round her, and drew her vigorously to his chest.

'This in exchange for Jocelyn,' drifted through Mrs. Luke's wretched and resisting mind.

But, even through her wretchedness and resistance she felt there was something rock-like, something solid and fixed, about Mr. Thorpe's chest, to which in the present catastrophe, with the swirling waters of bitterest disappointment raging round her feet, it might be well to cling.

IV

❁

And while these things were happening in Almond Tree Cottage, Jocelyn, in the private sitting-room of the Exeter hotel, was behaving, it seemed to Sally, in the most strange way.

If this was what married gentlemen were like, then she wondered that there should be any married ladies left. Enough to kill them off like flies, thought Sally, helplessly involved in frequent and alarming embraces. Still, she held on hard in her mind to what her father had said to her the evening before, when she was going up to bed,—'Sally,' her father had said, calling her back a moment and looking solemn, 'don't you take no notice of what Mr. Luke do or don't, once 'e's your 'usband. 'Usbands ain't gentlemen, remember—not ordinary, day-time gentlemen, such as you thinks they are till you knows better. And you just say to yourself as 'ow your mother went through it all before you was so much as born, and she was a bit of all right, warn't she? So you just remember that, my girl, if by any chance you should 'appen to get the fidgets.'

She did remember it, though it was Mr. Luke—so she thought of him—who had the fidgets. He didn't seem able to sit quiet for two minutes in his chair, and eat his supper, and let her eat hers. Such a lovely supper, too—a real shame to let it get cold. What was the good of ordering a lovely supper if one wasn't going to eat it properly?

More and more earnestly as the evening progressed did she wish herself back in the peaceful parlour behind the shop; less and less did the thought of her mother having been through all this too support her, because she became surer every minute that she hadn't been through it. Never in his life could her father have behaved as Mr. Luke was behaving. Entirely unused to kisses, except evenings and mornings, and then just

one on her cheek and over and done with at once, Sally couldn't get over the number and length of Mr. Luke's. Also, it surprised her very much to see a gentleman interrupt his supper—and such a lovely supper—to run round the table and go down on his knees and kiss her shoes,—new ones, of course, but still not things that ought to be kissed; it surprised her so much, that she came over quite queer each time.

She thought it a great mercy he had locked the door, so that the grand waiter couldn't get in, for the grand waiter, staring at her while he handed her the dishes and calling her Madam, alarmed her in his way very nearly as much as Mr. Luke alarmed her in his; yet, on the other hand, if the waiter was locked out she was locked in, so that it cut both ways, thought Sally, wishing she might be let eat the meringue the waiter had left on her plate before being locked out. But every time she tried to, Mr. Luke seemed to have to be kissed.

And the way Mr. Luke, when he did stay still a minute in his chair, never took his eyes off her, and the things he said! And he didn't seem a bit happy either, in spite of talking such a lot about heaven and the angels. If only he had seemed happy Sally wouldn't have minded so much, for then at least somebody would have been getting some good out of it; but he looked all upset, and as if he were going to be ill,—sickening for something, she concluded.

For a long time she kept up her manners, bravely clinging to them and trying hard to guess when was the right moment to say Yes and when to say No, which was very difficult because he talked so queerly, and she hadn't an idea what most of it meant; for a long time she was able to smile politely, if anxiously, every time she looked up and caught his fierce and burning eye; but all of a sudden, perpetually thwarted in her efforts to eat the meringue, and very hot and uncomfortable from so much kissing, she found she couldn't do anything any more that was proper, wasn't able to smile, said No when it ought to have been Yes, lost her nerve, and to her own surprise and excessive shame began to whimper.

Very quietly she whimpered, very beautifully, her head drooping exquisitely on its adorable little neck, while the meringue she had so badly

wanted to be allowed to eat for the last quarter of an hour was finally renounced, and left to waste and dribble away its expensive cream on her plate.

Jocelyn was appalled.

'Oh, Sally—oh, my angel—oh, my heavenly, heavenly child!' he cried, flinging himself once again at her feet, while she once again quickly drew them up beneath her frock, as she had done each time before.

She apologised humbly. She was really terribly ashamed,—and he so good to her, spending all that money on such a splendid supper.

'I ain't cried but once before in my life,' she explained, fumbling for her handkerchief, while the tears welled up in her enchanting sweet eyes. 'When mother died, that was, but I never didn't not else. Dunno what come over me, Mr. Luke—'

'Only once before! When your mother died! And now on your wedding day! Oh, Sally—it's me—I've made you—I, who would die a thousand deaths to spare a single perfect hair of your divine little head—'

'Don't say that, Mr. Luke—please now, don't say that,' Sally earnestly begged, much perturbed by this perpetual harping on death and angels. And having at last got out her handkerchief, she was just going to wipe her eyes decently when he snatched it from her and didn't let her do anything, but actually kissed away the tears as they rolled out.

'You ain't 'alf fond of kissin', are you, Mr. Luke,' murmured Sally miserably, helplessly obliged to hand over her tears to what seemed to her a really horrid fate, while to herself she was saying in resigned, unhappy astonishment, 'And them my very own eyes, too, when all's said and done.'

❁

It was three days later that Jocelyn, for the first time, said, 'Don't say that, Sally,' in a tone of command.

He had told her many times not to call him Mr. Luke, told her entreatingly, caressingly, playfully, that he was her husband Jocelyn, and no longer ever any more to be Mr. anything on her darling lips; and when she forgot, for habits in Sally died hard, smilingly and adoringly reminded her.

But this time, after three whole days' honeymoon and three whole nights, he commanded; adding in a tone of real annoyance, 'And for God's sake don't look at people when they pass.'

'I ain't lookin' at them,' protested Sally, flushing, who never wanted to look at anybody, besides having been taught by the anxious Pinners that no modest girl did. 'They looks at me.'

It was true. Jocelyn knew it was true, but nevertheless was angry, and caught hold of her arm and marched her up a side lane from the sea, up to the less inhabited hill at the back of the village.

For they were at St. Mawes, the little cut-off fishing village in South Cornwall which had lived in Jocelyn's memory ever since, two years before, on an Easter bicycling tour with his mother, he and she had suddenly dropped down on it from the hill above, unaware of its existence till they were right on it, so completely was it tucked away and hidden. It had lived in his memory as the most difficult spot to get at, and therefore probably the most solitary, of any he had come across. Miles from a railway, miles from the nearest town, only to be reached, unless one went to it by sea, along a most difficult and tortuous road that ended by throwing one down a precipice on to a ferry-boat which took one across the Fal and shot one out at the foot of another precipice,—or so the two hills seemed to Jocelyn and his mother, who had to push their bicycles up them—he considered it the place of places to hide his honeymoon in; to hide, that is, the precious and conspicuous Sally.

His recollection of it was just a village street along the sea, an inn or two, a shop or two, a fisherman or two, and in the middle of the day complete emptiness.

The very place.

He wrote, trembling with excitement, to its post office to get him rooms, rooms for his wife and himself—his wife; oh, my God! thought Jocelyn, still a week off his wedding day.

The post office got him rooms,—a tiny bedroom, almost filled by the bed, a tiny parlour, almost filled by the table, and a fisherman and his wife, who lived in the rest of the cottage, to look after them.

The first day they were out in a boat all day being shown coves by

the fisherman, who stared hard at Sally, and whenever they wanted to go back took them to see another cove instead; but the second day, the imperativeness of daily exercise having been part of Jocelyn's early training, he felt it his duty to exercise Sally, and emerged with her during the quiet hour after their mid-day meal for a blow along the sea front.

She had already said, when he asked her if she would like to go out, that she didn't mind if she did, and he had passed it over because he happened to be looking at her when she said it, and no one who happened to be looking at Sally when she said anything was able to pay much attention to her words. Jocelyn couldn't, anyhow, only three days married; but out on the sea front, walking side by side, his eyes fixed ahead in growing surprise at the number of people suddenly come out, like themselves, apparently, for blows, when in answer to his remark that the place seemed more populous than he had imagined, she said, 'It do, don't it, Mr. Luke,' he snapped at her.

Snapped at her. Snapped at his angel, his child of light, his being from another sphere, who ought, he had told her, making her fidget a good deal, for whatever did he mean? sit for ever on a sapphire throne, and be crowned by stars, and addressed only in the language of Beethoven's symphonies. But then there were these confounded people suddenly sprung from nowhere, and it was enough to make any man snap, the way they looked at Sally. Where did they come from? Where were they going? What did they want?

Jocelyn seized her, and hurried her up the side path that led over the hill to the quiet country at the back. He was excessively put out. The swine—the idle, ogling swine, he thought, rushing her up the steep path at such a rate that the willing Sally, obediently putting her best leg foremost, nevertheless, light and active as she was, arrived at the top so breathless that she couldn't speak.

Not that she wanted to speak. Never much of a hand at what her girl friends, when she still had them, used to call back-chat, the brief period of her honeymoon had taught her how safe and snug silence was compared to the draughty dangers of speech. Marriage, she already felt, groping dimly about in it, wasn't at all like anything one was used to. It seemed

swampy underfoot. You started walking along it, and it looked all right, when in you went. Husbands—difficult to know where one was with *them*, thought Sally. They changed about so. One moment on their knees as if one was a church, and the next rushing one off one's feet up a hill such as one couldn't have believed possible if one hadn't seen it for oneself, and their face all angry. Angry? What for? wondered Sally, who was never angry.

'It's that hair of yours,' said Jocelyn, got to the top, and standing still a moment, for he too was panting.

She looked at him uncomprehendingly, in a lovely surprise. He was frowning at the sea, and the bit of road along it visible at their feet, on which still crawled a few black specks.

"Ow?' Sally was injudicious enough to ask; but after all it was only one word—she was careful to say only one word.

One was enough, though.

'How, Sally—*how*, HOW. You really *must* learn to say *how*,' said Jocelyn, exasperated.

'I did say 'ow,' explained Sally meekly.

'Yes. You did. Exactly,' said Jocelyn.

'Ain't it right to say 'ow?' she asked, anxious for instruction.

'Haven't you *any* ear?' was Jocelyn's answer, turning to her with a kind of pounce.

Sally was still more surprised. What a question. Of course she had an ear. Two of them. And she was going to tell him so when his face, as he looked at her, changed to the one he had when he got talking about heaven and angels.

For how could Jocelyn stay irritated with anything like that? He had only to turn and look at her for all his silly anger to shrivel up. In the presence of her loveliness, what a mere mincing worm he was, with his precise ways of speech, and his twopenny-halfpenny little bit of superior education. As though it mattered, as though it mattered, thought Jocelyn.

'Oh, Sally, I didn't mean it,' he said, catching up her hand and kissing it, which made her feel very awkward and ashamed, somehow, having a thing like that done to her hand, and in broad daylight, too, and out of

doors. 'But you should try and tuck your hair more out of sight—look, this way,' he went on, gently taking her hat off and arranging her hair for her before putting it on again. 'You see,' he explained, 'it does catch the eye so, doesn't it, my beautiful, flaming seraphim—oh, my God,' he added under his breath, 'how beautiful you are!'

'It don't make no difference,' said Sally in a resigned voice.

'What doesn't?'

'If you tucks it in or don't. They always looks at me. We tried everything at 'ome, Father and Mother did, but they always looks at me.'

She spoke with deprecation and apology. Best let him know the worst at once, for she was thoroughly aware of her disabilities and the endless trouble she had given her parents; while as for their scoldings, and exhortations, and dark hints of bad things that might happen to her, hadn't they rung in her ears since she was twelve? But what could she do? There she was. Having been born like that, how could she help it?

And another thing she couldn't help, though she was unconscious that she did it, was that every time she caught the amiable eye of a stranger, and she had never yet met any stranger who hadn't amiable eyes, she smiled. Just a little; just an involuntary gratitude for the friendliness in the eye that had been caught. And as she had two dimples, otherwise invisible, the smile, which would anyhow have been lovely on that face, was of exceeding loveliness, and complications followed, and angry chidings from the worn-out Pinners, and, in Sally, a resigned surprise.

It was while she was trying to convey to Jocelyn that whatever he did with her hair she was doomed to be looked at, and was at the same time shaking it back so as to help him to get it neat—it looked startlingly vivid against the grey background of sea and sky—that a young man called Carruthers, out for a run with his dog after a stuffy Sunday family lunch, came round the bend of the path, whistling and swinging his stick, and stopped dead when he saw her.

His dog rushed on, however, and ran up to the spirit-thing, and sniffed and wagged round it, and seemed quite pleased; so it was real, it wasn't a spirit, it wasn't the beginning in his own brain of hallucinations on burning, Blake-like lines.

He stood gazing. He had never seen anything like that before,—no, by Jove, nor had most other people. 'Oh, I say—don't, don't, *don't* put it on yet!' he nearly cried out as he saw the hat in the dark, Iberian-looking youth's hands being raised quickly above the girl's head when that confounded dog disturbed them, and knew that in another instant it would descend and the light go out.

The Iberian's movements, however, were swift and decided, and the hat was not only put on but pulled on,—tugged on with vigour as far down over her eyes as it would go; and then, after a frowning glance round, the fellow drew her hand through his arm and walked her off quickly in the opposite direction.

There was nothing left for Carruthers but to call his dog—an attractive bitch, who would have been a Sealyham if it hadn't been for something its mother did once,—and it wasn't Carruthers' fault that it too should chance to be called Sally.

'Sally! Sally!' he therefore very naturally shouted, raising his voice as much as possible, which was a great deal. 'Sally! Come here! Sally! Come *here*, I tell you!'

The hills round St. Mawes reverberated with entreaties that Sally should come.

She did come, his Sally did, but behind it, running, came the Iberian as well. The girl was out of sight round the corner. Young Carruthers watched the hurrying approach of her companion with surprise, which increased when he saw the expression on his face.

'How dare you! How dare you!' shouted Jocelyn directly he was near enough; upon which Carruthers' surprise became amazement.

'What's up?' he inquired.

'How dare you call out Sally, and tell her to come here? Eh? What do you mean by it? You—'

'I say—hold on,' exclaimed Carruthers quickly, raising a defensive arm. 'Hold on a bit. Look—here she is, here's Sally—' and he pointed to the fawning sinner.

Jocelyn's fists fell limply to his sides. He flushed, and looked extremely foolish. 'I'm sorry,' he muttered.

'Don't mention it,' said Carruthers, with immense sarcastic politeness.

'It—it's my wife's name,' stammered Jocelyn, 'and I thought you knew her, and were incredibly cheeking her—'

Carruthers, staring at his nervous twitching face, didn't laugh, but simply nodded. Having seen Sally he simply nodded.

'That's all right,' he said gravely; and for some reason added impulsively, 'old man.'

He watched the thin figure hurrying off again. 'A bit of responsibility,' he thought. 'The poor chap looks all nerves and funk already—' for it was plain they couldn't have been married long, plain they were both too young to have been anything long.

Carruthers, who was as solid and matter-of-fact outside as he wasn't inside, turned away so as not again to interrupt, and went home across the fields whistling sad tunes in minor keys. Marvellous beyond imagining to be married to beauty like that, but—-yes, by God, one would be on wires the whole time, there'd be no end to one's anxieties. And his final conclusion was that Jocelyn was a poor devil.

❁

He might have concluded it even more emphatically if he could have followed him, and seen what he saw when he got round the corner where Sally had been left for a moment—only for a moment, mind you, said Jocelyn to himself indignantly,—and found her the centre of an absorbed group.

She was smiling at two men and a woman, who were smiling and talking to her with every appearance of profound and eager interest. She was, in fact, being polite; a habit against which Mr. Pinner had repeatedly warned her, but, for the reason that it wasn't a habit at all but her natural inability not to return smiles for smiles, had warned her in vain.

These people, climbing up the hill on its other side and finding her standing there alone, had asked her, their faces wreathed in smiles and their eyes wide with astonishment and delight, the way; and she had only

politely told them she was a stranger in those parts, and they were only asking her a few kindly questions, to which she had only answered, ''Ere on my 'oneymoon,' and they were only expressing hopes that she would have a good time, when Jocelyn descended, swift, lean and vengeful, on the otherwise harmonious group.

'Yes?' said Jocelyn, scowling round at them. 'Yes?'

'My 'usband,' introduced Sally, with a gesture of all-including friendliness.

But it was no use her being friendly. Jocelyn was rude. How not be rude, with those two men standing there staring as if their eyes would bulge right out?

'I was under the impression,' he said, glaring at them up and down, from the top of their badly hatted heads, along their under-exercised and over-coated bodies to their unsatisfactory feet, 'that it was possible in England to leave a lady alone for two minutes without her being subject to annoyance.'

'I'm sure—' began the woman of the party, turning very red, while the men looked both scared and sheepish.

'Don't mind ''im,' said Sally sweetly, desirous of mollifying.

'On the contrary, I assure you that you had much better—much better,' declared Jocelyn truculently. And again he pulled Sally's hand through his arm, and again he hurried her off.

'Really,' he said, when they were out of sight, and only green fields, empty of everything but cows, were visible. 'Really.'

He stopped and wiped his forehead.

''Ot?' ventured Sally, timid but sympathetic.

'To think that I can't leave you alone a minute!' he cried.

'They ask me the way,' Sally explained.

'Quite,' said Jocelyn. 'Quite. And what did you say, might I inquire?'

'Said as 'ow I didn't know it.'

'Quite,' said Jocelyn. 'Quite.'

'Bein', as one might say, a stranger in these parts,' Sally explained still further, for these repeated quites upset her into speech.

'Quite,' said Jocelyn. 'Quite.'

'Now don't say that, Mr. Luke—please don't, now,' she begged.

'Perhaps you, on your part, won't say Mr. Luke,' said Jocelyn. 'Not quite so often. Not more than a dozen times a day, for instance.'

Sally was silent. She mustn't think of him as Mr. Luke, she couldn't think of him by his outlandish other name, so she thought of him as Husband. 'Usband's cross,' she thought; and withdrew into a prudent dumbness.

He ended by scrambling her through the hedge, and across a field as far from the path as possible; and, sitting her down with her back to everything except another hedge, tried to tell her a few things of a necessary but minatory nature.

'Sally,' he began, lying down on the grass beside her and taking her hand in his, 'you know, don't you, that I love you?'

Sally, cautiously coming out of her silence for a moment, as one who puts a toe into cold water and instantly draws it back again, said, 'Yes, Mr.—' stopping herself just in time, and hastily amending, 'What I means is, yes.'

'And you know, don't you, that my one thought is for you and your happiness?'

Yes, she supposed she knew that, thought Sally, fidgeting uneasily, for though the voice and manner were the voice and manner of Mr. Luke there was somehow a smack about them that reminded her of her father when he was going to do what was known in the family as learning her.

'Don't you?' insisted Jocelyn, as she said nothing. 'Don't you?'

He looked up into her face in search of an answer, and his voice faltered, he forgot completely what he was going to say, and whispering 'Oh, I *worship* you!' began kissing the hand he held, covering it with kisses, and seizing the other one and covering it with kisses too, while his ears, she could see, for his head lay in her lap, went crimson.

And Sally, who had already discovered that when Jocelyn's ears turned crimson he did nothing but kiss her and murmur words that were not, however incomprehensible, anyhow angry ones, knew that for this time she was being let off.

V

He kept her indoors for the rest of the day, and decided that in future they would use the car as a means of getting well out of reach of St. Mawes, and then, leaving it in some obscure village, take the necessary exercise undisturbed. The boat would have done for getting away in, but the fisherman wouldn't let them have it without him, and he too stared persistently at Sally. His ridiculous name was Cupp. 'Serve him right,' thought Jocelyn, who disliked him intensely.

These difficulties considerably interfered with the peace of the honeymoon. Having to take precautions, and scheme before doing ordinary things such as go out for a walk, seemed perfectly monstrous to Jocelyn. He was inclined, though he struggled against it, to blame Sally. He knew it was grossly unfair to blame her, but then it was outside his theories that a modest woman, however lovely, shouldn't be able in England to proceed on her lawful occasions unmolested. There must be, he thought, something in Sally's behaviour, though he couldn't quite see what.

He took her away the next morning for the whole day in the car, and, leaving it at a lonely wayside inn, marched her off for the exercise they both needed. He needed it, he knew, for he was getting quite livery, and so, he dared say, was she; though it would have been as easy to imagine a new-born flower having a liver as Sally. Anyhow, she must be exercised; her health was now his concern, Jocelyn told himself. Everything of hers was now his concern. The lovely child had been miraculously handed over to him by Destiny—thus augustly did he dub Mr. Pinner—and there was no one but him to protect and guide and teach her. No one but him jolly well should, either, said Jocelyn to himself, baring his teeth at the mere thought, savagely possessive, strongly resembling a growling dog over a newly-acquired bone.

But it was trying, having to hide her like this. It came to that, that he had to hide her if he was to have any peace. Well, when he took her to London, and settled down there seriously, there wouldn't be this trouble, because he intended to live in the slums. Slums were the places, he felt sure, for being let alone in. Not, of course, the more cut-throat kind, but obscure streets where everybody was too busy being poor to be interested in a girl's beauty. To be interested in that, Jocelyn thought he knew, you have to have had and be going to have a properly filling dinner every day. No dinners, no love. One only had to think a little to see this must be so. In such a street, how peaceful they would be, he in one room writing, she in another room not writing. Nor would there be any servant difficulty for them either, because Sally was used to housework, and knew no other conditions than those in which she had to do it herself. He and she were going to lead simple lives, irradiated by her enchanting loveliness; and presently, when she had begun to profit by the lessons he would give her in the art of correct speech, she would be more of a companion to him, more able to—well, converse.

For the moment, he couldn't disguise from himself, she was weak in conversation. To look at her, to look at her strangely noble little head, with everything there that is supposed to go with mind—the broad sweep of the brow, the beautifully moulded temples, the radiance in the eyes, the light that seemed to play over the vivid face with its swiftly changing expressions, each one more lovely than the last, and the whole amazing creature a poem of delicate colouring, except where colour had caught fire and become the flaming wonder of her hair—to look at this, and then hear the meagre, the really most meagre and defective observations that came out of it all, was a surprise. A growing surprise. Frankly, a growingly painful surprise. Somehow he hadn't noticed it before, but now he every hour more plainly perceived a grave discrepancy between Sally's appearance and her reality. Or was what he saw her reality, and what he heard mere appearance?

At night he was sure this was so. Next morning he was afraid it wasn't. In any case, she didn't match.

Curious, thought Jocelyn a day or two later, how completely Sally didn't match. Perhaps he was getting livery, and beholding her with a jaundiced eye. It wouldn't be surprising if this were so, seeing the reversal of his ordinary habits that marriage had made. His life till then had been one of excessive intellectual activity, and excessive sexual inactivity. Now it was just the opposite. It seemed to him that he was living entirely on his emotions and his nerves, doing nothing but make love, and never thinking a single thought worth thinking. This preoccupation with Sally's discrepances, for instance—what, after all, were a girl's discrepances compared to the importance, the interest, of his brain work till he met her?

He would come down to breakfast, to the sober facts of bacon and grey morning light, in a highly critical mood, feeling very old, and wise, and mature, and of course—there could be no two opinions as to that—in everything, except just physical beauty, Sally's superior. Then she would come down, and, cautiously saying nothing, smile at him; and he would be forced, in spite of himself, to wonder, as he gazed at her in a fresh surprise, whether there could be anything in the world superior to such beauty. Not himself, anyhow, he thought, with his little inky ambitions, his desire to express and impress himself, his craving to find out and do. Sally had no cravings that he could discover; she was mere lovely acquiescence, content—and with what exquisiteness—to be.

Still, in this world one couldn't just sit silent, and serene, and wonderful; and the minute circumstances obliged her to say something her discrepances worried him again. It really was surprising: pure perfection outside, and inside—he hated to think it, but more and more feared he recognised—pure Pinner. He must take her in hand. He must teach her, train her in the manners expected in her new sphere of life.

He pulled himself together, and took her in hand. During the second week after their marriage she was, as it were, almost constantly in hand; and towards its end Jocelyn's consciousness of his responsibility and duty, which at first had faded away in the evening and disappeared entirely at night, stretched further and further across the day like a lengthening

shadow, till at last it reached right into his very bed. The image of his mother had begun to loom nearer,—his mother, whom he had forgotten in the first fever of passion, but to whom he would undoubtedly soon now have to show Sally. Show her? Nothing so easy and sure of its effect as showing Sally, but it was what would happen immediately after she had been shown that Jocelyn, daily more able to contemplate Sally objectively as his honeymoon grew longer, began to consider.

There was no time to lose. He took her in hand. He started by attacking her h's, whose absence had early become acutely distressing to him. Every day he devoted an hour the first thing after breakfast to them, making her talk to him, to her regret, for she by then well knew that little good came of talk, and patiently, each time she dropped one, picking it up and handing it back to her, so to speak, with careful marginal comments.

He found her most obtuse. Ordinary talk wasn't enough. He had to invent sentences, special sentences for her to learn by heart and practise on, with little pitfalls in their middles which she was to avoid.

She seemed incapable of avoiding anything. Into each pitfall Sally invariably fell; and unwilling to believe that she couldn't keep out of them if she really tried, Jocelyn said the sentences over and over again to her, obstinately persevering, determined she should learn.

Hefty Harry hurries after his hat. Sally drew in long breaths, and blew them out again at the beginning of each word, hoping they would turn into h's, though for the life of her she couldn't see any difference between the way she rendered *Hefty Harry* and the way Jocelyn did.

Husbands inhabit heaven. This was another one, worse than *Hefty Harry*, because it wasn't enough to blow out her breath at the beginning of each word, but she had somehow to get it out in the middle of the middle one as well; besides, husbands didn't inhabit heaven till they were dead, and Jocelyn's habit of harping on heaven upset her, for heaven meant death first, and ever since her mother's death, at which Sally had been present, she had had the poorest opinion of the whole thing.

During the lesson Jocelyn carefully gazed out of the window, keeping his eyes off her, because this was serious, this was important, and mustn't be interfered with by her face. There he sat, patient but determined,

holding her hand so as to reassure her, saying the sentences slowly and distinctly, while Sally, moist with effort, diligently blew. Why was it so important? she vaguely wondered. He seemed to love her a lot, especially in the evenings, and kept on telling her at the times when his ears were red how happy he was, so what more did he want? What was the use of bothering over things like h's, which he declared were there but of which she could see no sign? She and her father, they had never worried about them, and they had got along all right. But Sally was docile; Sally was obedient and good-natured; Sally earnestly wished to give people what they wanted; and if what Husband wanted was h's, then she would try her utmost to provide them. If only she were quite clear as to what they were! Perhaps, by plodding, she would some day discover.

She plodded; and the nearest she got to criticism of this new development in her life was occasionally, when after breakfast Jocelyn called her over to the window, where he had placed two chairs in readiness for the lesson and pulled down the blind below the level of her head, occasionally, very occasionally, to murmur to herself, 'Them h's.'

❀

But it wasn't only her h's, it wasn't only the way she pronounced the few words that seemed to be at her disposal; there were other things that disquieted Jocelyn, as he awoke more and more from the wild first worship of her beauty. He appeared to be surrounded, out of doors and in, by an increasing number of difficulties. There was that business of not being able to go out without becoming the instant centre of the entire attention of St. Mawes,—most painful to Jocelyn, who had a fixed notion, implanted in him early in the decent cover of Almond Tree Cottage, that the truly well-bred were never conspicuous. How unpleasant, how extraordinarily unpleasant when, the morning lesson over and the need for exercise imperative, he went round to the garage to fetch the car, to find on his return the sea-wall opposite their lodgings black with expectant loungers; how unpleasant, how extraordinarily unpleasant to have to hurry Sally into the thing, as if she were the centre figure of a

cause célèbre leaving the Law Courts; and the car, being an old one bought second-hand, sometimes wouldn't start—twice that happened—and then to see how those loungers sprang into life and flocked across to help! Jocelyn, used only to quiet comings and goings and no one taking the least notice of anything he did, used, in fact to being what his mother described as well-bred, felt as if he had suddenly turned into a circus.

And indoors, too, he had difficulties, apart from and in addition to the difficulties at the lessons, for Sally showed a tendency, mild but unmistakable, to coalesce with the Cupps. She wanted to help Mrs. Cupp make the bed in the morning, she tried to clear away the breakfast, so as to save her feet, as she put it, and once, on some excuse or other, she actually left Jocelyn by himself in the parlour and got away into the kitchen, where he found her presently, on going to look, kissing a fat and hideous child that could only be a little Cupp.

To do her justice Mrs. Cupp in no way that Jocelyn could see encouraged this; on the contrary, she seemed a particularly stand-offish sort of woman, who not only knew her own place but knew Sally's as well, and wished to keep her in it. Unfortunate that Sally should be, apparently, so entirely without that knowledge.

Jocelyn did his best to impart it. 'You belong to me now, Sally,' he explained, 'and my place and sphere is your place and sphere, and my relations and friends your relations and friends. I don't go and sit in kitchens, nor am I friends, beyond what every one is in regard to that class, with the Cupps. I don't, and therefore you mustn't.'

Was this speech snobbish? He hoped not; he trusted not. He despised snobbishness. His mother had most carefully taught him to. She would shudder at the mere word, and the shudder had got into his childhood's bones.

Sally gave herself great pains to understand, looking at him attentively while he spoke and coming to the conclusion that what Usband was driving at was that she had got to sit quiet and remember she was now a lady. She sat quiet, remembering it. She made no attempt at any further budging from her place, even when Mrs. Cupp dropped things off the overloaded tray at her very feet, and her fingers itched to pick them up.

She managed not to; she managed to take no notice whatever of them, and, bending her head over the paper Jocelyn had written her lesson out on in a fair round hand, would bury herself in it instead, saying it out loud as he had bidden her, conning it diligently.

The room re-echoed with *Hefty Harry,* and the deep preliminary drawings in and blowings out of breaths that were meant to become h's, and never did.

VI

❁

It was impossible for young Carruthers, having been vouchsafed a vision of Sally, to stop himself from trying to have another. He was drawn as by a magnet. His walks, after that Sunday, took him daily down to St. Mawes, where, having briskly gone the length of the front swinging his stick, he would lean awhile—as long as he dared without becoming conspicuous—against the sea-wall, smoking and ostensibly considering the horizon, but really missing nobody who came or went along the road. The Sealyham Sally was left at home, but other dogs were brought because they are such wonderful introducers, and the road to acquaintanceship, young Carruthers knew, is paved with good dogs.

He wasn't sure that any profit would come of it if he did see the honeymooners and get into conversation,—probably not; but he couldn't help it; he had to try; he was drawn. And very soon he discovered which house they were staying in, because the other loungers, smoking and gazing out to sea, rare figures at ordinary times and scattered sparsely over a quarter of a mile, were now considerably increased in numbers, and thickened into a knot at one particular point. That point, Carruthers unhesitatingly concluded, was where she lived.

Unwilling to be seen doing this sort of thing, he held himself aloof from the knot, smoking his pipe at a decent distance; but none the less nothing escaped him that happened at the windows or the door of the little house. The house, he knew, for his family had lived in the neighbourhood for many years, was the house of the fisherman Cupp. And he thought, thrice happy Cupp, and three times thrice happy Mrs. Cupp,—for she would be constantly in and out of the very room, and be able to look at—no, he wouldn't, he couldn't say Sally, not with his own four-legged Sally so grotesquely profaning the name.

He was all wrong, however, about the Cupps. They were not at all happy; at least, Mrs. Cupp wasn't, and unless Mrs. Cupp was happy Cupp, though he only dimly apprehended this truth and explained the fact of his discomfort in many ways that were not the right ones, couldn't be happy either. For Mrs. Cupp, who beheld Sally with astonishment on her first appearance, no one in the least like that ever yet having been seen in St. Mawes, quickly began to have doubts as to whether her lodgers were married. Everybody in St. Mawes was married, except those who were going to be or had been, and it disturbed Mrs. Cupp terribly, who all her life had held her head high and looked people in the face, to think she was perhaps harbouring and cooking for a person who was neither virgin, wife, nor widow.

For a brief time, so brief that it could be counted in hours, Sally's nightgown had reassured her, because it was essentially the nightgown of the really married, a nightgown that Mrs. Cupp herself might have worn, and the most moral laundress had not to blush over. Up to the chin, down to the toes, long-sleeved, stiff, solid, edged at the throat and wrists with plain scallops, this nightgown did at first help Mrs. Cupp to hope that her lodgers were all right; but back came her doubts, and more insistent than before, when she perceived that Cupp too was noticing the young person's appearance, and, though he said nothing, was beginning to behave all sly; and they deepened finally into certainty on her becoming aware of those thickening clusters of loungers constantly hanging about opposite her house. Even young Mr. Carruthers. Oh, she saw him plain enough, and knew all right what he was after; for she hadn't been to the pictures over at Falmouth for nothing, and she had learned from them that that sort of girl got men come buzzing round her as if she were a pot of honey and they just so many flies. Cupp shouldn't, though. Cupp shouldn't get buzzing. Cupp, after fifteen years of being a steady husband, wasn't going to be let buzz—not *much*, said Mrs. Cupp to herself, scouring her kitchen with violence.

She said nothing to him, however, for two, as she would soon show him, could play at his game of acting sly; but when at the end of the first fortnight of the Lukes' stay Jocelyn, on her coming in to clear away the

breakfast, got out his money and was preparing as usual to pay her the next week's lodging in advance, she told him without wasting words that the rooms were let.

'Let?' repeated Jocelyn, taken aback.

'There's an end to everything,' said Mrs. Cupp enigmatically, as she cleared the table with great swift swoops.

'But,' protested Jocelyn, annoyed and surprised, 'we intended to stay at least another week.'

'I say there's an end to everything,' said Mrs. Cupp even more emphatically, crowding the plates noisily on to a tray. 'And one of them's my patience.'

Jocelyn stared. Sally, raising her head from her daily task, on which she was at that moment engaged, looked on with the air of a mild, disinterested angel.

'But what on earth has happened? What's the matter?' asked Jocelyn.

'You only got to cast an eye out of the winder to see what's the matter,' said Mrs. Cupp, jerking her elbow in its direction. '*They* don't collect like that round parties that's respectable.'

And dropping some forks off the overloaded tray she clattered out of the room.

Jocelyn turned swiftly to Sally. 'You see?' he said.

'See wot?' asked Sally, who was about to stoop and pick up the forks, but remembered not to just in time.

Yes; see what, indeed. That it was her fault'? That this disgrace had been brought on him through her fault? Was that, Jocelyn asked himself, shocked at the tempest of injustice that had for an instant swept him off his feet, what he wanted her to see?

'I meant,' he said, ashamed of his unfairness, 'you heard. You did hear, didn't you, what the horrible woman was saying?'

Sally nodded. 'Thinks we ain't married,' she said. She seemed quite undisturbed. 'Well, it ain't much use thinkin' we ain't when we are,' she remarked.

'Unfortunately she's sure we're not, so that we are being turned out,' said Jocelyn, dropping her hand, which he had taken, for this placidity,

which seemed to him evidence of inability to grasp a situation, instead of soothing made him angry again.

He strode across to the window, and grabbing at the blind pulled it down still lower. How inexpressibly humiliating to be turned out, how unendurable to have people thinking Sally wasn't respectable, and that he, *he* of all people, would come off with a girl for that sort of loathsome lark.

'It ain't much use bein' sure, when I got my marriage lines,' said Sally with the same calm. 'Let alone my weddin' ring.' And she added complacently after a minute, 'Upstairs in my box.' And after a further minute, 'I mean, my marriage lines.'

Then, supposing that the interruption to the lesson might now be regarded as over, and that it would therefore be expected of her that she should get on with it, she applied herself once more with patient industry to her task.

'*H*-usbands *h*-in'abit *h*-eaven,' she began again, assiduously blowing.

'Oh, my God,' said Jocelyn, under his breath.

❁

They left St. Mawes during the dinner hour. When Jocelyn told her they were going to leave almost at once, and she had better pack, Sally merely said Right O, and went upstairs to do it.

Right O, thought Jocelyn. Right O. Not a question, not a comment of any kind. Convenient, of course, in a way, but was this companionship? Could there be much character behind such resistlessness? Yet if she had asked questions and made comments he would, he knew, have flown at her; so that he was being unfair again and unreasonable, and he hated himself.

He usedn't to be unfair and unreasonable, he thought, standing in front of the fireless grate, a wrathful eye on the loungers clotted on the other side of the road; and as for being angry, such a disturbance of one's balance, whenever he had observed it in others, had seemed to him simply the sign of imperfect education. The uneducated were swept by furies, not scientific thinkers. Now just the contrary was happening,

and the uneducated Sally remained serene, while he was in an almost constant condition of emotion of one kind or another. Marriage, he supposed gloomily; marriage. The invasion of the spirit by the flesh. So absurd, too, the whole thing—God, how absurd when he thought of it in the morning, and remembered the cringing worship of the night before. Absurd, absurd, this nightly abdication of the mind, this abject bowing down of the higher before the lower. ... The worst of it was he didn't seem able to help himself. Whatever his theories were in the daytime, whatever his critical detachment, he only had to be close to Sally at night. ...

And in the daytime, instead of at least in the daytime being tranquil and able to get back his balance, every sort of annoyance crowded on him. Were all honeymoons like this? Impossible. They hadn't got Sally in them. It was Sally who—

The door opened, and there she was again, not ten minutes after having gone up. For Sally's things being of the kind that are quick to pack, owing to their fewness, she was ready and down before he had had time, hardly, to be sure she was going to keep him waiting. So that he resented this too, because he wasn't able to be angry with her over something definite and legitimate. He wanted to have a legitimate excuse for being angry with her, for it was really all her fault that they had been insulted and turned out. Of course it was. If he had been with his mother, Mrs. Cupp would have been deference itself, and that confounded sea-wall empty. It was all Sally. Looking like that. Looking so different from any one else. Looking so entirely different from the accepted idea of a decent man's wife. Besides, she ought anyhow to have had more things to pack. That one small tin trunk of hers was a disgrace to him. Beastly thing, how he hated it. All yellow. He must get her a proper trunk, and fill it properly, before he could appear with her at Almond Tree Cottage. There certainly were drawbacks to taking a wife in her shift, as one's forbears called it.

Yet, when she came in ready to start, she looked so astonishingly *right*, tin trunk or not, and quite apart from her face. She looked right; her clothes did. She might have been a young duchess, thought Jocelyn, who had never seen a duchess. He hadn't an idea how the miracle was worked.

Not by dressmakers and cleverness, of that he was certain, for the poor Pinners would have to buy clothes off the peg. Perhaps because she was so reedy tall. Perhaps because of the way she moved. Perhaps because she was so slender that there hardly seemed to be anything inside the clothes, and they couldn't help, left in this way almost to themselves, hanging in graceful folds. But *he* knew well enough what was inside them—the delicate young loveliness, just beginning to flower; and at the thought his anger all left him, and he didn't care any more about the Cupps or the sea-wall, and the feeling of humility came over him that came over him each time he saw her beauty, and he went to her and took both her hands, her little red hands, the only part of her that had been got at by life and spoilt, and kissed them, and said, 'Forgive me, Sally.'

'Wot you been doin'?' asked Sally, surprised.

'Not loving you enough,' said Jocelyn, kissing her hands again.

'Now *don't*,' said Sally very earnestly, '*don't* you go thinkin' that, now—' for the idea that she, who had been being loved almost more than she could stand on this trip, and wouldn't have been able to stand if it hadn't been for knowing it was her bounden duty, might have to be loved still more if Mr. Luke got it into his head that she ought to be, excessively alarmed her.

❁

The departure was not unmarked, as is sometimes said, by incident. Cupp, when the luggage had to be brought down, wasn't to be found, Mrs. Cupp seemed incommunicably absorbed over a saucepan, and Jocelyn, with some sharpness refusing Sally's help, whose instinct after years spent doing such things was to lay hold of anything that had to be laid hold of and drag it, got the tin box and his suitcase downstairs himself, and said Damn very loud when he knocked his head at the turn of the little staircase.

Sally heard him, and was enormously surprised and shocked. This was swearing. This was what she had been most carefully taught to look upon as real sin. Nothing else had shocked her on the honeymoon, because she

– 59 –

had nothing to go by when it came to husbands other than her father's assurance that, except in the daytime, they weren't gentlemen, and her own solemn vows in church to obey; but she knew all about swearing. It was wrong. It was strictly forbidden in God's Holy Word. That and drink were the two evils spoken of most frequently in her home, and with most condemnation. They went hand in hand. Drink ruined people; and, on their way to ruin and when they had got to it, they swore.

This is what Sally had been brought up to believe, so that when, standing in the doorway of the parlour watching Jocelyn labouring down the stairs with her trunk and longing to give him a hand, she heard him, after knocking his head, say a most loud clear damn, she was horrified. Her husband swearing. And not been drinking, either. Just had his tea as usual at breakfast, and been with her ever since, so she knew he couldn't have. Next thing she'd have to listen to would be God's name being taken in vain; and at the thought of that the blood of all the Pinners, that strictly God-fearing, Sunday-observing, Bible-loving race, surged to her cheeks.

'Mr. *Luke!*' she exclaimed, throwing his teaching as to the avoidance of this name to the winds.

'Hullo?' said Jocelyn, stopping short on the stairs and peering down at her round the edge of the tin trunk, arrested by the note in her voice.

'You didn't ought to swear,' said Sally, taking all her courage in both hands, her face scarlet. 'There's no call for it, and you didn't ought to swear—you *know* you didn't ought to.'

'But I only said damn,' said Jocelyn. 'Wouldn't you, if you bashed your head against this confounded sticking out bit of ceiling?'

'Mr. *Luke!*' cried Sally again, her eyes filling with tears. That he should not only say bad words himself but think her capable of them. ... Often she had been bewildered by things he said and did, but now she looked up at him through the tears in her eyes in a complete non-comprehension. It was as though she were boxed away from him behind a great thick wall, or cut off across a great big river, alone on an island, while he stood far off and unreachable on the opposite bank, and she had somehow to get to him, to stay close to him, because he was her husband. Dimly

these images presented themselves to her mind, dimly and confused, but nevertheless producing a very clear anxiety and discomfort.

'I'm sorry,' said Jocelyn, carefully coming down the remaining stairs and depositing the trunk sideways in the narrow passage, for though the trunk, as a trunk, was small, the passage, as a passage, was smaller; and in his turn as he looked at her he grew red, for he had just remembered that he never said damn in the presence of his mother or of the other ladies of South Winch, which was a place one didn't swear in, however much and unexpectedly he chanced to hurt himself. Was this *laissez aller* in Sally's presence due to his consciousness that she wasn't a lady, or due to the fact that she was his wife? Jocelyn disliked both these explanations, and accordingly, in his turn, grew red.

'Forgive me, Sally,' he said for the second time within half an hour.

This time she had no doubt as to what had to be forgiven.

'Promise not to do it no more,' she begged. 'Promise now—do.'

'Oh Sally, I'll promise anything, anything,' said Jocelyn staring at her, caught again into emotion by the extraordinary beauty of her troubled face.

'Father says,' said Sally, still looking at him through tears, 'that if somebody swears, then they drinks. An' if they drinks, then they swears. An' it goes 'and in 'and, and they don't stop ever, once they starts, till they gets to—.'

She broke off, and stood looking at him in silence. The picture was too awful a one. She couldn't go on.

'What do they get to, my angel, my beautiful angel?' asked Jocelyn, kissing her softly, not listening any more.

''Ell,' whispered Sally.

'Now *you're* swearing,' murmured Jocelyn dreamily, no longer fully conscious, shutting her eyes with kisses. 'Your sweet, sweet eyes,' he murmured, kissing them over and over again.

No, Sally couldn't make head or tail of Mr. Luke. Better not try. Better give it up. *She* swearing?

❁

She longed very much for the company of Mr. Pinner.

'Father,' she thought, while Jocelyn was fetching the car, and she was standing alone in the passage watching the luggage, for she had been bred carefully never to leave luggage an instant by itself, 'Father—'e could tell me.'

What she wanted Mr. Pinner to tell her wasn't at all clear in her mind, but she was quite clear that he would tell her if he could, whereas Jocelyn, who certainly could, wouldn't. Mr. Luke, she felt in her bones, even if she had the courage to ask him anything would only be angry with her because she didn't already know it; yet how could she know it if nobody had ever told her? At home they usedn't to jump down one's throat if one asked a question. 'Snug,' thought Sally, her head drooping in wistful recollection, while with the point of her umbrella she affectionately stroked the sides of the tin trunk, 'snug at 'ome in the shop—snug at 'ome in the lil' shop—' and whatever else being married to a gentleman was, it wasn't snug.

Marriage to a gentleman—why, you never knew where you were from one moment to another; nothing settled about it; no cut and come again feeling; all ups and downs, without, as one might say, any middles; all either cross looks or, without warning, red ears, kisses, and oh-Sallyings. It was as if words weren't the same when a gentleman got hold of them. They seemed somehow to separate. Queer, thought Sally, wistfully stroking the tin trunk.

She groped round in her hazy thoughts. She was in a strange country, and there was a fog, and yet she had somehow to get somewhere. *She* swearing?

❀

The car came round, and Jocelyn came in.

'Hasn't Cupp turned up yet?' he asked.

Sally shook her head.

'I want him to help me cord the luggage on,' said Jocelyn, squeezing past between her and the trunk.

'I can,' said Sally.

'No you can't,' snapped Jocelyn, striding to the kitchen door and opening it.

'Is Mr. Cupp anywhere about?' he haughtily asked the figure bent over the saucepan. He needed his help, or nothing would have induced him to speak to Mrs. Cupp again.

'No,' said Mrs. Cupp, without ceasing to stir; but being a good woman, who tried always to speak the truth, she amplified this into accuracy. ''E's somewhere, but he ain't about,' said Mrs. Cupp.

For, having a short way with her when it came to husbands, she had turned the key that morning on Cupp while he was still asleep, well knowing that he wouldn't dare get banging and shouting lest the neighbours should find out his wife had locked him in, and his shame become public. Besides, he was aware of the reason, and would keep quiet all right, she having had a straight talk with him the night before.

Cupp had been discomfited.

'Don't you go thinkin' you're goin' to get adulteratin' at your age and after 'avin' been a decent 'usband these fifteen years,' said Mrs. Cupp.

''Oo's been adulteratin'?' growled Cupp, strong in the knowledge that he hadn't, but weak in the consciousness that he would have liked to have.

'In your 'eart you 'ave, Cupp,' said Mrs. Cupp, who had her Bible at her fingers' ends, 'and Scripture says it's the same thing.'

Cupp at this sighed deeply, for he knew it wasn't.

'Scripture says,' said Mrs. Cupp, sitting up very straight in bed and addressing Cupp's back as he lay speechless beside her, 'that 'ooso looks at a woman an' lusts after 'er 'as committed adultery with 'er in 'is 'eart. Ain't you been lookin' at that there girl and lustin' after 'er in your 'eart, Cupp? Ain't you? Why, I *seen* you. Seen you doin' it round doors, seen you doin' it out of winders. You been adulteratin' all over the place. *I'll* learn you to get lustin'—'

And when she went downstairs in the morning she locked him in.

So Jocelyn had to carry out the luggage himself, bidding Sally stay where she was and wait quietly till he called her, and cording it on without the assistance, curtly refused, of the loungers against the sea-wall.

His mother's luggage on their little holiday jaunts had been so neat, so easily handled, fixed on in two minutes; but the tin trunk was a difficult, slippery shape, and anyhow an ignoble object. Every aspect of it annoyed him. It was like going about with a servant's luggage, he thought, wrestling with the thing, which was too high and not long enough, and refused to fit in with his suitcase.

'Off?' inquired one of the loungers affably.

'Looks like it,' said Jocelyn, tugging at the cord.

What a question. Silly ass. 'Do you mind standing a little further back?' he said with icy anger. 'You see, if you come so close I can't get—' he tugged—'any—' he tugged, setting his teeth—'*purchase*—'

Nobody moved; neither the particular lounger he was speaking to, nor the others.

'Upon my word, sir,' said Jocelyn, jerking round furiously, ready to fight the lot of them.

But they were not attending to him. Their eyes were all fixed on the parlour window, to which Sally, so anxious not to keep Jocelyn waiting a minute when he called as to risk disobeying him, had stolen to see how near ready he was.

There she stood, almost full length, the blind, now that they were leaving, drawn up, and the sun shining straight on her. St. Mawes had not had such a chance before. Its other glimpses of her had been flashes. Nor had the place in all its history ever till now been visited by beauty. Pretty girls had passed through it and disappeared, or stayed in it and disappeared equally completely because of growing old, and there was a tradition that in the last century the doctor had had a wife who for a brief time was very pretty, and during that brief time caused considerable uproar; but no one living had seen her, it was all hearsay from the last generation. This at the window wasn't hearsay. This was the thing itself, the rare, heavenly thing at its most exquisite moment. Naturally the loungers took no further heed of Jocelyn; naturally with one accord they lifted up their eyes, and greedily drank in.

Jocelyn gave the cord one final and very vicious tug, knotted it somehow, and ran indoors.

'What on earth you must go and stand at the window for—' he exclaimed, hurrying into the room and catching her by the arm. 'I was going to fetch you in a minute. Come along, then—let's start, let's get out of this confounded place. Ready? Got everything? I don't want any delays once we're outside—'

Hastily he looked round the room; there was nothing there. Hastily he looked over Sally; she seemed complete. Then he rushed her out to the car exactly as if, head downwards, they were both plunging into something most unpleasant which had to be gone through before they could escape to freedom.

'Monstrous, monstrous,' said Jocelyn to himself. 'The whole thing is incredible and fantastic. I might be the impresario of a prima donna or a cinema star'—and he remembered, though at the time, like so many other things, it had drifted past his ears unnoticed, that that grotesque creature his father-in-law had said Sally had a gift for collecting crowds.

How painfully true, thought Jocelyn, plunging into the one waiting outside. What a regrettable gift. Of all gifts this was the one he could best have done without in anybody he was obliged to be with; for he hated crowds, he hated public attention, he was thin-skinned and sensitive directly anything pulled him out of the happy oblivion of his work. As far as he had got in life, and it seemed to him a long way, he judged that quite the best of all conditions was to sit in an eye-proof shell, invisible to and unconscious of what is usually called the world. And speculate; and discover; and verify.

Well, no use thinking of that now.

'Get in, get in,' he urged under his breath, helping Sally with such energy that she was clumsier at it than usual. 'Never mind the rug—you can arrange that afterwards. Here—I'll hold the umbrella—'

They got off. He could drive perfectly well, yet they got off only after a series of forward bounds and the stopping of his engine. But they did get off—through the loungers, past the windows with heads at them, round the sharp corner beyond the houses, up the extraordinarily steep hill.

Sally held her breath. This hill terrified her. Suppose the car, which

each time seemed very nearly to stop on it, stopped quite, couldn't go on at all, and they rolled down backwards, down, down, straight into the sea?

But they reached the top safely. It wasn't the car that rolled down backwards that day; it was the tin trunk, and with it Jocelyn's suitcase.

Unconscious, they drove on towards Truro.

VII

❁

They drove in total silence. Jocelyn had much to think of, and not for anything would Sally have opened her mouth when Mr. Luke's was shut in that particular tight line. He had see-sawed back again, she knew, and was at the opposite end to what she called his oh-Sally condition. Besides, she never did say anything when she was in the car, however much he tried to make her, for from the beginning, even before there were hills, it had frightened her. Cars hadn't come Mr. Pinner's way, and, except for the one drive with Jocelyn that first day of his courting, she had had no experience of them till now.

This one gave her little joy. It went so fast; it had hairsbreadth escapes at corners; it had twice run over chickens, causing words with other angry gentlemen, and it was full inside, where she had to sit, of important and dangerous-looking handles and pedals that had to have the rug and her dress and her feet and her umbrella carefully kept clear of them, or there would be that which she called to herself, catching her breath with fear, a naccident.

Jocelyn had said once, very peremptorily and making hurried movements with his left hand, 'For goodness sake don't let that rug get mixed up with the gears—' for the car was a Morris-Cowley, and what Sally thought of with anxiety as them 'andles were between her and Jocelyn, and it had been enough. The tone of his voice on that occasion had revealed to her that a combination of rug and gears, and therefore of anything else and gears, such as dress, feet or umbrella, would be instantly disastrous, and he never had to say it again.

For the rest of the honeymoon she sat squeezed together as far away from the alarming things as she could, the rug tucked with anxious care tightly round her legs, and her feet cramped up in the corner. She was very

uncomfortable, but that mattered nothing to Sally. Even if she hadn't been afraid of what might happen, her own comfort, when the wishes of her elders and betters were in question, wouldn't have been given a thought. The Pinners were like that. Their humility and patience would have been remarkable even in a saint, and as for their bumps of veneration, they were so big that that country would indeed be easy to govern which should be populated by many Pinners.

The late Mrs. Pinner, not of course herself a Pinner proper, but of the more turbulent blood of a race from Tottenham called Skew, had disliked these virtues in Mr. Pinner, and thought and frequently told him that a shopkeeper shouldn't have them at all. A shopkeeper's job, she often explained, was to leave off being poor as soon as possible, and Mr. Pinner never at any time left off being that—all because, Mrs. Pinner asserted, he had no go; and having no go was her way of describing patience and humility. But in Sally, when these qualities began to appear, she encouraged them, for they made for the child's safety, they kept her obedient and unquestioning, they sent her cheerfully to bed when other girls were going to the pictures, and caused her to be happy for hours on end by herself in the back parlour performing simple duties. Besides, though Mrs. Pinner would have been hard put to it to give it a name, in Sally patience and humility were somehow different from what they were in Pinner. They held their heads up more. They didn't get their tails between their legs. They were in fact in Sally, though Mrs. Pinner could only feel this dumbly, never getting anywhere near thinking it, not abject things that quivered in corners, but gracious things that came to meet one with a smile.

Filled, then, as ever, with these meek virtues, Sally, squeezed into as little space as possible, and bracing herself, having got safely to the top of the hill, to meet the next terror, which was the twisty, slippery, narrow steep road down to the ferry, and the twisty, slippery, narrow steep road up from it on the other side, and after that the terror of every corner, round each of which she was sure would lurk a broad-beamed charabanc,—was carried in the Morris-Cowley in the direction of Truro. Here, Jocelyn supposed, they had better stay the night. Here there were hotels, and he would be able to consider what he would do next.

He urged the little car along as fast as it would go, for he was possessed by the feeling that if he only got away fast enough he would get away altogether. But get away altogether from what? Certainly from St. Mawes, and Mrs. Cupp, and the loungers who all of course also supposed he and Sally weren't married. That was the first, the immediate necessity. He had not only been turned out, but turned out, he said to himself, with contumely,—no use saying it to Sally, because she wouldn't know what contumely was, and it did seem to him really rather absurd to be going about with somebody who had never heard even of such an ordinary thing as contumely.

It wasn't her fault, of course, but the turning out and the contumely were obviously because of her; there was no denying that. His mother would have been sitting in those rooms at this moment, the most prized and cherished of lodgers. Obviously the whole thing was Sally's fault, though he quite admitted she couldn't help it. But it merely made it worse that she couldn't, for it took away one's confidence in the future, besides making it unfair to say anything unkind.

Feeling that if he did say anything it might easily be unkind, he kept his mouth tight shut, and drove in total silence; and Sally, whenever the road was fairly straight and could be left for a moment unwatched, looked at him out of the corners of her eyelashes, and was very sorry for Usband, who seemed upset again.

'Stomach,' concluded Sally, who could find no other explanation for Jocelyn's ups and downs; and wondered whether she would ever dare bring to his notice a simple remedy her father, who sometimes suffered too but with less reserve, always had by him.

Well, there was one thing to be said for all this, thought Jocelyn, his stern eye fixed straight ahead, his brow severe, as he hurried the car along the road to the ferry—he was now awake. At last. High time too. Till then, from the day he first saw Sally, in spite of moments of grave spiritual disturbance and annoyance, he had been in a feverish dream. Out of this dream Mrs. Cupp's conduct had shaken him, and he believed he might now be regarded as through with the phase in which he thought of nothing but the present and let the future go hang. Now he had to

think. Decisions were being forced on him. Holidays end, but life goes on; honeymoons finish, but wives don't. Here he was with a wife, and upon his soul, thought Jocelyn, precious little else,—no career, no plans, no lodgings.

What a position. The lodgings, of course, were a small thing, but how being turned out of them rankled! His life had been so dignified. He and his mother had never once come across a member of the lower classes who was rude. At South Winch all was order, decency, esteem in their own set and respectfulness from everybody else. At Ananias what order, what decency, what esteem, what respectfulness. Impossible at Ananias, however modest one might be, not to know that one was looked upon as a present pride and a future adornment, with the Master at the top of the scale invariably remembering who one was and graciously smiling, and at the bottom the almost affectionate attentions of one's warm and panting bedmaker. Impossible, too, not to know, though this, except for the pleasure it gave his mother, was of no sort of consequence, that South Winch regarded him with interest. These attitudes hadn't at all disarranged Jocelyn's grave balance, hadn't at all turned his head, because of his real and complete absorption in his work; but they had been there—a fitting and seemly background, a sunny, sheltering wall against which he could expand, in quiet security, the flowers of his ambitions.

Now here he was, kicked out into the street—it amounted to that—by a person of the utmost obscurity called Cupp. Conceive it. Conceive having got into a position in which anybody called Cupp could humiliate him.

He banged his fist down on the electric born as an outlet to his feelings. It gave a brief squeak, and was silent.

'Horn's gone wrong,' he said, pressing it hard but getting nothing more out of it.

Sally's heart gave a thump. To have anything go wrong at such a moment! For they were on that road cut in the hillside, narrow, twisty, slippery and steep, which leads on the St. Mawes side down through a wood, charming that late March afternoon with the mild sun slanting through the pale, grey-green branches of naked trees across flocks of primroses, to the King Harry Ferry. Far down on Sally's side she could

have seen, if she had dared look, the placid waters of the Fal, unruffled in their deep shelter by the wind that was blowing along the open country at the top. Her anxious eyes, however, were not in search of scenery—at no time was she anything of a hand at scenery,—they were strained towards each fresh corner as it came in sight; for one day they had met a charabanc round one of those very corners, a great wide horror taking up nearly all the road. But luckily that day they were coming up the hill, not going down it, and so they had the inside, and not the unprotected, terrifying outside edge. Now they were outside, and suppose ...

'Horn's gone wrong,' said Jocelyn, just as she was thinking that.

But did it matter? she asked herself, seeking comfort. She tried to hope it didn't. Horns weren't like wheels. One didn't depend on them for getting along. They just made noises. Useful, as one's voice was useful, but not essential, like one's legs.

No, it didn't matter much, evidently, for Usband was saying he would put it right while they were on the ferry,—and then her heart gave a much bigger thump, and seemed to leap into her mouth and crouch there trembling, for there, round the very next corner, a few yards in front of them, was another charabanc.

'My gracious goodness,' thought Sally, the colour ebbing out of her face as she stiffened in her seat and held on tighter. 'My gracious *goodness*—'

But it was going down too; thank heaven it was going down too—making, even as they were making, for the ferry.

Jocelyn banged again on his horn, which gave another weak squeak and then was silent.

'Oh, 'e ain't goin' to try and pass it? 'E ain't goin' to try and pass it?' Sally asked herself, clutching the side of the car.

The charabanc, however, was unaware that anything had come down the hill behind it, and continued in the middle of the narrow road; and to Sally's relief Jocelyn stole quietly along close up to its back, for he thought that if he kept right up against it and made no noise the people in it wouldn't be able to see Sally, and he wouldn't have to sit there impotently watching the look spreading over their faces when they caught sight of her that by now he knew only too well.

All went smoothly till they were on the ferry. The charabanc drove straight to the farther end of it, and Jocelyn slipped along close behind, and then, getting out, still unobserved, opened his bonnet and began to deal with the horn.

He had no side-horn with him. It had been removed by an idiot who lived on his staircase at Ananias, and who constantly saw fun where no one else did. He saw fun in removing Jocelyn's horn; and though on serious representations being made he restored it, it hadn't been fixed on again, because Jocelyn soon after that met Sally, and everything else was blotted from his mind. Now he remembered it, and cursed the silly idiot through whose fault it wasn't at that moment on the car. Still, he would soon set the electric one right; there couldn't be much the matter with it.

He proceeded, his head inside the bonnet, to set it right, and Sally, feeling safe for a bit with Jocelyn outside the car, looked on sympathetically. She wanted to help, if only by holding something, but knew she mustn't move. The back of the great charabanc towered above their little two-seater as the stern of a finer towers above a tug. All was quiet up there. The tops of the heads of the last row of passengers were motionless, their owners no doubt being engaged in contemplating the scenery of the Fal.

Then suddenly under Jocelyn's manipulations the horn began to blow, and the row of heads, startled into attentiveness by this unexpected shrieking immediately underneath them, turned and peered down over the edge of the charabanc's back. Then they saw Sally, and their peering became fixed.

But Jocelyn had no time for that now; what was of importance at the moment was that the horn wouldn't stop. It shrieked steadily; and though he leapt backwards and forwards from the part of it that was in the bonnet to the part of it that was on the steering-wheel and did things rapidly and violently in both places, it went on shrieking.

Here was a nice thing, he thought, to happen to a man whose one aim was to be unnoticed. It was fortunate that the noise drowned what he was saying, for so Sally hadn't the shock of hearing him break his recent promise; and, much surprised at the conduct of the horn, she was shaken out of her usual prudent silence and was moved to draw Jocelyn's

attention to its behaviour by remarking, on one of his flying visits to the steering wheel, that it wasn't half hollering.

'Oh, shut *up*!' cried Jocelyn, beside himself; and who knows whether he meant Sally or the horn?

Sally took it that he was addressing the horn, and observed sympathetically that it didn't seem to want to.

'If only I had a small screwdriver!' cried Jocelyn, frantically throwing out the contents of his tool-box in search of what wasn't there. 'I don't seem to have a small screwdriver—a *small* screwdriver—has anybody got a *small* screwdriver?'

The ferryman had no screwdriver, big or small, and the driver of the charabanc, descended from his place to come and look on, had none small enough; while as for the passengers, now all standing on their seats and craning their necks, nothing was to be expected of them except absorption in Sally.

'Scissors would do—scissors, scissors!' cried Jocelyn, who felt that if the horn didn't stop he would go mad.

Nobody had any scissors except Sally, who got on her feet quickly and delightedly, because now she could help—the heads craned more than ever—and said she had a pair at the bottom of her trunk.

'No, no,' said Jocelyn, unable even for the sake of perhaps stopping the horn to face uncording and unpacking before the whole ferry that terrible tin trunk of hers. 'Sit still, Sally—'

And he began to hit whatever part seemed nearest to the noise with his clenched fist.

'*That* won't do no good,' said the driver of the charabanc, grinning.

The grin spread to the face of the ferryman, and began to appear on the faces piled up over the top of the charabanc.

Jocelyn saw it, and suddenly froze into icy impassiveness. Whatever the damned horn chose to do he wasn't going to provide entertainment for a lot of blasted trippers. Besides—was he losing his temper? He, who had supposed for years that he hadn't got one?

He slammed the bonnet to, flung the tools back into their box, got into his seat again, and sat waiting to drive off the ferry with a

completely expressionless face, just as if nothing at all were happening; and Sally, deluded by his calm into supposing that he thought the horn was now all right, after waiting a moment anxiously and seeing that he didn't do anything more, nudged him gently and told him it was still blowing.

'Is it?' said Jocelyn; and there was something in the look he gave her that made her more sure than ever that speech with Usband was a mistake.

It blew all the way to Truro. That was the nearest place where the thing could be taken to a garage, and kicked to pieces if nothing else would stop it. For ten miles it blew steadily. They streamed, shrieking, along the lanes and out on to the main road. The drive was a nightmare of astonished faces, of people rushing out of cottages, of children shouting, of laughter flashing and gone, to be succeeded by more and more, till the whole of every mile seemed one huge exclamation.

Sally squeezed terror-stricken into her corner. Such speed as this she had never dreamed of, nor had it ever yet been got out of the Morris-Cowley. She could only cling and hope. The noise was deafening. The little car leapt into the air at every bump in the road. Jocelyn's face was like a marble mask. The charabanc, being bound for Falmouth, turned off to the left at the main road, and the passengers rose as one man in their seats and waved handkerchiefs of farewell; while Sally, even at such a moment unable not to be polite, let go the side of the car an instant to search with trembling fingers for her handkerchief and wave it back.

❁

At Truro he stopped at the first garage he saw, a small one in the outlying part of the town, where there were few passers-by. The few there were, however, immediately collected round the car that swooped down the hill on them hooting, and still went on hooting in spite of having stopped.

How simple, if it had been his mother who was with him, to have asked her to walk on to an hotel or a confectioner's, and wait for him while he had the horn seen to. She would have proceeded through the town unobserved and unmolested, and the hotel or confectioner would

have received her without curiosity, and attended respectfully to her wants. Or she might have waited in the car, and there too she would have aroused neither interest nor comment. A lady, you see. A lady, turning, like a decent Italian house, her plain and expressionless side to the public of the street, and keeping her other side, her strictly private and delightful other side, for her family and friends.

He hurried Sally into the garage, into the furthermost depths of the garage. Not for her, he felt, were quiet walks alone through streets and unquestioning acceptance at hotels; not for him the convenience, the comfort, of a companion who in a crisis needn't be bothered about, who automatically became effaced. Nothing effaced Sally. Her deplorable conspicuousness made it impossible for her to go anywhere without him. She had to be accompanied and protected as watchfully as if she were the Crown Jewels. Yes, or a perambulator with a baby in it that could never be left alone for an instant, and was always having to be pushed about by somebody. That somebody was himself, Jocelyn Luke; Jocelyn Luke, who as recently as a month ago was working away, hopeful and absorbed, immersed in profoundly interesting and important studies, independent, with nothing at all to trammel him or hinder him—with, on the contrary, everything and everybody conspiring to leave him as untrammelled and unhindered as possible. What was he now? Why, the perambulator's nursemaid. Just that: the perambulator's attendant nursemaid.

This seemed to Jocelyn fantastic.

'Wait here, will you?' he said, hurrying her into the garage and depositing her like a parcel in the remotest corner. 'Don't move, will you, till I fetch you—'

And he left her there, safe as far as he could see, and went back to the shrieking car.

She sat down thankfully on a pile of empty petrol cans. If only she could be left there for a good long while, if only she could spend the rest of the day there. … 'Don't move,' Usband had said; as though she wanted to! Except that she was very hungry, really hungry now that her fears were over, for she had had no dinner yet, and it was two o'clock, how happy would she have been to stay there without moving for the rest of

the afternoon. The quiet corner, away from danger, away from having to guess what she ought to say to Usband, and away from the look he gave her when she had said it, seemed almost perfect. It would have been quite perfect if there had been anything to eat.

And as if in answer to her wish, the little door into a shed at the back opened, and in walked a youth, smudged and pasty-looking as those look who work much in garages, bearing in his hand a basin tied up in a crimson handkerchief.

This was young Mr. Soper, the most promising of the mechanics employed at the garage, who daily ate his dinner in that corner. There he could sit on the pile of empty petrol cans, out of sight and yet within earshot should his services suddenly be called for; and on this particular day, his firm having been by chance extra busy all the morning, he had gone later than usual into the private shed at the back to fetch the basin of food left there for him by his landlady's little son, so that when Jocelyn took Sally into the corner it was empty, because Mr. Soper, instead of being in the middle of his dinner as he would have been on other days, was in the act of collecting it in the shed.

'Beg pardon, Miss,' he said, staring at Sally, his mouth dropping open. 'Beg pardon, I'm sure, Miss—'

And he put his arm quickly back round the door he had just come through and whipped out a chair. 'Won't you—won't you sit more comfortable, Miss?'

'Don't mind if I do,' said Sally, getting up and smiling politely.

Mr. Soper's pasty face became bright red at that smile. He proceeded to dust the seat of the chair by rubbing the bottom of his handkerchiefed basin up and down it, and then stood staring at the young lady, the basin dangling-sideways in his hand, held carelessly by the knotted, corners of its handkerchief, and some of its gravy accordingly dribbling out.

'It do smell nice, don't it,' remarked Sally as she sat down, unable to refrain from sniffing.

'What do, Miss?' asked Mr. Soper, recognising with almost incredulous pleasure a manner of speech with which he was at his ease.

'Wot you got in that there basin,' said Sally, also recognising, and also

with pleasure, accents since her marriage become very dear to her because reminiscent of home.

She smiled with the utmost friendliness at him. Mr. Soper found it difficult to believe his eyes.

'It's my dinner,' said Mr. Soper, gazing at the vision.

'Well, I didn't suppose it was your Sunday 'at,' said Sally, pleased to find that she too, given a chance, could, say clever things. 'Tell by the smell it ain't a nat.'

Mr. Soper also seemed to think this clever, for he laughed, as Sally put it to herself, like anything.

'Stew?' she asked, her delicate nose describing little half circles of appreciative inquiry.

'That's right,' said Mr. Soper. 'Irish.'

'Thought so,' said Sally; and added with a sigh, 'the best of the lot.'

Mr. Soper being intelligent, though handicapped at the moment by not quite believing his eyes, thought he here perceived encouragement to untie the handkerchief. He put the basin on the floor at the young lady's feet, and untied it. She gazed at the lovely contents, at potatoes showing their sleek sides through the brimming gravy, at little ends of slender cutlets, at glimpses of bright carrots, at pearly-shouldered onions gleaming from luscious depths, with such evident longing that he was emboldened to ask her if she wouldn't oblige him by tasting it, and telling him her opinion of it as a stew.

'There's stews and stews, you know, Miss,' he said, hastily arranging it on an empty packing-case convenient for her, 'but my old woman's who looks after me is 'ard to beat——'

And he ran into the little shed he had come out of, and after a minute's rummaging brought her a spoon and plate. His own spoon was in his pocket. He didn't use a plate.

Sally tasted; and, having tasted, went on tasting. Soon there was danger that Mr. Soper's dinner would be so much tasted that there wouldn't be any left, but he cared nothing for that. If he had had a hundred stews, and he starving, they should all have been the young lady's.

Sally tried not to taste too much, but she was so hungry, and the stew

was so lovely. Besides, the young man kept urging her to go on. He was more like a friend than any one she had yet met. That he should never take his eyes off her didn't disturb her in the least, for she had been used to that all her life; and his language was her language, and he didn't make her feel nervous, and she knew instinctively that she could do nothing wrong in his sight, and she talked more to him during the half hour they ate the stew together—for she presently insisted on his getting another plate and joining in—than she had talked to Jocelyn the whole time they had known each other; talked more to him, indeed, than she had ever talked to anybody, except, when she was little, to those girl friends who had later fallen away.

How surprising, how delightful, the ease with which she said things to Mr. Soper, and the things that came into her head to say! Quite clever, she was; quite sharp, and quick at the take-up. And laugh—why, the young fellow made her laugh so that she could hardly keep from choking. Not in all her life had she laughed as Mr. Soper made her laugh. Bright, he was, and no mistake. While as for Mr. Soper himself, who could be much, much brighter, he was fortunately kept damped down to his simpler jokes by the effect the strange young lady's loveliness had on him; so that he who in Truro was known as the life of his set, as the boldest of its wits as well as the most daring of its ladies' men, was as mild and timid in his preliminary frisks with Sally as a lately born lamb exploring, for the first time, the beautiful strange world it had suddenly discovered.

❀

Jocelyn found them there, the empty basin on the floor between them, and, sticking up in it, two spoons.

'My 'usband,' introduced Sally, starting a little, for she had forgotten Jocelyn; and Mr. Soper had what he afterwards described as the turn of his life.

She with a husband? She who was hardly old enough, if you asked him, to have a father even? Got a husband all the time, and eaten his stew. He didn't grudge her the stew, but he did think she ought to have

told him she had a husband. Fancy eating his stew, and knowing she had a husband the whole time. It seemed to make it unfair. It seemed to make it somehow false pretences. And one of these blinking gentlemen, too; one of your haw-haw chaps with the brains of a rabbit, thought Mr. Soper, looking Jocelyn up and down, who took no notice of him whatever. See that written all over him, thought Mr. Soper, seeking comfort in derision,—a silly fool who couldn't even mend his own horn. Wicked, he called it, wicked, to thieve this girl away from her own lot, filch her, before she knew what she was about, from her natural mates, go-ahead chaps like, for instance, himself, when there were thousands of female rabbits in his own class who would have fitted him like so many blooming gloves.

'Class should stick to class,' said Mr. Soper to himself, who belonged to at least four societies for violently welding all classes into one, the one being Mr. Soper's.

Jocelyn ignored him. ('Haw, haw,' thought Mr. Soper derisively, hurt by this, and sticking out a chin that no one noticed.) Shutting his eyes to the hideous evidence of the two spoons in the basin, to which he would refer, he decided, later, he took Sally's arm and hurried her out to the now silent Morris-Cowley. This had not been his intention when he came in. He had intended to tell her that he had just discovered the loss of the luggage, that he was going back at once to look for it, and leave her there, where she was safe and private, till he came back.

The sight of the basin and spoons forced him to other decisions. She was obviously neither safe nor private. He said nothing at all, but gripping her arm with, perhaps, unnecessary vigour seeing how unresistingly she went, hurried her out of the place and helped her, again with, perhaps, unnecessary vigour into her seat, slamming the door on her and hastening round to the other side to his own.

Mr. Soper, however, was hard on their heels. Nothing if not nippy, he was determined to see the last of her who not only was the first human being he had met to whom he could imagine going down on his knees, but also—thus did romance and reality mingle in his mind—who contained at that moment at least three-quarters of his Irish stew. It seemed to give him a claim on her. Inside himself was the remaining quarter, and it did

– 79 –

seem to unite them. Mortified as he was, deceived as he felt himself to be, he yet couldn't help, in his mind, making a joke about this union, which he thought so good that he decided to tell it to his friends that night at the whist-drive he was going to—it need not be repeated here,—and he was so excessively nippy, such a very smart, all-there, seize-your-opportunity young man, that he actually managed to say in Sally's left ear during the brief moment Jocelyn was on his way round to the other side, bending down ostensibly to examine the near back tyre, 'Whatever did you want to go and marry one of them haw-haw fellers for, when there was—'

But what there was Sally never heard, for at that instant the car leaped forward, leaving him on the kerb alone.

There he stood, looking after it; apparently merely a pale, contemptuous mechanic, full of the proper scorn for a shabby little four-year-old two-seater—he could of course date it exactly—but really a baffled young man who had just been pulled up and thwarted in the very act of falling, for the first time in his life, passionately and humbly in love.

❁

The Thistle and Goat was where Jocelyn took her. It was the first hotel he saw. He had to deposit her somewhere; he couldn't take her with him in search of the luggage, and have her hanging round while he picked it up and corded it on again, and making friends with anybody who came along. Would she obey him and stay in the bedroom, or would he be forced to the absurdity of locking her in? He was so seriously upset by the various misfortunes of the day that he was ready to behave with almost any absurdity. He was quite ready, for instance, to fight that spotted oaf at the garage; he had itched to knock him down, and had only been restrained by a vision of the crowd that would collect, and a consciousness of how it would advertise Sally. To lock her in her room was, he admitted, a violent sort of thing to do, and violence, he had been brought up to believe, was always vulgar and ridiculous, but it would anyhow be effective. Definite and strongly simple measures were, he perceived, needful with Sally, especially when one was in a hurry. He couldn't, with the luggage lying

somewhere on the road between Truro and St. Mawes, probably burst open and indecently scattered and exposed, start explaining to Sally all the things she was on no account to do while he was away collecting it. He certainly would explain; and fully; and clearly; for the spoon and basin business had been simply disgusting, and he was going to put a stop to that sort of thing once and forever, but not now,—not till there was plenty of time, so that he really might have a chance of getting into her head at least the beginning of a glimmer of what a lady simply couldn't do. And he was so angry that he corrected this sentence, and instead of the word lady substituted the wife of a gentleman.

He locked her in.

'If any one knocks,' he told her before leaving her, 'you will call out that you have locked the door, as you wish to be undisturbed. You understand me, Sally? That's what you are to say—nothing else. Exactly and only that.'

'Right O,' said Sally, a little dejectedly, for his tone and expression discouraged cheerfulness, and preparing to lock the door behind him.

But it was he who locked it, much to her surprise, deftly pulling the key out of the inside of the door and slipping it into the outside before she realised what he was doing; and she heard him, having turned it, draw it out and go away.

Yes, she was locked in all right.

'Whatever—' began Sally in her thoughts; then gave it up, and sat down patiently on the edge of the wicker arm-chair to wait for the next thing that would happen to her.

'Glad I 'ad that there stew,' she reflected.

'My wife,' said Jocelyn to the lady in the office downstairs, as he went out still with the frown on his face caused by the realisation that he hadn't given Sally any reason for his suddenly leaving her, and that she hadn't asked for any—was that companionship?—'wishes to be undisturbed till I come back.'

'*I* see,' said the lady, with what seemed to him rather a curious emphasis, and she was about to inquire where his luggage was, for the Thistle and Goat liked to know where luggage was, when he strode away.

Now what did she see, Jocelyn asked himself. Nobody had ever said *I*

see like that to any orders given when he was travelling with his mother. The emphasis was marked. It sounded, he thought, both suspicious and pert. He went out to the car, strangling a desire to go back and ask her what she saw. Did she too think he wasn't really married? No, no— nonsense. Probably she saw and meant nothing. Really he was becoming sensitive beyond all dignity, he thought as he drove off on his unpleasant and difficult quest.

But the lady in the office had merely expressed herself badly. What was worrying her was not what she saw but what she didn't see, and what she didn't see was luggage. The Thistle and Goat, in common with other hotels, liked luggage. It preferred luggage to be left rather than ladies. Now the gentleman had gone off without saying a word about it, and she tried to reassure herself by hoping, what was indeed true, that he had gone to fetch it, and that she need do nothing about it, anyhow for the present. And hardly had she settled down to a cup of after-luncheon tea in the back office when the luggage arrived, brought in by a different gentleman, and one, to her great relief, whom she knew—young Mr. Carruthers, of Trevinion Manor.

Great was the confidence the Thistle and Goat had in the family of Carruthers, whom it had known all its life. No orders given by a passing tourist could have any weight when balanced against a Carruthers request. So that when young Mr. Carruthers, learning that Mr. Luke had lately left in his car, asked to see Mrs. Luke in order to hand over her luggage personally and desired his card to be sent up, regardless of the orders given by Mr. Luke the card was sent up and the message given; and Sally received both it and the message, for the chambermaid, finding the door locked and getting no answer, because Sally thought that by saying nothing she wouldn't be telling any lies, unlocked it with her pass-key; and Sally, having heard the message and received the card, issued forth obediently. Naturally she did. Usband had said nothing about not leaving the room. She wanted her tin box, and to get unpacked. Besides, when anybody sent for her she always went.

What had happened was that young Carruthers, strolling down as usual just before lunch across the fields to the sea-front, had found the

window of the Cupp parlour flung wide open, and Mrs. Cupp vigorously shaking the hearth-rug out of it. Evidently her lodgers had left; and he went in and began asking her about them, and very soon discovered that the lean chap was Jocelyn Luke—Luke of Ananias, as Carruthers, himself at Oxford, instantly identified him, for there couldn't well be two Jocelyn Lukes, and his reputation had ebbed across to Oxford, where he was known not unfavourably, and perhaps as on the whole the least hopelessly unpromising of the Cambridge crowd. And just as Mrs. Cupp was proceeding to tell him her opinion of the alleged Mrs. Luke, and how Cupp had only now been able to come out of his bedroom and have his dinner, there came news of the dropped luggage on the hill.

Carruthers felt that he was the very man to deal with that. He rushed off, thrust everybody aside, collected it reverently, for the tin trunk had indeed burst open, and its modest contents, of a touching propriety he thought, as he carefully put back things that felt like flannel, were scattered on the road, and then, fetching his car, took it into Truro.

It was easy, at the turn to Falmouth, to discover which way the Lukes had gone. It was also easy, on arriving in Truro, to discover which hotel they were in.

He only had to describe them. Everybody had noticed them. Everybody on the road had heard their horn, and everybody had seen the beautiful young lady. And because he went into the town by the direct road, and as Jocelyn coming out of it, and sure the luggage hadn't anyhow been dropped nearer than the top of the hill beyond the garage, took a round-about way, joining the main road only on the other side of the garage so as not again to have to set eyes on the loathsome oaf employed in it and risk being unable to resist going in and knocking him down, they missed each other precisely there; and accordingly when Jocelyn, having been all the way to St. Mawes, where he heard what had been done, got back about five, tired, very hungry, and wondering how on earth he was now going to find the officious person they said was trying to restore his belongings to him, he was told by the boots that young Mr. Carruthers had arrived just after he left, and was waiting to see him upstairs in the drawing-room.

'Thank heaven,' thought Jocelyn, feeling the key in his pocket, 'that I locked her in.'

And he went into the drawing-room, and there at a table in a corner by the fire, with the remains on it of what seemed to have been an extraordinarily good and varied tea, she was sitting.

❁

Carruthers—he recognised him at once as the man with the dog called Sally—was worshipping her. Decently, for Carruthers was plainly a decent chap, but worshipping her all right; it was written in every line and twist of him, as he leaned forward eagerly, telling her stories, apparently, for he was talking a great deal and she was only listening,—amusing stories, for she was smiling.

She never smiled with him, thought Jocelyn; not like that, not a real smile of just enjoyment. From the very first day, that day at tea in the Pinner parlour, she had seemed frightened of him. But she couldn't be much frightened, for here she was openly disregarding his injunctions, and somehow got out of her locked room. That seemed to Jocelyn anything but being frightened; it seemed to him to the last degree fearless and resourceful. And how strangely at variance with her apparent shyness and retiringness that twice in one day she should have allowed strange men to feed her.

He approached their corner, pale and grim. He was tired to death after the vexatious day he had had, and very hungry after not having had anything to eat since breakfast. Carruthers had watched his opportunity, of course—waited somewhere till he had seen him go, and then taken the luggage in and asked for Sally. And Sally, somehow getting out of that room, had defied his orders and come down. Well, he couldn't do anything with her at that moment. He was too tired to flare up. Besides—scenes; he couldn't for ever make scenes. What a revolting form of activity to have thrust upon him! But the amount of ideas that would, he perceived, have to be got into her head if life was to be even approaching tolerable was so great that his mind, in his fatigued state, refused to consider it.

She saw him first, and, much pleased with everything, with the beautiful tea, with Mr. Carruthers' funny stories and with her pleasant afternoon altogether, continued to smile, but at him now, and said to Carruthers, "Ere comes Mr. Luke.'

And on Carruthers getting up and Jocelyn arriving at the table, introduced them.

'My 'usband,' introduced Sally; explaining Carruthers to Jocelyn by saying, 'The gentleman as brought our traps.'

Jocelyn couldn't be angry with Carruthers; he looked at him so friendlily, and shook his hand with what surely was a perfectly sincere heartiness. And though he was obviously bowled over by Sally—naturally, thought Jocelyn, seeing that he had none of the responsibility and only the fun—there was something curiously sympathetic in his attitude to Jocelyn himself, something that seemed, oddly, to understand.

Sally, his wife, said, for instance, "Ad yer tea?'—just that, and made no attempt to give him any. But what Carruthers said, quickly going across and ringing the bell, was, 'I bet you haven't. You've had the sort of rotten day there's no time for anything in but swearing. They'll bring some fresh stuff in a moment. It's a jolly good tea they give one in this place,—don't they, Mrs. Luke.'

''Eavenly,' said Sally. And turning to Jocelyn she said, more timidly, ''Ad to come out of the bedroom. The servant—'

'Oh, that's all right,' interrupted Jocelyn hastily, earnestly desiring to keep from Carruthers the knowledge that he had locked her in. Things look so different, especially domestic actions, in the eyes of a third person unaware of the attendant circumstances, thought Jocelyn.

He dropped into a chair. What a comfort it was, after a fortnight of being dog alone with Sally, to hear that decent voice. It really was like music. He hadn't, at Cambridge, cared much for the Oxford way of speaking, but how beautiful it seemed after the Pinner way. He wanted to shut his eyes and just listen to it. 'Go on, go on,' he wanted to say, when Carruthers paused for a moment in his pleasant talk; and he sat there, listening and eating and drinking in silence, and Carruthers looked after him, and fed him, and talked pleasantly to him, and talked pleasantly to

Sally as well, and did, in fact, all the talking. There was something about Jocelyn that made Carruthers feel maternal. He was so thin. His shoulder blades stuck out so, and his lean, nervous face twitched. Carruthers thought, as he had thought on that first occasion, only this time, knowing who he was and aware of Sally's class, with ten times more conviction, 'Poor devil'; but he also thought, his eyes resting on the lovely thing in the corner—he had established her in the farthermost corner of the Thistle and Goat's drawing-room, for he too had instantly begun to hide her, and she lit up its gloom as a white flower lights up the dusk—he also thought, 'Poor angel.'

❁

Yes, she was an angel, and a poor one; he was sure of that. Carruthers, so romantic inside, so square and unemotional outside, told himself she was a forlorn child-angel torn out of her natural heaven, which obviously was completely h—less and obscure, but comfortable and unexacting, and pitched into a world of strangers, the very ABC of whose speech and behaviour she didn't understand.

After two hours *tête à tête* with Sally, two hours which seemed like ten minutes, so deeply was he interested, this was his conclusion. She hadn't been very shy, not after he left off being shy, which he was for a moment or two, confused by the sheer shock of her beauty seen close; but he had soon recovered and got into his stride, which was an easy one for her to keep up with, his one idea being to please her and make her happy.

It wasn't difficult to please Sally and make her happy; you had only to avoid frightening her. Mr. Soper hadn't frightened her, he had fed her,—always a good beginning with a woman. Carruthers knew this, and immediately ordered tea, in spite of its still being only three o'clock; and, since the Thistle and Goat specialised in teas, the one which was presently brought was of such a conspicuous goodness, with so many strange Cornish cakes and exciting little sandwiches, besides a bowl of the Cornish cream Sally liked altogether best of anything she had learned to

know on her honeymoon, that she soon felt as comfortable and friendly with Carruthers as she had with Mr. Soper.

She was at the age of jam. Cream was still enough to make her happy. And she wasn't used to quantities. In her frugal life there had never been quantities of anything, and they excited her. Quantities combined with kindness—what could be more delightful? She didn't suppose she had enjoyed anything so much ever as that tea. And it was sheer enjoyment, nothing to do with hunger at all, for hunger had been done away with by Mr. Soper's stew, and this was a deliberate choosing, a splendid unnecessariness, a sense of wide margin, of freedom, of power, and no need to think of putting away what was left over for next day.

So by the time that Carruthers said, with that simplicity which made his mother sure there was no one in the world like her Gerry, 'I've never seen any one as beautiful as you, and I didn't know there could be anybody,' Sally, unstiffened and lubricated by all the cream, was quite ready to discuss her appearance or anything else with him as far as she, restricted of speech as she was, could discuss at all, and he discovered to his deep surprise that she regarded her beauty as a thing to be apologised for, as a pity, as the same thing really as a deformity, forcing her to be conspicuous and nothing but a worry to those she loved and who loved her, and she not able to help it or alter it, or do anything at all except be sorry.

'Father,' she said, 'was in a state—you've no idea. If any one just looked my way. And they was always lookin'.'

Carruthers nodded. Just what he had been thinking when first he saw her on the hill behind St. Mawes, with Luke trying to cover her up, to extinguish her quickly in her hat,—the responsibility, the anxiety. ... But that she herself should regard it like that astonished him. Surely any woman ...

'And Mr. Luke—'e's frightened too. 'Ides me, same as Father and Mother used.'

'You're really imprisoned, then,' said Carruthers, staring at her. 'Imprisoned in your beauty.'

But seeing a puzzled expression come into her eyes he began to talk of other things, to tell her stories, to amuse her; for after all it wasn't very

fair to Luke, somehow, whose back happened to be turned, much against his will Carruthers was sure, to let her tell him about herself and her life. She was too defenceless. She was a child, who would talk to any stranger who was kind; and he could guess all he was entitled to know, he could see for himself the gift she held in her hands, the supreme gift for a woman, the gift beyond all others in power for the brief time it lasted, and he could see she was entirely unconscious of its value, of what might be done with it if only she knew how. And every time she opened her touchingly beautiful mouth of quick smiles and painstaking response, her h's dropped about him in showers.

Well, who cared? She might say anything she liked, and it wouldn't matter; in any voice, with any accent, and it wouldn't matter. Not even if she said coy common things, or arch common things, as he half expected she would when first she spoke and startled him with the discovery of her class, would it matter, For one needn't listen. One could always just sit and watch. Yes—who cared?

But the answer to that, he knew, wasn't simply Nobody, it was Jocelyn Luke. Luke would care. He quite obviously did care already, though they couldn't have been married more than two or three weeks; and she dumbly felt it, Carruthers was sure, for, after having been eager to get out of her imprisoning shell of illiteracy and say what she could while she was alone with him, directly Luke joined them she retired into a kind of anxious caution, looking at him before she said anything in answer to a question, and keeping as much as possible to Yes and No.

'He's been teaching her,' thought Carruthers. 'He's been going for her h's. She's on his nerves, and she knows it—no, not knows it, but feels it. She doesn't *know* anything about anything yet, but she feels a jolly lot, I'll swear.'

Deeply interesting Lukes. What would their fate be, he wondered.

❁

After Carruthers had gone, pensively driving himself back to St. Mawes in the pale spring twilight, Jocelyn, soothed by his agreeable talk and

manifest friendliness, and also by the good tea, felt quite different. He no longer wanted to admonish Sally. He didn't even want to ask her why she had come out of the bedroom. He was ashamed of that; ashamed of having locked her in, degrading her to God knew what level of childishness, of slavery, of, indeed, some pet animal that might stray—in fact, a dog. He shuddered a little, and looked at her deprecatingly, and leaning over the table took her hand and kissed it.

'Sally,' he murmured, suddenly for the first time since he grew up, feeling very young,—and how painfully young to be married!

Marriage. It wasn't just love-making, he thought as he kissed her hand; love-making, and then done with it and get on with your work. It was responsibility constant and lasting, not only for the other life so queerly and suddenly and permanently joined on to one, but also for oneself in a quite new way, a way one had never till then at all considered.

He kissed her hand again.

'Tea done 'im good,' thought Sally.

But it was the half hour with one of his own kind, and one who, while definitely charming to him, yet so obviously and with a kind of reverence admired Sally, that had done him good. It had restored him to a condition of tranquillity, and he felt more normal, more really happy—he didn't count his moments of wild rapture as happiness, because they somehow weren't—than he had done since the days, now so curiously far away, before he had met her. Carruthers had reassured him. His behaviour to Sally had immensely reassured him. The world was, after all, chiefly decent. It didn't consist solely of foul-minded Cupps, nor of impudent young men in garages. Just as there were more people in it healthy than sick, so there were more people in it who were appreciative and kindly than there were people who weren't. Carruthers had known all about him, too. Jocelyn hadn't credited Oxford with so much intelligent awareness. It was infinitely pleasant, after a fortnight with Sally who, wonderful as she was, uniquely wonderful he freely admitted, yet hadn't the remotest idea of what he had done and still hoped to do—yes, by God, still hoped to do. Why not? Why chuck Cambridge after all? Why not face it with Sally, and train her who was, he knew, most obedient and only needing showing,

to behave in such a way that no one, if she lived there, would dare make himself a nuisance?—it was infinitely pleasant after this to have been with somebody who knew all about him. He hadn't got very far, of course, in his work; nobody knew that better than himself. But it had been a good enough beginning for Carruthers and Oxford to have heard of him. And the desire to go on, to proceed along the glorious path, came back to him in a mighty flood as he sat in the Thistle and Goat's drawing-room, with that other desire appeased and seeming to be getting ready to fall into its proper place.

If Sally too could be got into her proper place, mightn't life even yet be a triumph?

❁

He wrote to his mother that night, after Sally had gone to bed. He sent her there early, and with a return of irritability, because of the way the people in the dining-room at dinner, and afterwards in the drawing-room where he and she sat in a remote corner while he had his coffee, behaved. It was really outrageous. This was his first experience of dining with her in a public place. And it was no good his glaring at the creatures, because they never gave him so much as a glance.

So he sent her to bed, and then he wrote to his mother. Better go home. Better now go home to South Winch, and not wander about in expensive hotels, with hateful old men in dinner jackets and fat women in beads staring their eyes out. Hotels were impossible with Sally; and so were lodgings, with the risk of another suspicious and insulting landlady. Besides, a fortnight was enough for a honeymoon, and for this particular honeymoon, with all its difficulties, quite enough. Home was the place. Almond Tree Cottage, and its quiet. He wanted to go home. He wanted to go home to his mother, and get her meeting with Sally over, and sit in that little study of his at the top of the house where not a soul could see him, and think out what was best to do next.

His mother would help him. She had always understood and helped. Never yet had she failed him. And she would help him, too, in the business

of looking after Sally,—take her off his hands sometimes, and perhaps succeed in getting her quite soon to talk like a civilised being.

It had been the last thing he had originally intended, to go with Sally to stay at his mother's. Introduce her, of course; take her down for a day; but not stay there, for well did he know his marriage would fall like a sword on his mother, cleaving her heart. Things, however, had changed since then. He had in his haste, in his blind passion, written to her that he was going to chuck Cambridge, and now that his passion was no longer blind and he wasn't going to chuck it—no, he'd be damned if he would; not anyhow till he had tried what it was like there with Sally—he was anxious to go to his mother and heal up at least one of the wounds he knew his letter must have made. He would ask her what she thought, having seen Sally, of the idea of her living in Cambridge. Perhaps—it flashed into his mind like light—his mother would live there too; give up Almond Tree Cottage, and live with them in Cambridge. What a solution. Then she could look after Sally, and be such a comfort, such a blessed comfort, to him as well. What a splendid, simple solution.

He threw down his pen, and stared straight in front of him. They would all be happy then—he going on with his work, Sally being taught by his mother, and his mother not separated from him.

When he went to bed, and Sally stirred in her sleep as if she were waking up, he took her in his arms and asked her if she would like to live in Cambridge.

'Yes,' murmured Sally, even though half asleep remembering to stick to monosyllables.

'It'll be better than London,' said Jocelyn, holding her close. 'Won't it, my love? Won't it, my *beautiful* love?' he added in a whisper, for there was something about Sally's hair, against which his face was, a softness, a sweetness …

'And perhaps my mother will come and live with us too there. You'd like that, wouldn't you, darling?'

There was a brief pause. Then, 'Yes,' murmured Sally.

He kissed her delicious hair. 'Darling,' he said tenderly, pleased by this

absence of all difficulty. 'You're half asleep,' he added in her ear, pushing aside the hair that lay over it with his mouth.

But was she? For, after another pause, she said, her face still turned away from him, something that sounded like Father.

'Yes, darling?' said Jocelyn, as she didn't go on.

''E might come too, p'raps,' murmured Sally.

'What?' said Jocelyn, not sure he could have heard right, bending his face nearer. 'Your father?'

'Yes,' murmured Sally.

'Your *father*?' said Jocelyn again.

'Yes,' murmured Sally. 'Then—we'd be tidy like—you'd 'ave 'er, and I'd 'ave 'im.'

'Go to sleep Sally,' said Jocelyn with sudden authority. 'Do you know what time it is? Nearly eleven.'

VIII

❀

Meanwhile, at Almond Tree Cottage, Jocelyn's mother had become Margery to Mr. Thorpe, and he to her was Edgar.

The idea she had played with, the possibility she had smiled at, was now fact. She had reacted to Jocelyn's marriage by getting involved, immediately and profoundly, in Mr. Thorpe. Without quite knowing how, with hardly a recollection of when, she had become engaged to him. He had caught her at the one moment in which, blind with shock, she would have clung to anything that offered support.

How could she face South Winch without support? For there was not only her inward humiliation to be dealt with, the ruin of her love and pride and the wreck of those bright ambitious dreams—surely of all ambitious dreams the most natural and creditable, the dreams of a mother for the future greatness of her son,—there was the pity of South Winch. No, she couldn't stand pity; and pity because of Jocelyn, of all people! Of him who had been her second, more glorious self, of him who was to have been all she would have been if she could have been. South Winch couldn't pity her if she married its richest man. There was something about wealth, when present in sufficient quantities, that silenced even culture; and everybody knew about Mr. Thorpe's house, and grounds, and cars, and conservatories. She therefore dropped like a fruit that no longer has enough life to hold on, into the outstretched hands of Mr. Thorpe.

Jocelyn didn't want her; Mr. Thorpe did. It was a deplorable thing, she thought, for she could still at intervals, in spite of her confusion and distress, think intelligently, that a woman couldn't be happy, couldn't be at peace, unless there existed somebody who wanted her, and wanted her exclusively; but there it was. Deplorable indeed, for it now flung her into Mr. Thorpe's arms prematurely, without her having had time properly to

think it out. No doubt she would have got into them in the end, but not yet, not for years and years. Now she tumbled in from a sheer instinct of self-preservation. She had to hold on to some one. She was giddy and staggering from the blow that had cut through her life. Jocelyn, her boy, her wonderful, darling boy, in whose career she had so passionately merged herself, doing everything, even the smallest thing, only with reference to him, wanted her so little that he could throw her aside, thrust her away without an instant's hesitation, and with her his whole future, the future he and she had been working at with utter concentration for years, for the sake of a girl he had only known a fortnight. He said so in the letter. He said it was only a fortnight. One single fortnight, as against those twenty-two consecrated years.

Who was this girl, who was this person for whom he gave up everything at a moment's notice? Mrs. Luke, shuddering, hid in Mr. Thorpe's arms; for the things that Jocelyn hadn't said in that letter on the eve of his marriage were more terrible almost to her than those he had said,—the ominous non-reference to the girl's family, to her upbringing, to her circumstances. Hardly had he mentioned her name. At the end, in a postscript, as if in his heart he were ashamed, he had said it was Salvatia—Salvatia!—and her father's name was Pinner, but that he really didn't know that it mattered, and he wouldn't have cared, and neither would anybody else who saw her care, if she hadn't had fifty names. And then he had added the strange words, ominously defiant, unnecessarily coarse, that he would have taken her, and so would any one else who saw her, in her shift; and then still further, and still more strangely and coarsely, he had scribbled in a shaky hand, as though he had torn open the letter again and stuck it in in a kind of frenzy of passion, 'My God—her shift!'

Mrs. Luke hid in Mr. Thorpe's arms. Coarseness had never yet got into Almond Tree Cottage, except the coarseness consecrated by time, which it was a sign of intelligence not to mind, the coarseness, for instance, of those marvellous Elizabethans. But coarseness from Jocelyn? Oh, blind and mad, blind and mad. Where had her boy got it from, this capacity for sudden, violent, ruinous behaviour? Not from her, very certainly. It must be some of the thick, sinister blood filtered down into him from the

Spanish woman her husband's great-grandfather—Mrs. Luke had been pleased with this great-grandfather up to then, because in her own family, where there should have been four, there hadn't been any—had married against his parents' wishes. She hid in Mr. Thorpe's arms. But—'This in exchange for Jocelyn?' she couldn't help repeating to herself that first day, trying to shut her eyes, spiritually as well as physically, trying to withdraw her attention, as even in this crisis she remembered Dr. Johnson had done in unpleasant circumstances, from Mr. Thorpe's betrothal caresses.

Mr. Thorpe was clean and healthy; for that she was thankful. Still, she suffered a good deal that first day. Then, imperceptibly, she got used to him. Surprising how soon one gets used to a man, she thought, on whom this one's substantial shape had made a distinctly disagreeable impression the first week she found herself up against it. By the end of a week she no longer noticed the curious springy solidity of Mr. Thorpe's figure, which had seemed to her when he first embraced her, used as she was to the lean fragility of her late husband, so unpleasantly much. And besides, the flood of his riches began to flow over her immediately, and it was a warm flood. She hadn't known how agreeable such a flood could be. She hadn't had an idea of the way it could bring comfort into one's every corner—yes, even into one's mind when one's mind was sore and unhappy. Riches, she had always held, were vulgar; but she now obscurely recognised that they were only vulgar if they were somebody else's. One's own—why, to what noble ends could not riches be directed in the hands of those who refused to use them vulgarly? Married to Mr. Thorpe, she would make of them as beautiful and graceful a thing as she had made of her poverty. And it did soothe Mrs. Luke, it did help her a great deal during these days of wreckage, that her life, which had been so spare and bony, was now becoming hourly, in every sort of pleasant way, more and more padded, more and more soft and luscious with fat.

For, if no longer precious to Jocelyn, she was precious to Mr. Thorpe, and it was his pride to pad out the meagreness of her surroundings; and though she cried herself to sleep each night because of Jocelyn, she awoke each morning comforted because of Mr. Thorpe. After twelve hours of not seeing Mr. Thorpe she could clearly perceive, what was less evident at

the end of a long evening with him, her immense good fortune in having got him. A decent, honourable man. Not every woman in the forties finds at the precise right moment a decent, honourable man, who is also rich. Where would she have been now without Mr. Thorpe? He was her rock, her refuge; he was the plaster to her wounded pride, the restorer of her self-respect.

'I can *rely* on him,' she said to herself while she sat in front of her glass in the morning, brushing her thick, black hair—in the evening when she brushed it she didn't say anything. 'I can entirely *trust* him. What, after all, is education? What has education done for Jocelyn? The one thing that matters is character.'

And she would come down to find her breakfast-table strewn with fresh evidences of Mr. Thorpe's hot-houses and love.

❁

Not a word from Jocelyn all this time, not a sign. He might be dead, she thought; and it would have hurt her less if he had been. For dead he would have been for ever hers; nobody then could touch him, take him away. Crushed and bitter, she crept yet closer to Mr. Thorpe. He liked it. He liked being crept close to. He was thoroughly pleased with what in his businesslike mind he referred to as his bargain.

She never mentioned Jocelyn to him, and he liked that too. 'Young fool,' he said, when he came round unexpectedly early one evening, and found her crying. 'No use worrying about a fool.'

And Mrs. Luke, still further crushed by hearing Jocelyn called a fool, and therefore being forced to the deduction that she had produced one— yes, and it was true, too, in spite of his brains—could only hang on to Mr. Thorpe, and say nothing.

He liked that. He liked to be hung on to, and he had no objection to a certain amount of saying nothing in a woman. Her late husband, could he now have seen her who was once his wife, would have been surprised, for in his day she had never hung on, and had been particularly good at conversation. But there was that about Mr. Thorpe which quenched

conversation. Even before her engagement, in the days of his preliminary assiduities after his wife's death, she had found it difficult, when he came round, to keep what she understood was sometimes described as the ball rolling; and she was completely in command of herself then, in the full flood of her happiness and satisfaction. Conversation with him, the kind she and South Winch knew and practised, was out of the question. There was no exchange of opinions possible with Mr. Thorpe, because he never exchanged his, he merely emitted them and stuck to them. And they came out clothed in so very few words that they seemed to Mrs. Luke, watching him with quizzical, amused eyes—ah, those detached days, when one looked on and wasn't involved!—almost indecently bare. Now she drooped. She bowed her head.

Mr. Thorpe liked that. He liked a woman to bow her head. Gentleness in a woman was what he liked: gentleness, and softness, and roundness. Margery was gentle all right, and soft enough in places—anyhow of speech; but she wasn't round. Not yet. Later, of course, after the cook at Abergeldie—his house was called Abergeldie—had had a go at her, she wouldn't know herself again. And meanwhile, to put an immediate stop to all this underfeeding, a stream of nourishment—oysters, lobsters, plovers' eggs, his own pineapples, his own forced strawberries, his own butter and fresh eggs, and, once, a sucking pig—thickly flowed across the daisied meadow dividing Abergeldie from Almond Tree Cottage.

The little maid turned yellow, and began to get up at night and be sick. Mrs. Luke, feeling it was both wrong and grotesque to bury lobsters in the back garden, and unable either to stop the stream or deal with it herself, was forced to send most of the stuff round to her friends; and so South Winch became aware of what had happened, for nobody except Mr. Thorpe grew pineapples and bought plovers' eggs, and nobody gave such quantities of them to a woman without being going to marry her afterwards.

Well, it was as good a way as any other of letting people know, thought Mrs. Luke, sitting in silence with Mr. Thorpe's arm round her waist, while every now and then he furtively felt to see whether she wasn't beginning anywhere to curve. Instead of sending round *billets de faire part* she sent

lobsters. Rather original, she thought, with a slight return to her detached and amused earlier self. 'Does he really think I can eat them all?' she wondered.

And the little maid, in whose kitchen much, even so, remained, fell from one bilious paroxysm into another.

❁

She was warmly congratulated. It soothed her afresh, this new importance with which she was instantly clothed. Money—she sighed, but faced it—money, even in that place where people really did try to keep their eyes well turned to the light, was a great, perhaps the greatest, power. She sighed. It oughtn't to be so; but if it was so? And who would not be grateful, really deeply grateful, to Edgar, and put up with all his little ways, when he was so generous, so kind, and so completely devoted? Besides, his little ways would, she was sure, later on become much modified. A wife could do so much. A well-bred, intelligent wife—it was simply silly not to admit plain facts—could do everything. When she was married …

And then she found herself shrinking from the thought of when she was married. She could restrain his affection now; it was her privilege. But when she was married, it would be his privilege not to be able to be restrained. And there appeared to be no age limit to a man's affectionateness. Here was Edgar, well over sixty and still affectionate. Really, really, thought Mrs. Luke, who even in her most ardent days had loved only with her mind.

And then one evening, nearly three weeks after the arrival of that letter of Jocelyn's that had brought all this about, Mr. Thorpe said, 'When's it going to be?'

'When is what going to be?' she asked, starting.

To this he only replied, 'Coy, eh?' and sat staring at her proudly and affectionately, a hand on each knee.

Pierced by the word, Mrs. Luke hastened to say in her most level voice, 'You mean our marriage? Surely there's plenty of time.'

'Time, eh? You bet there isn't. Not for you and me. We're no chickens, either of us.'

Mrs. Luke winced. She had never at any time tried, or wished, or pretended to be a chicken, yet to be told she wasn't one was strangely ruffling. If it were a question of chickens, compared with Edgar she certainly was one. These things were relative. But what a way of …

And then, as before, the little maid came in with a letter, and Mr. Thorpe, vexed as before by the interruption (why that servant—well, one could hardly call a thing that size a servant; that aproned spot, then—couldn't leave letters outside till they were wanted …), said, curbing himself, 'Letter, eh?'

'From Jocelyn,' said Mrs. Luke, who had flushed a bright flame-colour, and whose hands, as they held the letter, were shaking.

'Thought so,' said Mr. Thorpe in disgust.

❧

He learned with profound disapproval that Jocelyn was bringing his bride to Almond Tree Cottage. He didn't want brides about—none, that is, except his own; and he feared this precious son of hers, who had behaved to her about as badly as a son could behave, would distract Margery's attention from her own affairs, and make her even more coy about fixing the date of her wedding than she already was.

'Going to sponge on you,' was his comment.

She shrank from the word.

'Jocelyn isn't like that,' she said quickly.

'Pooh,' said Mr. Thorpe.

She shrank from this word too. Edgar was, as she well knew and quite accepted, a plain man and a rough diamond, but a man shouldn't be too plain, a diamond shouldn't be too rough. Besides, surely the expression was obsolete.

'My dear Edgar,' she protested gently.

Mr. Thorpe persisted. 'It's pooh all right,' he said. 'Young men with wives in their shifts'—he remembered every word of that first letter—'and

only five hundred a year to keep them on, always sponge. Or try to,' he said, instinctively closing his hands over his pockets. 'Got to live, you know. Must stay somewhere.'

'He is going to live in London,' said Mrs. Luke. 'You remember he said so in his first letter. Live there and do—do literary work.'

'Bunkum,' said Mr. Thorpe.

And this word seemed to her even more obsolete, if possible, than pooh.

But there was no time to worry about words. What was she going to do? Where was she going to put Jocelyn and his wife? How was she going to receive them? Had she better pretend to South Winch that she had known nothing about it till they had appeared on her doorstep and overwhelmed her with the news? Had she better pretend that Jocelyn had given up Cambridge because he had been offered a position in London too good to refuse? Or had she better hide them indoors till they had found rooms in London, and could be got away again without having been seen, and meanwhile go on behaving as if nothing had happened?

She lost her head. Standing there, with the letter in her shaking hands and Mr. Thorpe, who wouldn't go away, squarely in front of her, she lost her practical, cool head, and simply couldn't think what to do. One thing alone was clear—she was going to suffer. And presently another thing emerged into clearness, an absurd thing, but curiously difficult and unpleasant,—she had no spare-room, and in Jocelyn's room was only the little camp bed it had pleased him (and her too, who liked to think of him as Spartan), to sleep in. This was no house for more than just herself and Jocelyn. Oh, why hadn't she married Mr. Thorpe at once? Then she would have been established at Abergeldie by now, and able to let the pair have Almond Tree Cottage to themselves.

Abergeldie. The word brought light into her confusion. Of course. That was where they must go. Abergeldie, majestic in the size and number of its unused spare-rooms, magnificent in its conveniences, its baths, its staff of servants. She had been taken over it, as was fitting; had waded across the thickness of its carpets, admired its carved wardrobes, marble-topped

washstands and immense beds, gazed from its numerous windows at its many views, wilted through its hothouses, ached along its lawns, and knew all about it. The very place. And, given courage by the knowledge of the impossibility of housing more than one person beside herself in her own house, urged on by the picture in her mind of that tiny room upstairs and its narrow bed, she made her suggestion to Mr. Thorpe.

Nervously she made it, fearing that the reason for it, fearing that the merest most passing mention of such a thing as a bed, would bring out the side of him which she was forced to recognise as ribald. And it did. He said all the things she was so sorry to have been obliged to expect he would. But he was good-natured; he liked to feel he was helping Margery out of a fix. Also, the young fool would be away from his mother then, and perhaps some sense could be got into his head, and at the same time as sense was got in nonsense would be got out,—the nonsense, for instance, of no doubt supposing that he, Edgar Thorpe, was the sort of man who could be sponged upon beyond, say, a couple of days. Besides, he was proud of Abergeldie, and hardly anybody, what with first Annie's being alive and then with her not being alive, had ever seen it.

So it was settled, and he went away earlier than usual to give his orders to the housekeeper; and Mrs. Luke, creeping into bed with a splitting headache, lay for hours staring at nothing, and trying to forget Mr. Thorpe's last words.

For, after he had most affectionately embraced her, so affectionately that she was sure one of her tendons had snapped, he had said: 'No good his trying to milk *me*, you know.'

Milk him?

She lay staring into the dark. Was character, after all, better than education?

❀

The Canon said it was, and so did his wife. In fact at tea next day in Mrs. Luke's little garden, on that bit of lawn round the cedar, near the low fence across which grazed Mr. Thorpe's Jersey cows, they all three were

unanimous that it was. Wonderful how daylight, ordinary things, meals, tea-cups, callers, dispelled doubts.

'Better to have both, of course,' said the Canon, eating Mr. Thorpe's forced strawberries after covering them with the cream that had been, twenty-four hours earlier, inside those very cows, 'but if that's not possible, give me character. It's what *tells*. It's the only thing that in the long run *tells*.'

'Oh, well—one isn't seriously disputing it,' said Mrs. Luke. 'Only these theories, if one presses them—'

She paused, and poured out more tea for Mrs. Walker.

'For instance,' she went on, 'suppose a man had a cook of a completely admirable nature. If he married her, could he be happy? I mean, an educated man. Let us say a very *well* educated man.'

'Certainly, if she cooked nicely,' said the Canon, who thought he scented rather than saw the form of Mr. Thorpe lurking somewhere at the back of his delightful parishioner's remarks, and wasn't going to be caught.

He knew the importance of turning away seriousness, when it cropped up at the wrong moment, with a laugh. A man as valuably rich as Mr. Thorpe shouldn't be taken too seriously, shouldn't be examined and pulled about. His texture simply wouldn't stand it. He should be said grace over, thought the Canon, who fully realised what a precious addition Mr. Thorpe's wealth in Mrs. Luke's hands was going to be to South Winch, and gobbled up thankfully. Gobbled up; not turned over first on the plate.

Mrs. Luke hadn't invited the Walkers to tea. On the contrary, when first they appeared at the back door, ushered through it by the little maid who each time she saw the Canon's gaiters was thrown by them into a fresh convulsion of respectfulness, she had been annoyed. Because all day long she had been vainly trying to collect and arrange her thoughts, soothe her nerves, prepare her mind for the evening, when Jocelyn had said he would arrive—to supper, he wrote, somewhere round eight o'clock,—and define what her attitude was going to be both to him and to the girl with the utterly ridiculous Christian name; and not having one bit succeeded, and impelled by some vague hope that out of doors she might find quiet, that

in Nature she might find tranquility and composure, had said she would have tea in the garden.

Nature never did betray the heart that loved her. ...

Some idea like that, though she wasn't at all a Wordsworthian and regarded him at best with indulgence, drove her out to what her corner of South Winch held of Nature,—the bit of lawn, the cedar, the Kerria japonica against the wall by the kitchen window, the meadow across the railing, full of daisies and cows, and, on that fine spring afternoon of swift shadows and sunshine, the wind, fresh and sweet with the scent of young leaves.

But once the Walkers were there she found they did her good. They distracted her. And they liked her so much. It was always pleasant and restoring to be with people who liked one. The Canon made her feel she was good-looking and important, and his wife made her feel she was important. Also, they helped with the strawberries, from which, after a fortnight of them at every meal, she had for some time turned away her eyes. Later on, when she was alone again, there would still be at least a couple of hours to decide in what sort of a way she would meet Jocelyn; quite long enough, seeing how she couldn't, whenever she thought of the meeting, stop herself from trembling.

Oh, he had behaved outrageously to her—to her, his mother, who had given up her life to him. There had been men in past years she might have married, men of her own age and class, by whom she might have had other children and with whom she might have been happy all this time; and she had turned them down, dismissed them ruthlessly because of Jocelyn, because only Jocelyn, and his gifts and career, were to have her love and devotion. Wasn't it a shame, wasn't it a shame to treat her so? To behave to her as though she were his enemy, the kill-joy who mustn't be told and mustn't be consulted, who must be kept in the dark, shut out? And why, because he had gone mad about a girl, must he go still more mad, and ruin himself by throwing up Cambridge?

A wave of fresh misery swept over her. 'Go on talking—*please*,' she said quickly, when the Walkers, replete, fell momentarily silent.

They looked up surprised; and they were still more surprised when they

saw that her face, usually delicately pale, was quite red, and her eyes full of tears.

The Canon was affectionately concerned, and his wife was concerned.

'Are you not well, dear Mrs. Luke?' she inquired.

'My *dear* friend,' said the Canon, setting down his cup, tidying his mouth, and taking her hand. 'My dear, *dear* friend—what is it?'

Then, impulsively, she told them. 'It's Jocelyn,' she said. 'He's married, and given up Cambridge.'

And all her mortification and bitter unhappiness engulfed her, and she began helplessly to cry.

'Dear, dear. Dear me. Dear, dear me,' said the Canon.

'Dear Mrs. Luke—' said his wife.

They sat impotently looking on. Such excessive weeping from the poised, the unemotional, the serene Mrs. Luke, was most disconcerting. One shouldn't expose oneself like that, however unhappy one was, thought the Canon's wife, feeling terribly uncomfortable; and even the Canon had a sensation he didn't like, as of fig-leaves being wrenched off and flung aside.

Well, having behaved like this—really her nerves had completely gone—there was nothing left but to explain further, and after a few painful moments of trying to gulp herself quiet she told them all about it.

They were horrified. Jocelyn's behaviour, to the Walkers who had ripening sons of their own, seemed to the last degree disgraceful. That the girl was some one to be ashamed of was very plain, or why should he have come down voluntarily from Cambridge? Marriage by itself didn't stop a student from continuing there. He was ruined. He would never be anything now. And as representing South Winch, which had not yet in its history produced a distinguished man, the Canon felt this blighting of its hopes that some day it would be celebrated as the early home of Sir Jocelyn Luke, perhaps of Lord Luke—why not? hadn't there been Kelvin?—very keenly.

Poor mother. Poor, poor mother.

The Canon took her hand, and, raising it reverently to his lips, kissed it. His wife didn't mind this, because in sorrow, as in sickness, there is no

sex. Nobody enjoys kissing the hand of the sick. She minded nothing the Canon did so long as he didn't enjoy it.

'Yes—and he's bringing her here to-night,' gasped Mrs. Luke, struggling to keep down a fresh outburst.

'Here? Bringing her here? Without first asking your permission and forgiveness?' cried the Canon. 'Disgraceful. Outrageous. Unpardonable.'

'Oh, *isn't* it, *isn't* it—' wept Mrs. Luke into her handkerchief.

Never, never could she forgive Jocelyn. No, she never, never would. Let him manage for himself now. Let him lie as best he could on the miserable bed he had made. She would tell him so plainly, and though she couldn't help his coming there that night she would insist that he should go away again next morning and never, never come back. …

And then, over the top of her handkerchief, she saw him standing there, standing in the back-door looking at her: Jocelyn; the light of her eyes; the only thing really in her life.

'Jocelyn—oh, *Jocelyn!*'

She gave a kind of sobbing sigh; she struggled to her feet; she stood, swaying a moment, holding on to the table; and then simply ran to him.

❀

'Mother—'

'Oh—*Jocelyn!*'

He hugged her tighter than he had ever hugged her. He was raised quite outside his ordinary self, in this joy of getting back to her. And that she should run into his arms—she who never ran, who never showed emotion!

'You're not angry, Mother?' he asked, looking down at her upturned face, still wet and red from her recent weeping.

'Dreadfully,' she said, smiling up at him, the strangest transfigured, watery smile.

'Oh, Mother—I knew you wouldn't fail me!' he cried, infinitely relieved, infinitely melted and grateful.

'Fail you?'

'Oh, Mother—'

And they hugged again. His mother's love was a miracle. Her voice was an enchantment. Just to hear the words, the precious right words, said in the precious right voice. …

At the tea-table the Canon and his wife, who carefully didn't look but yet saw, were much shocked. This surely amounted to having duped them as to her real feelings, to having got their sympathy and concern on false pretences.

'Hadn't we better go home, John?' Mrs. Walker inquired of her husband.

'Much better,' said the Canon, who didn't see how to do it.

He looked about for a way of escape.

There wasn't one, except by climbing over to the cows, and that would involve them in trespass. Besides, retreat should be dignified.

'But where—?' Mrs. Luke was whispering, her cheek against Jocelyn's, while with one hand she still clung hold of his neck. 'Salvatia—?'

'In the sitting-room,' whispered Jocelyn. 'I put her there. I wanted to see you first alone. Why on earth those Walkers are here to-day of all days—'

He glanced at the scene on the lawn, where the Canon and his wife, marooned at the untidy tea-table, were trying to seem absorbed in something that wasn't happening up above their heads in the branches of the cedar.

'You said supper-time—'

'But I scorched to get to you quickly—'

'Then you wanted me?'

'Oh, Mother!'

And he hugged her again, and the Walkers looked about again for a way of escape, and again found none.

Sweet, sweet, delicious beyond dreams, was this restoration to all, to far more than all that had been apparent before, of her boy's need of her, and of his love. If this was the effect being married had on him, then she was glad he had married. How could she be angry with a wife who brought him closer than ever, more utterly than ever, back to his mother? So, she thought, must the Prodigal Son's father have felt about the swine his boy

had had such a dose of. He wouldn't have resented them; he must have quite liked them.

'You'll try and love her, won't you, Mother?' said Jocelyn. 'She is—very lovable.'

And taking his mother by the hand, he led her to the sitting-room.

❁

There stood the exquisite Sally; stood, because she was afraid to sit. Round her slender body she held tightly the new wrap Jocelyn, among other things, had bought her on their way through London and had instructed her to keep on till he told her to take it off. It was grey, so as to make her as invisible as possible, and was of the kind that has neither sleeves nor fastenings; and Sally, who had never been inside a thing like that before, clutched it with anxious obedience about her with both hands.

Extravagantly slender in this garment, which took on as if by magic the most delicious folds directly it got hold of Sally, and too lovely to be credible, she stood there, her lips parted in fright, and her eyes fixed on the entering Mrs. Luke.

'*Oh*—' said Mrs. Luke, catching her breath, who had read poetry, who had heard music, who knew what April mornings in the woods are like, when the sun shines through windflowers and the birds are wild with young delight.

Sally's knees shook. She clutched the grey wrap tighter still about her. Mr. Luke's mother was so terribly like Mr. Luke. Two of them. She hadn't bargained for two of them. And she was worse than he was, because she was a lady. Gentlemen were difficult enough, but they did every now and then cast themselves at one's feet and make one feel one could do what one liked for a bit, but a lady wouldn't; a lady would always stay a lady.

The word struck cold on Sally's heart. What did one do with a lady? And a lady, too, who seemed hardly older than her son, and as wide-awake and sharp as you please, Sally was sure. She had been imagining Jocelyn's mother old and stout and whitehaired, and perhaps not able to see or hear very well, and therefore comfortingly slow to mark what was done amiss.

And here was this thin, quick, almost young lady. No flies on *her* for dead certain, thought Sally, clutching her wrap.

Her heart, which felt as if it had already sunk as far as it could go, contrived to sink still farther. She stared at Mrs. Luke with the fascinated fear of a rabbit confronted by a snake; but her stare, which felt inside just as ugly and scared as that, was outside the most beautiful little look of gracious shyness, and Mrs. Luke, staring back, was for a moment quite unable to speak.

Who was this? Had Jocelyn caught and married some marvellous daughter of a patrician house? Had he been up to Olympus, and netted the young Aphrodite as, on that morning of roses, she stepped ashore from her shell?

She flushed scarlet. The perfect grace and youth, the dream-like loveliness ...

'Why,' she murmured under her breath, 'how *beautiful*—' and took a step forward, and held out both her hands.

'Are you really my new daughter?' she said in a low voice. 'You?'

With a great effort Sally managed to stand her ground, and not shrink away backwards before this alarming figure. She didn't know what to do about the held out hands, because if she let go of the wrap so as to shake them it would fall off, and Jocelyn had said she was on no account to let it do that.

She therefore stood motionless, and her tongue clove to the roof of her mouth.

Mrs. Luke came close. 'You wonderful child—*you're* Salvatia?' she murmured.

With a great effort Sally continued to hold her ground; with a great effort she unclove her tongue.

'That's right,' she said, clutching her grey wrap.

Two words; but enough. How many times had not Jocelyn told her not to say That's right? But he had told her not to say nearly everything; she couldn't possibly remember all the things she wasn't to say, however hard she tried. Indeed, Sally in her flustered soul was thinking what a mercy it

– 108 –

was she hadn't added 'mum.' It had been on the tip of her tongue, faced by a lady, and she had hung on to it just in time.

Mrs. Luke, startled, was arrested for an instant in her advance. Then, not after all quite certain that she had heard what she had heard—it seemed impossible that she should have—she went close up to Sally and kissed her. She had to reach up to her for Sally was half a head the taller, besides being rigid with fright.

'Sally, kiss my mother and make friends,' said Jocelyn.

'Yes, Mr. Luke—' said Sally, making a quick downward lunge of her head.

'Now, Sally—*please*,' protested Jocelyn. 'She can't,' he added, turning to his mother, 'get used to calling me by my Christian name.'

'Sorry,' said Sally; and felt so very warm that she had a queer conviction that even her stomach must be blushing.

Mrs. Luke stood looking at her, trying to smile. She now knew everything. No need for words from Jocelyn, for explanations. She knew, and she understood. Up to her to behave well; up to her to behave wonderfully, and make him more than ever certain there was no one in the whole world like his mother.

'She'll learn,' she said, smiling as best she could. 'Won't you—Salvatia?'

If only, thought Sally, she were back at Woodles; if only, only she were back safe and quiet with her father at Woodles.

'It was inevitable,' said Mrs. Luke, turning to Jocelyn. 'Absolutely inevitable.'

He caught hold of his mother's hands. That she should see that, that she should instantly understand. . . .

'And I congratulate you with all my heart, my dear son, and my dear daughter,' Mrs. Luke went on, continuing to be wonderful. 'You are both my dear, my very dear, children.'

And Jocelyn bent his head over her hand, and kissed it in a fervour of gratitude and relief.

And Sally, looking on at Usband in this new light, thought, 'Well, I'm blest.'

IX

Restored by the shock both of Sally's loveliness and language to her normal self, Mrs. Luke's tears dried up and her emotions calmed down, and she began to think rapidly and clearly.

This situation had to be dealt with. The only person who could deal with it with any hope at all of success was herself. She would, then, grasp it firmly, as if it were a nettle, and wear it proudly, as if it were a rose. Yes, that was the line to take: wear it proudly, as if it were a rose.

More clearly than if Jocelyn had explained for an hour she saw what had happened, what couldn't have helped happening, once chance had shown him Salvatia. From those few words of Sally's she reconstructed the Pinner family and its conditions, and as she stood gazing at her, with one hand still in Jocelyn's, she grouped the whole Pinner lot into the single word Gutter. Jocelyn had found and picked up beauty in a gutter. The gutter was as evident as the beauty, and as impossible to hide. Accept it, then; accept it, and make South Winch accept it. Treat it as quaint, as amusing, as completely excused by the beauty. She had made South Winch accept Tiepolo, when it didn't in the least want to, and now see into what an enthusiasm it had lashed itself! Even so would she make it accept Salvatia; and ceaselessly every hour, every minute, she herself would educate the girl, and train her patiently, and force her gently into proper ways of speech and behaviour. Seventeen, was she? Mrs. Luke felt that with seventeen all things were possible. A child. Wax. And she was so really exquisite, so really perfect of form and colour and movement, that it would be wonderful to watch her development, her unfolding into at least the semblance of a lady.

Salvatia—'No, no, dearest Jocelyn—not Sally, not Sally,' she begged on his calling her that, for she had a theory that names had the power of

making you be like them, and a Sally was foredoomed to unredeemable vulgarity—should have masters (perhaps mistresses would be better,) down from London, when once Mrs. Luke was married to Mr. Thorpe and could afford things; regular teachers who would give her lessons at stated hours, while she herself would give her lessons at all the unstated ones. And she would take her everywhere, to each of the South Winch festivities, whether tea-parties, or debates, or lectures, or concerts or plays, and wherever she went Salvatia should be her open glory. It would be a mistake in tactics, besides being an impossibility, to try to hide her. She should be flaunted. For, confronted by a bull, Mrs. Luke remembered, quite the best thing to do was to take it by the horns.

So swiftly do thoughts gallop through minds like Mrs. Luke's that she had planned out her attitude in those few instants in the sitting-room, while she stood gazing at Sally and holding Jocelyn's hand.

'We're going to be *great* friends, are we not Salvatia?' she said, laying her free hand on her daughter-in-law's delicate little shoulder.

Great friends? She and the lady? The bare suggestion produced in Sally that physical condition known to the Pinner family as fit to drop.

Directly questioned, however, she was forced to answer, so she said faintly, 'Right O,' and Mrs. Luke, smiling elaborately and patting the shoulder, said, 'You very quaint little girl,'—and in spite of the obvious inappropriateness of these adjectives as a description of the noble young angel standing before her, she was determined that they should, roughly, represent her attitude towards her.

'Now we'll all have tea,' she said, suddenly becoming gaily business-like. These children—it was she who must take them in hand. No more emotions, she decided. Her beloved Jocelyn needed her help again, couldn't do without her. ... 'Won't we, Jocelyn? Won't we, Salvatia? I've had some already, but I'll be greedy and have some more. Jocelyn, you go and tell Hammond—' Hammond was the little maid's surname, and by it, to her great astonishment who knew herself only as Lizz, she had been called since she entered Mrs. Luke's service—'to make fresh tea and bring it in here. You must both be dying for it. And then you can say goodbye to the Walkers for me, Jocelyn, will you?' she called after him. 'Tell them I've

– 111 –

got a most beautiful surprise for them—quite soon, perhaps to-morrow. *You're* the beautiful surprise, Salvatia,' she said, turning to Sally smilingly, who had made a sudden forward movement as if to follow Jocelyn, and who, on seeing him go out of the room and leave her alone with his mother, was so seriously alarmed that she again had a queer conviction about her stomach, but this time that it was turning what the Pinner family called as white as a sheet.

'Of course you know you're beautiful, don't you?' said Mrs. Luke, busily pulling out the little table the tea was to be put on in the absence of the proper table in the garden, and clearing Sir Thomas Browne off it, and also two bright tulips in a clear glass vessel. 'You must have heard that ever since you can remember.'

'But I can't *'elp* it,' said Sally, very anxious, her eyes on the door.

''Elp it? You quaint child. There's an h in help, Salvatia dear. Help it? But why should you want to? It's a wonderful gift, and you should thank God who gave it you, and use it entirely—' Mrs. Luke was quite surprised at her own words, for she wasn't at all religious, yet they came out glibly, and she concluded they were subconsciously inspired by the Canon in the garden—'entirely to His glory.'

'Yes, m—'

'No—stop there, stop there,' cried Mrs. Luke, quickly holding up her hand and smiling. 'You were going to say ma'am, were you not, Salvatia? Well, you mustn't. Not to me. Not to anybody. Except, of course,' she added, feeling she couldn't begin too soon to help the child, 'to the Queen, and other royal ladies.'

And before her eyes floated that vision she had so often contemplated of Sir Jocelyn Luke, of Lord Luke, and now was added to it Lady Luke, the lovely Lady Luke, being presented at Court, and by that time as perfect inside as out. Properly dealt with, Jocelyn's marriage, instead of being his ruin, might end by being one of his chief glories.

'Sit down, little girl'

Sally dropped as if she were shot on to the nearest chair, which was Mrs. Luke's.

'Not there—not that one,' said Mrs. Luke, smiling. 'No, dear child—nor

that one,' she added, as Sally having hastily got up again was about to drop on to the next nearest one, which was Jocelyn's—better get her into all the little ways at once. '*Any* chair, Salvatia dear, except just those two. Yes—that's a very comfortable one. Is not it too strange to think that this time yesterday you and I never had seen each other, and had no more idea—'

Sally, sitting down more cautiously on the edge of the third chair, didn't think that strange at all, but very natural and nice. There had been lots of yesterdays without the lady in them, and all of them had seemed quite natural. What really was strange was that they should have left off and landed her here, shut up alone with somebody so happily till then unknown. If only, thought Sally, she could now, having been introduced and that, go somewhere where the lady wasn't. For Mrs. Luke terrified her more than any one she had yet in her brief life come across. Worse, far worse, than her parents when, for her good, they used to give her What for, and worse even than Mr. Luke when he turned and just looked at her and didn't say anything after she had passed some remark, was this smiling lady who patted her. She couldn't take her eyes off Mrs. Luke, watching her with a fascinated apprehension, not knowing where she mightn't be going to be patted next.

Sitting sideways on the very edge of her chair, and still holding her wrap tightly about her, Sally's eyes followed Mrs. Luke's slightest movement. In any one else it would have been a stare, and Mrs. Luke would have explained that she mustn't, but there was nothing wrong to be found with the look in Sally's eyes,—nothing wrong, indeed, to be found in anything she did, thought Mrs. Luke, arranging things comfortably for everybody's tea, so long as it wasn't speaking.

Mrs. Luke knew she was being watched, but only, so it seemed, with a lovely and gracious attentiveness. She also knew Sally was sitting on the edge of her chair, with her legs drawn up under her just as if she were trying to keep them out of something not quite nice; but no need to disturb a position which somehow seemed sheer grace. What a pity, what a pity, flashed across Mrs. Luke's mind, that the child hadn't happened to be born dumb! Was that wicked? No, she didn't think so. She herself

– 113 –

could imagine being very happy dumb, with plenty of books, and not having to talk to bores.

'Wouldn't you like to take your hat off, Salvatia?' she asked, drawing Jocelyn's chair closer to the little table.

Sally started. 'No thank you, please—' she said hastily.

'Do,' said Mrs. Luke. 'I want you to.'

'Yes, m—yes, Mrs. Luke,' said Sally, instantly obeying.

'Not Mrs. Luke, dear—Mother. You must call me Moth—'

Her voice died away, and she stood staring in silence. How wonderful. How really amazingly beautiful. Like sunsets. And the girl, crowned with that bright crown of waving light, like some royal child.

She stood staring, her hands dropped by her sides. 'What a *responsibility*,' she whispered.

'Pardon?' said Sally, nervously.

❀

The Walkers were got rid of, and Jocelyn came back frowning. They had scolded him; him, who had been completely understood and unreproached by his mother, the one person with either a right or a grievance. Having known him since he was three didn't excuse them, he considered; and it seemed merely silly to rebuke him for leaving Cambridge when he wasn't going to leave it. He didn't attempt to enlighten them; he just stood and glowered, waiting till they should have done. What could old Walker know of the way one was forced to react to beauty? He had probably never set eyes on it in his life. And as for passionate love, the fiery love that had been burning him up for the last few weeks, one had only to look at Mrs. Walker to know he could never have felt that.

So he simply repeated, when the Canon paused a moment, that his mother had asked him to say good-bye for her, and then, this second time, he added, 'She can't come herself, because she is with my wife.'

'Conceited young monkey,' thought Mrs. Walker, who remembered him in petticoats, and even then giving himself airs. 'Wife, indeed.' Both Mrs. Walker's sons were without gifts.

'Your mother is an angel, sir,' said the Canon sternly.

'So is my wife,' said Jocelyn, glowering.

'No doubt, no doubt,' said the Canon, who didn't for a moment believe it. Angels weren't married in such a hurry. On the other hand, he was sure young devils frequently were. They got hold of one and made one. Jocelyn had been got hold of—lamentably, disastrously.

The Canon snatched up his hat. 'Come along, Margaret,' he said testily, squaring his shoulders.

And Margaret came along, and together they marched off into the house, along the passage, past the shut sitting-room door, accompanied by Jocelyn who showed them out in silence.

He had said no word of that pleasant part of his mother's message, that part about having a beautiful surprise for the Walkers, perhaps to-morrow, because he was annoyed with them, and they went away more indignant with him than before, besides feeling they had been treacherously treated by their hitherto dear friend, Mrs. Luke. And Mrs. Walker, when they were safely out in the road, said what a very disagreeable young man he had grown into, and the Canon said he hoped Mr. Thorpe would lick him into shape, and Jocelyn, all unconscious of Mr. Thorpe, went back frowning to his mother, who was in the act, when he opened the door, of stroking Sally's hair.

He forgot the tiresome Walkers, and his heart swelled with gratitude. That Sally should be taken at once to his mother's arms like this had been outside his wildest hopes. Indeed, he had had no hopes, no clear thoughts about it at all; he only, driven by weariness of the burden of complications Sally brought into the simplest things, had come back to his mother's feet as the Christian sinner, tired of or frightened by his sins, comes back to the feet of God. The analogy wasn't perfect, of course; Sally, so good and beautiful, couldn't be compared to sin. But he wanted to get back to his mother's feet, he had a tremendous, almost childish, longing to lie there and let her kick him if she chose. He had treated her badly. He well knew he deserved it. Let her do anything in the way of rebuke and chastisement, if only he might lie there, he and his burden, safely cast down, both of them, at her feet. '*I will arise and go to my Mother,*' had floated frequently

through his head as he set the bonnet of the Morris-Cowley eastward towards London and South Winch. Naturally he hadn't said it out loud. Sally was incapable of understanding even a simple reaction. This one, which was highly complicated, would have completely bewildered her. Besides, one can't well speak of a reaction to its cause.

But how happy was Jocelyn at the moment when he opened the door, and saw her and his mother in that attitude of mutual affection; how deeply relieved. The cords were loosened, the weight shifted. Here this calm room, with everything in it just right, just *so*—its restraints, its browns and ivories, its flashes of colour, its books, its one picture; and upstairs, up under the roof, his own attic waiting for him, with its promise of work to be resumed, to be carried on as it used to be in the tranquil, fruitful days before he met Sally.

Jocelyn stood a moment looking at the scene, smiling his rare smile because he was so content. How unlike the places he had suffered in since he last was here. How unlike the Pinner lair at the back of the shop, where he had burnt in torment, and the hideous dwelling of the Cupps, where he had been insulted, and the dingy expensiveness of the Thistle and Goat, and the other three or four cynically ugly and uncomfortable rooms through which he had trailed his passion. Impossible not to smile, not to laugh almost, with gladness at getting home again. He had, he knew, all his life loved his mother, but it seemed as if he hadn't loved her consciously till now, and he went quickly across to her and put his arm about her, and said, 'Mother, you must never leave me. I can't do without you. *We* can't. When I go back to Cambridge—and of course I'm going back—you must come too. You're going to live with us there. Everything depends on you. All my future, all my happiness—'

And Sally, over whose head these words were being tossed, sitting very rigid, for Mrs. Luke's hand was still on her hair, and wholly unaccustomed to displays of family affection, once again said to herself, just for company's sake and to keep her courage up, 'Well, I'm blest.'

❀

Mrs. Luke, however, was brought back by Jocelyn's words to a vivid sense of Mr. Thorpe. He had sunk aside in her mind during the emotions of the last half hour. He now became distinct; extremely distinct, and frightfully near. That very evening he would be coming round after supper—he had agreed that the meal itself should be given over to reunion—in order to collect his young guests.

Jocelyn, she knew, had no idea of his existence. Mr. Thorpe, though living in South Winch, had not till then been of it. His world had been different. His wealth had separated him, and his obvious disharmony— South Winch had only to look at him to perceive it—with the things of the spirit. Also, there had been his wife. So that if mentioned, which was rarely, it had merely been with vague uninterest as the rich man in the big house in Acacia Avenue.

Now he had to be mentioned, and Jocelyn's words made it difficult.

Mrs. Luke stood silent, her hand still on Sally's head, encircled by Jocelyn's arm, while he told her of the plans he had been making for the last two days, ever since it suddenly dawned on him that that was to be their future. How could she interrupt him with Mr. Thorpe? Yet Mr. Thorpe was, she was sure, the real solution. Salvatia was going to be expensive, very, if the gutter was to be properly scraped off her, and no further stretching could possibly be got out of her own income, while Jocelyn's, of course, would be all needed for Cambridge. Yes—Mr. Thorpe, who had begun by being a refuge, had now become a godsend. Jocelyn would see it himself, when he had had him properly explained.

But how difficult to explain him—now, with the sweet balm of her boy's dependence on her and his love being poured into her ears, her boy, who in his whole life hadn't shown so much of either as he had in the half hour since he came home. Yet it wasn't her fault, it was Jocelyn's. It was his marriage that had precipitated Mr. Thorpe into their lives. Still, she didn't blame Jocelyn, for no young man, let alone her imaginative, beauty-appreciating son, could have resisted Salvatia.

She stood silent, smiling nervously. To have to quench this happy hopefulness with Mr. Thorpe was most painful. She smiled more and more nervously. Apart from everything else, it embarrassed her, her

coming marriage, it embarrassed her dreadfully, somehow, faced by her grown-up son. The memory of that almost snapped tendon last night … suppose Jocelyn were to think she was marrying Mr. Thorpe for anything but convenience, with anything but reluctance … suppose he were to take up a Hamlet-like attitude to her, and think—he would never, she knew, say—rude things. …

'How delightful it all sounds,' she said at last, removing her hand from Sally's head, who at once felt better. 'Quite, quite delightful. But—'

'Now, Mother, there mustn't be any buts,' interrupted Jocelyn. 'It's all settled.' And rashly—but then he felt so happy and safe—he appealed to Sally. 'Isn't it, Sally,' he said. 'We want Mother, don't we. And we're going to have her, aren't we.'

'Yes—and Father,' said Sally, whose ideas were simple but tenacious.

'Father?' repeated Mrs. Luke, touched. 'Dear child, your poor Jocelyn has no—'

'Mother, you and I must really have a good talk together,' hastily interposed Jocelyn, who saw Sally's mouth opening again. She shouldn't *say* anything; she really shouldn't *say* anything; the less she said the better for everybody. 'You and I. By ourselves. This evening, when Sally—'

'Salvatia, Jocelyn. Please, please.'

'—has gone up to bed.'

'But you know, Jocelyn dear,' said Mrs. Luke, loosening herself from his clasp and withdrawing a little, 'that's just what the dear child can't go up to. Not here. Not in this tiny house. You didn't think, of course, but there isn't an inch of room really—not for three people. So I wanted to tell you—' she began putting his tie straight, her eyes on it, not looking at him—'what I've arranged. You're both going to be taken in next door.'

'Next door, Mother?' said Jocelyn, much surprised, for he couldn't at all recollect the next door people.

'Well, nearly next door,' said Mrs. Luke, diligent over his tie, and excessively annoyed to feel she was turning red. 'At Abergeldie.'

'Abergeldie?' echoed Jocelyn, to whom the name was completely unfamiliar.

'I tell you what we'll do,' said Mrs. Luke, as though she had suddenly

had a brilliant idea, on the little maid's appearing in the door bearing a tray that seemed twice as big as she was, and all but dropping it when she caught sight of the young lady on the chair. 'After tea Salvatia shall go and lie down in my bedroom and rest—won't you, Salvatia,—and you and I will have a quiet talk, dear Jocelyn—no, no, Hammond, not there; here, where I've put the table ready—and I'll tell you all about—we want three cups, Hammond, not two—I'll tell you all about—'

But she still couldn't bring herself to mention Mr. Thorpe, and again said Abergeldie.

'Is that lodgings?' asked Jocelyn, who didn't at all like the sound of it.

'Oh, no—it isn't *lodgings*,' said Mrs. Luke brightly, giving his tie a final pat.

❁

How was she to tell him about Mr. Thorpe? In what words, once she had got Salvatia upstairs out of the way, could she most quickly create in Jocelyn's mind the image she wished to have there of a good, and honourable, and wealthy man, a man elderly and settled down, who respected and esteemed her, and because he respected and esteemed her wished to make her his wife? A good man, who would be a solid background for them all. A good man, whose feeling for her—Mrs. Luke was most anxious that Jocelyn shouldn't suppose there was anything warm about Mr. Thorpe—was that of a kind, and much older, brother.

Preoccupied and perturbed, she poured out the tea and drank some herself, and hardly noticed what Sally was doing who, faced for the first time in her life by no table to sit up to and only her lap to put her cup and saucer and spoon and things to eat on, kept on either dropping them or spilling them.

'Well, Mother, you'll just have to be very patient,' said Jocelyn, himself deeply annoyed when Sally's spoon fell off for the third time, and for the third time made a noise on the varnished floor, which only had two rugs on it, and those far apart.

And Mrs. Luke smiled, and said 'Of course,' and hardly noticed, because of her deep preoccupation with Mr. Thorpe.

But when the cup itself slid sideways on the saucer and upset, and Sally's frock was soaked and the cup broken, she was startled into awareness again, and for the moment forgot Mr. Thorpe.

'Oh, *my*!' cried Sally, shaken into speech.

'It really isn't of the slightest consequence, Salvatia,' said Mrs. Luke, who was particularly fond of her teacups, of which none had ever yet been broken. 'Pray don't try to pick up anything. Hammond will do so. Jocelyn, ring the bell, will you? But I shouldn't,' she added, for naturally she was vexed at the set being spoilt, and though breeding, she knew, forbids vexation at such *contretemps* being shown, yet it has to get out in some form or other, 'I shouldn't say, "Oh, *my*," when anything unexpected happens.'

'Right O,' murmured Sally, shattered, all Jocelyn's teaching vanishing from her mind.

'Nor,' remarked Mrs. Luke, gently and very clearly, 'should I say, "Right O".'

'I've told her not to a hundred times,' said Jocelyn, wiping Sally's frock with his handkerchief.

'That's right,' murmured Sally, who had now lost her head, and only wanted to admit her evil-doing and be forgiven.

'Nor, dear Salvatia,' said Mrs. Luke, still more gently and clearly, 'should I, I think, say that.'

So then Sally said nothing, for there seemed nothing left to say.

'She'll be perfectly all right ultimately,' said Mrs. Luke, coming down to Jocelyn when presently she had taken her upstairs, and tucked her up on the bed, and told her she was tired and must rest. 'Perfectly.'

Jocelyn was waiting in the sitting-room. He and his mother were now, having got Sally out of the way, going to have their talk.

'You're wonderful, Mother,' he said.

'Darling Jocelyn,' smiled his mother. 'It's that child who is wonderful,' she added. 'Or will be, when she has been properly—' she was going to say scraped, the word gutter coming once more into her mind, but of

course she didn't, and substituted something milder. 'When she has been properly trained,' finished Mrs. Luke.

'It sounds like a servant,' said Jocelyn, who was sensitive because of the tin trunk (got rid of in Truro,) and the stiff nightgowns (got rid of in Truro too,) and several other distinct and searing memories.

'Servant? You absurd boy. She's a duchess, who happens not to have been born right—the most beautiful duchess the world would ever have seen. Now never,' said Mrs. Luke with much seriousness—she felt she must take this situation thoroughly in hand—'never, never let such a word as the one you just used enter your mind in connection with Salvatia again, my dear Jocelyn.'

No, he wouldn't tell his mother about the way Sally had seemed to drift, as if drawn, towards the Cupps, quite obviously wanting to make friends with them, nor about the way she actually had made friends with the spotted mechanic in the Truro garage. And as for Mr. Pinner, for whom he had a curious distaste and of whom the remembrance was definitely grievous to him, Jocelyn wouldn't tell his mother about him either. He would skim over Mr. Pinner. Why intrude him? Why dot the i's of Sally's beginnings? His mother had heard for herself how she spoke, and knew approximately what her father must be like. Let her knowledge remain approximate.

So they went together into the garden—again Mrs. Luke instinctively sought Nature,—Jocelyn determined to keep Mr. Pinner out of his mother's consciousness, and Mrs. Luke determined to get Mr. Thorpe into his.

❁

Arm in arm they paced up and down what Mr. Thorpe persisted in calling the drying ground, in spite of Mrs. Luke's steady reference to it as the lawn, and Jocelyn said, 'Her family come from Islington.'

'Suburbans. Like ourselves,' replied his mother, with a really heavenly tact, Jocelyn thought.

But she wasn't thinking of what he was saying and what she was

answering; she was seeking a formula for Mr. Thorpe. And, to gain yet a further moment's grace,—queer how nervous she felt—she stopped a moment in front of the Kerria japonica in the angle of the wall by the kitchen window, and asked him if he didn't think it was doing very well that year.

'Wonderful,' said Jocelyn. 'It's all perfect.'

He sighed with contentment at his mother's progressive and amazing tactfulness. How had she not from the first moment grasped the situation, and needed no explanation at all. Now she was grasping the Pinners, and dismissing them without a single question. 'Suburbans. Like ourselves.' At that moment Jocelyn positively adored his mother.

'Quite perfect,' he said, admiring the Kerria. 'Wherever you are, things grow as they should, and there's peace, and order, and exact *rightness*.'

'Marriage has turned you into a flatterer,' smiled Mrs. Luke, still putting off Mr. Thorpe.

'It has made me realise what a mother I've got,' said Jocelyn, pressing her arm.

'Darling Jocelyn. But surely rather an unusual result?'

'My marriage is unusual.'

'Yes,' said Mrs. Luke, bracing herself. 'Yes. I suppose—we had better talk about it.'

'But we *are* talking about it.'

'I mean the future.'

'Well, I've told you my plans.'

'But I haven't told you mine.'

'Yours, Mother?'

He turned his head and looked at her. Surely she was rather red?

'You know, Jocelyn,' she said, in a queer altered voice, 'I was very miserable. Very, very miserable. You mustn't forget that. I really *was*.'

❈

How differently Mrs. Luke had meant to introduce Mr. Thorpe; how clearly she recognised that in their present situation he was their only

hope, and that he should be explained with the appreciation and praise due to an only hope. And here she was prefacing him by a solemn declaration of her own unhappiness. It wasn't at all the proper beginning. It couldn't but be damaging to Mr. Thorpe. Besides, her pride had always been to appear before Jocelyn in every situation as completely content and calm. Breeding, she had preached to him ever since he was a tot, was invariably calm, and behaved very much like the great description of charity in St. Paul's first epistle to the Corinthians. Whatever it felt it didn't show it. But she had had a bad time lately, a bad, bad time, and her nerves had been tried beyond, apparently, their endurance.

'What is it, Mother?' asked Jocelyn, surprised and troubled. Had his mother been speculating, and lost?

She made a great effort to recover her self-control, and tried to smile. 'Really some very good news,' she said, resuming their walk. 'We'll go and sit under the cedar, and I'll—'

'Mother, what is it?' asked Jocelyn again anxiously as she broke off, a cold foreboding creeping round his heart. 'You're not going to—you're not going to fail me now?'

'I'm going to help you more than I've ever done. In fact, if it hadn't been for this—' she was going to say windfall, but found she couldn't think of Mr. Thorpe as a windfall,—'if it hadn't been for this, I could do very little for Salvatia. She will need—'

Had his mother been speculating, and won?

But what Salvatia would need Mrs. Luke didn't on that occasion explain, for as on their way to the cedar they passed below the open window of the bedroom Sally had been left in, they heard voices coming from it, and Mrs. Luke, much astonished, stood still.

Almond Tree Cottage was a small low house, and its first floor windows were not very far above the heads of those walking beneath them in the garden. Standing there astonished—for who could Salvatia possibly be talking to?—Mrs. Luke listened, her surprised eyes on Jocelyn's face. He too listened, but with less surprise, for from past experience he could guess—it was painful to him—what was happening, and he guessed that Sally was reverting to type again, and coalescing with the servant.

At first there was only a murmuring—one voice by itself, then another voice by itself, then two voices together; and his mother's face was frankly bewildered. But presently Sally's voice emerged, and it rose in a distinct, surprising wail, and they heard it say, or rather cry, 'Oh, Ammond—oh, Ammond—'

Twice. Just like that.

Whereupon Mrs. Luke let go suddenly of Jocelyn's arm, and hurried indoors and upstairs.

❁

'Are you unwell, Salvatia?' she asked quickly, opening the bedroom door.

On the edge of the bed, her stockinged feet trailing on the floor, sat Sally, and beside her, also on the edge of the bed, the little maid. Mrs. Luke couldn't believe her eyes. Their arms were round each other. She hadn't realised, somehow, that Hammond had any arms; not the sort that go round other people, not the sort that do anything except carry trays and sweep floors.

It came upon her with an odd shock. If Salvatia were ill, of course Hammond's arms would be in an explainable and excusable position. But Salvatia wasn't ill. Mrs. Luke saw that at once. She wasn't ill, for she was crying; and people who are ill, she had observed, do not as a rule cry.

The little maid jumped up, and stood, very red and scared, with alarmed eyes fixed on her mistress. Sally did just the opposite—she lay down quickly on the bed again, and pulled the counterpane up to her chin and tried to look as if she hadn't stirred from the position the lady had tucked her into when she left her. What she was ashamed of was crying; crying when everybody was so good to her and kind, patting and kissing her and that, even after she had broken the cup. It was terribly ungrateful of her to cry, thought Sally. But she wasn't ashamed of having put her arm round Ammond. Friendly, she was; friendly, and seemed to know a lot for her age, which was six months less than Sally's own. A bit shy she had been and stand-offish at first, but soon got used to Sally, who was feeling ever so lonely and strange, and when Ammond—of all the names for a

girl!—came in with hot water for the lady to wash in before the next meal, Sally, taken by her friendly eye, began talking to her, and it was as great a relief as talking to the young fellow in the garage, only with the young fellow she had laughed, and with Ammond, to her confusion and shame, she did nothing but cry. But then the lady … enough to make a cat cry, that lady … going to live with them, and never leave them any more … keeping on smiling smiles that looked like smiles, and weren't. …

'*I* know,' said the little maid, nodding gravely.

Knew a lot, Ammond did, for her age.

❂

Sally had been very thankful when that dreadful tea was somehow finished—they had actually tried to make her have more tea, and begin the cup and lap business all over again, but she wasn't to be caught a second time,—she had been very thankful to follow Mrs. Luke upstairs, and let herself be laid out on a bed and told she must rest till supper. Till breakfast next day she would rest if they liked, till kingdom come. She didn't want any supper. There were forks for supper, which were worse than spoons, and perhaps they had that too just sitting round with nothing but their laps. She didn't want anything, not anything in the world, except to be somewhere where the lady wasn't. And the lady had drawn the curtains, and then covered her up with a counterpane, and smoothed back her hair, and told her sleep would refresh her, and bent over her and kissed her, and at last had gone away—and how thankful Sally had been, just to be alone.

Kissed her. In spite of the cup, thought Sally, who lay still as she had been told, and reflected upon all that had been her lot that afternoon. They didn't seem able to stop kissing in that family, thought Sally, in whose own there had been a total absence of what the Pinner circle knew and condemned as pawings about. The Pinners never pawed, nor did any of their friends. Nice, that was, thought Sally wistfully; knew where you were. Among these here Lukes—so ran her dejected thoughts, with no intention of irreverence but unable, from her habit of language, to run otherwise—one never could tell where one wasn't going to be kissed

next. Hands, hair, face—nothing seemed to come amiss to them when they once got going. Kept one on the hop; made one squirmy. And Mr. Luke—*he* was different here. But then he kept on being different. While as for that there lady—

At this point of her meditations Sally had turned her face to the pillow and buried it, and to her surprise she found the pillow was wet, and on looking into this she discovered that it was her own tears making it wet. Then she was ashamed. But being ashamed didn't stop her crying; once she had begun she seemed to get worse every minute. And the little maid, coming in with the hot water, had found her crying quite hard.

❀

Mrs. Luke made short work of the little maid. She merely said, in that gentle voice before which all servants went down flat as ninepins, 'Hammond, I am surprised at your disturbing Mrs. Jocelyn's sleep—' and the little maid, very red and with downcast eyes, sidled deprecatingly out of the room.

Then Mrs. Luke took Sally in hand, sitting in her turn on the edge of the bed.

'Salvatia, dear—' she said, laying her hand on the arm outlined beneath the counterpane, and addressing the averted face. 'Salvatia, dear—'

Sally's tears dried up instantly, for she was much too much afraid to cry, but she buried her face still deeper, and kept her eyes tight shut.

'Don't make confidences to a servant, dear child,' said Mrs. Luke gently. 'Come to Jocelyn, or to me. We're the *natural* ones for you to come to in any of your little troubles. Oh, I know honeymoons are trying for a girl, and often, without knowing why, she wants a good cry. Isn't it so, Salvatia? Then come to me, or to your husband, when you feel like that, but don't say things to Hammond you may afterwards regret. You see, Salvatia dear, you're a lady, aren't you—a grown-up married lady now, and your place is with your husband and me. What, dear child? What did you say?'

Sally, however, hadn't said anything; she had only gulped, trying to

choke down her misgivings at this picture of where her place was. With the lady? 'Shouldn't be surprised,' she thought, in great discomfort of mind as she more and more perceived that her marriage was going to include Mrs. Luke, 'if I ain't bitten off more as I can chew—' and immediately was shocked at herself for having thought it. Manners were manners. They had to be inside one, as well as out. No good saying Excuse me, Pardon, and Sorry, if inside you were thinking rude. God saw. God knew. And if you were only polite with your lips, and it wasn't going right through you, you were being, as she remembered from her father's teaching, a whited sepulchre.

And Mrs. Luke, contemplating the *profit perdu* on the pillow, the tip of the little ear, the lovely curve of the flushed cheek, and the tangle of bright hair, bent down and kissed it with a view to comfort and encouragement, and Sally, trying not to shrink further into the pillow, said to herself, 'At it again.'

'Why did you cry, Salvatia?' asked Mrs. Luke, gently.

'Dunno,' murmured Sally, withdrawing into the furthermost corner of her shell.

'Then, dear, it was simply childish, wasn't it—to cry without a reason, and to cry before a servant too. Things like that lower one's dignity, Salvatia. And you haven't only your own dignity to consider now, but Jocelyn's, your husband's.'

'Oh dear,' sighed Sally to herself, recognising from the tone, through all its gentleness, that she was being given What for—a new kind, and one which it was extremely difficult to follow and understand, however painstakingly she listened. Which parts, for instance, of herself and Mr. Luke were their dignities? 'Good job I ain't a nursin' mother,' she thought, for she knew all about nursing mothers, 'or the lady'd turn my milk sour'—and immediately was much shocked at herself for having thought it. Manners were manners. They had to be inside one, as well as out. 'Never think what you wouldn't say,' had been her father's teaching; and fancy saying what she had just thought!

'*Oh Gawd,*' silently prayed Sally, who had been made to repeat a collect every Sunday to Mr. Pinner, and in whose mind bits had stuck, '*send*

– 127 –

down the 'Oly Spirit and cleanse the thoughts of my 'eart with 'im forasmuch as
without thee I ain't able to. …'

'Perhaps, dear,' said Mrs. Luke, finding it difficult in the face of Sally's silence to go on—not for want of things to say, for there were so many and all so important that she hardly knew where to begin,—'the best thing you can do is to bathe your eyes in the nice hot water Hammond has put ready, and tidy yourself a little, and then come downstairs. What do you think of that? Isn't it a good idea? It is dull for you up here alone. But bathe your eyes well. We don't want Jocelyn to see we've been crying, do we, dear child—'

And in the act of stooping to give Sally a parting kiss she heard her name being called, loud and cheerily, downstairs in the hall.

She started to her feet.

'Margery! Margery!' called the voice, with the cheerful insistence of one who, being betrothed, has the right to be cheerful and insistent in his fiancée's hall.

Edgar. Come hours before his time.

❁

'Oh, hush, *hush*—' besought Mrs. Luke, hurrying down to him.

'Hush, eh?'

'Jocelyn—'

She glanced fearfully along the passage to the backdoor.

'He's arrived,' said Mr. Thorpe, not hushing at all. 'Know that. Saw his—well, you can hardly call it a car, can you—his contraption, outside the gate.'

'But I haven't had time yet to tell him—'

'That he's been a fool?' interrupted Mr. Thorpe.

'Come in here,' said Mrs. Luke, taking him by the arm and pressing him into the parlour, the door of which she shut.

'Brought you this,' said Mr. Thorpe, holding up a fish-basket, a big one, in front of her face. 'Salmon. Prime cut. Thought it would be a bit of something worth eating for your—well, you don't have dinner, do

you—meal, then, to-night. Came back early from the City on purpose to get it here soon enough.'

'How kind, how kind,' murmured Mrs. Luke distractedly.

'Plenty of it, too,' said Mr. Thorpe, slapping the basket.

'Too much, too much,' murmured Mrs. Luke, not quite sure whether it were the salmon she was talking about.

'Too much? Not a bit of it,' said Mr. Thorpe. 'I hate skimp.'

And he was going to put down his present on the nearest chair and then, she knew, fold her in one of those strong hugs that scrunched, when she bent forward and hastily took the basket from him. She couldn't, she simply couldn't, on this occasion be folded—not with Jocelyn sitting out there, all unsuspecting, under the cedar.

'Never mind the basket,' said Mr. Thorpe, who felt he had deserved well of Margery in this matter of the fish.

'I must take it to the kitchen at once,' said Mrs. Luke, evading his wide-opened arms, 'or it won't be ready in time for supper.'

'What? No thanks, eh?'

'Yes, yes—afterwards,' said Mrs. Luke, slipping away to the door. 'Jocelyn doesn't know yet. About us, I mean. I haven't had time—'

'Time, eh? Not had time to tell him, you've netted me?'

Mr. Thorpe took out his watch. 'Five minutes,' he said. 'Two would be enough, but I'll give you five. Trot along now, and come back to me sharp in five minutes. If you don't, I'll fetch you. Trot along.'

Trot along. ...

Mrs. Luke, shutting him into the parlour, asked herself, as she went down the passage bearing the heavy basket in both her delicate hands, how long it would take after marriage to weed out Mr. Thorpe's language. To be told to trot along, however, was so grotesque—she to trot, she, surely the most dignified of South Winch's ladies!—that it seemed to restore her composure. She would not trot. Nor would she, in the emotional sphere, do anything that corresponded to it. She would neither trot nor hurry; neither physically, nor spiritually. She declined to be bound by five minutes, and a watch in Edgar's hand. Really he must, somehow, come up more to her level, and not be so comfortably certain that she was coming

down to his. And what a way to speak of their marriage—that she had netted him!

Frozen, then, once more into calm by Mr. Thorpe's words, she proceeded down the passage with almost more than her usual dignity, and as she passed the kitchen door she held out the fish-basket to the little maid, who came out of the shady corner where the sink was with reluctance, merely saying, 'Boil it.' Then, with her head held high as the heads of those are held who face the inevitable, she went out into the garden, and crossed the grass to where Jocelyn was waiting for her on the seat beneath the cedar.

This took her one minute out of the five. In another four Mr. Thorpe would come out too into the garden, to see why she didn't return. Let him, thought Mrs. Luke, filled with the courage of the cornered. This thing couldn't be done in five minutes; it couldn't be fired off at Jocelyn's head like a pistol. Foolish Edgar.

❁

'Well, Mother?' said Jocelyn, getting up as she approached.

He had been smoking, content to leave whatever it was Sally had been doing in his mother's capable hands, yet wishing to goodness Sally hadn't done it. This trick of wanting to be with servants must revolt his mother. It revolted him; how much more, then, his fastidious mother.

'I can guess what it is, I'm afraid,' he said, as she sat down beside him.

'No,' said Mrs. Luke. 'You haven't any idea.'

'*What* has she been doing, Mother?' he asked, seriously alarmed, and throwing away his cigarette.

'Salvatia? Nothing. Nothing that matters, poor dear child. It's not about her I want to talk. It's about Mr. Thorpe.'

'Mr. Thorpe?'

'Yes. Abergeldie. That's Mr. Thorpe's. That's why you are going there—because it is Mr. Thorpe's.'

'But why should we—?'

'Now Jocelyn,' she interrupted, 'please keep well in mind that Mr.

Thorpe is the most absolutely reliable, trustworthy, excellent, devoted man. I can find no flaw in his character. He is generous to a fault—really to a fault. He has a perfect genius for kindness. Indeed, I can't tell you how highly I think of him.'

Jocelyn's heart went cold and heavy with foreboding.

There was a little silence.

'Yes, Mother. And?' he said, after a minute.

'And he is rich. Very.'

'Yes, Mother. And?' said Jocelyn, as she paused.

'When I got your first letter I was, of course, very much upset,' said Mrs. Luke, looking straight in front of her.

'Yes, Mother. And?' said Jocelyn, for she paused again.

'Everything seemed to go to pieces—all I had believed in and hoped for.'

There was a longer pause.

'Yes, Mother. And?' said Jocelyn at last, keeping his voice as level as possible.

'I'm not a religious woman, as you know. I hadn't got God.'

'No, Mother. So?'

'So I—I turned to Mr. Thorpe.'

'Yes, Mother. Quite.'

The bitterness of Jocelyn's soul was complete. A black fog of anger, jealousy, wounded trust, hurt pride and cruellest disappointment engulfed him.

'Why not say at once,' he said, lighting another cigarette with hands he was grimly determined should be perfectly steady, 'that you are going to marry him?'

'If it hadn't been for your marriage it never would have happened,' said Mrs. Luke.

'Quite,' said Jocelyn, very bitter, pitching the newly-lit cigarette away. 'Oh, quite.'

Sally again. Always, at the bottom of everything, Sally.

Then he thought, ashamed, 'My God, I'm a mean cur'—and sat in silence, his head in his hands, not looking up at all, while his mother did her best to make him see Mr. Thorpe as she wanted him to be seen.

In her low voice, the low, educated voice Jocelyn had so much loved, she explained Mr. Thorpe and his advantages, determined that at this important, this vital moment she would not allow herself to be vexed by anything Jocelyn said.

He, however, said nothing. It simply was too awful for speech—his mother, who never during her whole life had shown signs of wanting to marry, going now, now that she was at an age when she might surely, in Jocelyn's twenty-two year old vision, be regarded as immune, to give herself to a complete stranger, and leave him, her son who needed her, God knew, more than ever before, to his fate. That he should hate this Thorpe with a violent hatred seemed natural. Who cared for his damned money? Why should Sally—his mother kept on harping on that—be going to be expensive? As if money, much money, according to what his mother was saying, now that Sally had come on the scene, Sally who was used to being penniless, was indispensable. Masters? What need was there for masters? His mother could teach her. Clothes? Why, whatever she put on seemed to catch beauty from her—he had seen that in the shop in London where he bought the wrap: every blessed thing the women tried on her, however unattractive to begin with, the minute it touched her body became part of beauty. And how revolting, anyhow—marriage. Oh, how he hated the thought of it, how he wanted now beyond anything in the world to be away from its footling worries and complications, away from women altogether, and back at Cambridge, back in a laboratory, absorbed once more in the great tranquil splendours of research!

'He is in the sitting-room,' said Mrs. Luke, when she had said everything she could think of that she wished Jocelyn to suppose was true.

'Who is?' said Jocelyn.

'Ah, I was afraid you would be angry,' she said, putting her hand on his arm, 'but I hoped that when it was all explained you would understand, and see the great, the immense advantages. Apparently you don't, or—' she sighed—'won't. Then I must be patient till you do, or will. But Mr. Thorpe is waiting.'

'Who cares?' inquired Jocelyn, his head in his hands; and it suddenly struck Mrs. Luke that Mr. Thorpe was waiting very quietly. The five

minutes must have been up long ago; she must have been sitting there quite twenty, and yet he hadn't come after her as he had threatened. Knowing him, as she did, for a man absolutely of his word, this struck her as odd.

'Dear Jocelyn,' she said, remembering the fits of dark obstinacy that had at times seized her boy in his childhood, and out of which he had only been got by the utmost patience and gentleness, 'I won't bother you to come in now and see Mr. Thorpe. But as he is going to be your host to-night—'

'He isn't,' said Jocelyn, his head still in his hands, and his eyes still fixed on the grass at his feet.

'But, *dearest* boy—'

'I decline to go near him.'

'But there's *positively* no room here for you both—'

'There's London, and hotels, I suppose?'

'Oh, Jocelyn!'

She looked at him in dismay. He didn't move. She again put her hand on his arm. He took no notice. And aware, from past experiences, that for the next two hours at least he would probably be completely inaccessible to reason, she got up with a sigh and left him.

Well, she had told him; she had done what she had to do. She would now go back to Mr. Thorpe.

And she did go back; and opening the parlour door slowly and gently, for she was absorbed in painful thought, she found Mr. Thorpe sitting on the sofa, busily kissing Sally.

X

The following brief dialogue had taken place between him and Sally, before he began to kiss:

'Crikey!' he exclaimed, on her appearing suddenly in the doorway.

'Pardon?' said she, hesitating, and astonished to find a strange old gentleman where she had thought to find the Lukes.

'It's crikey all right,' he said, staring. 'Know who I am?'

'No, sir.'

'Sir, eh?'

He took a step forward and shut the door.

'Father—that's who I am. Yours. Father-in-law. Same thing as father, only better,' said he. 'What does one do to a father, eh? Kisses him. How do, daughter. Kiss me.'

Sally kissed him; or rather, having no reason to doubt that the old gentleman was what he said he was, docilely submitted while he kissed her, regarding his behaviour as merely another example of the inability of all Lukes to keep off pawings; and though she was mildly surprised at the gusto with which this one gave himself up to them, she was pleased to notice his happy face. If only everybody would be happy she wouldn't mind anything. She hadn't felt that the lady's kisses were expressions of happiness, and Mr. Luke's, when he started, made her think of a funeral that had got the bit between its teeth and couldn't stop running away, more than of anything happy. Father-in-law, on the contrary, seemed as jolly as a sand-boy. And anyhow it was better than having to talk.

This was the way the situation arose in which Mrs. Luke found them.

'Making friends with my new daughter,' said Mr. Thorpe, not without confusion, on perceiving her standing looking on.

'Quite,' said Mrs. Luke, who sometimes talked like Jocelyn.

Now to have caught Mr. Thorpe kissing somebody else—she didn't like it when he kissed her, but she discovered she liked it still less when it was somebody else—was painful to Mrs. Luke. Every aspect of it was painful. The very word *caught* was an unpleasant one; and she felt that to be placed in a position in life in which she might be liable to catch would be most disagreeable. What she saw put everything else for the moment out of her head. Edgar must certainly be told that he couldn't behave like this. No marriage could stand it. If a woman couldn't trust her husband not to humiliate her, whom could she trust? And to behave like this to Salvatia, of all people! Salvatia, who was to live with them at Abergeldie during term time, while Jocelyn pursued his career undisturbed at Cambridge— this had been another of Mrs. Luke's swift decisions,—live with them, and be given advantages, and be trained to become a fit wife for him,—how could any of these plans be realised if Edgar's tendency to kiss, of which Mrs. Luke had only been too well aware, but which she had supposed was concentrated entirely on herself, included also Salvatia?

And if the situation was disagreeable to Mrs. Luke, it was very nearly as disagreeable to Mr. Thorpe. He didn't like it one little bit. He knew quite well that there had been gusto in his embrace, and that Margery must have seen it. 'Damn these women,' he thought, unfairly.

The only person without disagreeable sensations was Sally, who, unconscious of anything but dutiful behaviour, was standing wiping her face with a big, honest-looking handkerchief, observing while she did so that she wasn't half hot.

'Jocelyn is in the garden, Salvatia,' said Mrs. Luke.

Regarding this as mere news, imparted she knew not to what end, Sally could think of nothing to say back, though it was evident from the lady's eyes that she was expected to make some sort of a reply. She searched, therefore, in her *répertoire*, and after a moment said, 'Fancy that,' and went on wiping her face.

'Won't you go to him?' then said Mrs. Luke, speaking very distinctly.

'Right O,' said Sally, hastily then, for the lady's eyebrows had suddenly

become rather frightening; and, stuffing the handkerchief yard by yard into her pocket as she went, she exquisitely slid away.

'I'll be off too,' said Mr. Thorpe briskly, who for the first time didn't feel at home with Margery. 'Back on the tick of ten to fetch 'em both—'

'Oh, but please—wait just one moment,' said Mrs. Luke, raising her hand as he began to move towards the door.

'Got to have my wigging first, eh?' he said, pausing and squaring his shoulders to meet it.

'What is a wigging, Edgar?' inquired Mrs. Luke gently, opening her clear grey eyes slightly wider.

'Oh Lord, Margery, cut the highbrow cackle,' said Mr. Thorpe. 'Why shouldn't I kiss the girl? She's my daughter-in-law. Or will be soon.'

'Really, Edgar, it would be very strange if you didn't wish to kiss her,' said Mrs. Luke, still with gentleness. 'Anybody would wish to.'

'Well, then,' said Mr. Thorpe sulkily; for not only didn't he see what Margery was driving at, but for the first time he didn't think her particularly good-looking. Moth-eaten, thought Mr. Thorpe, eyeing her. A lady, of course, and all that; but having to sleep later on with a moth-eaten lady wouldn't, it suddenly struck him, be much fun. 'Need a pitch dark night to turn *her* into a handsome woman,' he thought indelicately; but then he was angry, because he had been discovered doing wrong.

'I wanted to tell you,' said Mrs. Luke, ignoring for the moment what she had just witnessed, 'that I have told Jocelyn.'

And Mr. Thorpe was so much relieved to find she wasn't pursuing the kissing business further that he thought, 'Not a bad old girl, Marge—' in his thoughts he called her Marge, though not to her face because she didn't like it—'not a bad old girl. Better than Annie, anyhow.'

Yes, better than Annie; but less good—ah, how much less good—than young beauty.

'That's all right, then,' he said, cheerful again. 'Nothing like coughing things up.'

No—Edgar was too rough a diamond, Mrs. Luke said to herself, shrinking from this dreadful phrase. She hadn't heard this one before. Was there no end to his dreadful phrases?

'He is much annoyed,' she said, her eyebrows still drawn together with the pain Mr. Thorpe's last sentence had given her.

'Annoyed, eh? Annoyed, is he? I like that,' said Mr. Thorpe vehemently, his cheerfulness vanishing. Annoyed because his mother was making a rattling good match? Annoyed because the richest man for miles round was taking her on for the rest of her life? Of all the insolent puppies …

Mr. Thorpe had no words with which to express his opinion of Jocelyn; no words, that is, fit for a drawing-room—he supposed the room he was in would be called a drawing-room, though he was blest if there was a single stick of stuff in it to justify such a name—for, having now seen Sally, his feeling for Jocelyn, which had been one of simple contemptuous indifference, had changed into something much more active. Fancy *him* getting her, he thought—him, with only a beggarly five hundred a year, him, who wouldn't even be able to dress her properly. Why, a young beauty like that ought to be a blaze of diamonds, and never put her feet to the ground except to step out of a Rolls.

'I'm very sorry, Edgar,' said Mrs. Luke, 'but he says he doesn't wish to accept your hospitality.'

'Doesn't wish, eh? Doesn't wish, does he? I like that,' said Mr. Thorpe, more vehemently still.

That his good-natured willingness to help Marge out of a fix, and his elaborate preparations for the comfort of the first guests he had had for years should be flouted in this way not only angered but hurt him. And what would the servants say? And he had taken such pains to have the bridal suite filled with everything calculated to make the young prig, who thought his sorts of brains were the only ones worth having, see for himself that they weren't. Brains, indeed. What was the good of brains that you couldn't get enough butter out of to butter your bread properly? Dry-bread brains, that's what this precious prig's were. Crust-and-cold-water brains. Brains? Pooh.

This last word Mr. Thorpe said out loud; very loud; and Mrs. Luke shrank again. It strangely afflicted her when he said pooh.

'And I'm afraid,' she went on, her voice extra gentle, for it did seem to her that considering the position she had found him in Edgar was

behaving rather high-handedly, 'that if he knew you had kissed his wife, kissed her in the way you did kiss her, he might still less wish to.'

'*Now* we've got it!' burst out Mr. Thorpe, slapping his thigh. '*Now* we're getting down to brass tacks!'

'Brass tacks, Edgar?' said Mrs. Luke, to whom this expression, too, was unfamiliar.

'Spite,' said Mr. Thorpe.

'Spite?' repeated Mrs. Luke, her grey eyes very wide.

'Feminine spite. Don't believe a word about him not wanting to come and stay at my place. You've made it up. Because I kissed the girl.'

And Mr. Thorpe in his anger inquired of Mrs. Luke whether she had ever heard about hell holding no fury like a woman scorned—for in common with other men who know little poetry he knew that—and he also called her Marge to her face, because he no longer saw any reason why he shouldn't.

'My *dear* Edgar,' was all she could find to say, her shoulders drawn up slightly to her ears as if to ward off these blows of speech, violence never yet having crossed her path.

She didn't get angry herself. She behaved with dignity. She remembered that she was a lady.

She did, however, at last suggest that perhaps it would be better if he went away, for not only was he making more noise than she cared about—really a most noisy man, she thought, gliding to the window and softly shutting it—but it had occurred to her as a possibility that Salvatia, out in the back garden, might be telling Jocelyn that Mr. Thorpe had kissed her, and that on hearing this Jocelyn, who in any case was upset, might be further upset into coming and joining Edgar and herself in the sitting-room.

This, she was sure, would be a pity; so she suggested to Mr. Thorpe that he should go.

'Oh, I'm *going* all right,' said Mr. Thorpe, who somehow, instead of being the one to be wigged, was the one who was wigging.

'We'll talk it all over quietly to-morrow, dear Edgar,' said Mrs. Luke, attempting to placate.

'Dear Edgar, eh?' retorted Mr. Thorpe, not to be shaken by fair words from his conviction that Marge regarded herself as a woman scorned, and therefore that she outrivalled the worst of the ladies of hell. 'Fed-up Edgar's more like it,' he said; and strode, banging doors, out of the house.

❀

Mrs. Luke stood motionless where he had left her. What an unexpected turn things had taken. How very violent Edgar really was; and how rude. A woman scorned? Feminine spite? Such expressions, applied to herself, would be merely ludicrous if they hadn't, coming from Edgar in connection with Salvatia, been so extraordinarily rude.

In connection with Salvatia. She paused on the thought. All this was because of Salvatia. From beginning to end, everything unpleasant and difficult that had happened to her during the last few weeks was because of Salvatia.

But she mustn't be unfair. If Salvatia had been the cause of her engagement to Edgar, she was now being the cause of its breaking off. For surely, surely, breaking off was the only course to take?

'Let me *think*,' said Mrs. Luke, pressing her hand to her forehead, which was burning.

Yes; surely no amount of money could make up for the rest of Edgar? Surely no amount, however great, could make up for the hourly fret and discomfort of having to live with the wrong sort—no, not necessarily the wrong sort, but the entirely different sort, corrected Mrs. Luke, at pains to be just—of mind? Besides, of what use could she be to Jocelyn and Salvatia, married to Edgar, if Jocelyn wouldn't go near him, and Salvatia couldn't because of his amorousness? It would merely make the cleavage between herself and Jocelyn complete at the very moment when he more than ever before in his life needed her. And the grotesqueness of accusing *her*, who had remained so quiet and calm, of being a fury, the sheer imbecility of imagining *her* actuated by feminine spite! Really, really, said Mrs. Luke to herself, drawing her shoulders up to her ears again at the recollection. And then there was—no, she turned her mind away from

those expressions of his; she positively couldn't bear to think of cough it up, bunkum, and pooh.

She went to her little desk and sat down to write a letter to Mr. Thorpe, because in some circumstances letters are so much the best; nor did she want to lose any time, in case it should occur to him too to write a letter, and it seemed to her important that when it comes to shedding anybody one should get there first, and be the shedder rather than the shed; and she had got as far as *Dear Edgar, I feel that I owe it to you*—when Jocelyn appeared in the doorway, with blazing eyes.

❀

What had taken place in the garden between Jocelyn and Sally was this:

She had gone out obediently to him, as she had been told. 'Do as you're told,' her father and mother had taught her, 'and not much can go wrong with you.' Innocent Pinners. Inadequate teaching. It was to lead her, before she had done, into many difficulties.

She went, then, as she had been told, over to where she saw Jocelyn, and sat down beside him beneath the cedar.

He didn't move, and didn't look up, and she sat for a long while not daring to speak, because of the expression on his face.

Naturally she thought it was his stomach again, for what else could it be? Last time she had seen him he was smiling as happy as happy, and kissing his mother's hand. Clear to Sally as daylight was it that he was having another of those attacks to which her father had been such a martyr, and which were familiar to the Pinners under the name of the Dry Heaves. So too had her father sat when they came on, frowning hard at nothing, and looking just like ink. The only difference was that Jocelyn, she supposed because of being a gentleman, held his head in his hands, and her father held the real place the heaves were in. But presently, when the simple remedy he took on these occasions had begun to work, he was better; and it seemed to Sally a great pity that she should be too much afraid of Usband to tell him about it,—a great pity, and wrong as well. Hadn't she promised God in church the day she was

married to look after him in sickness and in health? And here he was sick, plain as a pikestaff.

So at last she pulled her courage together, and did tell him.

'Father's stomach,' she began timidly, 'was just like that.'

'What?' said Jocelyn, roused from his black thoughts by this surprising remark, and turning his head and looking at her.

'You got the same stomachs,' said Sally, shrinking under his look but continuing to hold on to her courage, 'you and Father 'as. Like as two peas.'

Jocelyn stared at her. What, in the name of all that was fantastic, had Pinner's stomach to do with him?

'Sit just like that, 'e would, when they come on,' continued Sally, lashing herself forward.

'Do you mind,' requested Jocelyn with icy politeness, 'making yourself clear?'

'Now, Mr. Luke, don't—please don't talk that way,' begged Sally. 'I only want to tell you what Father did when they come on.'

'When what comes on, and where?'

'These 'ere dry 'eaves,' said Sally. 'You'd be better if you'd take what Father did. 'Ad them somethin' awful, 'e did. And you'd be better—'

But her voice faded away. When Jocelyn looked at her like that and said not a word, her voice didn't seem able to go on talking, however hard she tried to make it.

And Jocelyn's thoughts grew if possible blacker. This was to be his life's companion—his *life's*, mind you, he said to himself. Alone and unaided, he was to live out the years with her. A child; and presently not a child. A beauty; and presently not a beauty. But always to the end, now that his mother had deserted him, unadulterated Pinner.

'There's an h in heaves,' he said, glowering at her, his gloom really inspissate. 'I don't know what the beastly things are, but I'm sure they've got an h in them.'

'Sorry,' breathed Sally humbly, casting down her eyes before his look.

Then he became aware of the unusual flush on her face,—one side was quite scarlet.

'Why are you so red?' he asked suddenly.

'Me?' said Sally, starting at the peremptoriness in his tone. 'Oh—*that*.'

She put up her hand and felt her burning cheek. 'Father-in-law,' she said.

'Father *who?*' asked Jocelyn, astonished out of his gloom.

'In-law,' said Sally. ''Im in the 'ouse. The old gentleman,' she explained, as Jocelyn stared in greater and greater astonishment.

Thorpe? The man who was to be his stepfather? But why—?

A flash of something quite, quite horrible darted into his mind. 'But why,' he asked, 'are you so very red? What has that to do—?'

He broke off, and caught hold of her wrist.

'Daresay it ain't the gentleman's day for shavin',' suggested Sally.

And on Jocelyn's flinging away her wrist and jumping up, she watched him running indoors with recovered complacency. 'Soon be better now,' she said to herself, pleased; for her father always ran like that too, just when the heaves were going to leave off.

❁

And she was right. Next time she saw him, which was at supper, he was quite well. His face had cleared, he could eat his food, and he kissed the top of her head as he passed behind her to his chair.

'Well, *that's* over,' thought Sally, much relieved, though still remaining, through her lowered eyelashes, watchful and cautious. With these Lukes one never knew what was going to happen next; and as she sat doing her anxious best with the forks and other pitfalls of the meal, and the little maid came in and out, free in her movements, independent, able to give notice and go at any moment she chose, Sally couldn't help comparing her lot with her own, and thinking that Ammond was singularly blest. And then she thought what a wicked girl she was to have such thoughts, and bent her head lower over her plate in shame, and Mrs. Luke said gently, 'Sit up, dear child.'

That night a bed was made for Jocelyn on the sitting-room sofa, Sally slept upstairs in the tiny Spartan room he used to sleep in, and Abergeldie

wasn't mentioned. Nor did they have Mr. Thorpe's salmon for supper, because the idea of eating poor Edgar's gift seemed, in the circumstances, cynical to Mrs. Luke; so Hammond ate it, and never afterwards could be got to touch fish.

Mr. Thorpe had now become poor Edgar to Mrs. Luke. Only a few hours before, he had been thought of as a godsend. Well, he shouldn't have kissed Salvatia. But indeed what a mercy that he had, for it brought clarity into what had been troubled and obscure. Without this action—and it wasn't just kissing, it was enjoyment—Mrs. Luke would, she knew, have gone stumbling on, doing her duty by him, trying to get everybody to like each other and be happy in the way that was so obviously the best for them, the way which would quite certainly have been the best for them if poor Edgar had been as decent as, at his age, it was reasonable to expect. She could, she was sure, have managed Jocelyn, for had she not managed him all his life? And after marriage she could, she had no doubt, have managed Edgar too; but what hard work it would have been, what a ceaseless weeding, to take only one aspect of him, of his language!

The enjoyment—it was the only word for it—with which he had kissed Salvatia had spared her all these pains. Certainly it was beneath her dignity, beyond her patience, altogether outside any possible compensation by wealth, to marry and manage a man who enjoyed kissing other women. That she couldn't do. She could do much, but not that. Like the Canon's wife, she would have forgiven everything except enjoyment. And she wrote an urbane letter—why not? Surely finality can afford to be urbane?—after having had a talk with Jocelyn when he arrived with blazing eyes in the sitting-room, a talk which began in violence—his,—and continued in patience—hers,—and ended in peace—theirs; and by the time they sat down to supper the letter, sealed—it seemed to be the sort of letter one ought to seal—was already lying in the pillar box at the corner of the road, and the last trying weeks were wiped out as though they had never been.

At least, that was Mrs. Luke's firm intention, that they should be wiped out; and she thought as she gazed at Jocelyn, so content again, eating a supper purged of the least reminder of Mr. Thorpe, that the *status quo ante* was now thoroughly restored. Ah, happy *status quo ante*, thought Mrs.

Luke, whose mind was well-furnished with pieces of Latin, happy *status quo ante*, with her boy close knit to her again, more than ever unable to do without her, and she in her turn finding the very breath of her being and reason for her existence in him and all his concerns. Not a cloud was now between them. She had quickly reassured him as to Salvatia's red cheek,—Mr. Thorpe's greeting, she had explained, was purely perfunctory, and witnessed by herself, but the child had such a delicate skin that a touch would mark it.

'You mustn't ever bruise her,' she had said, smiling. 'It would show for weeks.'

'Oh, Mother!' Jocelyn had said, smiling too, so happy, he too, to know he had been lifted out of the region of angers, out of the black places where people bruise hearts, not bodies, and in so doing mangle their own.

Yes, she could manage Jocelyn. Tact and patience were all that was needed. Never, never should he know of Edgar's amorousness, any more than he was ever, ever to know of Edgar's other drawbacks. Let him think of him in the future as the kind, reliable rich man who once had wanted to marry her, but whom she had refused for her boy's sake. She made this sacrifice willingly, happily, for her darling son—so she gave Jocelyn to understand, during the talk they had alone together in the sitting-room.

The truth? No, not altogether the truth, she admitted as she sat eating her supper, her pure, pure supper, with all those horrible gross delicacies, under which she had so long groaned, banished out of sight, her glance resting fondly first on her boy, and then in amazed admiration, renewed with a start each time she looked at her, on the flame of loveliness that was her boy's wife. No; what she had said to Jocelyn in the sitting-room wasn't altogether the truth, she admitted that, but the mutilated form of it called tact. Or, rather, not mutilated, which suggested disfigurement, but pruned. Pruned truth. Truth pruned into acceptability to susceptibility. Was not that tact? Was not that the nearest one dared go in speech with the men one loved? They seemed not able to bear truth whole. Children, they were. And the geniuses—she smiled proudly and fondly at Jocelyn's dark head bent over his plate—were the simplest children of them all.

Yes, she thought, the *status quo ante* was indeed restored, and everything was going to be as it used to be. The only difference was Salvatia.

❀

Before a week was over Mrs. Luke left out the word 'only' from this sentence, and was inclined to say—again with Wordsworth; curious how that, surely antiquated, poet cropped up—*But oh, the difference*, instead. Salvatia was—well, why had one been given intelligence if not to cope, among other things, with what Salvatia was?

That first night of reunion with Jocelyn, Mrs. Luke had lain awake nearly all of it, making plans. Very necessary, very urgent it was to get them cut and dried by the morning. The headache she had had earlier in the evening vanished before the imperativeness of thinking and seeing clearly. Many things had to be thought out and decided, some of them sordid, such as the question of living now that there was another mouth to feed, and others difficult, such as the best line to take with South Winch in regard to Mr. Thorpe. She thought and thought, lying on her back, her hands clasped behind her head, staring into the darkness, frowning in her concentration.

Towards morning she saw that the line to take with South Winch about poor Edgar was precisely the line she had taken with Jocelyn: she had given up the hope of marriage, she would say, so as to be able to devote herself exclusively to her boy and his wife.

'See,' she would say, indicating Salvatia, careful at once to draw attention to what anyhow, directly the child began to speak, couldn't remain unnoticed, 'how this untrained, delicious baby needs me. No mother, no education, no idea of what the world demands—could I possibly, thinking only of myself, selfishly leave her without help and guidance? I do feel the young have a very great claim on us.' And then she would add that as long as she lived she would never forget how well, how splendidly, Mr. Thorpe had behaved.

Pruned truth, again. And truth pruned, she was afraid, in a way that would cover her with laurels she hadn't deserved. But what was she to do?

One needs must find the easiest and best way out of a difficulty,—easiest and best for those one loves.

In order, however, to indicate Salvatia and explain things by means of her, Mrs. Luke would have to produce her, have to show her to South Winch, and in order to do that she would have to give a party. Yes; she would give a party, a tea-party, and invite every one she knew to it—except, of course, Mr. Thorpe.

Mrs. Luke had hitherto been sparing of parties, considering them not only difficult with one servant, and wastefully expensive, but also so very ordinary. Anybody not too positively poor could give tea-parties, and invite a lot of people and let them entertain each other. She chose the better way, which was to have one friend, at most two, at a time, and really talk, really exchange ideas, over a simple but attractive tea. Of course the friends had to have ideas, or one couldn't exchange them. But now she would have a real party, with no ideas and many friends, the sort of party called an At Home, and at it Salvatia should be revealed to South Winch in all her wonder.

The party, however, couldn't be given for at least a week, because of first having to drill Salvatia. A week wasn't much; was, indeed, terribly little; but if the drill were intensive, Mrs. Luke thought she could get the child's behaviour into sufficient shape to go on with by the end of it.

Hidden indoors—and in any case they would both at first hide indoors from a possible encounter with poor Edgar—she would devote the whole of every day to exercising Salvatia in the art of silence. That was all she needed to be perfect: silence. And how few words were really necessary for a girl with a face like that! No need whatever to exert herself,—her face did everything for her. Yes; no; please; thank you; what couldn't be done with just these, if accompanied by that heavenly smile? Why, if she kept only to these, if she carefully refrained from more, from, especially, the use of any out of her own deplorable stock, it wouldn't even be necessary for Mrs. Luke to say anything about her having had no education; and if she could be trained to add, 'So kind of you,' at the proper moment, and perhaps, 'Yes, we are very happy,' her success would be overwhelming.

But almost immediately on beginning the drill, which she did the next day, Mrs. Luke perceived that this last sentence must be dropped. Poor Salvatia. The poor child was precluded from speaking of happiness, because of its h. Really rather sad, when one came to think of it. She could, relatively easily, be taught to speak of sorrow, of pain, of misfortune, of sickness and of death, but she couldn't be taught, not in a week Mrs. Luke was afraid, to speak of happiness.

Well, Rome wasn't built in a day. 'We must be patient,' she said, smiling at Sally, who seemed to tumble over herself in her haste to smile back.

Almond Tree Cottage was now the scene of tireless activity. The At Home was fixed for the following Thursday week,—eight days ahead; and Mrs. Luke sent Jocelyn off to Cambridge the very morning after he arrived, in order to rearrange matters with his College and look about, as he seemed bent on it, for a suitable little house for them all, though she privately was bent on staying where she was, and keeping Sally with her. But it did no harm to let him look, and it kept him out of the way for a couple of days, in case Mr. Thorpe should think fit to come round in person, instead of writing. And, having cleared the field, she settled down to devoting herself entirely to Sally.

But Sally, seeing Jocelyn preparing to depart—for some time she couldn't believe her eyes—without going to take her too, was smitten into speech.

'You ain't goin' to leave me 'ere, Mr. Luke?' she asked in tones of horrified incredulity, when at last it began to look exactly as if he were.

'Two days only, darling,' said Jocelyn. 'And you'll be very happy with my mother.'

'But—can't I come with you? I wouldn't be no trouble. I—I'd do anything sooner than—'

She looked over her shoulder; Mrs. Luke, however, was in the kitchen giving her orders for the day.

'—be as 'appy as all that,' she finished, under her breath.

'I shall be much too busy, darling,' said Jocelyn, pleased at the way she was taking their first separation, and not hearing the last words because he was rummaging among coats.

'There's Father,' persisted Sally anxiously. ''*E* could take me in. I wouldn't be no trouble to nobody—'

'Darling, I'm afraid it can't possibly be managed,' said Jocelyn, very thankful to leave her safe with his mother; but she looked so enchanting in her obvious sorrow at being parted from him that he took her in his arms, and kissed her warmly.

'*Kissin's* no good,' said Sally. 'Goin' too's what I'd like.'

'And if I took you too, my beautiful one,' whispered Jocelyn, naming up at the touch of her, 'I'd do nothing but kiss you instead of doing my business—' which wasn't true, but with Sally in his arms he thought it was; besides, they had been separated for a whole night.

'Turtle doves—oh, *turtle* doves!' exclaimed Mrs. Luke, managing to smile, though she didn't like it, when she came out of the kitchen and found them locked together; for this was happening in what Mr. Thorpe refused to call the hall.

And later on when Jocelyn had gone, she put her arm through Sally's, who was standing at the window staring after him as though it couldn't be true that he had really left her, and drew her away into the little dining-room at the back of the house, because of its greater privacy— she had to consider the possible movements of Mr. Thorpe—and at once began to put the plans she had made in the night into practice, not only taking immense pains with the child's words and pronunciation, but leaving no stone unturned—'As the quaint phrase goes,' she said, smiling at Sally, for why hide her intentions?—in order to win her confidence and love.

Sally was most depressed. She didn't want to love—'Too much of that about as it is,' she thought,—and she hadn't an idea what her confidence was.

The table was arranged with paper and ink, and Mrs. Luke began by kissing her affectionately, and telling her that they were now going to be very busy and happy. 'Like bees,' said Mrs. Luke, looking cheerful and encouraging, but also terrifyingly clever, with her clear grey eyes that seemed to see everything all at once and never were half as much pleased as her mouth was.

'You know how bees store up honey—the bright, golden honey, don't you, dear. Say honey, Salvatia dear. Say it after me—'

Sally was most depressed. Mixed up with her efforts to say honey were puzzled thoughts about her husband's having left her. She understood, from her study of the Bible, that one of the principal jobs of husbands was to cleave to their wives. Till death, the Bible said. Nobody had died. It wasn't cleaving to go away to Cambridge and leave her high and dry with the lady. And though Usband was often very strange, he wasn't anything like as strange as the lady; and though he often frightened her, there were moments when he didn't frighten her at all—when, on the contrary, she seemed able to do pretty much as she liked with him. And she had great hopes that some day she and he would get on quite nicely together, once they had set up housekeeping and he went off first thing after breakfast to his work, and she got everything tidy and ready for him when he came back to his dinner. Yes; she and Usband would settle down nicely then. And later on, when she had a little baby—Sally thought frequently and complacently of the time when she would have a little baby, several little babies—things would be as pleasant as could be. All she wanted, so as to be happy, was no lady, a couple of rooms, Usband to do her duty by, God's Word to study, and every now and then a little baby. It was all she asked. It was her idea of bliss. That, and being let alone.

'Peace an' quiet,' she said to herself, as she sat painfully trying, at Mrs. Luke's request, to discuss with her the habits of bees. She hadn't known they had any habits. She doubted whether she would know a bee if she saw one. There were no bees in Islington. Wasps, now—she knew a thing or two about wasps. Raw onion was the stuff for when they stung. ... 'Peace an' quiet,' she said to herself. 'All one asks. This ain't neither.'

In an agony of application Sally perspired through the two days of Jocelyn's absence. Lessons didn't leave off when the paper and ink were cleared away because of the rissoles of lunch and the poached eggs of supper, but went on just as bad while she was eating. 'Salvatia dear, don't 'old your fork like that—' 'Salvatia dear, don't go makin' all that there noise when you drinks—' so did Mrs. Luke's admonishments present themselves to Sally's ill-attuned ear. And after that the lessons were

continued in the garden, where she was walked up and down, up and down, till her head, as she said to herself, fair reeled. Never before had Sally been walked up and down the same spot. She used to walk straight sometimes to places, and then come home again and done with it, but never up and down and keeping on turning round. No escape. The lady had her by the arm. Exercise, she called it. And talk! Not only talk herself, but keep on dragging her into it too. Education, the lady called it. Lessons, that's to say. What ones these Lukes were for lessons, thought Sally, remembering her experience at St. Mawes. And there, through the kitchen window every time she passed it, she could see Ammond, washing up as free as air.

The garden was small; the turnings accordingly frequent; and Sally's head, strained by the excessive attention Mrs. Luke insisted on, did indeed reel. Her head ... How was it, Mrs. Luke was asking herself by the evening of that first day, ostensibly pleasantly chatting, but carefully observing Sally, who, pale and beautiful, with faint shadows under her eyes, sat looking at her lap so as not to see the lady looking at her,—how was it that so noble a little head, with a brow so happily formed, one would have supposed, for the harbouring of intelligence, should apparently be without any?

Apparently. Mrs. Luke was careful not to come to any hasty conclusion, but by this time she had been drilling Sally ceaselessly for a whole day, and she had been so clear and patient, and so very, very simple, that she began to think her vocation was probably that of a teacher; yet no sign of real comprehension had up to then appeared. Goodwill there was; much goodwill. But no real *grasp*. And, of course, most lamentably little ear. Those h's—it would have been disheartening, if Mrs. Luke hadn't refused to be disheartened, the way Salvatia didn't even seem to know if they were in a word or not. She simply didn't hear them.

'Do you like music, Salvatia?' said Mrs. Luke, getting up and preparing to test her ear on the clavichord at the other end of the room, an instrument which gave her great pleasure because it wasn't so gross as a piano.

'Yes,' said Sally, who had been strictly drilled that day in naked monosyllables.

'Do you sing, dear child?'

''Ymns,' said Sally.

'Ah, dear, *dearest* child!' cried Mrs. Luke, drawing her shoulders up to her ears, for after all the pains and labours of the day she was tired, and she couldn't help being, perhaps, a little less patient. 'How do you spell that poor small word? It is such a tiny, short word, and can't afford to lose any of its letters—'

And in the kitchen, Sally knew, with her hearth swept and neat, and everything put nicely away for the day, sat Ammond, doing her sewing as free as air.

❀

Jocelyn came home on the evening of the third day. He hadn't found a house, and seemed dispirited about that, and looked a great deal at Salvatia, Mrs. Luke thought,—almost as if he had never seen her before; indeed he looked at her so much that he hardly had eyes or attention for anything else.

Mrs. Luke didn't like it.

Certainly the girl was quite extraordinarily beautiful that evening, and seemed even more alight than usual with the strange, surprising flame-effect she somehow made, but one would have supposed that these outwardnesses, once one knew that they were not the symbols of any corresponding inwardnesses, could hardly be sufficient for a man like Jocelyn.

A little pang of something that hurt—it couldn't of course be jealousy, for the very word in such a connection was ludicrous—shot through Mrs. Luke's heart when she more than once caught a look in her boy's eyes as they rested on his wife that she had never seen in any man's eyes when they rested on her herself, but which she nevertheless instantly recognised. The love-look. The look of burning, impatient passion. She had been loved, but never like that, never with that intent adoration.

Sally sat quietly there, neither speaking nor moving, but over her face rippled gladness. Nice, she thought, to get Usband back. It hadn't been

half awful without him. Finished now, though; wouldn't happen again. 'Let's forget it,' she said to herself.

And that night, after every one was in bed, Mrs. Luke heard cautious steps creaking up the stairs, and the door of the room Sally slept in across the little landing was softly opened, and some one went in and softly shut it again; and Mrs. Luke didn't like it at all, and ended by crying herself to sleep.

Next day, however, Jocelyn was restored to the self she knew, and was reasonable and detached. They talked over the house in Cambridge question, and he quite agreed with his mother that when he went up, which he was due to do in nine days time, while he continued in his spare moments there to search for one she would keep Sally with her at Almond Tree Cottage.

'And even if you find one, dearest,' said Mrs. Luke, 'remember we can't afford to take it till I have got rid of this one.'

'Quite, Mother,' said Jocelyn—so reasonable, so completely detached.

'And meanwhile, the best thing will be for Salvatia to stay quietly here with me.'

'Far and away the best, Mother,' said Jocelyn, whose thoughts had gone off with renewed eagerness to his work, to the two spacious months of undisturbed labour ahead of him in those quiet rooms of his in Austen's Court.

What was Sally's surprise to find that Jocelyn's return made no difference to the lessons. They went on just the same; indeed, they seemed every day to get worse, and he, except at meals and when he crept into her room at night, stayed at the top of the house shut up by himself, or went out for his daily walk after lunch and didn't take her with him.

At night she tried to ask him about these things, because this was the time he was most likely to answer, but he only whispered, 'Hush—Mother will hear.'

'Not if you whispers,' whispered Sally.

'She'd hear the whispers,' whispered Jocelyn.

Why Mother shouldn't hear whispers Sally was unable to make out.

And there at night was Usband, all for being friendly and loving, and

in the day didn't seem to know she was alive. Warmed up a bit, he did, towards evening, but else sat hardly opening his mouth, his eyes looking at something that wasn't there. Was this, Sally might well in her turn have asked if she had been able to formulate such a question, companionship? But even if she had formulated it she wouldn't have asked it, because she was so meek.

Strange, however, how the meek go on being meek till the very moment when they do something from which bold persons would shrink. This is what Sally did, after having progressed that week steadily towards despair.

Gradually but steadily, by piecing together bit by bit the things Mrs. Luke and Jocelyn said to each other at meals and in the evening, she became aware of what was in store for her. First, a party; an enormous party, at which everybody who wasn't a gentleman was going to be a lady; and she was to be at it too, and it was for this that her mind and manners were being fattened up so ceaselessly by Mrs. Luke. Then, two days after the party, Jocelyn, her husband who had promised in church to cherish her, was going away to Cambridge, and going to stay there by himself till the summer, just as if he weren't married. How could he cherish her from Cambridge? It was evident even to Sally that it couldn't be done. Finally, she was to be left at Almond Tree Cottage alone with Mrs. Luke, being educated, being made fit, being fattened inside just as you fatten animals outside. What for? She hadn't married Mrs. Luke. Wasn't she able, just as she was, to be a good wife to Usband, and a good mother later on to the little babies? What more could a girl do than be ready to work her fingers to the bone for him? And she could cook so nicely, give her a chance; and she could mend as well as any one; and as for keeping the house clean, hadn't her mother taught her never to dream of sitting down and taking up her sewing while there was so much as a single speck of dirt about?

With growing horror, and steadily increasing despair, Sally listened to the talk at meals. She had learned to say nothing now but yes, no, thank you, and please, and either kept her eyes on her plate or, through her eyelashes, watched with pangs of envy the happy Hammond's free entrances and departures. She herself never moved without Mrs. Luke's arm through hers or round her shoulders,—'We are quite inseparable,'

Mrs. Luke would say, smiling at Jocelyn, when the meals were over and the time had arrived for going somewhere else, as she either encircled Sally's shrinking shoulder or put her hand through her limp arm. 'Aren't we, Salvatia?'

And Sally, starting—she had got into a curious habit, which Mrs. Luke much deplored, of starting when she was spoken to, however gently— hurriedly said, 'Yes.'

Queer, thought Mrs. Luke, who noticed everything but was without the power of correct deduction, seeing that the child so obviously was anxious to please and she herself so certainly was anxious to help her, queer how difficult it was to do anything with her in the way of confidence and love. And to Jocelyn in the evenings, after Sally had been told she was tired and must wish to go to bed, which she quickly learnt meant that she was to get up at once and say goodnight and go to it, Mrs. Luke would talk about her lovingly and humorously, and laughingly describe what she called the intensive methods of cultivation she was applying to the marvellous child.

'You'll see how beautifully she'll behave at our little party,' she said. 'And as for what she'll be like after a few months—well, dearest, all I can say is that I promise to hand her over to you fit to be your real companion, and not only—' Mrs. Luke shivered slightly at the thought of the creaking stairs—'just a wife.'

Two evenings before the day of the party, Mrs. Luke, who had made, she knew, no headway at all in spite of the most untiring efforts in winning the confidence and love she expected, remarked hesitatingly, when she and Jocelyn were alone together after Sally's departure for bed, that the child appeared to have rather curious and disconcerting resistances.

'Do you mean she doesn't obey you?' asked Jocelyn, much surprised.

'Oh, with almost too much eagerness. No. I mean something mental. Or rather,' amended Mrs. Luke, who by this time was definitely disappointed in Sally's mind but was still prepared to concede her a soul, 'spiritual. Spiritual resistances. Disconcerting *spiritual* resistances. She seems to shut herself up. And I ask myself, what in? A child like that, with a—well, really rather blank mind at present. What is she withdrawing into? Where does she *go*, Jocelyn?'

And that night when, having given his mother time to go to sleep and the house was quiet, Jocelyn stole upstairs to Sally, full of nothing but love for her, she made a scene. He called it a scene; she called it mentioning. She had screwed herself up to mentioning to him that it was wrong to leave her, as she now beyond any possibility of doubt knew that he was going to leave her, and go away by himself to Cambridge.

A scene with Sally. Jocelyn was as much amazed, and correspondingly outraged, as if his fountain-pen had turned on him and declared that what he was making it write was all wrong. For Sally took her stand on the New Testament, on the Gospel of St. Mark, Chapter X, Verses 7 and 8, and not only declared there was no mistaking the words, and that it wasn't his wife a man had to leave but his father and mother, and that he had to leave them so as to cleave to his wife, and that they two were to be one flesh, but asked him how he could either cleave or be one flesh if he were in Cambridge and she in South Winch?

It was past midnight and pitch dark, so he couldn't see her face, and accordingly wasn't bewitched. Also, he had found her waiting up for him, not gone to bed at all, but dressed and sitting in a chair, so that, again, he wasn't bewitched. When one neither saw nor touched Sally it was quite easy not to be bewitched.

'For heaven's sake don't *talk*,' he said in a low voice, when he had got over his first astonishment. 'Don't you know Mother will hear?'

Sally couldn't help that. She had got to say it. God was on her side. His laws were going to be broken, and nothing made Sally so brave as having to take up the cudgels in defence of God's laws. Besides, if the dark prevented Jocelyn from seeing her beauty it saved her from seeing the icy displeased look on his face that made her falter off into silence. And she was in despair. Apart from the right or the wrong of it, she felt she couldn't possibly be left alone with Mrs. Luke. Therefore, having mentioned God's laws to him, she proceeded to entreat him to take her with him, it didn't matter into what hole, or let her go to her father's, and he come and see her whenever he had time.

'I told you—I told you the other day,' said Sally, trying to subdue her voice to a whisper, but it kept on breaking through, 'when you was only

goin' to be away for two days that I didn't 'alf like it. 'Ow do you suppose I'm goin' to like weeks and weeks? And it ain't *right*, Mr. Luke—it ain't *right*. You only got to read St. Mark—'

Jocelyn was amazed. Sally talking like this? Sally suddenly making difficulties, and having an opinion, and judging? Dragging in the Bible, too, just like somebody's cook.

'You don't understand,' he said in a low voice because of his mother, but a voice quite as full of anger as if he had been shouting. 'How can you? What do you know about anything?'

'I know what ain't bein' one flesh,' persisted Sally, greatly helped in the matter of courage by the dark.

He gathered his dressing-gown round him; it sounded exactly as if a servant were daring to talk familiarly to him.

'This isn't the time,' he whispered, infinitely disgusted, 'to argue.'

'P'raps you'll tell me when the time is, then,' said Sally, who knew she could never be alone with him in the day because of Mrs. Luke; and really in the dark, unable to see her, Jocelyn had the impression of some woman of the lower classes confronting him with arms akimbo.

'Certainly not at one in the morning,' he said freezingly. 'I shall go downstairs again. I didn't come up here to listen to outrageous rot.'

'Mr. *Luke*! Rot? When it's God's Word I'm talkin' about? Ain't you my 'usband? Didn't you vow—'

There was a tap at the door.

'You see?' said Jocelyn, starting and extraordinarily put out that Mrs. Luke should know he was in there. 'You *have* disturbed my mother.'

'What is it, Jocelyn?' his mother's voice asked anxiously from outside.

He opened the door. She too was in a dressing-gown, and her long hair hung down in thick plaits.

'What is it, Jocelyn?' she asked again.

'Only that Sally has gone out of her senses,' he said shortly; and he stalked away downstairs, ashamed to have been caught by his mother upstairs, angry with himself for being ashamed, and seriously enraged with Sally.

'Salvatia, Jocelyn dearest—*do* remember,' called Mrs. Luke plaintively after him.

'Oh, Christ!' muttered Jocelyn, banging the sitting-room door behind him and throwing himself on the hard narrow sofa from which, only a quarter of an hour before, he had got up, all warm with love, to go to his wife.

And in the room overhead Mrs. Luke put her arms round Sally, and did her best, while tactfully asking no questions, to soothe and calm the child. But how can one soothe and calm anything that behaves exactly as if it were a very rigid, unresponsive, and entirely dumb stone?

❊

There were explanations next day. Mrs. Luke put the whole situation patiently and clearly before Sally. It wasn't fair, she said to Jocelyn, after a private talk with him during which he had told her the sorts of things Sally had said in the night, it wasn't fair to keep the child quite in the dark as to their arrangements. Even if she weren't altogether able to understand, she should, Mrs. Luke said, be given the opportunity of doing so.

So when breakfast was cleared away, and Jocelyn had withdrawn to his attic, Mrs. Luke shut herself up as usual with Sally in the dining-room, and spent the morning patiently explaining.

Sally said nothing. This made it difficult for Mrs. Luke to know whether she had understood. And yet how simple it was. Jocelyn's work, the paramount importance of his work, on which both his and Salvatia's future and perhaps—who knew?—the world's, depended; their present, but no doubt temporary, poverty, which made it out of the question for them to follow him to Cambridge till Almond Tree Cottage had been let; the necessity of teaching Salvatia, during long, quiet, uninterrupted days, all the little odds and ends, so small and yet so indispensable, that go to make up the wife of a gentleman; and the impossibility of asking Jocelyn to leave his rooms in College and live in anything as uncomfortable and makeshift as the sorts of lodgings within their means were bound to be. Of course had Salvatia been alone in the world, and with nowhere at all to

go to, some such arrangement would have had to be made. But she wasn't alone. She had her husband's mother, and her husband's mother's home, and affection, and sympathy, and the warmest welcome.

'Just a little patience, Salvatia dear,' said Mrs. Luke, 'and our little problems will all quite naturally solve themselves. We shall have got a tenant for this house, Jocelyn will have found a nice home for us in Cambridge, you will meanwhile have learnt everything necessary to make you able to be its perfect little mistress, and we'll all live happily ever after.'

Now wasn't this kind? Surely it was very kind, thought Mrs. Luke. And wasn't it loving? Surely it was altogether loving. Yet Salvatia said never a word.

Indeed, Sally was necessarily dumb. She had too few words to enter into controversy with Mrs. Luke, and knew that if she tried to she would only collapse into tears. But after lunch, through which she sat saying nothing, when Mrs. Luke sent her out into the garden alone because she herself had to go down that afternoon to the shops to see about the cakes for her party next day, Sally went to the one corner which wasn't overlooked by the windows of the house, owing to an intervening tool-shed, and, leaning against the iron rails that separated Mrs. Luke's property from Mr. Thorpe's, wept bitterly.

She clutched the top rail with both hands, and laying her head on them wept most bitterly; for it was plain now to her that her dream of two rooms and no lady was never to come true, and that meanwhile—what was the good of blinking facts?—her husband had deserted her. And she had no money; only five shillings her father had given her as a wedding present,—that was all. Handsome as a present, but not enough, she was sure, to get her home to him. If only she could go home to him, and escape any more of Mrs. Luke, and escape the terrible, the make-you-come-over-all-cold-to-think-of party! Then, when Usband arrived at his college, she could turn up there and give him a surprise, and find a room for herself somewhere close, and live in it as quiet as a mouse, not bothering him at all or interrupting, but near enough to feel still married.

Sally's body was shaken by sobs; even the rail on which she leant her head, her head with its bright, tumbled hair, whose ends, getting into her

eyes, were wet and darkened by her grief, was shaken. She could bear no more. She couldn't bear any more of anything in the house behind the tool-shed. Yet what was she to do? Five shillings would get her nowhere—

'Crying, eh?' said a voice on the other side of the fence.

And looking up with a great start, Sally beheld Father-in-law.

XI

❁

Mr. Thorpe, being a man accustomed all his life to success in everything he undertook—except in the case of Annie, but even she had been a success at first—had spent a week of bitterness.

He was aggrieved, deeply aggrieved; and he hated the hole and corner way Mrs. Luke had hidden from him, refusing to see him, refusing any sort of explanation, turning him down with a single letter, and not answering when he wrote back.

He, who was very well aware that he was conferring everything, that he was giving her a chance in a million, when he called was shown the door; and all he had done for her, the affection he had bestowed, the gifts he had lavished, were as though they had not been. In the sight of South Winch and of his own household he was humiliated. But it went deeper than that: he knew himself for kind, and no one wanted his kindness; he knew himself for generous, and no one wanted his generosity either. Naturally he was full of resentment; so full, that he hadn't even gone to his office regularly that week, but had hung about his house and grounds instead, fault-finding.

Where he hung about most was that part of his plantations which abutted on the meadow dividing Abergeldie from Mrs. Luke; and wandering among his conifers he could see, without himself being seen, anything that went on in her miserable plot of ground. If he had been told that such behaviour was undignified he would have replied that dignity be damned; for not only was he smarting under Mrs. Luke's ingratitude, not only was he annoyed beyond measure at not going to get the wife he no longer really wanted—who would wish to be tied up to a jealous, middle-aged woman, when there were so many pretty, cheerful girls

about?—but he longed, with a simple longing he hadn't felt since he first went sweethearting as a boy, to see Sally again.

He did see her; always, however, arm in arm with Hell's Fury, as he now called her who had so recently been his Marge. Then, on this Wednesday afternoon, more than a week after Mrs. Luke had shown herself in her true colours—a jolly good thing he had found her out before and not after marriage, thought Mr. Thorpe, who yet was enraged that he had,—as he wandered among his conifers after luncheon, nursing his grievances and glancing every now and then at the little house across the meadow, so insignificant and cheap and nevertheless able to play such a part in his life, he saw young beauty at last come out alone, and go round to the back of the tool-shed, and behave as has been indicated.

For a few minutes Mr. Thorpe stayed where he was, in case the H.F.— so, for convenience sake, did he abbreviate the rude nickname he had given Mrs. Luke—should come out too; but when some time had passed and nobody appeared, he concluded that the two highbrows had gone for a walk, and Beauty for once was alone. Crying, too. What had they been doing to the girl, that precious pair of hoity toity treat-you-as-dirters, Mr. Thorpe asked himself. Then, climbing cautiously over the fence, and crossing the field close to the belt of firs, he arrived unseen and unheard to where Sally, her head bowed over her hands, was standing crying.

How kind he was. What a comfort he was. And how clear in his instructions as to what she was to do. It was quite easy to say things to Father-in-law; he seemed to understand at once.

Nobody had told Sally he wasn't her father-in-law. The Lukes' habit of silence towards her about their affairs had left her supposing he was what he said he was, and she herself had heard him not being contradicted by Mrs. Luke when she came into the drawing-room that day and he told her he was making friends with his new daughter.

Sally was aware that Jocelyn's own father was dead, and she had at first supposed Mr. Thorpe was Mrs. Luke's second husband. In the confusion of mind in which she had been since arriving at Almond Tree Cottage, she had had no thoughts left over for wondering why, if he were, he lived somewhere else. Dimly the last few days, not having seen

him again, she had begun to think, though with no real interest, that perhaps Mrs. Luke hadn't quite married him yet, but only very nearly. Anyhow it didn't matter. He said he was her father-in-law, and that was good enough for her. Such a kind old gentleman. Much older than her own father. Might easily have been her grandfather, with all that bald head and grey moustache.

And Mr. Thorpe's pleasure, nay, delight, at being able to help Beauty and at the same time give those two high-brows something to talk about, was very great. This was indeed killing two birds with one stone—and what birds! He listened attentively to all she brokenly and imperfectly said; he entirely applauded her idea of going back to her father for a bit, and assured her there was no place like home; he told her he would send her there in one of his cars, quite safe from door to door; he advised her to stay with her father till her husband did his duty, which was to make a home for her and live with her in it; he asked why she should allow herself to be deserted, to be left alone with Mrs. Luke, who would do nothing but try and cram her head with rubbish—

'Don't you like 'er?' asked Sally, surprised.

'No,' said Mr. Thorpe stoutly.

'But you're goin' to marry 'er,' said Sally, more surprised.

'Catch *me*,' said Mr. Thorpe.

'But then you ain't my father-in-law,' said Sally, more surprised than ever.

'Yes I am,' said Mr. Thorpe hastily. 'Once a father-in-law always a father-in-law,' he assured her,—and hurried her off this subject by asking her why she should be treated by her husband as if she weren't married at all, and by what right young Luke thought he could behave differently from any husband any one had ever heard of. Scandalous, said Mr. Thorpe, to leave her. Shocking. Incomprehensible. And that so-called husband of hers with his marriage vows not yet had time to go cold on his lips!

In fact, Mr. Thorpe said out loud and beautifully everything Sally had thought and not been able to get into words.

The result was that, encouraged and supported, indeed urged and driven, she took one of those desperate steps characteristic of the very

meek, and, acting according to Mr. Thorpe's clear and precise instructions, stole out of the house at five next morning—the very day of the party, from which he, who knew all about it from his housekeeper, and had tried to console himself by thinking of the piles of strawberries and peaches and quarts of cream he wasn't going to send to it, insisted that she should at all costs escape—carrying only a little bag, with her five shillings in it and her comb and toothbrush; and, creeping down the stairs holding her breath, got out without a sound through the kitchen window, anxiously listening for a moment as she passed the shut sitting-room door on the other side of which Jocelyn lay asleep,—Jocelyn, who that night, being still much annoyed with her, had very fortunately not been upstairs.

At the corner of the road was Mr. Thorpe's car. He himself remained discreetly in bed. No use overdoing things. Besides, he could wait. He knew where to find Beauty when the time came, which was more than those damned Lukes did; and he had given his chauffeur the necessary orders the night before, and could rely on their being carried out to the letter; so that Sally found, when she got into the car, which was more splendid outside and more soft inside than she could have believed possible, not only a lovely rug of the silkiest fur, which the chauffeur, a most attentive young gentleman, wrapped round her legs as carefully as if they were the Queen's, but a basket full of everything for breakfast, even hot coffee, and an enormous box of chocolates which were for her to keep, the chauffeur said, with Mr. Thorpe's compliments. And such was the effect on her of all this moral and physical support that she no longer, as she was smoothly and deliciously borne along through sleeping South Winch, across awakening London, past sunshiny fields and woods just flushing green, on and on, into Essex, into Cambridgeshire, smooth and swift, with a motion utterly different from the one Jocelyn's car made and completely confidence-inspiring, she no longer felt as if she were doing anything that was frightening, and also, perhaps, wrong. Could anybody be doing anything very wrong who had such a splendid car to sit in, and such a respectful and attentive young gentleman driving it?

❀

Mr. Pinner disillusioned her.

For many years he hadn't tasted such quiet happiness, such contentment and well-being, as during the four weeks he had been without Sally. Her marriage to a gentleman, to one of the scholars from Cambridge, was known to every one in the village, and he was proud of it, very proud. Sally, besides having been handed over safe and sound to some one else's care, had risen in life and was now a lady. He had every reason to be proud of her, and no further bother. Now for the first time he could live, after forty years of the other thing, free from females. Was it sinful, he asked himself occasionally, and at variance with God's Word, to be so very happy all alone? He didn't think it could be. He had served his time. Forty years in the wilderness he had had—just like the Israelites, who had come out of it too, just as he had, and enjoyed themselves too at last, as he was enjoying himself, quietly and nicely. No husband or father could have been fonder of his wife and daughter than he had been of his, or done his duty by them more steadily. Surely now, both of them being safely settled, it couldn't be wrong to like having a rest? He loved Sally, but she had been a back-breaking responsibility. For four weeks now he had enjoyed himself, and with such relish that when he got up in the morning and thought of the quiet, free hours ahead of him, he had often quavered into song. Then came the day when, peacefully dusting the toffee in his window, and thinking how prettily the birds were singing that fine spring morning, and of the little bit of mutton he was going to do in capers for his dinner, he saw an enormous closed car coming down the village street, and with astonishment beheld it stop in front of his shop, and Sally get out.

Mr. Pinner knew enough of what cars cost to be sure this one wasn't anyhow Mr. Luke's. Things like that cost as much as two of Mr. Luke's five hundreds a year; so that the car, of which Sally had been so proud, far from impressing him only frightened him. And when, after the chauffeur had handed her a bag, he saw him turn the car round and disappear, going away again without her while she came running up the steps, he was more frightened than ever.

What had happened? Not a month married, and back again by herself with a bag.

'I come 'ome,' said Sally in the doorway, still bright with the sheer enjoyment of the ride, yet, faced by her father's amazement, conscious of a slight lowering of her temperature. 'My! You ain't 'alf small, Father,' she added, surprised, after looking at the tall Jocelyn and the broad Mr. Thorpe, by how little there was of Mr. Pinner. 'Almost count you on the fingers of one 'and,' she said.

'Want more fingers than I got to count *you*,' retorted Mr. Pinner, retreating behind the counter and feeling that these words somehow constituted a smart preliminary snub.

He didn't offer to kiss her. He stood entrenched behind his counter and stared up at her, struck, after having got out of the habit of her beauty, into a new astonishment at it. But it gave him no pleasure. It merely frightened him. For it blew up peace.

'Where's your 'usband?' he inquired, afraid and stern.

'Oh—'*im*,' said Sally, trying to look unconcerned, but flushing. "E's with 'is mother, 'e is. Ain't you pleased to see me, Father?' she asked, in an attempt to lead the conversation off husbands at least for a bit; and tighter to her side she hugged the box of chocolates, because the feel of it helped her to remember Father-in-law's approval and encouragement. And he was a gentleman, wasn't he? And a lot older even than Father, so must know what was what.

'Oh, indeed. With 'is mother, is 'e,' said Mr. Pinner, ignoring her question. "Oos car was that?' he asked.

'Father-in-law's,' said Sally, hugging her chocolates.

'Oh, indeed. And 'oo may father-in-law be?'

'The gentleman as is—as was goin' to marry Mr. Luke's mother.'

'Oh, indeed. And you ride about in 'is car meanwhile. *I* see.'

'Lent it to me so I can come 'ome.'

'What do 'e want to send you 'ere for, then?' asked Mr. Pinner, leaning on his knuckles, his blue eyes very bright. 'Ain't your 'ome where your 'usband's is? Ain't that a married woman's 'ome?'

'I only come on a visit,' faltered Sally, whose spirits were by now in her shoes. Her father had often scolded her, but she had never been afraid of him. Now there was something in his eye that made her feel less sure that

she had taken, as Mr. Thorpe had told her, the one possible and completely natural step. 'I only come for a few days, while Mr. Luke—'

'Mr. Luke know you're 'ere?' interrupted her father.

''E don't know yet,' said Sally. 'But I—'

'That's enough,' said Mr. Pinner, holding up a hand. 'That's quite enough. No need for no more words. You go back right away to your 'usband, my girl. Come to the wrong box, you 'ave, for 'arbourin' runaway wives.'

'But, Father—' she stammered, not yet quite able to believe that in coming back to him she had only got out of the frying pan into the fire, 'you got to listen to *why* I come—'

He held up his hand again, stopping her. He had no need to listen. He could see for himself that she was a runaway wife, which was against both man's and God's laws.

Sally, however, persisted. She put her bag down on the counter, behind which he firmly remained, and facing him across it tried to give him an idea of what had been happening to her, and what had been going to happen to her much worse if she had stayed.

He refused to be given an idea of it. He turned a deaf ear to all explanations. And he was merely scandalised when she said, crying by this time, that she couldn't, couldn't, be left alone with Mr. Luke's mother, for where a husband thinks fit to leave his wife, said Mr. Pinner, always supposing it is respectable, there that wife must remain till he fetches her. This he laid down to Sally as a law from which a married woman departs at her peril, and he laid it down with all the more emphasis, perhaps, because of knowing how unlikely it was that he himself would ever have had the courage to enforce it in the case of Mrs. Pinner, and that, if he had, how certain it was she wouldn't have stayed five minutes in any place he tried to leave her in.

Sally was in despair. What was she to do? The little shop looked like paradise to her, a haven of peaceful bliss after the life she had led since last she saw it. She cried and cried. She couldn't believe that her father, who had always been so kind really, wouldn't let her stay with him for the two days till Jocelyn got back to Cambridge.

But not even for one night would Mr. Pinner, who was secretly terrified of Jocelyn, and sure he would be hot on his wife's tracks and make a scene and blame him if he gave her so much as an inch of encouragement, harbour her. Back she should go by the very next train to her husband and her duty; and the breaking of marriage vows, and the disregard of the injunctions in the New Testament which had so much shocked her in Jocelyn, were now thrown at her by Mr. Pinner, who accused her of precisely these. Useless for Sally, clinging to the hope of somehow being able to justify herself and be allowed to stay, to say through her tears that the Gospel didn't mention what a woman had to do but only what a man had to, because to that Mr. Pinner replied that no Gospel could be expected to mention everything, and that in any case, when it came to sinning, the sexes couldn't be kept apart.

❀

He walked her off to the little station three miles away. The bag the respectful chauffeur had wanted to carry for her up those few steps she now carried three miles herself.

'Pity you was in such a 'urry to let that there car go,' Mr. Pinner remarked sarcastically, as they trudged almost in silence along the lanes.

Sally gulped; delicately, because even her gulps were little gulps,— gentle, delicate little things. She didn't know what was to become of her, she really didn't. Go back to that dreadful house, and arrive in the middle of the party? Face real wrath, real deserved wrath, from those who even when they were being kind had terrified her? So thoroughly had Mr. Pinner's horror at what she had done cleared her mind of Mr. Thorpe's points of view that she felt she hadn't a leg to stand on, and would do anything, almost, sooner than, covered with shame, go back to the anger of the Lukes. But what? What could she do except go back? Yet if she had been miserable there while she was still good, how was she going to bear it now that she had become wicked? She shuddered to think of what Mrs. Luke would be like really angry—and Mr. Luke, who had the right not to leave her alone even at night. ...

Sadly did Sally gulp from time to time, and every now and then emit a faint sob, as she walked in silence that morning beside the adamant Mr. Pinner to the branch-line station. She hadn't been in the Woodles district very long, but it seemed to her as she passed along its quiet lanes that she loved every stick and stone of it. It was what she understood. It was peace. It was home. Her father went with her as far as Cambridge, so as to put her safely into the express to Liverpool Street, and his instructions were, after buying her a first class ticket—he felt that Mr. Luke would wish her to travel first class, and it gave him a gloomy pride to buy it—that she was to take a taxi from Liverpool Street, and go in it all the way to South Winch.

He then, with the ticket, gave her a pound note.

'It can't be more than ten miles out,' said Mr. Pinner, who had never in his life before squandered money, let alone a pound, on a taxi, but who tried to console himself with the thought that it would have been well spent if only it got Sally safe back to where she belonged; and though he was depressed he was also proud, for it, too, gave him a kind of sombre satisfaction.

'Been an expensive day for me, this,' he said, gloomy, but proud.

Sally gulped.

He kept her in the waiting-room at the station till the last moment, for she was attracting the usual too well-remembered attention, and beauty in tears was even more conspicuous than beauty placid, and then he hurried her along to the front of the train, and put her in a carriage in which there was only one lady—a real lady, of course, thought Mr. Pinner, anxiously taking stock of her, or she wouldn't be travelling first class.

'Beg pardon, Madam,' he said in his best behind-the-counter manner, taking his hat off. 'You goin' to London by any chance?'

Seeing that the train didn't stop till it got there, the lady couldn't say anything but yes; and then Mr. Pinner asked her if she would mind keeping an eye on his daughter, who, though a married lady too—the lady made a little bow of acknowledgement of this tribute to her evidently settled-down appearance, though she was, in fact, a spinster—yet didn't know her way about very well.

Then when the train began to move, and Sally's face, as she leant out of the window to say goodbye, was a study in despair, Mr. Pinner relented enough to pat her tear-stained cheek, and running a few steps beside the carriage bade her not take on any more.

'What's done's done,' he called out after the train, by way of cheering her.

And Sally, dropping back into her corner, pulled out her handkerchief and wept.

❁

Yes. What was done was done true enough, she thought, mopping the tears as they rolled down her face, including her having married Mr. Luke and his mother; for she now regarded him and his mother as all of a piece.

The lady at the other end of the carriage, who, however hard she tried, couldn't take her eyes off her—and she did try very hard, for she hated staring at grief—ventured after a while to repeat Mr. Pinner's advice, and suggested, though in more Luke-like language, that Sally shouldn't take on. Whereupon Sally, the voice being sympathetic and the face kind, took on more than ever.

'Oh, *please* don't,' said the lady, much concerned, moving up to the seat opposite her. Such liquefaction she had never seen, nor such loveliness in spite of it. When she herself cried, which was very rarely—what was the good?—she became a swollen thing of lumps. 'You mustn't, really,' she begged. 'Your eyes—you simply *mustn't* do anything to hurt them. What is it? Can I help at all? I'd love to if I could—'

By the time they were rushing through Bishops Stortford Sally had told her everything. Incoherent and sobbing at first, there was something about this lady that comforted her into calmness. She wasn't at all like Mr. Thorpe, yet she took his sort of view, not Mr. Pinner's, and was even more sympathetic, and even more understanding. It really seemed, from the questions she asked, as if she must know the Lukes personally. She said she didn't, when Sally inquired if this were so, and laughed. She was very cheerful, and laughed several times, though she was so kind and sorry about everything.

– 169 –

'You can't go back there today, anyhow,' she said at last. 'Not into the middle of that party—' she laughed and shuddered, for Sally had explained with a face of horror that nobody at all was going to be at the party who wasn't either a lady or a gentleman except herself. 'You shall come and stay with me for a few days till your Mr. Luke goes to Cambridge, and then we'll see what happens. But I'm not going to let you go back into the clutches of that Mrs. Luke.'

And she leant forward and took her hand, and smiled so kindly and cheerfully, and said, 'You'll come for a day or two to our house, won't you? My father isn't there just now, and I've got it all to myself. Come till we have made up our minds about what to do next.'

This really seemed too good to be true. Sally turned scarlet. Was she saved? Saved, at the very last minute, from horror and disgrace?

'Just for a day or two,' said her new friend, who couldn't take her eyes off Sally's face, 'till your husband can find somewhere for you to live. We'll help him to look. I'll come with you, and help to find something. No, it doesn't matter a bit about your not having any luggage—I can lend you everything. And we'll write to him if you like, and tell him you can't and won't stay with his mother. Don't you think this is quite the best plan? Don't you, Sally?'

And she smiled, and asked if she might call her Sally.

'But,' hesitated Sally, for she didn't want to get anybody into difficulties, 'Father says I'm a runaway wife, and 'e wouldn't 'arbour me 'imself because of that.'

'Oh, but somebody must. And I'm the very one for it, because I'm so respectable, and not a wife. Don't you worry, you lovely thing. We really must bring your Mr. Luke to his senses. By the way, hasn't he got a Christian name?'

'You never *eard* such a name,' said Sally earnestly, who felt, to her own great surprise, almost as comfortable and easy with this strange lady as she had with Mr. Soper. 'Outlandish, I call it.'

Her new friend laughed again when she told her it was Jocelyn. 'Aren't you delicious,' she said, her bright eyes screwed up with laughter.

Sally liked being called delicious. It gave her assurance. Jocelyn had

called her lots of things like that in his red-eared moments, but they hadn't done her much good, because they never seemed to go on into next day. This lady was quite in her ordinary senses, her ears were proper pale ears, and what she said sounded as though it would last. And how badly Sally needed reassurance after the things Mr. Pinner had said to her that morning!

'Now you come along with me,' said her friend, jumping up as the train ran into Liverpool Street, her eyes, which were like little black marbles, dancing. 'And please call me Laura, will you? Because it's my name.'

She leaned out of the window, and waved. A chauffeur came running down the platform and opened the door; a car was waiting; and in another minute Sally was in it, once more sunk in softness, and once more with a lovely fur rug over her knees, while sitting next to her, talking and laughing, was her new friend, and sitting opposite her, neither talking nor laughing, a smart young lady in black, carrying a bag, who had appeared from nowhere and wasn't taken any notice of, and who looked steadily out of the window.

'What a *day* I'm 'avin', thought Sally.

But when presently the car stopped at a big house in a great square with trees in the middle, and a footman appeared at the door, and in the hall Sally could see another one just like him, and then another, and yet another, she was definitely frightened.

'Oh lor,' she whispered, shrinking back into the car.

'No—Laura,' said her new friend, laughing and taking her hand; and drawing it through her arm she led her up the steps of the house, and into the middle of the first real fleshpots of her life.

❁

Fleshpots.

She had thought her honeymoon was a honeymoon of fleshpots; she had been sure Almond Tree Cottage was the very home of them; but now she saw the real thing: fleshpots *in excelsis*.

Her father had said, 'Beware of fleshpots,' when he was expounding the

doings of the Children of Israel to her of a Sunday afternoon, 'they don't do no one no good.' And she had been brought up so carefully, so piously, so privately, that she had never come across that literature of luxury, those epics of fat things, that are lavishly provided for the poor and skimped. The flunkeys and the frocks, the country castles and the town palaces, the food, the jewels and the dukes, had remained outside her imaginative experience. What she had read had been her Bible, and a few books of her mother's childhood in which people were sad, and good and ill, and died saying things that made her cry very much. There was nothing to set her dreaming in these. Life, she thought, was like that, except for the lucky ones such as herself, who had kind parents and a nice back parlour to sit and sew in when their work was done. There were the gentry, of course; they existed, she knew, but only knew vaguely. Entirely vague they had been in her mind till she became a Luke, and found herself engulfed by them; and what an awe-inspiring engulfing it had seemed to her, with Ammond handing round everything at meals, and tea on a table you didn't sit up at!

Now, as her new friend's arm propelled her past the blank-faced footmen, across the great marble-floored and columned hall, she realised that Almond Tree Cottage had been the merest wheelbarrow in size and fittings compared to this. This was grand. More—this was terrible. It was her idea of a cathedral or a museum, but not of a place human beings washed their hands in, and talked out loud.

'P'raps,' she murmured to the lady called Laura, holding back as she was about to be taken into a room which she could see at once she would never feel comfortable in, and where far away in the distance was another of those tables with tea on it that one didn't sit up at, 'p'raps, if you don't mind, I'd better be gettin' along after all—' for, being polite, she had forced herself to bow with a nervous smile to a gentleman in black, who was standing about and whose eye had met hers, and he hadn't taken any notice but looked as blank-faced as everybody else, and the rebuff had terribly embarrassed her.

'Come along,' was all Laura said to that, calling out over her shoulder to the same gentleman in black to see that a room was got ready for Mrs.

Luke; and he answered, as polite and mild as milk, 'Very good, m'lady—' so he was a servant, and Laura was one of those ladies Sally had heard her parents sometimes allude to with awe, who are always being told they're ladies every time any one speaks to them, and who were, so Mr. and Mrs. Pinner declared, the pick of the basket.

'P'raps,' murmured Sally again, faintly, for the thought of having got among the pick of the basket unnerved her, 'I'd best do what Father said, and take a taxi …'

'You shall if you really want to,' said Laura, 'but let's have tea first. And think of that party! It's raging at this minute. Oh, Sally—could you bear it?'

Sally sat down on the chair Laura pushed up for her. She sat down obediently, but only on the edge of it, her long slender legs tucked sideways, as one sits who isn't at ease. No, she couldn't bear to go back to that party; nor could she, waiting till it was over, go back after it and face Mrs. Luke. It was more than flesh and blood could manage.

Then, that being so, and seeing that her father wouldn't have her, the only thing to do was to stay where she was till Usband went to Cambridge on Saturday, and be thankful she had this kind lady to be with, and try and swallow all the servants and marble, and do her best to behave grateful. It was only for a couple of days, for directly Usband got to Cambridge she would go after him as a wife should. Fallen on her feet wonderfully she had, Sally anxiously assured herself; but nevertheless, as she sat on the edge of her chair, and great pictures looked down at her from vast walls, she felt excessively uneasy.

'Tell me some more about the Lukes,' said Laura gaily, arranging a little table in front of her on which her cup and plate had a nice lot of room, and nothing got spilt or dropped. 'I think they're such fun.'

'Fun?' echoed Sally, her lips parting.

She stared at Laura. Fun? The Lukes?

'I never 'eard of a 'usband bein' fun,' she said in a very low voice, her head drooping.

'Perhaps that isn't quite the word,' said Laura, 'though I believe it's a very good way of approaching them.' And then she paused, teapot in

hand, her eyes on Sally's face. 'I suppose,' she said, 'you know you're *the* most utterly beautiful thing?'

Whereupon Sally started, for this was the way Mrs. Luke had begun with her, and said quickly, even as she had said then, 'But I can't 'elp it.'

'Help it?' echoed Laura, astonished.

'People begins,' said Sally anxiously, 'with "Oh my, ain't you beautiful," and ends with bein' angry. It ain't as if I could *'elp* it,' she said, looking up at her new friend with eyes in which tears were gathering, for it would be more than she could bear on her empty stomach—she had had no food since her breakfast in Mr. Thorpe's car—if she too were going to be angry with her.

Really such an extraordinary piece of good fortune as this had never yet come Laura's way.

❁

Now was Sally shovelled up by chance from the bottom of the social ladder to the top, for Laura was the spinster daughter of a duke. He was so aged that, by sheer going on living, everything he had ever done, good and bad, had been forgotten, and at last he had become an object of universal respect. Ninety-three next birthday; a great age. And his eldest son, the prospective duke, was sixty-five,—a great age too for anything that is still prospective. He was a marquis, Sally learned with surprise presently, when she was having her tea and Laura, who perceived she needed soothing, was trying to distract her by telling her about her relations; for she failed to understand why he shouldn't be a duke. Pinners produced Pinners; why not dukes dukes?

But Laura said these things couldn't be explained, and hurried on.

The old duke had married three times, and Laura was the product of what the neat-phrased French would call the third bed. All the beds, first, second, and third, had long vanished, and of the third, which had been very fruitful, Laura, and her brother Charles, and her married sister Terry, were the only surviving traces. The second bed had been barren; the first had provided the heir, and three ancient ladies old enough to

be Laura's mothers, who were scattered over England in varying degrees of resignation, one being the widow of a bishop, another the widow of a Cabinet Minister, and the third not yet the widow of a club man and expert bridge-player, who never came home till next day.

'Why don't 'e?' asked Sally, manners seeming to demand that she should say something when, for an instant, her friend paused.

But Laura said these things couldn't be explained, and hurried on.

Much the liveliest of the beds had been the one she herself came out of, and her blood pressure—except during the last year of the War, when unceasing hard work, combined with a diet of practically continual boiled fish, reduced it to a comfortable normal—had always been higher than was convenient. This led her into excesses. She must be up and doing; she found it impossible to sit still. Vitality bubbled in her quick speech and danced in her black eyes. She was now thirty-five, round and stubby, fleet of foot and swift of reply, and her past was strewn with charities she had organised, dressmakers she had established, hat shops she had run, estate agencies she had started, hospital beds she had endowed, arts she had supported, geniuses she had discovered, and four lovers.

Four weren't many, she thought, considering the piles her sister Terry had got through. Laura's lovers had come and gone, as lovers do, and she hadn't minded much, because neither had they. There was something too electric about her for love. She seemed to crackle in their very arms. This disconcerted them; and each in his turn married some one else.

For a long time now she had been bored, and bored violently, and by the time she came across Sally she had seen everything, been everything, heard everything and done everything; and the prospect of seeing and being and hearing and doing over and over again, till her joints cracked and her hair fell out, was boring her into fits.

Her father's three wives had been the daughters of millionaires, whose pride it was to leave them all their money. Her father, rich before, had thus become incredibly richer. England was full of him. And the war had only made him richer, because he owned coal mines. Such riches, Laura considered, were disgusting, and she had plunged into Socialism, and come up dripping Labour. But whatever she did, whatever she was,

her chief job was to look after her father, and see that his last years were peaceful; and she had now only left him in Cambridgeshire, where they had been spending Easter, for a day or two, and rushed up to London because of being obliged to go to a charity ball of which she was a patroness, to the first night of a play whose author she was encouraging, to a bazaar in aid of the Black and Blue League, of which she was vice-president and whose aims were the assistance of wives, and, if possible, to look in at a concert being given by a young violinist she had helped to have trained: and she had been thinking, as she sat in the empty railway carriage between Crippenham and Cambridge—the expresses stopped at Crippenham when the Duke was in residence—that all this was a great bore.

What was the good of it, really? Oughtn't charity to be approached quite differently? Weren't bazaars essentially vicious? Did wives need assistance more than husbands? And there was her own stupid supper-party that night after the play, with the author coming to it, and the leading lady, and Streatley her elder brother, who thought he admired the leading lady, and Terry her sister, who thought the author admired her, and Charles her younger brother, who was sure he admired nobody, and one or two others, including a dramatic critic; and how too perfectly awful if the play was a failure, and there they all were, boxed up with the person who had written it.

'Silly life,' she had been thinking as the train ran into Cambridge. 'Round and round in a cage we go, and nothing is ever different except our whiskers, which keep on getting greyer.'

'But then,' she said leaning forward, her eyes twinkling and dancing as she looked at Sally, who by this time had finished her tea, 'the door opened and *you* got in. Too marvellous, Sally. Divinely beautiful. And not an h in your whole delicious composition.'

'Pardon?' said Sally, who hadn't quite got that.

❁

She hadn't understood more than a word here and there of all the words Laura had rattled off at her, and in her heart, while she steadily ate sandwiches, she had slowly come to the conclusion that the pick of the basket was a queer fish. An affectionate and friendly fish, but queer all right, thought Sally; and in spite of the good tea—the best she had ever had, outdoing the one at Truro, and infinitely better than any at Mrs. Luke's,—in spite of the calming and balancing effect of nourishment after not having had a bite to eat since five o'clock that morning, in spite of Laura's kindness and cheerfulness, Sally felt uneasy.

She oughtn't to be there. She oughtn't to have come with Laura. It was only for two days, but two days were enough to do wrong in. What would her father say, who thought she was at that moment in a taxi, paid for by his pound, if he could see her? What would Mrs. Luke say? What *was* Mrs. Luke saying, anyhow? As for Mr. Luke, what he would say didn't so much matter, because almost before he had finished saying it she would have joined him in Cambridge, and started acting as a wife should. Of course he on his side must act as a husband should, and not try and send her away from him to his mother,—that was only fair, wasn't it? Sally anxiously asked herself.

And her uneasiness became acute when Laura, having taken her up a whole lot of stairs, every one of which looked like pure marble, and into a room she could only guess was a bedroom because there was a bed in it, but which was otherwise unidentifiable to Sally as such, sat down at a table and began telephoning to people to send round somebody at once with dresses and shoes to be tried on a young lady, who had to wear them that very evening.

Sally listened in alarm. Impossible not to guess that she was the young lady; impossible not to gather that there was to be a party, and she was to be at it. Had she after all only escaped Mrs. Luke's party to find herself caught in another? Was Laura, who had so much sympathised with her earnest wish not to be present at the one, going to plunge her into the other?

Standing afraid and conscience-stricken in front of the blazing wood fire, while Laura telephoned—this all came of not obeying her

father—Sally wondered whether anything could save her. Laura had saved her from Mrs. Luke, but who was going to save her from Laura? Laura lived in the middle of marble. She had servants at her beck and call, and could make the gentleman in black do anything she chose. And the smart young lady, who had sat on the small seat of the car and looked out of the window, presently, on Laura's telling her to, crawled round the floor at Sally's feet with her mouth full of pins, doing something to a petticoat of Laura's that Sally, it seemed, was going to have to wear that evening.

'All you've got to do, Sally,' said Laura, having finished telephoning, and coming briskly over to where her newest discovery was standing meekly without her frock and hat, while the petticoat was pinned narrower, 'is to enjoy yourself. Oh, you lovely, *lovely* thing!' she burst out, beating her hands together with delight; for the more one took off Sally the more exquisite she became.

Enjoy herself? She, a married woman? 'Wonder 'ow,' thought Sally.

'Say what you like, do what you like,' said Laura, her eyes bulging with admiration, 'and don't care about anybody or anything. Don't you bother about h's, or silly things like that. Just say whatever comes into your darling, delicious head, and enjoy yourself.'

In the presence of the young lady crawling on the floor, Sally was dumb. Laura, on the other hand, talked just as if she weren't there; but when for a moment Sally found herself alone with Laura, she did make a mild protest.

'Might 'ave gone back to that there other party after all,' she said, 'an' done what Father tell me, if I got to be at one any'ow.'

'Oh, but this isn't a party,' Laura hastily assured her, for Sally was distinctly drooping. 'This is a theatre. You like going to a play, don't you, Sally? Of course you do. I simply don't believe the girl exists who doesn't.'

Yes; Sally liked going to a play. She hadn't ever been to one, and the idea of a theatre did cheer her up. And Laura said nothing about the supper afterwards, because why say everything?

❁

They went, then, to the first night of Mr. Gillespie's new play. Sally was astonished when Laura, and the maid, and the head lady from Paquille's and her two assistants, had finished with her and bade her look at herself in the glass.

'That me?' she asked, her lips parting and her eyes widening, for it might have been a real grand lady. And she added doubtfully, 'I ain't 'alf bare.'

Laura, however, was just as bare, and there was ever so much more of her to be bare with, so she supposed it must be all right; but she did wonder what her father would say if he could see her now—'Oh, my *goodness*,' shuddered Sally, her mind slinking away from the thought.

They had dressed her in a cloud of blue tulle over a cloud of green tulle. Her loveliness was startling. It was like nothing either Laura or the lady from Paquille's had ever seen, and they had seen most of what there was of existing beauty. Even the maid, an expert in repression, showed excitement. And presently when the Paquille lady wrapped the cloak round her that went with that frock, and, swathed in its green and silver, she looked like a white flower in a slender sheath of green, Laura fairly danced with delight to think what Terry would say, who was used to being so much prettier than anybody else, and what Charles would say, who long had declared there was no such thing as real beauty, and Streatley, who said the women nowadays couldn't hold a candle to the women of his youth, and everybody.

Such a find, such a haul, such a piece of luck had never yet befallen Laura. And the mischievous pleasure she took in thinking of the effect it was going to have on her relations and of the upsetting results it was going to produce, was all the more surprising because, at the bottom of her heart, she was devoted to them.

❁

Among the opera-glasses that raked Sally as she followed Laura into the stage box three minutes before the curtain went up on Mr. Gillespie's new play, were Terry's. She was in the stalls, with the young man who just then

was, as the Pinners would have said, walking out with her. He too was looking at Sally.

'Laura's latest,' remarked Terry, turning to him after a prolonged incredulous stare at the astonishing contents of the box; for Laura was well known for her successive discoveries of every kind—saints, geniuses, rugged men of labour—each of which, after a brief blare of publicity, disappeared and was not heard of again.

The young man's face, however, had the kind of expression on it as he looked at Sally that is apt to annoy the woman one is with; and Terry, who was strictly monogamous during each of her affairs, and expected the other person to be so too, didn't like it.

'Who is she?' asked her young friend.

'God knows,' said Terry, shrugging her shoulders.

The curtain went up and the lights went down, and Sally disappeared into the darkness. When next she was visible, Charles Moulsford and Lord Streatley had joined their sister in the box. They were talking to Sally. She was politely smiling. The house had eyes for nothing else.

'Who *is* she?' asked Terry's young friend again, with a warmer insistence.

'You'd better go and ask her,' said Terry, cross.

'All right, I will,' said her young friend; and got up and left her; for by this time she had been monogamous with him for six months, and he long had wished she would love him less.

The other three acts of the play took place in bright summer weather, and the glorious sunshine on the stage lit up Sally too in the stage box. The house had eyes only for her. Mr. Gillespie's play accordingly fell flat. Nobody called for him at the end, what applause there was was absent-minded, and next morning the leading newspaper, after a perfunctory *résumé* of that which it unkindly described as the alleged plot, ended by remarking languidly, 'Mr. Gillespie must try again.'

It was a strange evening. The actors, who began well, seemed to get more and more bloodless as the play proceeded. Mr. Gillespie, crouching in the darkest corner of the box above Laura's, a shelter out of which nothing would have dragged him except the most frenzied cries of enthusiasm, couldn't imagine what was the matter with his players; but they had felt

almost at once that no notice was being taken of them, and presently, discovering the reason, a blight settled on them, and its ravages, as the evening went on, became more marked. By the end there was practically complete anaemia, and Mr. Gillespie, fleeing from the theatre before the final curtain so as to see and hear nothing more, so as to get away, so as to meet neither managers nor actors, so as to wipe from his mind that he had ever written plays, or ever hoped, or ever believed, or ever had dreams and ambitions, went straight for comfort to his friend Lady Laura Moulsford, who had been so kind and encouraging, and who had told him to come round to her that evening, laughingly promising to have the laurels ready.

Laurels! Poor Mr. Gillespie now only wanted to hide his head in her kind lap. He winced to remember how happily he too had laughed, how sure he had been. But that was because of the great success of his first play; and this one, his second, was twenty times better, and was going to be twenty times greater a success.

And so it would have been except for Sally. When, presently, after he had waited three quarters of an hour alone in the library at Goring House because Sally was being so much crowded round coming out of the theatre that it took all that time to extricate her and get her away, she came in with Laura and Laura's brothers, he instantly realised what had happened; and even as Mr. Soper hadn't grudged her his stew, though feeling aggrieved, so did Mr. Gillespie, though feeling heartbroken, not grudge her the laurels that should have been his.

He turned very red; he bent low over her hand when Laura introduced him; he murmured, 'I lay my failure at your feet and glory in it,'—this being the way Mr. Gillespie talked; and Sally, nervous and bewildered, but indomitably polite, said, 'Pardon?'

❀

She kept on saying 'Pardon?' that evening. She found it difficult to follow the things they all said. They were kind, and seemed to want to make her happy, but their language was obscure. So was Mr. Luke's, if it came to that, only he, except at intervals, wasn't kind. No, she couldn't call Mr.

Luke a kind man; but then he was her husband, and these weren't, though they all behaved, she thought, rather as if they would like to be,—that is, there were curious and unmistakable resemblances between their way of looking at her and speaking to her and Jocelyn's when he was courting. Lords, too, two of them. Who would have thought lords would forget themselves like this? For they knew she was married, and that it was sheer sin to look at her as though they were going to be husbands. And they so grand and good in the newspapers, making speeches, and opening hospitals! Sally was much shocked. One of them was very old; he couldn't, she decided, be far off his dying breath. Oughtn't he to be thinking what he was going to do about it, instead of sitting up late at a party behaving as if he would like to be a husband?

The only thing that comforted her for being at a party after all was that Jocelyn wasn't there. She felt she could manage parties much best single-handed, without him watching and being angry. None of these people were angry, or minded about how she spoke; on the contrary, they seemed to like it, and laughed,—except one, the younger lord, who sat as grave as a church. There was, when all was said and done, a certain feeling of space in being without one's husband; and after she had drunk a little champagne,—a very little, because it was so nasty, and reminded her of fizzy lemonade gone bad—this feeling of space increased, and she was able to listen to the things the gentlemen kept on saying to her with the same mild patience, tinged with regret, with which on her one visit to the Zoo she had contemplated the behaviour of the monkeys. Laura's relations seemed to Sally, as she sat listening to them, as difficult to account for as the monkeys. One couldn't account for them. But even as these, she reminded herself, they belonged to God.

'They're God's,' Mr. Pinner had said that day at the Zoo, when asked by her to explain why the monkeys behaved in the way they did; and that being so there was nothing further to worry about.

As for Laura, whose heart, being a Moulsford's, was good, though it sometimes in moments of excitement forgot to be, she had several qualms during that evening, and soon began to think that perhaps she oughtn't to have kidnapped Sally, or, having kidnapped her, ought to have kept

her hidden till she took her to Cambridge and handed her over to her husband.

Yet she was even more of an overwhelming success than Laura had expected. Streatley was idiotic about her, Charles had fallen in love at last, Mr. Gillespie worshipped and forgave, the dramatic critic was fatuous, Terry was indignant, and the leading lady had been so furious when she saw Sally in the box, and knew why she herself and the play were being failures, that she had refused to come round to supper.

'What a success,' thought Laura, looking round her table, the vacant place at which was filled by Lady Streatley, who had drifted in unexpectedly because she didn't see why Streatley should make a fool of himself with that actress woman unchecked. She had come to check him, and found him needing checking at an entirely different pair of feet. 'What a *success*,' thought Laura, suddenly ashamed.

'And so you ought to be,' said her brother Charles after supper, when she—they were great friends—took him aside and told him she somehow felt ashamed. 'You're a little fool, Laura, and never see further than the end of your silly nose. I should get rid of a few of your good intentions if I were you.'

'But she was so unhappy,' said Laura, trying to justify herself.

'You wouldn't have cared in the very least if she had been plain,' said Charles.

'Am I as bad as all that?' asked Laura.

'Every bit,' said Charles, who was annoyed because of the way Sally was disturbing him.

Indeed, the way Sally was disturbing everybody was most unfortunate. Here was a united and affectionate family, the three younger ones almost filially devoted to their elder brother, all four of them with the warmest hearts, which, though they led them into situations Terry's husband and Streatley's wife might dislike, never for an instant dimmed their fraternal affections and loyalties. Not one of them would willingly have hurt the others. All were most goodnatured, doing what they could to make everybody happy. Laura was really benevolent; Theresa was really kind; Charles was really unselfish; and Streatley so really affectionate

that he could still, at sixty-five, love several women at once, including his wife.

How annoying for Charles, for instance, who was so fond of his brother, and had looked on with bland detachment at his successive infatuations, suddenly to find he was competing with him. Competing with Streatley! And not only competing, but saying to himself that he was an ancient ass. Charles was horrified to find himself thinking Streatley an ancient ass; but he was even more horrified when he quite soon afterwards discovered he was definitely desirous of strangling him. That was because of the way he looked at Sally. It made Charles's hitherto affectionate fingers itch to strangle him.

And how annoying for Lady Streatley to see her elderly husband making yet another fool of himself. He had made so many fools of himself over women that it was to be supposed she would by now have got used to it. Not at all. She was each time as profoundly upset as ever. And this time it was really dreadful, because the girl was hardly more than a child. Oughtn't he to be thoroughly ashamed of himself?

'I wish you could see the expression on your face,' she murmured acidly to him, as they got up from the supper-table and gathered round the fire.

'Leave my face alone,' he growled, looking at her furiously; and that she should be acid and he should growl and look at her furiously was distressing to Lady Streatley, who was the most amiable of women, and knew that he was the most naturally kind of men.

And then Terry, so affectionate and faithful to her young friend Robert,—for her to have to look on while he forgot her very existence and sat on the floor at somebody else's feet, his rapt gaze fixed unswervingly on a face that wasn't hers, was most annoying. He had insisted on coming round with her to Laura's party, though she refused at first to bring him. So violently determined was he, however, that he assured her she would never see him again if she didn't take him round with her; and Terry, cowed, as many a fond woman had been before her by this threat, gave in, and spent the evening in a condition of high indignation.

It was Laura, though, with whom she was indignant,—Laura, the sister she had always so much loved, who had arranged the whole thing

so as to set everybody by the ears. She forgave Robert—they had got to the stage when she was continually forgiving him, and he was continually hoping she wouldn't—for how could he help it if this artful young woman from the slums laid herself out to beguile him? It was all Laura's fault. Terry couldn't have believed her goodnatured sister had it in her to be so wickedly mischievous. What devil had taken possession of her? First dressing the girl up and spoiling poor Jack Gillespie's play with her, and then getting them all there to supper, so as to make fools of them. ...

'I hope you're pleased with your detestable party,' she said, leaning against the chimney piece, staring in wrathful disgust at the circle round Sally, who, glancing shyly and furtively every now and then at the lovely dark lady dressed like a rose, thought she must surely be the most beautiful lady in the whole world, but feeling, judged Sally, a bit on the sick side that evening,—probably eaten something.

'I'm not at all pleased,' snapped Laura, 'and I wish to goodness you'd all go home.'

That, however, was exactly what they couldn't bear to do. Hours passed, and Laura's party still went on. The men were unable to tear themselves away from Sally, whose every utterance—she said as little as possible, but couldn't avoid answering direct questions—filled them with fresh delight, and the two women, Terry and her aggrieved sister-in-law, were doggedly determined to stay as long as they did.

'If she weren't so lovely,' murmured Lady Streatley to the indignant Terry, when a roar of laughter, in which the loudest roar was Streatley's, succeeded something Sally, tired and bewildered, had said in answer to a question, 'I suppose they wouldn't see anything at all in that Cockney talk.'

'They'd think it unendurable,' said Terry shortly.

'But you see,' said Laura, who was cross with Terry, 'she happens to be the most beautiful thing any of us have ever seen.'

'Oh, I quite see she's very beautiful,' said poor Lady Streatley, who had given Streatley seven children and was no longer the woman she was.

'If one *likes* that sort of thing,' said Terry, descending in her anger to primitive woman.

'Which one evidently does,' said Laura maliciously, glancing at the infatuated group.

'Men are such fools,' said Terry.

'Babies,' sighed Lady Streatley.

Only once did Charles, who was the greatest contrast to his brother, being lean and brown and goodlooking and not much past thirty, besides remaining grave on all the occasions that evening when his brother laughed, for Charles was fastidious as well as sympathetic, and Sally's accent didn't amuse him, and he hated to see her unwittingly amusing the other four infatuated fools,—only once did he get her a moment to himself, and then only for a minute or two, while there was some slight rearrangement of positions because of the bringing in of a tray of drinks.

When he did, this was the conversation:

'I believe,' said Charles in a low voice, 'you're every bit as beautiful inside as you are out.'

'Me?' said Sally with weary surprise—by this time she was deadly tired—for she hadn't thought of bodies as reversible. 'Ain't I all pink?'

'Pink?' echoed Charles, not at first following. Then he said rather hastily, being queasy and without Streatley's robust ability to enjoy anything, 'I mean your spirit. It's just as divinely beautiful as your face. I'm sure it is. I'm sure you never have a thought that isn't lovely—'

And he went on to murmur—why on earth he should say these inanities he couldn't think, and was much annoyed to hear them coming out—that he hoped her husband loved her as she deserved.

'You never *see* such lovin',' said Sally earnestly, who didn't mind this one of the gentlemen as much as the others.

'Oh, I can imagine it,' said Charles, again hastily; and wanted to know whether, then, her husband wouldn't be excessively unhappy, not having an idea where she was.

'Dunno about un'appy,' said Sally, knitting her brows a little—Charles was deeply annoyed to discover how much he wished to kiss them—for she hadn't thought of unhappiness in connection with her brief and strictly temporary withdrawal. 'Angry's more like it.'

'Angry?' said Charles, incredulously. 'Angry with you?'

'Gets angry a lot, Mr. Luke do,' said Sally, bowing her exquisite little head in what Charles regarded as a lovely but misplaced acquiescence. 'Except,' she added, anxious to be accurate, 'when 'e begins oh-Sallyin'.'

This ended the conversation. Charles couldn't go on. He was queasy. He didn't need to ask what oh-Sallying was. He could guess. And, as he shuddered, the desire he had to strangle Streatley was supplemented by a desire to save Sally,—to seize and carry her off, out of reach of indignities and profanities, and hide her away in some pure refuge of which only he should have the key.

XII

He couldn't, however, do that; but he could carry her off next day in his car into the country for a few hours, away from London and the advances Streatley would be sure to try to make, and everybody else would be sure to try to make who should meet her if she stayed with Laura.

Next day was Friday; and his chief, one of the leading lights of the Cabinet, to whom he was the most devoted and enthusiastic of private secretaries, was going away for the week-end. Charles would be free. Walking up and down his room, unable to go to bed, he decided he would drive his car himself round to his father's house the first thing in the morning, not taking the chauffeur, and get hold of Sally before anyone else did. For one whole day he would be alone with her. One day. It wasn't much to take out of her life, just one day?

Charles was in love. How not be? He was in love from the first moment he saw the radiant beauty in Laura's box at the play, and his love had survived, though it took on a tinge of distress, their brief conversation. But it became a passion when she broke up Laura's party at last by suddenly tumbling off her chair in a faint and lying crumpled on the floor at his feet, her eyes shut and her mouth a little open, and her hands flung out, palm upwards, in a queer defencelessness.

There had been a rush to help, and he had actually shoved Streatley away with a vicious intention of really hurting him, so unendurable had it been to him to think of those great hairy hands, besmirched by a hundred love affairs, touching the child; and it was he who had picked her up and carried her upstairs, followed by Laura, and laid her on her bed.

'I'm *ashamed* of you,' he had said to Laura under his breath as he turned and walked out of the room, shocked at such brutal exploiting of an exhausted child.

'But so am I, so am I—' Laura had answered distractedly, running to the bell and frantically ringing for her maid; and Sally lay on the bed like a folded flower, thought Charles, stirred by passion into poetic images, and at least for the moment safe in unconsciousness from the screaming, tearing, grabbing world.

The next morning, then, when Laura came down punctually at nine o'clock to breakfast—for however late she went to bed her restless vitality, once it was broad daylight, prevented her being able to stay there, which made her unpopular in country houses,—she found Charles in the dining-room, standing with his back to the fire.

'How much you must love me,' she remarked sarcastically, being, after a bad night, a little cross.

'I don't love you at all at this moment,' said Charles.

'Then is it breakfast you want?'

'No,' said Charles.

'Can it be Sally?'

'Yes,' said Charles.

'Fancy,' said Laura; and poured herself out some coffee.

'How is she?' asked Charles after a pause, ignoring such silliness.

'Oh, quite well,' said Laura. 'She was tired last night.'

'Tired! I should think so,' said Charles severely. 'I've come to ask her if she will let me take her into the country for the day. It's my intention to get her away from your crowd for a few hours.'

'Rescue her, in fact,' said Laura, munching, her back to him.

'Exactly,' said Charles, who was angry.

'I expect Tom'—Tom was Lord Streatley—'will be here soon, wanting to rescue her too,' remarked Laura, glancing out of the window to where she could see Charles's touring car standing, and no chauffeur. '*He* won't bring his chauffeur either. Have some?' she asked, holding up the coffee-pot.

'Can't you be a little beast when you give your mind to it,' said Charles.

'Well, you scolded me last night because *I* had rescued her, and now here you are—'

Laura broke off, and hastily drank some coffee. She didn't really want

to quarrel with Charles; she never had yet. In fact, till Sally appeared on the scene she had never quarrelled with any of her family. Besides in her heart, though she was cross that morning, not having slept well for the first time for years because of being worried and conscience-stricken and anxious, she was glad that Charles should take Sally off her hands. She had so much to do that day, so many important engagements; and if Sally went with her everybody would instantly be upset, and if she left her at home she would be a prey to Streatley. Other people wishing to prey on her could be kept out by a simple order to the servants, but not her own brother. And Streatley, when he was infatuated, was a gross creature, and there would be more trouble and wretchedness for poor Kitty his wife, let alone God knowing what mightn't happen to Sally.

If Sally had to be with one or the other of them, Charles was far the better; but what a very great pity it was, Laura thought as she pretended to be absorbed in her breakfast, that she hadn't let her go back the day before to where she belonged. It wasn't any sort of fun quarrelling with her dearest brother Charles, and seeing him look as if he hadn't slept a wink. Besides, Sally was going to have a baby. At least, so she had informed Laura during the night, basing her conviction on the close resemblance between her behaviour in fainting, and her subsequent behaviour when she came to in being violently sick, and the behaviour of somebody called Mrs. Ooper, who had lived next door at Islington, and every spring, for seven years running, had fainted just like that and then been sick,—and sure as fate, Sally had told Laura in a feeble murmur, there at Christmas in each of those seven years had been another little baby.

'*I* don't want no doctor,' she had whispered, putting out a cold hand and catching at Laura's arm when, dismayed at Sally's sickness just as they had at last been able to undress her and get her into bed, she was running to the telephone to call hers up.

'But, my darling,' Laura had said, bending over her and smoothing back the hair from her damp forehead with, quick, anxious movements, 'he'll give you something to make you well again.'

'No,'e won't,' Sally had whispered, looking up at her with a faint, proud smile, ''cos I ain't ill. *I* know wot's 'appenin' all right. It's a little baby.'

And then she had told Laura, who had to stoop down close to hear, about Mrs. Ooper.

Well, Laura didn't know much about babies before they were born, but she was sure a person who was expecting any ought to be with her husband. She couldn't kidnap whole families; she hadn't bargained for more than one Luke. And during the few hours that remained of the night, after she had seen Sally go off to sleep with an expression of beatitude on her face, she had tossed about in her own bed in a fever of penitence.

When would she learn not to interfere? When would she learn to hang on to her impulses, and resist sudden temptation? Up to then she had never even tried to. And a vision of what Sally's unfortunate young husband must be feeling, and of course his mother too, who might be tiresome but hadn't deserved this, produced the most painful sensations in Laura's naturally benevolent heart.

She would make amends,—oh, she would make amends. She would take Sally to Cambridge herself on Saturday, when she was through with her London engagements, and find rooms for her, and explain everything to the young man, and beg his pardon. Perhaps, too, she could tell him a little of Sally's fear of his mother, and perhaps she might be able to persuade him not to let her live with them; for Laura had often noticed, though each time, being a member of the Labour Party, with shame and regret, that the persuasions of the daughter of a duke are readily listened to. But she didn't want to make amends that day,—she was too busy; and she couldn't send a telegram, or anything like that, letting the Lukes know where Sally was, because it would only bring them about her ears in hordes, and she simply hadn't time that day for hordes. Laura's intentions, that is, were admirable, but deferred.

'Isn't she coming down?' asked Charles at last, for Laura, with her back to him pretending to eat her breakfast, had said no more.

'She's having breakfast upstairs,' said Laura.

'Why didn't you tell me?' he asked, annoyed.

'Because you say I'm a little beast, so I may as well do the thing thoroughly.'

Charles went across to the bell.

'No—don't ring,' said Laura jumping up. 'I'll go and tell her.' And she went to the door, but hesitated, and came back to him, and laid her hand on his arm.

He withdrew his arm.

'Charles—are you so angry with me?' she asked.

'You've behaved simply disgracefully,' he answered in a voice of deep disgust. 'You would sacrifice anybody to provide your friends with a new sensation.'

Laura looked at him. It was true; or had been true. But she wasn't going to ever any more, she was going to turn over a new leaf—next day, when she had finished with all her tiresome and important engagements.

'You sacrificed that child'—began Charles, passionately indignant when he thought of the unconscious figure on the floor.

'Don't *you* sacrifice her,' interrupted Laura. And when Charles stared at her, too angry for speech, she added hastily, 'Oh, don't let's quarrel, Charles darling. I'm sure you'll take the greatest care of her. I'll go and fetch her. Drive slowly, won't you—and bring her back safe. Tomorrow I'm going to hand her over to her husband.'

❀

Now in his heart Charles knew that this was the only right thing to do. Sally ought never to have been taken away from her husband, and, having been taken, ought to be returned to him. At once. Not tomorrow, but at once. He didn't know the circumstances, except what Laura had hurriedly told him the night before after supper, about having found her in a train, dissolved in tears because her father was sending her back to a mother-in-law who was awful to her, and she had brought her home with her just to comfort her, just to let her recover; but it was plain that such conduct on Laura's part was indefensible. If ever anybody ought to be safe at home it was Sally. She should be taken there without losing a moment. Disgraceful of Laura to put it off for another day and night, while she kept her fool

engagements. Having behaved so wickedly, she ought, without losing an hour, to set things straight again.

Charles felt strongly about Laura's conduct; yet, though he himself could have set things straight by simply driving Sally back to the Lukes that morning, he didn't do so. That was because he couldn't. He was in love, and therefore couldn't.

There are some things it is impossible to do when you are in love, thought Charles, who recognised and admitted his condition, and one is to hand over the beloved to a brute. Luke was a brute. Clearly he was, from what Sally had said the night before. He was either angry—angry with that little angel!—or he oh-Sallied. A cold shudder ran down Charles's spine. The thought made him feel really sick, for he was a tender-stomached as well as a tender-hearted young man, and possessed an imagination which was sometimes too lively for comfort. It wouldn't be *his* hand that delivered her up to a young brute; nor, he suddenly determined, on the butler's hurrying out to Laura, who was standing on the steps seeing him and Sally off, and saying with urgency, 'Lord Streatley to speak to Mrs. Luke on the telephone,' would it be his hand that delivered her up to an old one. At once on hearing the message he started the car, and was out of the square before Laura could say anything. There was Sally, tucked up beside him in Laura's furs, and looking more beautiful in broad sunshine even than he remembered her the night before,—a child of light and grace if ever there was one, thought Charles, a thing of simple sweetness and obedience and trust; and was he going to bring her back to another evening's exploitation by his sister and her precious friends, with that old scoundrel, his elder brother, all over her?

Never, said Charles to himself; and headed his car for Crippenham.

❁

Crippenham was where his father was. What so safe as a refuge for Sally as his father? He was ninety-three, and he was deaf. A venerable age; a convenient failing. Convenient indeed in this case, for the Duke, like Charles, took little pleasure in the speech of the lower classes. Also he

was alone there till Laura should come back to him on the following day, because nobody was ever invited to Crippenham, which was his yearly rest-cure, and nobody ever dared even try to disturb its guarded repose.

Charles felt that it was, besides being the only, the very place. Here Sally could be kept remote and hidden till Laura—not he; he wouldn't be able to do such a thing—restored her to where she belonged; here she would be safe from the advances of Streatley, who couldn't follow her anywhere his father was, because the old man had an aversion to the four surviving fruits of his first marriage, and freely showed it; and here he would have her to himself for a whole evening, and part at least of the next day.

Also, it would serve Laura right. She would get a fright, and think all sorts of things had happened when they didn't come back. Well, thought Charles, she deserved everything she got. Under the cloak of protecting and comforting Sally she had been completely selfish and cruel. Charles was himself astonished at the violence of his feelings towards Laura, with whom he had always been such friends. He didn't investigate these feelings, however; he didn't investigate any of his other feelings either, not excepting the one he had when he asked Sally, soon after they had turned the corner out of the square, if she were warm enough, and she looked up shyly at him, and smiled as she politely thanked him, for his feelings since the evening before no longer bore investigation. They were a mixed lot, a strong lot. And it vexed Charles to know that even as early in the day as this, and not much after half past nine in the morning, he wished to kiss Sally.

This wasn't at all the proper spirit of rescue. He drove in silence. He couldn't remember having wished to kiss a woman before at half past nine in the morning, and it annoyed him.

Sally, of course, was silent too. Not for her to speak without being spoken to, and she sat mildly wondering that she should be going along in a car at all. Laura had come up to her bedroom and said her brother was there, wanting to take her out for a little fresh air. Do her good, Laura had said, though Sally had never known good come of fresh air yet; but, passive as a parcel, she had let herself be taken. Why, however, she should

be going for a joy-ride with this lord she didn't know, though she supposed it was as good a way as another of getting through the intimidating day among the picks of the basket, and anyhow this way there was only one of them, and anyhow he wasn't the big old one with the hairs on his hands.

Queer lot, these picks, thought Sally. Didn't seem to have anything to do to keep them at home; seemed to spend their time going somewhere else. Fidgety. And a vision of her own life as it was going to be once she was settled in those rooms at Cambridge, getting ready for her little baby, and cleaning up, and making things cosy for her man, flooded her heart with a delicious warmth. Lama had promised to help her find the rooms, and take her to where Mr. Luke would be. Mr. Luke wouldn't be angry any more now, thought Sally—he'd be too pleased about the little baby; and Laura seemed to know exactly where they would find him, and had assured her he wouldn't want to have Mrs. Luke living with them. Laura was queer too, in Sally's eyes, but good. Indeed Sally, feeling very much the married woman after what had happened the evening before, feeling motherly already, feeling exalted by the coming of her baby to a height immensely above mere spinsterhood, went so far as to say to herself of Laura, with indulgent affection, 'Nice kid.'

❀

They lunched at Thaxted. It was still only half past twelve, and Charles had managed to be three hours doing the forty odd miles. There was a beautiful church at Thaxted in which he could linger with her, for he didn't want to get to Crippenham till tea-time, and Crippenham was only about nine miles beyond Cambridge, off the Ely road between Waterbeach and Swaffham Prior.

Up to Thaxted, Charles was filled with an embarrassingly strong desire to appropriate Sally for ever to himself. He hadn't an idea how to do it, but that was his wish. She sat there silent, beautiful beyond his dreams—and how often and how wistfully had he not dreamt of what a woman's beauty might be!—pathetic, defenceless in the midst of a rudely jostling, predatory world, like a child with a priceless pearl in its hand among the

poor and hungry, and he passionately loved her. As the miles increased, so did Charles's passion. He looked at her sideways, and each time with a fresh throb of wonder. He wove dreams about her; he saw visions of magic casements and perilous seas, and she behind them, protected, guarded, worshipped by him alone; his soul was filled with poetry; he was lifted above himself by this Presence, this Manifestation; he thought in terms of music; the whole of England sang.

But at Thaxted he felt different, and began to think Sally ought to be with those she belonged to; and by the time it was evening, and he was meditating alone in the garden at Crippenham, he was quite sure of it.

At Thaxted he ordered the best lunch he could—Sally's mouth watered as she listened,—and while it was being got ready he took her into the church. She was inattentively polite. The brisk movements of a big, close-cropped man in a cassock, who strode busily about and made what seemed to Sally a curtsey each time he crossed the middle aisle, appeared to interest her much more than Charles's remarks on the clear, pale beauty of the building. It was rather like taking a dog to look at things. Charles didn't consciously think this, but there was an unawareness about Sally when faced by the beauties of Thaxted Church, and when faced, coming down, by the beauties of certain bits of the country that singing April morning, which was very like, Charles subconsciously thought, the unawareness of a dog. Ah, but how far, far more beautiful she herself was than anything else, he thought; how exquisite she looked in Laura's chinchilla wrap, with the exalted thoughts of the men who had built the church, thoughts frozen into the delicate greys, and silvers, and rose-colours of that fair wide place, for her background.

The man in the cassock left off doing whatever he was doing on catching sight of Sally, and, after looking at her a moment, came up and offered, his eyes on her face, to show them round the church; a little cluster of Americans dissolved, and flowed towards her; and a woman dressed like a nun broke off her prayers, and presently sidled up to where she stood.

Charles removed her.

Thaxted is a quiet place, and he strolled with her through its streets till

their food should be ready. Its streets, quiet to begin with, didn't stay quiet. The people of Thaxted, for some reason incomprehensible to Charles, because no two women could be more unlike, seemed to think Sally was Mary Pickford. He heard whispers to that effect. Did they then think, too, that he was the person known, he understood, as Doug?

He removed her a second time.

Perhaps the inn was as good a place as any to wait in. He had, however, to engage a private room for their lunch, because so many people came in and wished to lunch too; and it was when Sally had eaten a great deal of greengage tart and cream—bottled greengages, Charles feared, but she said she liked them—and drunk a great deal of raspberry syrup which had, he was sure, never been near real raspberries and couldn't be very good for her, and then, while he was having coffee and she tea—he had somehow stumbled on the fact that she liked tea after meals, and he watched with concern the strength and number of the cups she drank—it was then that she began to thaw, and to talk.

Alas, that she should. Alas, that she didn't remain for ever silent, wonderful, mysterious, of God.

Once having started thawing, it wasn't in Sally's generous nature to stop. She thawed and thawed, and Charles became more and more afflicted. Lord Charles—so, the night before, she had learned he was called—was evidently a chip off the same block as her friend Laura; kind, that is. See what a lovely dinner he was giving her. Also he had been much more like a gentleman that day, and less like somebody who wanted to be a husband; and after the greengage tart she began to warm up, and by the time she had got to the cups of tea she felt great confidence in Charles.

'Kind, ain't you,' she said with her enchanting smile, when he suggested, much against his convictions, another pot of tea.

'Isn't everybody?' asked Charles.

'Does their best,' said Sally charitably. 'But it's up 'ill all the way for some as I could mention.'

By this time Charles was already feeling chilled. The raspberry syrup and the cups of strong tea had estranged him. This perfect girl, he thought, ought to be choice too in her food, ought instinctively to

reject things out of bottles, and have no desire for a second helping of obviously bad pastry. Still, she was very young. He too, at Eton, had liked bad tuck. After all, queer as it seemed, she had only got to the age he was at then.

He made excuses for her; and, it appearing to him important that he should be in possession of more facts about her than those Laura had told him the evening before, said encouragingly, 'Do mention them.'

Sally did. She mentioned everybody and everything; and soon he knew as much about her hasty marriage, hurried on within a fortnight to the first man who came along, her return from her honeymoon to South Winch, the determination of her mother-in-law to keep her apart from her husband, her flight, helped by her father-in-law, back to her father, his rejection of her, and her intention to rejoin her husband next day at Cambridge whether he liked it or not, as he could bear.

He couldn't bear much. It wasn't only how she said it, but what she said. Charles, who had at first been afflicted by her language, was now afflicted by her facts. He shifted uneasily in his chair. He smoked cigarette after cigarette. His thin brown face was flushed, and he looked distressed. In that strange, defective, yet all too vivid speech which he so deeply deplored, she drew for him a picture of what seemed sheer exploitation, culminating in his own sister's flinging herself hilariously into the game. This child; this helpless child, who would obey anybody, go anywhere, do anything she was told—in Charles's eyes, as he listened and drew her out, she became the most pathetic thing on earth. Everybody, it appeared, first grabbed at her and then wanted to get rid of her. Everybody; himself too. Yes, he too had grabbed at her, under a mealy-mouthed pretence of helping her, and now he too wanted—not to get rid of her, that seemed too violent, too brutal a way of putting it, but to hand her over, to pass her on, to send her back to that infernal young Luke, who himself was trying to escape from her and leave her to his mother. And the courage of the child! It was the courage of ignorance, of course, but still it seemed to Charles a lovely thing, that was afraid of nothing, of no discomfort, of no hard work, if only she might be with her husband in their own home. Charles discovered that that was Sally's one wish, and that her simple

ambition appeared to be to do what she called work her fingers to the bone on behalf of that odious youth.

'Mr. Luke,' said Sally, who was unacquainted with any reason why she shouldn't say everything she knew to anyone who wished to hear, 'Mr. Luke, 'e thinks 'e can't afford a 'ome yet for me, and so—'

'Then he oughtn't to have married you,' flashed out Charles, infuriated by the young brute.

'Seemed 'e couldn't 'elp it,' said Sally. 'Seemed as if it 'ad to be. 'E—'

'Oh yes, *yes*,' interrupted Charles impatiently, for he hated hearing anything about Jocelyn's emotions. 'Of course, of course. That was a quite foolish remark of mine.'

'Five 'undred pounds a year 'e got,' went on Sally, 'and me able to make sixpence go twice as far as most can. Dunno wot 'e's talkin' about.'

And indeed she didn't know, for she shared Mr. Pinner's opinion that five hundred a year was wealth.

'Fair beats me,' she added, after a thoughtful pause.

Well, thought Charles, the Moulsford family had behaved badly, and, under the cloak of sympathy and wishing to help, his and Laura's conduct had been most base; but they were certainly going to make up for it now. By God, yes. Crippenham, which he had at first thought of from sheer selfishness as the very place to get Sally to himself in, was evidently now the place of all others from which she could be helped. Quite close to Cambridge, within easy reach of young Luke, and in it, all-powerful even now in spite of his age, certainly all-powerful when it came to putting the fear of God into an undergraduate, or whatever he was, his ancient but still inflammable father. Naturally at ninety-three the old man consisted principally of embers; but these embers could still be fanned into a partial glow by the sight of a good horse or a beautiful woman, and Charles would only need to show Sally to him to have the old man on her side. Not able to hear, but able to see: what combination could, in the case of Sally, possibly be more admirable?

He drove on after lunch, his conscience clear; so clear that before leaving Thaxted he sent Laura a telegram telling her they were going to Crippenham, because he no longer wanted her to be made

anxious,—for those only, thought Charles, are angry and wish to make others uncomfortable who are themselves in the wrong. He was no longer in the wrong; or, rather, he was no longer thinking with rapture of the wrong he would like to be in if Sally could be in it with him. Her speech made a gulf between them which his fastidious soul couldn't cross. There had to be h's before Charles could love with passion. Where there were none, passion with him collapsed and died. On this occasion it died at the inn at Thaxted towards the end of lunch; and he was grateful, really, however unpleasant at the moment its dying was. For what mightn't have happened if she had gone on being silent and only saying yes and no, and smiling the divine, delicious smile that didn't only play in her dimples but laughed and danced in her darling eyes? Charles was afraid that in that case he would have been done for. Talking, she had saved him; and though he still loved her, for no man could look at Sally and not love her, he loved her differently,—kindly, gently, with a growingly motherly concern for her welfare. After Thaxted there was no further trace in his looks and manner of that which had made Sally suspect him of a wish to be a husband.

But she was surprised when he asked her, as they drove along, whether she would mind if he took her to his father in the country for the night, instead of back to what he called noisy London. Laura was in London; why should she be taken somewhere else, away from her? And to his father too—to more picks, fresh ones; just as she was beginning to shake down nicely with the ones she knew. Surely the father of the picks would be the most frightening of all?

So she said, 'Pardon?' and looked so much alarmed that Charles, smiling, explained that his father was staying at that moment quite near Cambridge, and it would be convenient for the search for rooms she had told him Laura had promised to undertake with her next day.

'He's quite harmless,' Charles assured her, for she continued to look alarmed—if where she was to be taken to next was near Cambridge, it must also be near Woodles, and suppose her father were to happen to see her?—'and he's all alone there till Laura goes back to him tomorrow. It will cheer him up to have us. He's ninety-three.'

Ninety-three? 'Oh, my,' said Sally politely. ''E ain't 'alf old. Poor old gentleman,' she added with compassion, old people having been objects of special regard and attention in the Pinner circle.

But for the rest of the drive she was silent, for she was trying to thread her way among her indistinct and entangled thoughts, all of which seemed confusedly to press upon her notice that she oughtn't to be where she was at all, that if she was anywhere it ought to be with her husband, and that with every hour that passed she was sinking deeper and deeper in wrong-doing.

'Soon be in right up to the neck,' she said to herself with resigned unhappiness; and sincerely wished it were that time tomorrow, and she safely joined up with Mr. Luke, and finished for good and all with these soft-spoken but headstrong picks.

XIII

While they, along the roads, were drawing every minute nearer, the unconscious Duke was sitting in his plain study, having his plain tea, which had been set beside him by his plain parlourmaid. This is not to say that the parlourmaid was ill-favoured, but only that she wasn't a footman.

There were no footmen at Crippenham. There was hardly anything there, except the Duke. For years it had been his conviction that this annual fortnight of the rest that is obtained by complete contrast prolonged his life. Something evidently prolonged it, and the Duke was sure it was Crippenham. There he went every Easter alone with Laura, because it was a small house, and an ugly house, and a solitary house, and had nothing to recommend it except that it was the exact opposite of every other Moulsford possession.

Only Charles could come and go as he pleased; only he could dare break in without notice on the sacred yearly business of prolonging life. Although he had had ninety-three years of it, the Duke still wanted more. He liked being alive, and it pleased him to keep Streatley waiting. Streatley, and the other three children of his first marriage—absurd, he thought, to have to refer to those four old things as children—were unpopular with their father. He had never at any time cared much for them, and had begun to be really angry with them when he was a lively seventy, and perceived that the possession of children bordering on a heavy fifty made him seem less young than he felt himself to be. Now that they were practically seventy themselves, and old seventies too, and he not looking a day different, he hoped, from what he had looked thirty years before, he was angrier with them than ever. He admitted that other people might be old at ninety-three, but he wasn't; he was the exception. He didn't feel old, and he didn't, he considered, look old, so what was all this talk of age? The press never

mentioned him without the prefix venerable; people pretended he was deaf, when he could hear as well as any man if he wasn't mumbled at; Laura, was continually making him sit out of draughts, just as if he were a damned invalid; arms were offered him if he wanted to walk a few steps—he couldn't appear in the House without some officious member of it, usually that ass Chepstow, who was eighty if a day himself, ambling across to help; and every time he had a birthday the newspapers tumbled over each other with their offensively astonished congratulations. Couldn't a man be over ninety without having it perpetually rubbed into him that he was old?

What he loved was his brood of young ones—Laura, Terry, and Charles; and of this lively trio the dearest to him was Charles. So that, looking up from his seedcake and seeing his last born coming into the room, not only entirely unexpectedly but with a young woman, though he was surprised he wasn't angry; and when on their coming close to him he perceived the exceeding fairness of the young woman, his surprise became pleasurable; very pleasurable; in fact, pleasurable to excess.

He stared up at Sally a moment, not listening to what Charles was saying, and then struggled to get on to his feet. Younger than his three young ones ... much, much younger than his three young ones ... youth, ah, youth ... lovely, lovely youth. ...

Charles wanted to help him, but was thrust aside. 'Poor old gentleman,' said Sally, catching him by the arm as he seemed about to lose his balance and drop back into the chair.

'Married?' asked the Duke, breathing hard after his exertion, and looking at Charles.

Charles shook his head.

''Course I'm married,' said Sally with heat.

'He means us,' said Charles.

'Us?' repeated Sally, much shocked.

'You're going to be, then,' said the Duke, looking first at her and then at Charles, his face red with pleasure.

Charles shook his head again, and laughed.

But the Duke didn't laugh. He stared at him a minute, and then said, 'Fool.'

'I *got* a nusband,' said Sally indignantly.

'He can't hear,' said Charles. 'He's very deaf.'

'What does she say?' asked the Duke. 'Speak clearly, my dear—no, don't shout,' he added; though Sally, far from going to shout, wasn't even opening her mouth. Poor old gentleman, she thought, gazing at him in silent compassion; fancy him still being anybody's father.

The Duke took her hand in a dry, cold grip.

'Like shakin''ands with a tombstone,' thought Sally.

And she was filled with so great a pity for anything so old that she didn't feel shy of him at all, and in the coaxing voice of one who is addressing a baby she said, ''Ave yer tea while it's 'ot—do, now.'

Charles looked at her astonished. Nearly everybody was afraid of his father. She reminded him of the weaned child in Isaiah, who put its hand fearlessly on the cockatrice's den.

'What does she say?' asked the Duke, gazing at her with delight.

'This is Mrs. Luke, Father—a friend of Laura's,' shouted Charles, 'and I've brought her—'

'Write it down, my dear,' said the Duke, not heeding Charles, and drawing Sally into a chair next his own and pushing paper and a pencil towards her with his shaking old hands. 'Write down what you were saying to me.'

Charles became anxious. He felt sure Sally couldn't write anything down. Nor could she; for if her spoken words were imperfect her written ones were worse, so that to be given a pencil and paper by the Duke and told to write might have been embarrassing if she hadn't, owing to his extreme age and evident dilapidation, felt he wasn't, as she said to herself, all there. Poor old gentleman, she thought, full of pity. What she saw, sitting heavily in the chair, breathing hard and blinking at her so kindly, was just, thought Sally, the remains, the left-overs; like, she said to herself, her images being necessarily domestic, Sunday's dinner by the time one got to Friday,—not much good, that is, but had to be put up with. No; there was nothing frightening about *him*, poor old gentleman. More like a baby than anything else.

''Ave yer tea while it's 'ot,' she said again, gently putting the paper and pencil aside. 'Do you good,' she encouraged, 'a nice 'ot cup of tea will.'

'He can't hear, you know,' said Charles, much relieved by Sally's attitude. But with what confidence, he thought, couldn't a thing so gracious approach the most churlish, disgruntled of human beings; and his father wasn't either churlish or disgruntled,—he only looked as if he were, and frightened people, and when he saw they were frightened he didn't like them, and frightened them more than ever.

The Duke, watching Sally's every movement with rapt attention, thought when she put her hand on the teapot to feel if it was still hot that she wanted tea herself, and bade Charles ring the bell and order more to be brought, and meanwhile he took the cup she offered him obediently, his eyes on her face. He hadn't got as far, being still in too great a condition of amazement at her beauty, as wondering which of the ancient families of England had produced this young shoot of perfection, and not being able to hear a word she said took it for granted that the delicate-ankled—he was of the practically extinct generation that looks first at a woman's ankles,—slender-fingered creature belonged to his own kind. True her hands were red hands; surprisingly red, he thought, on her presently taking off her gloves, which she rolled up together into a neat tight ball, compared to the flawless fairness of her face; but they were the authentic shape of good-breeding, even if her nails—

The Duke was really surprised when his eyes reached Sally's nails.

Charles drew a chair close up to his father, and began his explanations. He was determined the old man should attend, and shouted well into his ear as he told him that he had motored Laura's friend, Mrs. Luke, down from London, where she had been staying with Laura at Goring House, to Crippenham for the night because it was quieter, and she hadn't been well—

'*I'm* all right,' interrupted Sally, who had been listening in an attitude of polite attention.

'Oh, my dear child—when you fainted,' protested Charles in his ordinary voice, raising a deprecating hand.

'Speak up,' said the Duke, impatiently.

''Course I fainted,' said Sally, looking pleased.

'What does she say?' asked the Duke.

'Yes—and were unconscious for at least half an hour,' said Charles.

'That's right. *And* sick,' said Sally, looking proud.

'Sick? Were you sick as well? Then see how really ill—'

'Speak up, speak up,' said the Duke testily.

But Sally said nothing further, and merely smiled indulgently at Charles.

'What did she say?' asked the Duke, not wishing to lose a word that fell from that enchanting mouth.

'She said,' shouted Charles, 'that she is quite well now.'

'Of course she is,' said the Duke, staring at her face and forgetting her nails. 'Anyone can see she is as perfectly well as she is perfectly beautiful.'

'Oh lor,' thought Sally, 'now *'e's* goin' to begin.'

❁

That afternoon and evening were a triumph for her if she had known it, but all she knew was that she was counting the hours to next day, and Jocelyn, and the settling down at last to her home and her duties. The old man was her slave. Crippenham and everything in it was laid at her feet, and the Duke only lamented that it should be to this one of his houses that she had come, where he couldn't, he was afraid, make her even decently comfortable. Positively at Crippenham there was only one bathroom. The Duke seemed to regard this as a calamity, and Sally listened with mild wonder to the amount he had to say about it.

'Fair 'arps on it, don't 'e, poor old gentleman,' she remarked to Charles; and bending over to the Duke's ear—Charles looked on in astonishment at the fearless familiarity of the gesture—she tried to convey to him that it wasn't Saturday night till the next night, and that by then she'd be in Cambridge, so there was no need for him to take on.

'Eh?' said the Duke. 'What does she say?' he asked Charles.

'She says,' shouted Charles, 'that it doesn't matter.'

How very glad he was that his father was so deaf. Often he had found

his deafness trying, but how glad he was of it now. Not Saturday night. …
Charles fell silent. It was then Friday. Could it be that since the previous
Saturday—?

The Duke, however, knew nothing of Sally except what his eyes told
him, and accordingly he was her slave. When she presently went up
to Laura's room with the housekeeper, who had instructions to place
everything of Lady Laura's at Mrs. Luke's disposal—Crippenham had
no spare rooms, only a room each for the Duke, and Charles, and Laura,
the other six or seven bedrooms being left unfurnished and kept locked
up—and Charles, who from long practice could make his father hear
better than anyone except Laura, settled down to telling him as much
about Sally as he thought prudent, the old man listened eagerly, his
hand behind his ear, drinking in every word and asking questions which
showed that if he was really interested in a subject he still could be most
shrewd.

He was delighted that Sally should have run away from her mother-
in-law, said it was proof of a fine, thoroughbred spirit, and asked who her
father was.

Charles said his name was Pinner.

The Duke then inquired whether he were one of the Worcestershire
Pinners, and Charles said he didn't know.

The Duke then rambled off among his capacious memories, and
presently brought back a Pinner who had been at Christchurch with
him, and who had married, he said, one of the Dartmoors, an extremely
handsome woman, fair too, who was probably the girl's grandmother.

Charles merely bowed his head.

The Duke then asked who the Lukes, apart from this boy-husband
at Ananias, were; for, he said, except the fellow in the Bible, he couldn't
recollect ever having heard of a Luke before.

Charles said all he knew was that they lived at South Winch.

'What?' cried the Duke. 'Has she married beneath her?'—and was so
really upset that for a time he blinked at Charles in silence. Because he felt
that if only this dear son of his had secured the beautiful young creature
he could have died content; and it seemed to him a double catastrophe

that not only should his boy have missed her, but that she should have been caught into a misalliance with some obscure family in a suburb.

'Upon my word, Charles,' he said, after a dismayed silence, 'that's a pity. A very great pity.'

And rambling off into his memories again, he said it was a good thing that poor Jack Pinner was dead, for no man had a keener family feeling than he, and it would have broken his heart to think his grand-daughter had made a mistake of that kind.

He couldn't get over it. He had never, in the whole of his long life, seen anyone to touch this girl for beauty, and that she should, at the very outset of what ought to have been a career of unparalleled splendour and success, have dropped out of her proper sphere and become entangled in a suburb really shocked him. Kings at her feet, all Europe echoing with her name—this seemed to the Duke such beauty's proper accompaniment.

'Tut, tut,' he said, his hands, clasped on the top of his stick, shaking more than usual, 'tut, tut, tut. What was her mother thinking of?'

'Her mother is dead,' said Charles.

'Her father, then. Jack Pinner was no fool. I don't understand how his son—where is he, by the way? I heard something about the Worcestershire estates having been sold after the war—'

Charles said he didn't know where her father was, because, although Sally had told him the shop was at Woodles, he had never heard of Woodles, which indeed is not marked on any map, so that he felt he wasn't lying in saying he didn't know.

The Duke, however, appeared to be seized by a sudden fierce desire to track down his old friend's reprehensible son and tell him what he thought of him, and Charles was dismayed, for no good, he was sure, could come of tracking down Mr. Pinner. Sally, he knew, was anxious her father shouldn't find out her disobedience to his orders, and though of this disobedience Charles held Laura guilty, not Sally, yet he didn't suppose Mr. Pinner would look at it like that, and it was, besides, important, Charles considered, that his father, who had always had a rooted objection to any woman who wasn't well-bred, should go on thinking Sally was a Worcestershire Pinner.

It seemed, then, to Charles a good thing to keep his father and Mr. Pinner apart, and it was therefore with regret that he listened to the old man asking Sally the moment he next saw her, which wasn't till dinner, for she stayed up in her room till fetched down by the scandalised housekeeper, to whom it was a new experience that His Grace should be kept waiting even a minute after the gong had sounded, where her father was.

"Im?' said Sally, turning pale but forced by nature and her upbringing to an obedient truthfulness. "E's at Woodles, 'e is.' And, 'Oh my gracious,' she added to herself, 'they ain't goin' to tell 'im I'm 'ere?'

'What does she say?' the Duke asked Charles.

'She says,' shouted Charles, following his father, who was shuffling along leaning on Sally's arm, to the dining-room, and shouting with outward composure but inward regret, 'that he is at Woodles.'

'Woodles? Woodles?' repeated the Duke. 'Never heard of it. Is it in Worcestershire?'

Sally shook her head. She didn't know where Worcestershire was, but she felt pretty sure Woodles wasn't in it.

'*I* dunno wot it's in,' she said. And then, impelled as always to the naked truth, she added, 'Close by 'ere, any'ow.'

'What does she say?' inquired the Duke, turning again to Charles.

'She says,' shouted Charles, obliged to hand on the answer correctly with Sally listening, but doing so with increased regret, 'that it isn't far from here.'

'How very lucky,' said the Duke, 'and how very odd that I shouldn't have known he was so near.' And he added, when he had been lowered into his chair at the head of the table by the parlourmaid, who held one arm, and his servant, who held the other, 'I'd like to have a talk with that father of yours, my dear.'

Sally turned paler.

'Your grandfather was one of my oldest friends,' continued the Duke, with difficulty unfolding his table-napkin because of how much his hands shook.

'I ain't *got* no grandfather,' said Sally anxiously, who had never heard of him till that moment.

'What does she say?' asked the Duke.

'She says,' began Charles reluctantly—'You know,' he muttered quickly to Sally, for how could he tell the old man what she had said? 'you *have* a grandfather—or had. You must have. Everybody has them.'

'What? What?' said the Duke impatiently. 'Send a message round tonight, Charles, and say with my compliments that I'd very much like to see Pinner. Tell him I'm too old to go to him, so perhaps he'll be obliging enough to come to me some time tomorrow. You can say his father was at Oxford with me if you like, and that I've only just heard he is in the neighbourhood. Say his daughter—'

'Now don't—now *don't* go doin' a thing like that,' Sally faintly begged of Charles.

'What does she say?' asked the Duke.

'Do you think it's wise to break your rule of never seeing anybody while you're here?' shouted Charles. 'You shouldn't,' he added to Sally, 'have told him about Woodles.'

'But 'e *ask* me,' said Sally, distressed.

'You're not obliged to tell everybody everything,' said Charles.

'But if they *asks* me—' said Sally, almost in tears.

The Duke became suddenly cross. 'I hate all this muttering,' he said. 'Why on earth can't you speak up, Charles?'

Charles spoke up. 'It's impossible to send tonight, Father,' he shouted. 'If you won't keep servants here you can't send messages.'

'Then you can go yourself tomorrow,' said the Duke.

'Now don't—now *don't* go doin' a thing like that,' implored Sally again.

'And bring him back in your car,' said the Duke.

'I believe Mrs. Luke would rather not see her father,' shouted Charles.

'That's right,' said Sally, nodding her head emphatically. It did sound awful though—not wanting to see one's father. 'Ain't I gettin' wicked *quick*,' she thought; and hung her head.

He didn't seem to think so, however, the old gentleman didn't, for he leant across to her looking as pleasant as pleasant, and patted her shoulder with his poor shaky old hand, and said she was quite right. Right? Poor old gentleman, thought Sally—past even knowing good from bad.

The Duke bent across and patted her shoulder, a broad smile on his face. Such spirit—running away from her mother-in-law, and kicking at seeing her father—delighted him. She was a high-stepper, this lovely, noble little lady, and all his life he had admired only those women whose steps were high.

'You shan't see him, my dear,' he said. 'Quite right, quite right not to wish to.' And just as she was heaving a sigh of thankfulness he added, 'But *I* will. I really must have a talk with him.'

Strange, thought Charles, this determination to talk with Sally's father. How much better, how much more really useful, to talk with her husband, or her mother-in-law.

❁

After dinner, which Sally ate reluctantly, for she well knew by now that her ways with knives and forks were somehow different from the ways of people like Lukes and dukes, and she felt, besides, that the old gentleman's eye was on her—which it was, but her face, for she was of course now without her hat, engrossed his whole attention, and he saw nothing that her hands were doing—after dinner, after, that is, the small cups of clear soup and the grilled cutlets with floury potatoes which were the evening meal at Crippenham during the severity of the retreat, Charles went into the garden to smoke.

It was a small garden, with nothing in it but a plot of rough grass, some shrubs, a tree or two, and in one comer the shut up four-roomed cottage his father had had built for him and Laura and Terry twenty-five years ago, when first he bought Crippenham, to play at housekeeping in. For years it had been unused; a melancholy object, Charles thought whenever he went into the garden and saw it there, smothered in creepers and deserted, a relic of vanished youth, a reminder that one was getting old.

Beneath its silent walls he wandered up and down, thinking. Every now and then, drawn by the light streaming out through the uncurtained window of his father's study, he crossed the grass and stood a moment looking in, fascinated by the picture inside,—the two figures brilliantly

lit up, the hunched-up old man, with his great bald head glistening in the light, talking, talking, and the exquisite girl, her head bowed in a divine courtesy and patience, listening, though her angelic little face was distinctly troubled. That was because of the fear of her father, Charles knew. She needn't be afraid. If the old man insisted on seeing Pinner he would have to go to Woodles himself, for Charles certainly wasn't going to fetch the creature. Charles didn't at all like Mr. Pinner—imagine turning down a daughter, and such a daughter, when she fled to him for sanctuary!—but though he didn't like him, and quite shared his father's opinion that he should be talked to, wisdom told him that the best thing to do with Mr. Pinner was to leave him alone. The Lukes were the ones needing talking to. The Lukes were the people to deal with. The Lukes—

Yes; what line had he best take with his father in the conversation he meant to have after their adorable guest had gone to bed? He wandered up and down the path beneath the shuttered windows of the deserted cottage, deep in reflection. It was clear to him that nobody except his father could really help Sally. Laura, though she was provided with everything, and more than everything, that she wanted, had no separate income of her own, and could do nothing beyond giving moral support. He himself couldn't lift a finger without at once causing scandal. His father could; his father was the only person who could; and his father, Charles determined, should. There were, then, after all, thought Charles, back at the window again and staring through it, compensations in being so old: one could help Sally. His father was revoltingly rich. It would be nothing to him to set her on her feet. True, there was no earthly reason why he should, but sometimes—great God, couldn't a man sometimes come out of the narrow ring of reason, get outside the circle of just claims, forget his cautious charities, be unbusinesslike, break traditions, shock solicitors, and for once in his life do something absurd, and beautiful, and entirely for nothing?

Charles threw away his cigarette, and with his hands in his pockets took a few quick strides about the little garden, excited, stirred out of his customary calm. Why, even if the old man did as little for her as interrupt his rest-cure for a few hours and take her into Cambridge himself, just for

the girl to be seen with him, just for her to appear under his wing, would knock every obstacle out of her path, except that one obstacle of young Luke's poverty. His father knew the Master of Ananias; his father knew everybody. They all listened when he spoke. The merest indication of a wish would be attended to. It was, of course, regrettable that there should be this attentiveness to a man merely because he was rich and a duke, but by God, thought Charles, how damned convenient.

He walked quickly about the little garden. His father must be made to understand the situation. He would sit up all night if necessary, getting it into his head. He would tell him everything Sally had told him, adding anything that should seem in his judgment effective, and only keeping Mr. Pinner back, and the fact that the darling, lovely girl was not at her best in conversation and no good at all at writing things down. His father must take the Lukes by the hand; he must be led to desire to do so above all things. Tact, skill, judgment,—Charles would sit up all night exercising these. Mrs. Luke must be suppressed. The unpleasant youth, who dared be angry, must be taught his incredible good fortune in getting such a wife. Those Lukes—

Suddenly Charles stood still.

Those Lukes …

Queer, but the words had sounded in his ears like a cry of pain.

He was down at the edge of the garden, which ended in a ditch, and on the other side stretched flat, empty fields divided from each other by hedges and rows of elms, darker than the darkness. The air smelt of damp grass. The sky was wonderful, thick strewn with stars. A great peace lay over the fields. They seemed folded in silence. He could hear nothing but the croak of a far away frog. Why, then, had it seemed to him as if—

Charles stood motionless.

Those Lukes … what must they not, since yesterday, have suffered?

Extraordinary, that he hadn't thought of it before.

XIV

Speaking of this time later on, Mrs. Luke was accustomed to say, 'It was a *mauvais quart d'heure*,' and to smile; but in her heart, when she thought of it, there was no smile.

She never forgot that coming down to breakfast on the morning of Sally's flight, so unconscious of anything having happened, pleased that it was a fine day for her party, pleased with the pretty frock she had had sent from Harrods for the child to wear, excited at the prospect of presenting her to a dazzled South Winch, confident, somehow, with that curiously cloudless confidence that seems to lay hold of those about to be smitten by fate, that her beautiful daughter-in-law would behave perfectly, and the whole thing be a great success. Fate was about to smite her; and with more than the disappearance of a daughter-in-law, for that disappearance was but the first step to having to give up, renounce entirely and for always, her son.

Jocelyn came down to breakfast in a good humour too. He had slept like a log, after his series of interrupted nights.

'Sally's late,' he said presently.

'She is, isn't she,' said his mother. 'You won't call her Sally this afternoon, will you, dearest,' she added, giving him his coffee.

'Sorry, Mother. No. I'll remember.'

And soon after that they made their discovery.

'Now what,' Mrs. Luke asked herself, pressing her cold hands together, when an hour or two later it became evident beyond doubt that Sally hadn't merely gone, unaccountably, for an early walk, but had gone altogether, 'now what, what have I done to deserve this?'

And the period of torment began, the period of distress and anxiety,

of anger at first which soon flickered out, and of ever-growing, sickening fear, which she afterwards spoke of quietly as a *mauvais quart d'heure.*

It took some time before she and Jocelyn could be convinced that this wasn't just a before breakfast walk. They clung to the hope that it was, in spite of their knowledge of Sally's lack of initiative. Yet how much more initiative would be needed, they thought, looking at each other with frightened eyes, to do that which it became every moment more and more apparent that she had done.

'But why? But why?' Mrs. Luke kept on asking, pressing her cold hands together.

Jocelyn said nothing.

At eleven o'clock, when it was plain she wasn't coming back, he went out and fetched his car.

'She's gone to her father,' he said.

'But why? Oh, Jocelyn—why?'

'We've made her unhappy,' he said, pulling on his gloves, his face set.

'Unhappy?'

'*I* have, anyway. I've been an infernal cad—I tell you I *have*,' he said, turning on his mother. 'It's no good your telling me I haven't—I *have*.'

And he drove off, leaving her at the gate pressing her cold hands together, and staring after him with wide-open eyes.

But his coming back was worse than his going. It was after six before he got home, tired and dusty, at the fag end of the terrible party.

Mrs. Luke hadn't seen how not to have the party, and had told her friends—ah, how much she shrank from them—when they trooped in punctually at half-past four, eager to see Jocelyn's bride, that her daughter-in-law very unfortunately had had to go that morning to her father, who had suddenly fallen ill.

'An old man,' said poor Mrs. Luke—after dreary and painful thought she had come to the conclusion that if she said it was Sally who had fallen ill, Hammond would be sure sooner or later to give her away,—'an old man, I'm afraid, and liable to—liable to—'

What was he liable to? Mrs. Luke's brain wouldn't work. Her lips, forced into the continual smile of the hostess, trembled. She wanted to

cry. How badly, how badly she wanted just to sit down in a corner alone, and cry.

Then Jocelyn came back. There were still the Walkers there, and Miss Cartwright, and old Mrs. Pugh. Why wouldn't they go? Why did they hang on, and hang on, and never, never go?

They all heard the car. They all knew it was his, because it made so much more noise than anybody else's, and they all knew, because Mrs. Luke had told them, that he had motored his wife himself that morning to her sick father.

'Ah. *Now* we shall have the bulletin,' said the Canon cheerfully; for the illness, probably slight, of an unknown young lady's almost certainly inglorious father couldn't be regarded, he felt, as an occasion for serious gloom. 'No doubt it is a good one, and Jocelyn has been able to bring his wife back with him.'

'I'll go and see,' said Mrs. Luke, getting up quickly, and almost running out of the room.

'What a lot of trouble there is in the world, to be sure,' said old Mrs. Pugh, shaking her head, 'what a lot of trouble.'

'Do you mean the father?' asked Mrs. Walker.

'Who *is* the father?' asked Miss Cartwright.

'Nobody knows,' said the Canon.

'Not really?' said Miss Cartwright.

'Hush—' said the Canon, raising his hand.

Outside the window, which was open, Jocelyn was speaking, and holding their breaths they heard him say, 'Well, Mother? What time did she get back?'

❁

He had been to Mr. Pinner. He had heard what Mr. Pinner had to say. The man had behaved well, had done his duty and sent her straight home; but she hadn't got there.

Fear now descended on Jocelyn's and his mother's souls,—fear ten times greater than the fear of the morning; such fear that they were hardly

aware of the Walkers, and Miss Cartwright, and old Mrs. Pugh, and said goodbye to them mechanically, and hadn't an idea what any of them were saying, and the dusk deepened, and night came, and it grew late, and they sat listening and watching at the window, the window wide open so as to catch the first sounds of a footstep on the path, and they sat in almost complete silence, for they were too much frightened to speak.

That child—somewhere out there in the darkness—that beautiful, ignorant child, by herself in London—Sally, who had only to appear to collect a crowd—Sally, so trustful, so ready to obey anybody. ...

But what did one *do*? Who did one go to? What *could* one do but still, in the dark, not speaking, hardly breathing so intently were they listening, wait?

Fragments of what Mr. Pinner had said drifted in and out of Jocelyn's brain—

'Told 'er to take a taxi all the way ...'

'Give 'er a pound, I did ...'

'Mistake was, lettin' that there car go ...'

That car? What car?

'Mother,' he said suddenly, 'what car?'

'What car, my darling?'

'She arrived there in a car. Her father said so. I forgot to tell you.'

'A car?'

Mrs. Luke got up quickly. So did he. She turned on the light, and it shone on their pale faces staring at each other. He hadn't remembered the car till that moment.

Then without a word she went into the passage, snatched up a coat, wrapped it round herself, and before he could speak was out of the house. 'Wait there,' she called over her shoulder, 'wait there—she might come—'

A car. Whose car but Edgar's? Had Edgar—? Was Edgar—?

No, no. Impossible. She had arrived alone at her father's, and the car had left her there.

But Edgar must know—he could tell her. ...

❁

The butler hadn't wanted to let her in, seeing her looking so wild on the steps when he answered the ring, and no hat on, and an old coat pulled round her shoulders, and he well knowing the affair with his master was off; but what did she care for butlers? She simply pushed past him, and went straight to the library—the handsome, Turkey-carpeted, leathery library she so vividly remembered—and there, as she expected, sat Mr. Thorpe.

He was in a deep chair before a great wood fire, with beside him, on a little Moorish table, his coffee and his liqueur, in his hands the evening paper, and in his mouth a huge cigar. He didn't look in the least unhappy, nor did he look in the least as if he were still angry. On the contrary, he looked contented and pleased. But this expression changed when, turning his head on hearing the door open, he saw Mrs. Luke.

'Edgar,' she said, coming quickly across to him, holding Jocelyn's coat together at her neck with shaking fingers, 'where is Salvatia?'

And it was no use his staring at her as if she were a ghost, which indeed at first he thought she must be, so totally unlike the nicely dressed, ladylike Margery of his misplaced love was this white-faced, ruffled-haired woman,—it was no use his staring at her openmouthed and not answering, and then getting up with deliberation and ostentatiously going towards the bell, for she took no notice of any of that, and went on to say that Salvatia wasn't with her father, who had sent her back to South Winch at once that morning, and hadn't come home. Did he know where she was?

Then Mr. Thorpe, in his turn, was frightened. Not with her father? Not come home?

He stared at Mrs. Luke. What had he done? What, if that were the case, had he done? And instead of the agreeable vision he had been so much pleased with of paying out Margery and her stuck-up son, and the still more agreeable vision of visiting Sally secretly and comfortably at her father's, and developing his friendship with her to almost any extent, he saw, as he stood staring, a picture that really frightened him, a picture of young beauty lost somehow in London, and quite peculiarly defenceless.

What had he done?

But Mr. Thorpe was a man of action. Not his to wring his hands and wait and hope; not his to waste time, either, confessing that he had behaved abominably, and begging Margery's pardon. He did both, but quickly, economising words, and within five minutes was round at Almond Tree Cottage, and within ten minutes his car was round there, and within an hour he and Jocelyn were at Scotland Yard—Jocelyn, who also had no time for anger with Mr. Thorpe, who had no time for anything but searching for and rescuing Sally.

Nor did Mr. Thorpe say much to Jocelyn. His longest speech was to remark, looking out of the window on his side of the car as they tore up to London, that it was a pity one couldn't get out of the habit of behaving first and thinking afterwards. He could go no nearer than this to apologising. He had done Jocelyn a great wrong, he knew, but he couldn't bring himself to say so. To the mother, yes; somehow it was easier to eat humble pie to a woman. Contrition welled up in Mr. Thorpe, but stuck in his throat. It wouldn't come out.

'Damned pity, eh?' he repeated, though not as one who requires an answer.

'It's so beastly *dark*,' was all Jocelyn said, huddled, whitefaced and sick, in the other corner.

❀

Scotland Yard took down particulars.

'Expense no object,' said Mr. Thorpe.

'I can't pay,' said Jocelyn, who was shivering.

'But I can,' said Mr. Thorpe. 'What you've got to do,' he continued to the official, 'is to find her instantly—*instantly*, do you hear? Get a move on. Not a minute to lose. If you'd seen her you'd understand—eh?' he said, turning to Jocelyn for confirmation, who only shivered.

This great place—all the policemen they had met—all the being passed on from one official to another—nothing but officials, officials everywhere—it struck his heart cold. Sally in connection with this? He couldn't speak. His lips were dry. He felt sick.

'Upset,' said Mr. Thorpe confidentially to the official. 'Husband. Bound to be.'

The official nodded, and began telephoning.

'I'll let you know,' he said to Mr. Thorpe, the receiver at his ear. 'It's no use your waiting here. Where can I—that you, Williams? Just one moment—where can I ring you up?'

And he wrote down the name of the hotel Mr. Thorpe gave him, for Mr. Thorpe wasn't going to leave London till he had found Sally, not if he had to stay in it ten years, and then bowed his head in abstracted dismissal, his eyes gone absent-minded while he rapidly conversed with the person at the other end of the telephone.

'Come on,' said Mr. Thorpe, laying hold of Jocelyn's arm.

He took him away to the hotel. The hotel was the Carlton. 'Know me at the Carlton,' said Mr. Thorpe, who in the first year of his widowerhood, before he felt justified in beginning to court Mrs. Luke, had sometimes consoled himself with the cooking of the Carlton. And thus it was that Mrs. Luke presently found herself too at the Carlton, for Jocelyn, who no more than Mr. Thorpe would leave the neighbourhood of Scotland Yard, was concerned for his mother, left alone at Almond Tree Cottage. So Mr. Thorpe sent the car back for her, and also for the necessary luggage. He couldn't quite see himself appearing next morning at the Carlton in the dinner-jacket he put on every night at Abergeldie because of the butler.

❁

She arrived at one in the morning. Mr. Thorpe by that time had taken three bedrooms, and a sitting-room.

'I can't pay,' said the unhappy Jocelyn on seeing these arrangements.

'But I can,' said Mr. Thorpe.

'I don't know why—' began Jocelyn, shrinking under the accumulating weight of obligations.

'But *I* do,' said Mr. Thorpe, cutting him short.

Mrs. Luke never forgot that pink sitting-room at the Carlton, for it was there that Jocelyn, walking up and down it practically demented, cast

himself adrift from her for ever. And yet what had she done but try to help him? What had she ever done all his life but love him, and try to help him?

'There's been too much of that—there's been too *much* of that,' Jocelyn raved, when she attempted, faintly, for she was exhausted, to defend herself.

She soon gave up. She soon said nothing more at all, but sat crying softly, the tears dropping unnoticed on her folded hands.

Before this, however, while the car was fetching her from South Winch, Mr. Thorpe, bracing himself to his plain and unshirkable duty, invited Jocelyn into the sitting-room he had engaged, and ordered whiskies and sodas. These he drank by himself, while Jocelyn, his head sunk on his chest, sat stretched full length in a low chair staring at nothing; and having drunk the whiskies, Mr. Thorpe felt able to perform his duty.

Which he did; and in a series of brief sentences described the girl's state of mind when he accidentally found her down by his fence, and how it was the idea of being left alone with Jocelyn's mother till the summer that she couldn't stand, because she simply couldn't stand his mother. Frightened of her. Scared stiff. Just simply couldn't stand her.

At this Jocelyn, roused from his stupor, looked round at Mr. Thorpe with heavy-eyed amazement.

'Couldn't stand my mother?' he said in tones of wonder, his mouth remaining open, so much was he surprised.

'That's the ticket,' said Mr. Thorpe; and drank more whiskey.

He then, after explaining that he wasn't an orator, told Jocelyn in a further series of brief sentences that it was unnatural for wives to live with their mothers-in-law instead of with their husbands, that his wife knew and felt this, and that she was, besides, having been brought up on the Bible and being otherwise ignorant of life, genuinely and deeply shocked at what she regarded as his disobedience to God's laws.

'But my mother,' said Jocelyn, 'has been nothing but—'

'Sees red about your mother, that girl does,' interrupted Mr. Thorpe.

'But *why?*' said Jocelyn, sitting up straight now, his brows knitted in the most painful bewilderment.

'Don't ask *me*,' said Mr. Thorpe; and drank more whiskey.

He then told Jocelyn, in a third and last series of brief sentences, for after that not only had he said his say but the young man didn't seem able to stand any more, that if—no, when—his wife was restored to him, he had better see to it that his mother was as far off and as permanently off as possible; and then, Jocelyn by this time looking the very image of wretchedness, he gave him, poor young devil, the bit of comfort of telling him that his wife had only meant to leave him till she knew he was in Cambridge, and that then she had been going to join him there, and live in some rooms somewhere near him. It wasn't him she was running from, it was his mother.

'All that girl asked,' said Mr. Thorpe, bringing his fist, weighty now with whiskey, down shatteringly on the table, 'was a couple of rooms, and you sometimes in them. A girl in a thousand. If she'd been as ugly as sin she'd still have been a treasure to any man. But look at her—*look* at her, I say.'

'Oh, damn you!' shouted Jocelyn, springing to his feet, unable to bear any more, 'Damn you—damn you! How dare you, how dare you, when it's you—*you*—'

And he came towards Mr. Thorpe, his arms lifted as if to strike him; but he suddenly dropped them to his sides, and turning away gripped hold of the chimney-piece, and, laying his head on his hands, sobbed.

❁

Charles Moulsford, then, was right, and the Lukes suffered. So did Mr. Thorpe, for it was all his fault really. He was amazed at the ease and swiftness with which he had slipped away from being evidently and positively a decent man into being equally evidently and positively an evil-doer. That he had done evil, and perhaps irreparable evil, was plain. Yet its beginning was after all quite small. He had only helped the girl to go to her father. Such an act hadn't deserved this tremendous punishment. Mr. Thorpe couldn't help feeling that fate was behaving unfairly by him. If all his impulses and indiscretions throughout his life had been punished like this, where would he have been by now?

But that was neither here nor there. This terrible thing had happened, and it was his fault. Without him she couldn't have budged; and, weighed down by his direct responsibility, when Jocelyn advanced on him with his fists uplifted ready to strike him he rather hoped he would actually do it, and when instead the poor devil broke down and began to cry, Mr. Thorpe was very unhappy indeed. Perhaps he hadn't been quite tactful in the things he had said to him. Perhaps he had been clumsy. Whiskey was tricky stuff. He had only meant—

Then Margery arrived, with her white face and great, scared eyes, and found her son standing there holding on to the chimneypiece and crying, and—well, Mr. Thorpe felt he had overdone the getting even business altogether, and discovered with a shock that he could no longer regard himself as a decent man.

He went away to his bedroom, leaving them alone. He didn't know what they were saying to each other, but he could hear that Jocelyn seemed to be talking a good deal. Couldn't stop, the poor devil couldn't; went on and on.

Mr. Thorpe sat down to think out plans, the ceaseless sound of that voice in his ears. It was he who had lost the girl, and it was he who was going to find her. If Scotland Yard found her first so much the better, but he wasn't going to sit still till they did, he was going off on his own account next morning. He'd begin by sending Margery home, who was doing no good here, he could tell by the sounds coming through the door, pack Jocelyn, who was doing no good here either raving like that, off to Cambridge because of the remote chance that the girl was going to be able after all to do what she said and join him there, and he himself would meanwhile make a bee-line for her father.

Pinner was the man. Pinner was the point to start from. Pinner and Woodles. She had said his name was Pinner, and that he lived at Woodles. Woodles? Funny sort of name that, thought Mr. Thorpe, trying to cheer himself up by being amused at it. The sounds coming through the door weren't very cheering. Raving, the poor young devil was,—raving at his mother. Mr. Thorpe feared he had perhaps been quite beastly tactless, telling him of Sally's not being able to stand his mother. He felt very

uncomfortable about it, sitting there with those sounds in his ears. And meanwhile the night was slipping along, and where was that girl?

There were so many possible answers to this question, and all of them so very unpleasant, that Mr. Thorpe couldn't, he found, sit quiet in his chair. Three o'clock. Fourteen hours now since last she was seen …

He got up and walked about. In the next room he could hear Jocelyn doing the same thing. No—dash it all, thought Mr. Thorpe after listening for some time to the ceaseless voice, he couldn't be allowed to go on at his mother like that. He'd had close on a couple of hours of it. All very well being heartbroken, all very well being out of one's senses, but he couldn't be allowed—

Mr. Thorpe opened the door and went in. There was Jocelyn, striding about the room, up and down, round and round, enough to make one giddy just to see him, his words pouring out, his face convulsed, and there sitting looking at him, not saying a word, with tears rolling down her face, was his mother.

No—damn it all—there were limits—

'Better shut up now, eh?' said Mr. Thorpe firmly to the demented young man. 'Said all there's to say long ago, I bet. Won't help, you know—this sort of thing.'

'I'm telling my mother—I'm making it clear to her once and for all,' raved Jocelyn, who indeed no longer had the least control of himself, 'that if I ever find Sally never again as long as I *live* shall she come between us, never shall she set *foot*—'

'Oh, shut up. We know all that, don't we, Margery. Who's going to come between you, you silly young ass? Look here—no good crying, you know,' said Mr. Thorpe, going to Mrs. Luke and putting his arm round her. It seemed natural. For two pins he would have kissed her. Habit. Can't get away from habits.

But Mrs. Luke didn't appear to know he was there.

Her eyes, from which the tears dropped slowly and unnoticed, were fixed only on Jocelyn.

'He's so tired—so tired,' she kept on whispering to herself. 'Oh, my darling—you're so *tired*.'

It was Mr. Pinner's turn next day to have a bad time, and he had it. He had a most miserable day, from noon on, when the same car that had brought Sally drew up in front of his shop, and a stout elderly gentleman with a red face and a bristly moustache got out, and came and spent half an hour with him.

What a half hour that was; but all of a piece with the life he seemed now to be living. The day before there had been first Sally, and then Mr. Luke, and now there was this gentleman. Mr. Luke had soon been pacified, and only wanted to be getting home again, but the stout gentleman came in and sat down square to it, and at the end of half an hour Mr. Pinner felt as if he had been turned inside out, and wouldn't ever be able to look himself in the face again.

For Sally hadn't gone home, and it was his fault that she hadn't. These were the facts; the gentleman said so. Terrible, terrible, thought Mr. Pinner, shrinking further than ever into his trousers. The first fact was terrible enough, but the second seemed even worse to Mr. Pinner. Responsibility, again—and he who had supposed when he got Sally safely married that he had done with it for good and all!

At first he had tried to make a stand and hold up his head, and had said politely—nothing lost by manners,—'Excuse me, sir, but are you by any chance the gentleman my daughter mentioned to me as 'er father-in-law?' And when the gentleman, after a minute, said he was, Mr. Pinner told him that in that case it was he who was responsible for her loss, for it was he who had lent her the car in which she had left her husband.

Wasn't this true? Anybody would have thought so; but before Mr. Pinner could say knife the boot had been put on the other leg, and he found that it was his fault and his only that she was lost, because he hadn't, as the gentleman said was his plain duty, taken her back himself to the very door.

Mr. Pinner, constitutionally unable not to feel guilty if anybody told him loud enough that he was, at once saw the truth of this. Terrible. Awful. Fancy. Yes, indeed—a daughter like that. Yes, indeed—*any* daughter, but

a daughter like that, a daughter in a million. No, indeed—he didn't know how he came not to do such a thing—

And the more Mr. Thorpe cross-examined him about the details of that seeing-off at the station, the more did Mr. Pinner's conduct appear criminal; for, under Mr. Thorpe's searching questions, Mr. Pinner somehow began to be sure the lady in the carriage hadn't been a lady at all, but something quite different, something terrible and wicked, who had carried Sally off into the sort of place one doesn't mention. He remembered her black eyes, and how they rolled—

'Rolled, eh?' said Mr. Thorpe, who was snatching at Mr. Pinner's words almost before they appeared, trembling, on the edge of his mouth.

Yes—rolled. And bold-looking, she was too,—bold-looking, and pat as you please at answering. Not Mr. Pinner's idea at all of a modest woman. Yes, and the compartment smelt of scent, now he came to think of it— yes, he dared say it was cheap scent. And powdered, her face was—he had remarked on it to himself, after the train had gone.

Thus did Mr. Thorpe's own fears get by cross-examination into Mr. Pinner's mind, and by the end of the half hour Mr. Pinner was as much convinced as Mr. Thorpe that Sally had fallen into the hands of somebody of whom Mr. Thorpe used an expression that Mr. Pinner wouldn't have soiled his lips with for any sum one cared to mention. And then, after swearing at him, and asking him what sort of a father he thought he was, and Mr. Pinner, who by this time was wishing with all his heart that he wasn't a father at all, tremblingly begging him not to blaspheme, Mr. Thorpe went away.

'What 'ad I better do now, sir?' Mr. Pinner asked, following him out on to the steps in much distress, clinging to him in spite of his horrifying language.

'You? What can *you* do? You've done your damnedest—'

'Sir, sir—'

And he got into his car, and Mr. Pinner heard him tell the chauffeur to drive like the devil to London and go to Liverpool Street Station; and it seemed as if in a flash the street were empty, and he alone.

That afternoon Mr. Pinner himself arrived at Liverpool Street Station—an anxious little man in his Sunday clothes, his blue eyes staring with anxiety. He couldn't just stay in his shop, and as likely as not never hear anything more, either one way or the other. He must do something. He must ask questions. Nobody would tell him if Sally were found or not, if he didn't. She herself might some day perhaps drop him a line, but she wasn't much of a one for writing, and besides he had been harsh to her. 'Don't believe you loves me,' she had said, crying bitterly when he scolded her so and wouldn't let her stay with him. Love her? He loved her dearly. She was all he had in the world. If anything had happened to that girl—

He timidly stopped a porter, and began to inquire. The porter, who was busy, stared at him and hurried on. He then tried a guard, who said, 'Eh?' very loud, looked past him along the platform, waved a green flag, jumped on to a train, and departed.

He then tried another porter; several porters; and at last, more timid than ever by this time, approached a ticket-collector.

Nobody seemed to have time for Mr. Pinner. His trousers were against him. So was his hat; so was everything he said and did. The ticket-collector, who didn't like shabbiness and meekness, ignored him. He knew perfectly well who Mr. Pinner was talking about, for the whole station was invariably aware of any of the Duke's family passing through it, and everybody the day before had seen Lady Laura and the young lady. Mr. Pinner hadn't got beyond his first words of description before the ticket-collector knew what he was driving at, but he only looked down his long nose at the flushed little man in the corkscrew trousers, and said nothing. Give a thing like that information about her ladyship's movements? Not much.

Yet this same ticket-collector, only an hour or two before, had been wax in the gloved hands of Mr. Thorpe, and with these words had parted from him:

'Thank you, sir. Don't mention it, sir. No trouble at all. Yes—a very striking young lady indeed, sir. Her ladyship was going to Goring House

for a couple of days, so the chauffeur told me. Much obliged, sir. Yes, sir—Lady Laura Moulsford. That's right, sir—the Duke of Goring's daughter.'

This same ticket-collector had said all that; and to Mr. Pinner he said not a word. He merely down his long nose looked at him, and when the little man explained that he was the fair young lady's father he looked at him more glassily than ever. So that presently for very shame Mr. Pinner couldn't go on standing there asking questions that got no answers, and after lingering awhile uncertainly in the ticket-collector's neighbourhood, for something told him that this man could throw light on Sally's disappearance if he would, he went sorrowfully, but unresentfully, away.

Presently he found himself in South Winch. He seemed to have drifted there, not knowing what to do or where to go next, and unable to bear the thought of his lonely shop and of nobody's letting him know about anything. He had thought it fine and peaceful at first to be independent and at last alone, but it didn't seem so now. He missed his wife. Nobody now to mind what he did, good or bad. Nobody.

In South Winch he sought out the grocer, so as to get Jocelyn's address, preferring him to the Post Office because the smell of currants and bacon made him feel less lonely, and, having followed the directions the grocer gave him, found the road and the house, and opened the white gate with deferential trepidation. Timidly at the door he asked if he might say a word to Mr. Luke, and the little maid, at once at ease with his sort of clothes, inquired pleasantly if Mrs. Luke wouldn't do just as well; better, suggested the little maid, because she was there, and Mr. Jocelyn wasn't. In fact she offered Mrs. Luke to Mr. Pinner, she pressed her upon him,—a lady he wouldn't have dreamt of disturbing if left to himself.

So that Mr. Pinner, without apparently in the least wanting to, found himself in a beautiful drawing-room, and there by the fire sat a lady, leaning back on some cushions as though she were tired.

At first he thought she was asleep, and he was beginning to feel extremely awkward when she turned her head and looked at him.

A pale lady. A very pale lady; with a face that seemed all eyes.

'Beg pardon, mum,' said Mr. Pinner, wishing he hadn't come.

The lady went on looking at him. She didn't move. Her hands were

– 228 –

hanging down over the arms of the chair as though she were tired. She just turned her head, but didn't move else.

'It's about Sally,' said Mr. Pinner. "'Appened to be passin', and thought I'd—'

He stopped, for now he came to think of it he didn't rightly know what he had thought.

The lady leant forward in her chair. 'Do you know where she is?' she asked quickly.

'No, mum. Do you?' asked Mr. Pinner.

'No,' said the lady in a queer sort of voice, her head drooping.

Mr. Pinner stood there very awkward indeed.

'Are you her father?' she asked, after a minute.

'That's right, mum,' said Mr. Pinner.

Then she got up and came across to him.

'I'm afraid you are very unhappy,' she said, looking at him.

'That's right, mum,' said Mr. Pinner.

She held out her hand, her eyes on his face.

He shook it respectfully, but without enthusiasm.

'Why, you're cold,' she said.

'That's right, mum,' said Mr. Pinner.

'Won't you come to the fire and get warm?' she said; and before he had time to consider what he ought to do next, Mr. Pinner found himself sitting on the edge of the low chair the lady pushed up for him, warming his knees and not saying anything.

The lady talked a little. She had some nice hot tea made for him, and while he drank it talked a little, and said she was sure they would hear good news soon, and he mustn't worry, because she was sure ...

Then she fell silent too, and they sat there together looking into the fire; and it was funny, thought Mr. Pinner, how just to sit there quietly, and know she was sorry too about everything, seemed to make him feel better. A kind lady; a good lady. What did Sally mean, saying he wouldn't be able to stand her either, if he knew her? The only thing wrong with her that Mr. Pinner could see, was that she looked so ill. Half dead, thought Mr. Pinner.

And after being with her he had more courage to go back to the lonely shop, and she promised faithfully to let him know the minute there was any news, and again told him not to worry and everything would come all right, and he went away comforted.

And she, watching him as he trotted off down to the gate, felt somehow comforted too; not quite so lonely; not quite so lost.

❁

Meanwhile Mr. Thorpe, having lunched and tidied and generally freshened himself up, was on the steps of Goring House, asking for Lady Laura Moulsford.

'Her ladyship is hout,' said the footman haughtily, for he knew at once when Mr. Thorpe added the word Moulsford that he was what the footman called not one of Our Lot. No good his having a car waiting there, and a fur coat, and suede gloves; he simply wasn't one of Our Lot. And the footman, his head thrown back, looked at Mr. Thorpe very much as the ticket-collector was at that moment looking at Mr. Pinner.

'Out, eh?' said Mr. Thorpe. 'When will she be in?'

'Her ladyship didn't say,' said the footman, his head well back.

'You've got a young lady here of the name of Luke. She in?'

'Mrs. Luke is hout,' said the footman, beginning to shut the door.

'Is anybody in?' asked Mr. Thorpe, getting angry.

'The family is hout,' said the footman; and was going to shut the door quite when Mr. Thorpe went close up to him and damned him. And because Mr. Thorpe's temper was quick and hot he damned him thoroughly, and the footman, as he heard the familiar words, strongly reminiscent not only of Lord Streatley but also of the different sergeants he had had during the war, who, however unlike each other to look at, were identical to listen to, thought he must be one of Lady Laura's friends after all, and began to open the door again; and Mr. Thorpe advancing, damning as he went and saying things about flunkeys that were new to the footman, entered that marble hall which had struck such a chill into Sally's unaspiring soul.

The butler appeared. The butler was suave where the footman had been haughty. He had heard some of the things Mr. Thorpe was saying as he hurried from his private sitting-room into the echoing hall, and had no doubt that he was a friend of the family's.

Lady Laura had been in to lunch, but had gone out again; Mrs. Luke was motoring with Lord Charles—who the devil was *he*, Mr. Thorpe wondered—down to Crippenham, where she was going to stay the night. Her ladyship had had a telegram from his lordship to that effect, and she herself was going down the following morning.

'Where's Crippenham?' asked Mr. Thorpe.

The butler was surprised. Up to that moment he had taken Mr. Thorpe for a friend, if an infrequent one, of Lady Laura's.

'His Grace's Cambridgeshire seat,' he said, in his turn with *hauteur*. 'His Grace is at present in residence.'

'Crikey!' thought Mr. Thorpe. 'Got right in with the Duke himself, has she?' And he felt fonder of Sally than ever.

❀

At this point Mr. Thorpe, who had been behaving so well, began to behave less well. The minute the pressure of anxiety was relaxed, the minute, that is, that he no longer suffered, he became callous to the sufferings of the Lukes; and instead of at once letting them know what he had discovered he kept it to himself, he hugged his secret, and deferred sending till some hours later a telegram to each of them saying, '*Hot on her tracks.*'

Quite enough, thought Mr. Thorpe, as jolly again as a sand-boy, and immediately unable to imagine the world other than populated by sand-boys equally jolly,—quite enough that would be to go on with, quite enough to make them both feel better. If he told them more, they'd get rushing off to Crippenham and disturbing the Duke's house-party. The whole thing should now be allowed to simmer, said Mr. Thorpe to himself. Sally should be given a fair field with her duke, and not have relations coming barging in and interrupting.

But what a girl, thought Mr. Thorpe, slapping his knee—he was in his

car, on the way to his club—what a girl. She only had to meet dukes for them to go down like ninepins at her feet. Apart from her beauty, what spirit, what daring, what initiative, what resource! It had been worth all the anxiety, this magnificent *dénouement*. Safe, and sounder than ever. A glorious girl; and he too had at once seen how glorious she was, and at once, like the Duke, fallen at her feet. That girl, thought Mr. Thorpe, who began to believe she would rise triumphant even over a handicap like Jocelyn, might do anything, might do any mortal thing,—no end at all, there wasn't, to what that girl couldn't do. And, glowing, he telephoned to Scotland Yard, and later on, after having had his tea and played a rubber of bridge, sent his telegrams.

Then he went quietly home. Things should simmer. Things must now be left to themselves a little. He went quietly home to Abergeldie, and didn't let Mrs. Luke know he was there. Her feelings, he considered, were sufficiently relieved for the present by his telegram; things must now be allowed to simmer. And he took a little walk in his shrubbery, and then had a hot bath, and dressed, and dined, ordering up a pint of the 1911 *Cordon Rouge,* and sat down afterwards with a great sigh of satisfaction by his library fire.

He smoked, and he thought; and the only thing he regretted in the whole business was the rude name he had called Lady Laura Moulsford to that fool Pinner. But, long as he smoked and thought, it never occurred to him to resent, or even to criticise, the conduct of the Moulsford family. Strange as it may seem, considering that family's black behaviour, Mr. Thorpe dwelt on it in his mind with nothing but complacency.

XV

At Crippenham next morning it was very fine. London and South Winch were in a mist, but the sun shone brightly in Cambridgeshire, and the Duke woke up with a curiously youthful feeling of eagerness to get up quickly and go downstairs. He knew he couldn't do anything quickly, but the odd thing was that for years and years he hadn't wanted to, and that now suddenly he did want to; and just to want to was both pleasant and remarkable.

He had been thinking in the night,—or, rather, Charles's thoughts, placed so insistently before him, had sunk in and become indistinguishable from his own; and he had thought so much that he hadn't gone to sleep till nearly five. But then he slept soundly, and woke up to find his room flooded with sunshine, and to feel this curiously agreeable eagerness to be up and doing.

The evening before, when Charles came in from the garden and packed his bewitching guest off to bed, he had been very cross, and had listened peevishly to all his son was explaining and pointing out; not because he wasn't interested, or because he resented the suggestions being made, but simply because the moment that girl left the room it was as if the light had gone out,—the light, and the fire. She needn't have obeyed Charles. Why should she obey Charles? She might have stayed with him a little longer, warming him by the sight of her beauty and her youth. The instant she went he felt old and cold; back again in the condition he was in before she arrived, dropped back again into age and listlessness, and, however stoutly he pretended it wasn't so, into a deathly chill.

Now that, thought the Duke, himself surprised at the difference his guest's not being in the room made, was what had happened to David too towards the end. They didn't read it in the Lessons in church on Sundays,

but he nevertheless quite well remembered, from his private inquisitive study of the Bible in his boyhood, how they covered David when he was old with clothes but he got no heat, and only a young person called the Shunammite was able, by her near presence, to warm him. The Duke didn't ask such nearness as had been the Shunammite's to David, for he, perhaps because he was less old, found all he needed of renewed life by merely looking at Sally; but he did, remembering David while Charles talked, feel aggrieved that so little as this, so little as merely wishing to look at her, should be taken from him, and she sent to bed at ten o'clock.

So he was cross, and pretended not to understand, and anyhow not to be interested. But he had understood very well, and in the watches of the night had come to his decision. At his age it wouldn't do to be too long coming to decisions; if he wished to secure the beautiful young creature—Charles said help, but does not helping, by means of the resultant obligations, also secure?—he must be quick.

He rang for his servant half an hour before the usual time. He wanted to get up, to go to her again, to look at her, to sit near her and have her fragrant, lovely youth flowing round him. The mere thought of Sally made him feel happier and more awake than he had felt for years. Better than the fortnight's cure of silence and diet at Crippenham was one look at Sally, one minute spent with Sally. And she was so kind and intelligent, as well as so beautiful—listening to every word he said with the most obvious interest, and not once fidgeting or getting sleepy, as people nowadays seemed to have got into the habit of doing. It was like sitting in the sun to be with her; like sitting in the sun on a warm spring morning, and freshness everywhere, and flowers, and hope.

Naturally, having found this draught of new life the Duke wasn't going to let it go. On the contrary, it was his firm intention, with all the strength and obstinacy still in him, to stick to Sally. How fortunate that she was poor, and he could be the one to help her. For she, owing all her happiness to him, couldn't but let him often be with her. Charles had said it would be both new and desirable to do something in one's life for nothing; but the Duke doubted if it were ever possible, however much one wished to, to do anything for nothing. In the case of Sally it was manifestly

impossible. Whatever he did, whatever he gave, he would be getting far more back; for she by her friendship, and perhaps affection, and anyhow by her presence, would be giving him life.

'Come out into the garden, my dear,' he said, when he had been safely helped downstairs—the stairs were each time an adventure—putting his shaking hand through her arm. 'I want to see your hair in the sun, while I talk to you.'

And leading him carefully out, Sally thought, 'Poor old gentleman,' and minded nothing at all that he said. Her hair, her eyes, all that *Oh my ain't you beautiful* business, of which she was otherwise both sick and afraid, didn't matter in him she called the Jewk. He was just a poor old gentleman, an ancient and practically helpless baby, towards whom she felt like a compassionate mother; and when he said, sitting in the sunny sheltered seat she had lowered him on to and taking her hand and looking at her with his watery old eyes, that he was going to give her Crippenham, and that the only condition he made was that he might come and do a rest-cure there rather often, she smiled and nodded as sweetly and kindly as she smiled and nodded at everything else he said.

Like the croonings of a baby were the utterances of the Duke in Sally's ears; no more meaning in them, no more weight to be attached to them, than that. Give her Crippenham? Poor old gentleman. Didn't know what he was talking about any more, poor old dear. She humoured him; she patted his arm; and she wished to goodness Laura would be quick and come and take her to her husband.

Sally now longed to get to Jocelyn as much as if she had passionately loved him. He was her husband. He was the father of the little baby. Her place was with him. She had had enough of this fleshpot business. She was homesick for the things she knew,—plain things, simple things, duties she understood. Kind, yes; kind as kind, the picks were, and they meant well; but she had had enough. It wasn't right it wasn't, at least it wasn't right for her, to live so fat. What would her father have said if he had seen her in the night in Laura's bedroom, among all that lot of silver bottles and brushes and laces and silks, and herself in a thin silk nightgown the colour of skin, making her look stark naked? What would he have said if he had

seen her having her breakfast up there as though she were ill,—and such a breakfast, too! Fleshpots, he'd have said; fleshpots. And he would have said, Sally, strong if inaccurate in her Bible, was sure, that she had sold her husband for a mess of fleshpots.

This was no life for her, this was no place for her, she thought, her head bowed and the sun playing at games of miracles with her hair while the Duke talked. She drew impatient patterns with the tip of her shoe on the gravel. She hardly listened. Her ear was cocked for the first sounds of Laura. She ached to have done with all this wasting of time, she ached to be in her own home, getting on with her job of looking after her man and preparing for her child. 'Saturday today,' she mused, such a lovely look coming into her eyes that the Duke, watching her, was sure it was his proposed gift making her divinely happy. 'We'd be 'avin' shepherd's pie for dinner—or p'raps a nice little bit of fish. ....'

And, coming out of that pleasant dream with a sigh, she thought, 'Oughtn't never to 'ave met none of these 'ere. All comes of runnin' away from dooty.'

Apologetically she turned her head and looked at the Duke, for she had forgotten him for a moment, besides having been thinking on lines that were hardly grateful. Poor old gentleman—still keeping on about giving her Crippenham. Crippenham? She'd as soon have the cleaning of Buckingham Palace while she was about it as of that great, frightening house—or, come to that, of a prison.

But how like a bad dream it was, being kept there with the morning slipping past, and she unable to reach him across the gulf of his deafness. By eleven o'clock she was quite pale with unhappiness, she could hardly bear it any longer. Would she have to give manners the go-by and take to her heels once more? This time, though, there would be no kind father-in-law to lend her a car; this time she would have to walk,—walk all the way, and then when she got there find Jocelyn unaided. And the old gentleman kept on and on about Crippenham being hers, and everything in it. ...

"'E's nothin' but a nimage,' she said to herself in despair. 'Sits 'ere like a old idol. Wot do 'e know about a married woman's dooties?'

'Where's Charles?' asked the Duke.

Sally shook her head. She hadn't seen a sign of him that morning.

'I want him to get my solicitor down—no time to lose,' said the Duke. 'You're to have the place lock, stock and barrel, my dear, such as it is—servants and all.'

Servants and all? Poor old gentleman. Why, she wouldn't know which end of a servant to start with. She with servants? And these ones here who, however hard she tried up there in the bedroom, wouldn't make friends. They called her Madam. She Madam? Oh, my gracious, thought Sally, shrinking in horror from such a dreadful picture.

'It's a hole of a place,' went on the Duke, 'and quite unworthy of you, but we can have more bathrooms put in, and it'll do till we find something you like better. And Charles tells me you married rather suddenly, and haven't got anywhere to go to at present. He also says you have to live close to Cambridge, because of your husband's studies. And he also says, and I entirely agree with him, my dear, that you oughtn't to be in Cambridge itself, but somewhere more secluded—somewhere where you won't be seen quite so much, somewhere hidden, in fact. Now I think, I really do think, that Crippenham, in spite of all its disadvantages, does exactly fulfil these requirements. And I want you to have it, my dear—to take it as my wedding present to you, and to live in it very happily, and bless it and make it beautiful by your presence.'

Thus the Duke.

''E don't 'alf *talk*,' thought Sally, quivering to be gone.

❁

Charles, on being sent for by the Duke, was nowhere to be found. That was because he was in South Winch. He had gone off at daybreak in his car, and at the very moment his father woke up to the fact of his absence and asked where he was, he was standing in the drawing-room at Almond Tree Cottage, his eyes fixed eagerly on the door, waiting for Mrs. Luke.

He hadn't been able to sleep for thinking of her. Somehow he had got it into his head that she, more than her son, would suffer through Sally's disappearance, and be afraid. Because, thought Charles, she would feel

that it was from her the girl had run, and that any misfortune that might happen to her would be, terribly, laid at her door. For two whole days and two whole nights that unfortunate woman must have gone through torture. What Charles couldn't understand was why he hadn't thought of this before. Indeed his and Laura's conduct had been utterly unpardonable. The least he could now do, he thought, as he lay wide awake throughout the night, was to get to South Winch without losing a minute, and put Mrs. Luke out of her misery, and beg her forgiveness.

She was in the garden when he arrived. The little maid, staring at the card he asked her to take to her mistress, said she would fetch her, and ushered him into the drawing-room, where he waited with the books, the bright cushions, the Tiepolo, and two withered tulips in a glass from which nearly all the water had dried away; and while he waited he fought with a feeling he considered most contemptible, in face of the facts, that he was somehow on an errand of mercy, and arriving with healing in his wings,—that he was somehow a benefactor.

Sternly he told himself he ought to feel nothing but shame; sternly he tried to suppress his glow of misplaced self-satisfaction. There was nothing good about him and Laura in this business. They had, the pair of them, been criminally impulsive and selfish. He knew it; he acknowledged it. Yet here he was, secretly glowing, his eyes watching the door, as much excited as if he were going to bestow a most magnificently generous, unexpected present.

Then it opened, and Mrs. Luke came in. He was sure it was Mrs. Luke, for no one else could look so unhappy; and the glow utterly vanished, and the feeling of shame and contrition became overwhelming.

'She's safe,' said Charles quickly, eager to put a stop at once to the expression in her eyes. 'She's at my father's. She's going to Cambridge today to your son. She's been with us the whole time—'

And he went to her, and took her hand and kissed it.

'If it weren't so ridiculous,' he said, his face flushed with painful contrition, still holding her hand and looking into her heavy, dark-ringed eyes, 'I'd very much like to go down on my knees to you, and beg your pardon.'

❧

And while Charles was in South Winch, Laura was in Cambridge, dealing with Jocelyn. She, like Charles, had become conscious of the sufferings of the Lukes, and, like him, was obsessed by them and lost in astonishment that she hadn't thought of them sooner; but for some obscure reason, or instinct, her compunctions and her sympathies were for Jocelyn rather than for his mother, and after a second sleepless night, during which she was haunted by the image of the unfortunate young husband and greatly tormented, she went down, much chastened, to Cambridge by the first possible train, with only one desire now, to put him out of his misery and beg his forgiveness.

So that Jocelyn, sitting doing nothing, his untouched breakfast still littering the table, sitting bent forward in the basket-chair common to the rooms of young men at Cambridge, his thin hands gripped so hard round his knees that the knuckles showed white, his ears strained for the slightest sound on the staircase, his eyes hollow from want of sleep, sitting as he had sat all the previous afternoon after getting Mr. Thorpe's telegram and most of the night, sitting waiting, listening, and perhaps for the first time in his life, for his mother had not included religious exercises in his early education, doing something not unlike praying, did at last hear a woman's step crossing Austen's Court, hesitating at what he felt sure was his corner, then slowly coming up his staircase, and hesitating again at the first floor.

All the blood in his body seemed to rush to his head and throb there. His heart thumped so loud that he could hardly hear the steps any more. He struggled out of his low chair and stood listening, holding on to it to steady himself. Would they come up higher? Yes—they were coming up. Yes—it must be Sally. Sally—oh, oh, *Sally!*

He flew to the door, pulled it open, and saw—Laura.

'It's all right,' she panted, for the stairs were steep and she was fat, 'it is— about Sally—don't look so—' she stopped to get her breath—'so dreadfully

disappointed. She's safe. If you'll—oh, what *stairs*—' she pressed her hand to her heaving bosom—'come with me, I'll—take you—to her—'

And having got to the top, she staggered past him into his room, and dropped into the basket-chair, and for a minute or two did nothing but gasp.

But how difficult she found him. Jocelyn, whose reactions were always violent, behaved very differently from the way his mother at that moment was behaving, placed in the same situation of being asked forgiveness by a Moulsford. Instead of forgiving, of being, as Laura had pictured, so much delighted at the prospect of soon having Sally restored to him that he didn't mind anything, he appeared to mind very much, and quarrelled with her. She, accustomed to have everything she did that was perhaps a little wrong condoned and overlooked by all classes except her own, was astonished. Here she was, doing a thing she had never done before, begging a young man to forgive her, and he wouldn't. On the contrary, he rated her. Rated her! Her, Laura Moulsford. She knew that much is forgiven those above by those below, and had frequently deplored the practice as one that has sometimes held up progress, but now that the opposite was being done to herself she didn't like it at all.

'Oh, what a nasty disposition you've got!' she cried at last, when Jocelyn had been telling her for ten impassioned minutes, leaning against the chimney-piece and glowering down at her with eyes flashing with indignation, what he thought of her. 'I'm glad now, instead of sorry, for what I did. At least Sally has had two days less of you.'

'If you're going to rag me as well—' began Jocelyn, taking a quick step forward as if to seize and shake this fat little incredibly officious stranger,—so like him, his mother would have said, to waste time being furious instead of at once making her take him to Sally.

But Laura, unacquainted with his ways, was astonished.

Then he pulled himself up. 'It's not you I'm cursing really at all,' he said. 'It's myself.'

'Well, I don't mind that,' said Laura, smiling.

'I've got the beastliest temper,' said Jocelyn.

'So I see,' said Laura.

'Do you think,' he asked, for in spite of his anger he was all soft and bruised underneath after his two days of fear, and when the fat stranger smiled there was something very motherly about her, 'I shall ever get over it?'

'Perhaps if you try—try hard.'

'But—look here, I don't care what you say—what *business* had you to make away with my wife?'

'Now you're beginning all over again.'

'Make away with my wife, smash up everything between me and my mother—'

'Oh, *oh*—' interrupted Laura, stopping up her ears, and bowing her head before the storm.

❈

It was ten more minutes before she got him out of his rooms and into a taxi.

'We've lost twenty minutes,' she said, looking at her watch. 'You've lost twenty kisses you might have had—'

'For God's *sake* don't rag me!' cried Jocelyn, gripping her by the arm and bundling her into the taxi.

'But what,' asked Laura, who had tumbled in a heap on the seat, yet who didn't mind being thrown in because she knew she deserved worse than that, 'what else can one do with a creature like you?'

And she told him very seriously, as they heaved along towards Crippenham, that the real mistake had been Sally's marrying beneath her.

'Beneath her?' repeated Jocelyn, staring.

'Isn't it apparent?' said Laura. 'Angels should only marry other angels, and not descend to entanglements with perfectly ordinary—'

'No, I'm damned if I'm ordinary,' thought Jocelyn. 'And who the devil is *she*, anyhow?'

'Bad-tempered,' continued Laura.

'Yes, I'm beastly bad-tempered,' he admitted.

'Conceited—'

'I swear I'm not conceited,' he said.

'Aren't you?' said Laura, turning her head and scrutinising him with bright, mocking eyes.

And then, coming swift and silent as an arrow along the road towards their taxi, she saw her father's car.

'Oh, stop!' she cried, leaping to her feet and thrusting as much of herself as would go through the window. 'Here's my father—yes, and Sally. Stop—oh, *stop!*' she cried, frantically waving her arms.

❀

It had been decreed by Fate that Jocelyn should be reunited to Sally in the middle of the road just beyond Waterbeach, at the point where the lane to Lyddiatt's Farm turns off; for such was the Duke's desire to help his lovely friend and such his infatuation, that he had actually broken his rule of never emerging from Crippenham, once he got there, till the day appointed for his departure, and was himself taking her to Ananias to hand her over in person to her husband, afterwards lunching with the Master,—a thing unheard of, this lunching, for the Duke disliked the Master's politics and the Master disliked the Duke's, but what wouldn't one do to further the interests, by saying a good word for them, of the young couple?

This he had arranged that morning before coming downstairs, his amazed servant telephoning the message and receiving the Master's hypocritical expressions of pleasure in return, for apart from the Duke's politics the Master was no fonder of a deaf guest than anybody else; and just as Sally, on that garden seat, was coming to the end of her patience and submissiveness and was seriously thinking of jumping up and taking to her heels, the parlourmaid appeared on the path; and when she was quite close she stood still, and opened her mouth very wide, and roared out that the car was at the door; and the Duke, with a final pat of benediction, bade Sally fetch her hat, and come with him to her husband.

So there it was that they met,—the taxi and the Rolls Royce, Laura and Jocelyn, Sally and the Duke. And on the Swaffham Prior side of Waterbeach, where the crooked signpost points to Lyddiatt's Farm, the dull, empty road was made radiant for a moment that day by happiness.

'Stop! Stop!' cried Laura, frantically waving.

'Sally! Oh—oh, *Sally*!' shouted Jocelyn, standing up too, and trying too, behind Laura, to wave.

The chauffeur recognised Laura, and pulled up as soon as he could; the taxi pulled up with a great grinding of its brakes; Jocelyn jumped out of one door, and Laura of the other; and both ran.

'Why,' said Sally, who didn't know what had happened, turning her head and looking in astonishment at the two running figures coming along behind, 'why,' she said, forgetting the Duke was deaf, ''ere *is* Mr. Luke—'

And in another instant Jocelyn was there, up on the step of the car, leaning over the side, dragging her to him with both arms, hugging her to his heart, and kissing her as if there were no one in the world except themselves.

'Sally—oh, my *darling*! Oh, Sally—oh, oh, *Sally*!' cried Jocelyn, raining kisses on her between each word. 'How could you—why did you—oh, yes—I know, I know—I've been a beast to you—but I'm not going to be any more—I swear, I swear—'

'Now don't, Mr. Luke,' Sally managed to say, stifled though she was, 'don't get swearin' about it—'

And pulling her head away from him she was able to attend to the proprieties, and introduce him.

'My 'usband,' introduced Sally, looking over his arm, which was round her neck, at the old man beside her. 'The Jewk,' she said, turning her face back to Jocelyn, who took no notice of the introduction, who didn't indeed hear, because the moment she turned her face—oh, her divine, divine little face!—back to him, he fell to kissing it again.

And Laura, coming panting up just then, got up on the step on the other side of the car, and shouted in her father's ear, who could always hear everything she said, 'This is Jocelyn Luke, Father—Sally's husband.'

And the Duke said, 'I thought it must be.'

XVI

Now the end of this story, which is only the very beginning of Sally, the merest introduction to her, for it isn't to be supposed that nothing more happened in her life,—the end of it is that she did as she was told about Crippenham, and if the Duke had been less than ninety-three there would have been a scandal.

But after ninety there is little scandal. The worst that was said of the Lukes was that they had got hold of the old man, and nobody who saw Sally believed that. Indeed, the instant anyone set eyes on her the Duke's behaviour was accounted for, and after five minutes in her company it became crystal clear that she was incapable of getting hold of anybody. So young, so shy, so acquiescent,—absurd to suppose she ever had such a thing as an ulterior motive. And the husband, too; impossible to imagine that silent scholar, also so young, and rather shy too, or else very sulky,—impossible to imagine him plotting. On the contrary, he didn't seem to like what had happened to him much, and showed no signs whatever either of pleasure or gratitude. But of Jocelyn no one thought long. He was without interest for the great world. He was merely an obscure young man at Cambridge, somebody the Duke's amazing beauty had married.

Sally did, then, as she was told about Crippenham. It was given her, and she took it; or rather, for her attitude was one of complete passivity, it became hers. But she had an unsuspected simple tenacity of purpose, which was later to develop disconcertingly, and she refused to live anywhere except in the four-roomed cottage in the corner of the garden, built years before as a playhouse for Laura and Charles.

On this one point she was like a rock; a polite rock, against which persuasions, though received sweetly and amiably, should beat in vain. So the Duke had the little house fitted up with every known labour-saving

appliance, none of which Sally would use because of having been brought up to believe only in elbow-grease, and two bathrooms, one for her and one for Jocelyn; and he attached such importance to these bathrooms, and he insisted so obstinately on their being built, that Sally could only conclude the picks must need a terrible lot of washing. Whited sepulchres they must be, she secretly thought; looking as clean as clean outside, fit to eat one's dinner off if it came to that, but evidently nothing but show and take-in.

The Duke, much concerned at first, settled down to this determination of Sally's, and explained it to himself by remembering Marie-Antoinette. She had her Trianon. She too had played, as Sally wished to play, at being simple. He consoled himself by speaking of the cottage as Little Trianon; a name Sally accepted with patience, though she told Jocelyn—who was so much stunned at the strange turn his life had taken that she found she could be quite chatty with him, and he never corrected, and never even said anything back—she wouldn't have thought of herself. Some day, the Duke was sure, the marvellous child would grow up and get tired of her Trianon, and then, when she wanted to move into the house, she should find Versailles all ready for her, and very different from what it used to be.

So, on the excuse of seeing to the alterations, he was hardly ever away from Crippenham, and if he had been less than ninety-three there would certainly have been a scandal.

But Jocelyn, who woke up after the wild joy and relief of being reunited to Sally to find himself the permanent guest of a duke, didn't know whether to be pleased or annoyed. The problems of his and Sally's existence were solved, it was true, but he wasn't sure that he didn't prefer the problems. He rubbed his eyes. This was fantastic. It had no relation to real life, which was the life of hard work and constant progress in his cloister at Ananias. Also, its topsy-turviness bewildered him. Here was the Duke, convinced that Sally had married beneath her, and so unshakably convinced that Jocelyn had enormous difficulty in not beginning to believe it too. He couldn't help being impressed by the Duke. He had never met a duke before, never come within miles of meeting one, and was impressed. That first afternoon, when he had been

carried off in the Rolls Royce to Crippenham, he had spent the time between luncheon and tea shut up in the old man's study being upbraided for having taken advantage, as he was severely told, of Sally's youth and inexperience and motherlessness to persuade her into a marriage which was obviously socially disastrous for her; and he couldn't even if he had wished to, which he certainly didn't, tell him about Mr. Pinner, because he couldn't get through the barrier of his deafness. There the old man had sat, with beetling brows and great stern voice, booming away at him hour after hour, and there Jocelyn had sat, young, helpless, silent, his forehead beaded with perspiration, listening to a description, among other things, of the glories which would have been Sally's if he hadn't inveigled her into marrying him. And so sure was the Duke of his facts, and so indignant, that gradually Jocelyn began to think there was something in it, and every moment felt more of a blackguard. In the old man's eyes, he asked himself, would there be much difference between him and Pinner? And was there, in anybody's eyes, much difference? More education; that was all. But of family, in the Duke's sense, he had as little as Pinner, and if Pinner had been to a decent school, as Jocelyn had, and then gone to Cambridge—no, Oxford for Pinner—he would probably have cut quite as good a figure, if not in science then in something else; perhaps as a distinguished cleric.

He sat dumb and perspiring, feeling increasingly guilty; and if he could have answered back he wouldn't have, because the Duke made him feel meek.

This meekness, however, didn't last. It presently, after a period of bewilderment, gave way to something very like resentment, which in its turn developed into a growing conviction that he had become just a cat's paw,—he who, if left to himself, could have done almost anything.

Naturally he didn't like this. But how, for the moment, could he help it? Sally was going to have a baby. They had to live somewhere. It was really heaven-sent, the whole thing. Yet—Sally, whom he had been going to mould, was moulding him. Unconsciously; nothing to do with any intention or desire of her own. And what she was moulding him into, thought Jocelyn, as he drove himself backwards and forwards every day

between Crippenham and Cambridge, between his domestic life and his work, between the strange mixture of emotions at the one end and the clear peace and self-respect at the other, turning over in his mind with knitted brows, as he drove, all that had happened to him in the brief weeks since he had added Sally to his life—what she was moulding him into was a cat's paw.

Yes. Just that.

Were all husbands cat's paws?

Probably, thought Jocelyn.

❁

Mrs. Luke also reacted to the Moulsfords in terms of meekness. Hers, however, lasted. She found them permanently dazzling. Besides, there was nothing to be done. Jocelyn had gone; she had lost him for ever; he would never come back, she very well knew, to the old life of dependence on her. And if he must go, if she must lose him, there really was no one in the world she would more willingly lose him to than the Duke of Goring. For certainly it was a splendid, an exalted losing.

When she had had time to think after that visit from Lord Charles— he had, she considered, a curious attractiveness—and was more herself again, when she had recovered a little from the extreme misery she had gone through and began not to feel quite so ill, she found it easy to forgive her *mauvais quart d'heure*. The Moulsfords were heaping benefits on her boy. They were settling all his difficulties. That morning when she was so unhappy, Lord Charles had been most delightfully kind and sympathetic, and had told her that the Duke, his father, intended to help the young couple,—'You know my son won this year's Rutherford Prize,' she had said. 'Indeed I do,' he had answered in his charming, eager way, adding how much interested his father was in the careers of brilliant young men, especially at Cambridge, helping them in any way he could—and who would not, in such circumstances, forgive?

Mrs. Luke forgave.

The fact, however, remained that she was now alone, and she couldn't

think what her life was going to be without Jocelyn. For how, she wondered, did one live without an object, with no *raison d'être* of any sort? How did one live after one has left off being needed?

That year the spring was late and cold. The days dragged along, each one emptier than the last. There was nothing in them at all; no reason, hardly, why one should so much as get up every morning and dress for days like that,—pithless, coreless, dead days. She tried to comfort herself by remembering that at least she wasn't any longer beaten down and humiliated, that she could lift her head and look South Winch in the face, and look it in the face more proudly than ever before; but even that seemed to have lost its savour. Still, she mustn't grumble. This happened to all mothers sooner or later, this casting loose, this final separation, and to none, she was sure, had it ever happened more magnificently. She mustn't grumble. She must be very thankful. She *was* very thankful. Like Toussaint l'Ouverture—Wordsworth, again—she had, she said to herself, sitting solitary through the chilly spring evenings by her fire after yet another empty day, great allies; only fortunately of a different kind from poor Toussaint's, for however highly one might regard, theoretically, exultations and agonies and love and man's unconquerable mind, she, for her part, preferred the Moulsfords.

But did she?

A bleak little doubt crept into her mind. As the weeks passed, the doubt grew bleaker. Invisible Moulsfords; Moulsfords delightful and most friendly when one met them, but whom one never did meet; Moulsfords full of almost intimacies; Moulsfords who said they were coming to see one again, and didn't come; Moulsfords benignant, but somewhere else: were these in the long run, except as subjects of carefully modest conversation in South Winch—and South Winch, curiously, while it was plainly awe-struck by what had happened to Jocelyn yet was also definitely less friendly than it used to be—were these in the long run as life-giving, as satisfying, as fundamentally *filling* as Toussaint's exultations and agonies?

Ah, one had to *feel*; feel positively, feel acutely. Anything, anything, any anger, any pain, any anxiety, any exasperation, anything at all that stabbed

one alive, was better than this awful numbness, this empty, deadly, settled, stagnant, back-water calm. ...

And one evening, when it had been raining all day, after a period of standing at the drawing-room window looking out at the dripping front garden, where the almond-tree by the gate shivered in the grey twilight like a frail, half-naked ghost, she turned and went to her writing-table, and sat down and wrote a little note to Mr. Thorpe, and asked if he would not come in after his dinner, and chat, and show that they could still be good friends and neighbours; and when she had finished it, and signed herself Margery, with no Luke, she rang for the little maid, and bade her take it round to Abergeldie and bring back an answer.

'For after all,' she said to herself while she waited, standing by the fire and slowly smoothing one cold hand with the other, 'he has *sterling* qualities.'

❁ ❁ ❁

Afterword

❁

What would happen if the impossibly beautiful heroine of fairy tale and myth were actually a real person? And not just a real person, but an ordinary one, with no riches, high status or brilliant mind to go alongside her extraordinary good looks?

That is, in essence, the premise of Elizabeth von Arnim's *Introduction to Sally*. The improbably named Salvatia is considered by everyone to be above her humble station in life because of her appearance, but doesn't fit anywhere else. It is an idea which lends itself equally to tragedy or comedy – and, in von Arnim's novel, manages to be both.

How to convince the reader that Sally is so stunning that every man she encounters is bowled over? Only fifteen years earlier, Max Beerbohm's eponymous heroine of *Zuleika Dobson* had found herself in the same position, inadvertently bewitching all the undergraduates of Oxford University to lose their hearts (and sometimes their lives). In Beerbohm's description, Zuleika is 'not strictly beautiful. Her eyes were a trifle large, and their lashes longer than they need have been […] her features were not at all original'. It is a clever technique, giving little explanation for why people fell for her so universally. Von Arnim goes a step further, and tells us hardly anything that is precise about Sally's appearance. For the most part, von Arnim sticks to generalisations or metaphors: we are simply told that Sally is 'amazingly pretty' and her 'loveliness was startling'. We hear that she is comparable to the goddess

⚙ ⚙ ⚙

Aphrodite, 'she was in a continual condition of radiance'. The most complete description given is:

> She was beauty itself. From the top of her little head, with its flame-coloured hair and broad low brow and misty eyes like brown amber, down along the slender lines of her delicate body to where her small feet were thrust into shabby shoes, she was, surely, perfect.

Even here, we learn that she has red hair and brown eyes and is slender. There is no detailed inventory of her features, nor explanation about exactly what makes Sally so attractive. If beauty is in the eye of the beholder, the reader is largely left to superimpose their own standard of perfection onto this brief sketch.

A contemporary such standard is mentioned late in the novel and adds complication rather than any conclusion:

> The people of Thaxted, for some reason incomprehensible to Charles, because no two women could be more unlike, seemed to think Sally was Mary Pickford. He heard whispers to that effect. Did they then think, too, that he was the person known, he understood, as Doug?

From this addition, the reader can learn that Sally either looks very like – or very unlike – the famous Canadian actress Mary Pickford.

At the time that *Introduction to Sally* was published, Mary Pickford was probably the most popular and recognisable actress in the world, nicknamed the 'Queen of the Movies', while the 'Doug' Charles mentions is her husband Douglas Fairbanks, a famous actor nicknamed 'the King of Hollywood'. Mary Pickford most commonly played *ingénues* in silent films, with her hair styled in long curls for several years after many actresses of the 1920s had opted for the bob. When she did eventually chop off her hair (two years after *Introduction to Sally* was published) it made front-page news in the *New York Times*. Her career

❀ ❀ ❀

would dwindle after the advent of the 'talkies', when spoken dialogue became an option and the silent film era ended (though Pickford herself had suggested that 'adding sound to movies would be like putting lipstick on the Venus de Milo'). But when this novel was published, the comparison doesn't simply tell us that Sally has long ringlets – she is being compared to a woman who was shorthand for innocence and purity.

And that, along with Sally's beauty, is what makes her feel like an other-worldly or angelic creation forced to step into flawed reality. Sally is 'good and modest', 'she liked everyone very much', and she is 'never angry'. Encountering Salvatia is described – appropriately, given her name – as an almost divine experience. When Jocelyn Luke meets her, 'all the things he had thought, and hoped, and been interested in up to then, seemed, directly he saw Sally, dross'. It is the language of a conversion moment. There are echoes of St Paul's words in his letter to the Philippians: 'I consider everything a loss because of the surpassing worth of knowing Christ Jesus my Lord, for whose sake I have lost all things. I consider them garbage, that I may gain Christ' (Philippians 3:8). One biographer of von Arnim has even suggested that Sally is intended to be a Christ figure in the book.

Elizabeth von Arnim's thorough knowledge of the Bible is a thread through *Introduction to Sally*, with the most overt moment of scriptural reference coming from a minor character: '"Scripture says," said Mrs Cupp, sitting up very straight in bed and addressing Cupp's back as he lay speechless beside her, "that 'ooso looks at a woman an' lusts after 'er 'as committed adultery with 'er in 'is 'eart."' Mrs Cupp's reference is to Jesus's Sermon on the Mount, specifically Matthew 5:28 in the King James Version: 'That whosoever looketh on a woman to lust after her hath committed adultery with her already in his heart.'

While Mrs Cupp has biblical basis for blaming the men who can't resist staring at Sally, one of the central themes in the novel is the misogyny which leads to Sally being blamed for this unrequested

⊗ ⊗ ⊗

attention. Though chiefly a comic novel, von Arnim has a lot to say about the way that women are treated, and Sally is the victim of censure from both her father and her husband, among others. Jocelyn, at least, struggles against it:

> He was inclined, though he struggled against it, to blame Sally. He knew it was grossly unfair to blame her, but then it was outside of his theories that a modest woman, however lovely, shouldn't be able in England to proceed on her lawful occasions unmolested. There must be, he thought, something in Sally's behaviour, though he couldn't quite see what.

The idea that there is 'something in [a woman's] behaviour' to blame, rather than finding the ogling men culpable, is sadly a viewpoint that hasn't entirely disappeared in the near-century since *Introduction to Sally* was published.

When the novel was published, von Arnim reported that 'Apparently the American end thinks there is too much sex in the Lukes. I am amazed. Really amazed. It seems to me totally without any love making.' While we are not privy to much that happens behind the bedroom door after the Lukes' marriage, there are plenty of quite daring euphemisms that come earlier in the book. Part of Mr Pinner's desperation to marry off his daughter is to keep her virginity intact before marriage: 'from experience he knew that everybody had wanted to do something badly with Sally, but it had hardly ever been marriage.' Even after Jocelyn has proposed, Mr Pinner lives 'in a fearful state of watchfulness' to ensure that Sally and Jocelyn aren't left to themselves, because 'there was that in Mr. Luke's eye, he told himself, which could only be got rid of by marriage; nothing but the Church could make the sentiments the young gentleman appeared to entertain for Sally right ones'. He considers this desire to be one-sided, despite recollections of his own wife, left very vague, but perhaps enough to alarm those early

American audiences: 'she sometimes frightened him in bed, and he was sure it wasn't at all respectable for a wife to do that'.

Sally is demoted from human being to inanimate object in Mr Pinner's keenness to get her respectably wed: 'her father was tying her up with trembling haste, as if she were a parcel to be got rid of in a hurry'. It's not the only time that a woman is compared to an object in *Introduction to Sally*. Jocelyn's ideal woman is compared to a building: 'A lady, turning, like a decent Italian house, her plain and expressionless side to the public of the street, and keeping her other side, her strictly private and delightful other side, for her family and friends.'

Most of the men in the novel are not shy in prescribing what they do and do not want in a woman. Mr Thorpe demands 'gentleness, and softness, and roundness', while the narrator is not quite innocent of this belittling treatment herself, describing Sally as 'hardly [having] what could be called thoughts but only feelings'. There seems to be a consensus among the dominant voices of the novel that the perfect woman should be mostly silent.

Indeed, when Sally does speak, Jocelyn's opinion of her begins to shake.

"Well," said Sally shyly, "I don't mind if I do—." And for the first time Jocelyn heard the phrase he was later on to hear so often, uttered in the accent he was to try so hard to purify.

Similarly distressing to Jocelyn's ears is the word 'pardon'. As recently as 2017, *Tatler* magazine's etiquette expert wrote that '"Pardon" is a bit like a matching sofa and armchairs; de rigueur in some circles, déclassé in others', but gave its nod to the use of the word. 'Pardon' is unlikely to raise many eyebrows today, but it was a cultural divider in the early and mid-twentieth century and a shibboleth of class. In Nancy Mitford's influential and controversial 1955 essay, 'The English Aristocracy', later published in *Noblesse Oblige* (1956), she gave a glossary of words that were

'U' (upper class) or 'non-U' – with 'pardon' among them. According to Mitford, the correct, 'U' term to use is 'What', or simply silence.

Jocelyn's attempts to alter his wife's accent, vocabulary and elocution bear strong similarities to the plot of George Bernard Shaw's play *Pygmalion*, which debuted on the English stage in 1914. Its tale of young Cockney flower girl Eliza Doolittle (played by the widely beloved Mrs Patrick Campbell, despite being almost 50) and phonetics professor Henry Higgins was well-reviewed and successful and was revived twice in the 1920s.

Higgins promises to Eliza, 'You are to live here for the next six months, learning to speak beautifully, like a lady in a florist's shop.' Sally, meanwhile, enters into a similar bargain unknowingly and perpetually. It takes her a while to even realise the 'problem' that her husband is trying to fix:

"How, Sally—*how*, ʜᴏᴡ. You really *must* learn to say *how*," said Jocelyn, exasperated.

"I did say 'ow," explained Sally meekly.

"Yes. You did. Exactly," said Jocelyn.

Later, she is given a series of 'h' heavy sentences to practise, though Jocelyn seems to have none of Higgins' expertise in conveying exactly how to go about it. Elizabeth von Arnim preempts the famous line 'In Hertford, Hereford, and Hampshire, hurricanes hardly ever happen', which doesn't appear in Shaw's *Pygmalion* though it is included in a 1938 film version and later, more famously, the stage and film musical adaptation *My Fair Lady*.

Hefty Harry hurries after his hat. Sally drew in long breaths, and blew them out again at the beginning of each word, hoping they would turn into h's, though for the life of her she couldn't see any difference between the way she rendered *Hefty Harry* and the way Jocelyn did.

If Jocelyn sees Sally's beauty being in opposition to her voice and vocabulary, it is because of the unspoken belief that beauty equates class. To find a goddess among the lower classes – or, as Jocelyn's mother phrases it, 'beauty in a gutter' – is considered by almost all the novel's characters to be an extraordinary paradox. Even a mechanic whom they encounter doesn't believe he will be able to speak to Sally because of her appearance, but once he hears her voice feels much more able to share an unsophisticated meal with her. In a characteristically dry moment, von Arnim uses the narrative voice to take a swipe at the mechanic:

> "Class should stick to class," said Mr Soper to himself, who belonged to at least four societies for violently welding all classes into one, the one being Mr. Soper's.

Class is not the same as wealth, of course. Jocelyn has £500 a year, which seems riches to Sally and her father. But it is probably insufficient for the lifestyle Jocelyn believes himself fit for, and, similarly, his mother recognises the need of more funds for herself. While Jocelyn is marrying Sally, Mrs Luke is courting her neighbour who is both rich and unmannerly. It seems to matter less in a man, the novel suggests.

If Sally is a creation more commonly found in a fairy tale, then she is also given a fairy-tale ending. The munificence of the elderly Duke changes the course of her future, and the elevation of her circumstances to match her beauty help iron out any confusion in the people who see her. The novel may only be an introduction to Sally, but it also gives us a conclusion that, while not strictly likely, will please any reader who wishes to see her secure and content.

Simon Thomas

Series consultant **Simon Thomas** created the middlebrow blog Stuck in a Book in 2007. He is also the co-host of the popular podcast Tea or Books? Simon has a PhD from Oxford University in Interwar Literature.

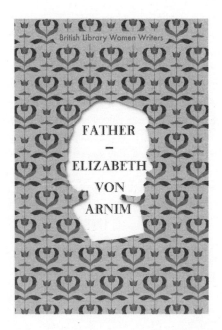

*Ah – there they were, the words to be expected, the immemorial
words. Right to freedom. Words bound, thought father watching her
icily, to occur sooner or later in the speech of persons whose
ambitions outran their talents – usually disaffected female relatives.*

Since her mother's death Jennifer has devoted years of her life to
her father, managing the home and acting as his secretary. After the
sudden announcement that he has remarried, Jennifer, at 33, seizes
the opportunity to lead an independent life. With a humorous tone,
this novel explores the familial and societal expectations placed on
single women during the interwar years.

304 PAGES
978 0 7123 5318 2

ALSO AVAILABLE

… after years of anxiety and distress there would once more be a home. She would make it, alone, untrammelled, a free human being.

Originally published in 1971, this searing novel looks at the experience of a woman escaping a faithless marriage and trying to establish a new home for grown-up children who no longer need her. Eleanor's emotional journey is often raw and dark, but there is humour and absurdity as she grapples with her newfound singledom. Fiercely capturing the tone of the 70s, it shines a light on the reality faced by so many women of the period when forced to re-assess their roles as wife and mother.

224 PAGES
978 0 7123 5492 9

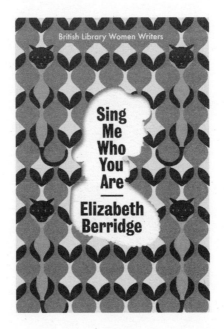

So she had had a shock, things weren't as they seemed. How had they seemed, then? Now it was her turn; this was for herself.

Harriet Cooper crawls up a pot-holed lane in a Hillman crammed with everything she owns. She is taking possession of a large green bus, an inheritance from her aunt, which now sits on her cousin Magda's land. Harriet is making a new start – her intention is to live a solitary, frugal life in the bus with her two cats.

This is a timely reissue of a 60s novel that deals with the lingering trauma of the Second World War and the dark secrets that families carry, as well as touching on environmental concerns that feel prescient today.

224 PAGES
978 0 7123 5487 5

For more Spinsters Ink titles please visit:

www.BellaBooks.com

Bella Books and Distribution
P.O. Box 10543
Tallahassee, FL 32302

Phone: 800-729-4992

As always, my forever admiration and gratitude to the late, great woman in the annals of our literary history, Barbara Grier, and to her partner and spouse, Donna McBride, for creating Naiad Press, birthplace of my work and that of so many of my sister authors.

Much loving gratitude to Linda and Jessica Hill at Bella Books for picking up the baton from Naiad Press, for all they've done and continue to do for us all, for warmly welcoming me home again where it all began. Dorothy was so right with all her iterations of "There's no place like home."

It's been a great ride. I'm proud and grateful to have been a lesbian writer creating books for my community over four decades of momentous history. I remain forever grateful to all of you, my readers, who have been with me on our wondrous journey together.